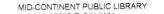

WE FIVE

WE FIVE

A NOVEL OF UNINTENDED COLLABORATION

Mark Dunn

DZANC BOOKS

DZANC BOOKS

5220 Dexter Ann Arbor Rd.
Ann Arbor, MI 48103
www.dzancbooks.org

Designed by Steven Seighman

Library of Congress Cataloging-in-Publication Data
Dunn, Mark, 1956-
    We five : a novel of unintended collaboration / Mark Dunn.—First edition.
        pages ; cm
    ISBN 978-1-938103-12-4 (hardcover)
    1. Authorship—Fiction. 2. Women authors--Fiction. 3. Female friendship—
    Fiction. I. Title.
    PS3604.U56W4 2015 813'.6—dc23   2015015292

First U.S. Edition: October 2015

Printed in the United States of America

10 9 8 7 6 5 4 3 2 1

For the four Weekley sisters:
Mary, Leslie, Laura, and Julia

All life is just a progression toward,
and then a recession from,
one phrase—"I love you."

—F. SCOTT FITZGERALD, "THE OFFSHORE PIRATE"

WE FIVE

Foreword

I fell in love with Elizabeth Gaskell's secret back-drawer novel *We Five* in the early nineties when I was looking for a work of Victorian fiction to adapt to the musical stage in partnership with a composer and a lyricist, who have since left the theatre and now raise Jerusalem artichokes. In the course of my investigation into what has happened to Gaskell's story of five young female friends who fall prey to five young men of predatory purpose, I discovered that since the posthumous publication of Gaskell's book in 1867, it has—over the succeeding decades—been adapted by three other novelists of some literary stature:

Grady Larson—*We Happy Five*, published in 1910.

Gail Lowery—*Five Saints, Five Sinners*, published in 1930.

Daphne Rourke—*Songs and Sirens*, published in 1952.

Swift upon the heels of the publication of my first novel *I Am a Time Bomb* in 2000, I tried my own hand at retelling Gaskell's story (set outside of Manchester, England, in 1859); I placed my version of this story, *Five Came Running*, in north Mississippi in 1997. It sold respectably well—not quite as well as my first novel, but better than my third, published in 2009, *The Dithering Heart*.

Given the similarities to be found among *We Five* and its four subsequent adaptations (including my own), I felt that this story might do with one more telling, an amalgamation of all five auctorial voices, each of the five versions of the story coming into violent collision at its climax.

Perhaps a word or two should be said about the book's epilogue, which is taken from an upcoming sixth version of the story...

Or not.

Mark Dunn
March 2015

Dramatis Personae

WE FIVE

Jane (Janie) Higgins
Maggie (Margaret, Mag, Mags) Barton
Carrie (Caroline, Car) Hale
Ruth (Ruthie) Thrasher
Molly Osborne

THE MEN

Tom (Thomas, Tommy) Catts/Katz ... *who pursues Jane*
Jerry (Jeremiah) Castle ... *who pursues Maggie*
Will (William, Willy) Holborne ... *who pursues Carrie*
Cain Pardlow ... *who is supposed to pursue Ruth*
Pat (Patrick, Paddy) Harrison ... *who pursues Molly*

Family Folk

Lyle Higgins ... *Jane's younger brother*
Clara Barton ... *Maggie's mother*
Sylvia Hale ... *Carrie's mother*
Herbert (Bert, Herb) & Lucile (Lucille) Mobry ... *Ruth's guardians*
Michael Osborne ... *Molly's father*
Jemma Spalding ... *Molly's cousin*

Other Players

Vivian (Vivien, Viv) Colthurst ... *We Five's employer (or manager or immediate supervisor)*
Reginald (Reggie) & Mirabella (Bella, Mira) ... *Carrie's neighbors and friends of We Five*
Lydia DeLash Comfort ... *famed evangelist in the Aimee Semple McPherson mold*
Miss (Abigail) Dowell ... *Miss/Ms. Colthurst's assistant*

Chapter One

Tulleford, England, August 1859

(from We Five, *by Mrs. Elizabeth Cleghorn Gaskell)*

Jane was the oldest of the five. She was also the tallest (with or without the clackety pattens). Though she was thought at times to be the most outspoken of the five, yet her friend Maggie was *also* possessed of an opining nature, which rivaled—sometimes even surpassed—Jane's characteristic candour.

As for Ruth, let it be said that when she was not repairing in quiet solitude to her books and her biscuits and her beefsteak pudding, she was given to speak her own mind in a clarion voice that tended to call a room to silence.

And what of Carrie and Molly, the remaining points on this pentagram of interlocking friendship? They would enter the lists on occasion themselves, but only for just cause, or if defence of personal honour demanded it, *or*, in the case of Molly, if the little girl within her was put into a mope. Consequently, Jane Higgins and her friends Maggie and Ruth and Carrie and Molly were given to occasional conversational skirmishes—skirmishes that sometimes disrespected Jane's seniority (and imposing height)—on a variety of topics, each, thankfully, of minor consequence.

Except when they should be of *major* consequence.

Yet disputation was the natural order of things, and had come to be accepted, as one comes to accept that shawls will fray and draggle, and stays will pinch, and white muslin will soil, but that is no reason to toss aside one's entire wardrobe, which otherwise serves.

For Jane and Maggie and Carrie and Ruth and Molly, having become friends in early girlhood, found a kinship of the heart, which was underpinned by the following sad verity: that with the untimely youthful demises of Maggie's two sisters, and the crib death of Molly's younger sister, there was not a single living female sibling to be claimed amongst the quintet (and no siblings *at all* for four of its members—or shall we say, no siblings at all for four of its members of which they were *aware*). In effect, five sisterless friends became sisters of a different sort, their sisterhood constituting a melding of several hearts that was fixed and enduring—a most remarkable thing for five women of an age in which beauty and animal spirit tended to engender the building up of permanent little walls of jealousy and mistrust, as might be readily glimpsed amongst the many other clutches of young maidens who worked and played together in Tulleford, the mill town of their birth. But in this special circle of similarly situated seamstresses, one noticed no such fatuous partitions, despite the inevitable differences in character and temperament to be found amongst them, and if they were at times to disagree and dispute as all sisters will disagree and dispute, there ensued without exception a cleansing aftermath of repentance and the putting of things to rights with a demonstration of only the most tender species of affection.

They called themselves "Circle Sisters," or "Sisters of the Heart," *or*, when an economy of self-denomination was required, simply "We Five." And each of the young women, having attained in the previous two years the age of one-and-twenty, and each being neither married nor affianced, but, in fact, wholly unattached in *any* romantic sense, owned a different opinion with regard to her present state of singularity, it being an *intolerable lot* in the short run for one of their number, *tolerable but preferentially undesirable by degrees* for three of their number, and *utterly and blissfully convenient* for the fifth member (who had no desire whatsoever to wed)—each of these views to be sorted out and properly assigned for the reader as our story unfolds.

Jane Higgins was, by her own admission, "the sage observer." She would not deny the astute observation that she was the wisest member of the group in *every* aspect of her nature (so long as the contention was voiced out of earshot of any other member of her circle who might disagree). However, Jane was not, by any measure, the most comely of the five, nor ever could she be deemed anything beyond "palatable in appearance" and "pretty after a fashion" by the prevailing consensus, her face being attenuated, arguably equine, her eyes deeply set. These attributes might be appropriate for a Transylvanian or Mediterranean exotic, but for a young woman of English stock, they constituted somewhat of a demerit, for they gave the impression of one fixed to a perpetually sombre, even lugubrious mien, or one robbed of restful sleep, or, more unkindly, one given to occasional neighing and clopping of the hooves. In reality, Jane, though crippled by a diminished upbringing, had overcome a great number of personal difficulties, such triumphs of mettle earning her the right to hold her head high and to wear her pride as a badge of honour, and not to be thought of in any negative way whatsoever, save by one generally unacquainted with all her *redeeming* traits.

Who *was* the fairest of the five? Perhaps it was the circle's youngest member, Molly Osborne, whose flaxen hair set her apart from her dark-tressed circle-sisters. Molly of the long lashes and wispy brows and oh-so-not-very-English softly rounded chin, indented with a dainty, almost capricious cleft. Molly of the arresting milk-blue eyes and the enchaining smile, which curled the plump lips with every glad thought or in response to even the smallest demonstration of spontaneous kindness, or whenever she found herself tickled by the wand of mischievous delight. (For Molly had an impish streak, which drew humour from circumstances not always conducive to the production of jocularity.) Molly, who turned the head of every young mill-working lad in the town of Tulleford and captured the eye of all their fathers as well (the men giving themselves license to partake in a furtive glance, which did little harm and which tended, in the main, to uplift the soul for some time thereafter). Molly was a chatterer and Molly was the one least shorn of her girlhood, and the coquettish nature that sometimes presented itself was nothing more, in fact, than the flit and flutter of a girl not yet molded fully into womanhood, though everything about her look and carriage might argue to the contrary.

Carrie Hale was the musical one, skilled at playing on both the pianoforte and violin, and blessed with an angel's voice. Carrie's face was music of a different sort, composed of full bright lips and cheeks, crimsoned by nature's rouge, and set with hazel eyes that trilled their own song through glimmer and sparkle. There was drama and mystery in these eyes, as well, just as there was drama and mystery in the heart and soul of this lyrical creature, who was Carrie to everyone but her mother, for whom Carrie would always be Caroline ("singer of carols"—or at least this was the derivation assumed by Sylvia Hale, who knew little of the name's monarchial pedigree).

Ruth Thrasher, by contrast, was quiet and retiring, save for those occasions when, in the company of her friends, she animated herself with clever observations and opinions. Ruth was a little plump (and had been at times quite a bit plumper), possessed of a pillowy frame and doughy cheeks, and a face that might give openness and light in one moment and the adumbrative appearance of brooding introspection in the very next. Whenever there was a matter to be decided, Ruth kept her own counsel until such point as it became necessary to break a tie, and then what Ruth said would rule the day, and that was the way she liked it, for keeping herself in detachment and studying a matter from every aspect was the best way for her to maintain her habit of feeding her intellect (alongside her equally insistent alimentary tract).

Ruth, unlike her circle-sisters, had been an orphan from birth. She was the daughter of an unmarried cook, employed by two maiden sisters of advanced age and truculent disposition. (The identity of Ruth's father was never discovered.) When Ruth's mother expired upon the parturition bed, the sisters allowed the baby Ruth to remain in their house, to be nursed with only the greatest of reluctance and to be fed sparingly. To compensate for this act of self-sacrificial Christian charity, Ruth was put into service at a very early age. The two women who superintended her youth were coarse and cruel and overworked her in Cinderella-stepmother fashion. At the age of fourteen, having had her fill of back-breaking chores and lumpy gruel and living in a house without a mote of love to be found within, Ruth ran away and became maid-of-all-work for a Dissenting minister and his sister on the other side of town, who subsequently taught her to read and to respect herself and to love God and do His will, and to sew. The minister and his sister, seeing the need to rescue their maid from a long, dull life of washing linens and scouring floors, sent her to the dressmaker and milliner, for whom she now worked in the company of her four circle-sisters. It was Ruth herself who, in response to Mrs. Colthurst's promptings, invited her four childhood friends to join her in employment there. (Mrs. Colthurst, you see, had worked in Manchester as an assistant to a successful modiste until she was disfigured in a terrible carriage accident and was no longer able to model the gowns her employeress designed. Having saved a few guineas over the years, the enterprising dressmaker ventured out under her own industry and opened a dress shop in neighbouring Tulleford.)

And what of Maggie Barton? She was passionate and smart and decisive and often precipitant, her manner bold (sometimes when boldness was hardly required). There was something enviably admirable in her determinate stubbornness and her steadfast unwillingness to admit to even the occasional miscalculation. But even for those who may see such wilfulness as a deficiency of character, the flames of her incandescent nature were seldom caustic, and one could scarcely look into her dark smoldering eyes, or take in the contemplative expression of serious purpose, or attend the eruption of mirth from her laughing lips that found ridiculousness in everything not overshadowed by death and illness and the other misfortunes of life, without falling helplessly subservient to her galvanic temperament. Maggie Barton wasn't beautiful, her face having been pocked (though, fortunately, not deeply so) by a childhood bout with the scourge of smallpox. But there was voluptuous heat and pulchritudinous passion in her soul, and if Molly was the one who turned the male head and put a fluttering butterfly kiss upon the male heart, then it was Maggie Barton who, to put it indecorously, inflamed the male loins.

"Maggie? Maggie, dear, is that you?" The voice, which belonged to Maggie's widowed mother, was more robust than usual, though it emanated from the bed of an intermittent invalid.

"Can it be anyone else?" returned Maggie, her own voice raised in volume. Maggie, having just shut the front door behind her, was now standing at the foot of the narrow staircase that led to the two companion bedchambers of the diminutive family cottage.

"Have you returned from the market?"

"No, Mamma. I'm still there. Oh, Lor, how my words do carry!"

Maggie chuckled. She set her bundle of greens upon the vestibule chair and mounted the stairs. As she stepped into her mother's tiny apartment, she found the drapes opened wide and the room flooded with radiant early morning sunshine. (It was clear to Maggie that her mamma had previously risen to welcome the day, and then promptly retreated to her bed, slipping indulgently beneath the cool sheets.)

"Don't you look pretty this morning? Tell me how long I may have you before you dash off to spend the balance of the day with Mrs. Colthurst."

"Scarcely any time at all, Mamma. And it's all Mrs. Lumley's fault, if you must blame someone. She detained me with a most long-winded story about her son—the one who serves in the Royal Navy, not the one who mends umbrellas and chases dogs. Mrs. Lumley still fancies that one day Henry and I will wed and I'll give her eight sturdy grandchildren, all of whom, she has no doubt, will look exactly like *him*. How are you feeling this morning, Mamma? Mrs. Forrest said she'd be happy to look in on you later. What should I tell her?"

"You may tell that meddlesome woman she needn't come at all," bolted out Mrs. Barton as Maggie descended languidly onto the bed, taking care to spread out her skirts with both hands to keep them unruffled. "I feel quite myself this morning," Mrs. Barton went on, "and have it in mind to spend most of this beautiful summer's day *out* of bed. I may even pay a visit to the tittle-tattling *Mrs. Forrest* for a change."

"She'll be most surprised to see you," laughed Maggie. "Only last week she summoned me to her doorstep to tell me in a most grave and despairing tone that in her studied estimation you are living on borrowed time."

"What a deliciously morose woman!" exclaimed Mrs. Barton, who signed her desire for a morning embrace from her only child by extending her arms and twiddling her fingers.

Maggie obliged. The two held themselves thusly across the bed until Maggie felt pinioned and succeeded in wriggling herself free and then popping up from the bed like the little clown sprung from the box. Mrs. Barton took this opportunity to give her daughter a good looking-over. "Tut, tut, tut. You're much too pretty to spend your day in the back of that woman's dreary dress shop, stitching away with those other girls like prisoners in a women's gaol."

"You mustn't speak so unkindly of Mrs. Colthurst. She's a good woman and a generous and thoughtful taskmistress. Only last week she rewarded us with yet another twenty-minute interval in the fresh air and fortifying sunshine; we are now permitted *three* opportunities during the workday to leave that windowless workroom and take a bit of a stretch."

"Permit me, then, to disparage her for the *opposite* reason. I shall mark the very odd stripe of liberality to her character."

"Do as you wish, Mamma, but I believe Mrs. Colthurst's kindness devolves from her great fondness for us. And in my mind, there is not a thing odd or *wrong* about it."

"Then I shall confine myself to my feelings about your daily absence from this house. Surely, I cannot be singular in pining away for a missing daughter. Doesn't Carrie's mother feel similarly deprived?"

"I suspect, Mamma, that it isn't my *society* you are missing so much as my lack of attendance to your every hourly need. Which distinguishes you from Mrs. Hale. Carrie's mother doesn't lie abed all day as you are wont to do, with sufficient opportunity for indulging in troubling contemplations. She occupies herself in her solitary hours with industrious and conscientious endeavours. She plays upon the harp. She bakes muffins for the poor. Then in the evening, when Carrie returns, the two are pleasantly restored to the company of one another, but neither will have considered the separation as any sort of trial. To be quite honest, Mamma, I've never seen such *sensible* affection demonstrated betwixt a mother and daughter."

Mrs. Barton's eyes flashed; her nostrils dilated. It was a look half put up and half sincere. "I noted three, perhaps four, things in that last peroration which pricked this particular mother's soul—the last being the most distressing. Have we *nothing* between us which remotely resembles the affection shown by Carrie and Sylvia Hale for one another?"

"I've seen little evidence of it."

Mrs. Barton flung a palm to her chest and gasped.

"Hold, Mamma. Let me finish. We haven't the same affection because its character bears no similarity to our own. Carrie and her mother are in some ways more like friends than relations. *We* are different. You are the mother and I am the daughter, and we know our rôles and we do credit to them." Maggie cleared her throat. "After a fashion."

Mrs. Barton's frown transformed into a fully blown pout. "I think that I should like to be *your* friend someday."

"And yet, with all candour, Mamma, I would not choose you for a friend. I simply would not."

Clara Barton rose from her bed and then promptly put herself down upon the edge. Her hands made themselves into little fists that bunched and clutched the folds of the counterpane with straitened vexation. "Such a thing to say to one you love! Or *do* you love me?"

Maggie sate down next to her mother. She took one of Clara's hands and laid it within the cradle of her own unturned palms. "Stuff! Of course I love you. I simply mean that as much as I esteem Carrie, I could never *be* Carrie, and as much as, I'm certain, you esteem Mrs. Hale, you could never *be* Mrs. Hale. The idea, for example, of spending the entirety of one's evening reading aloud to one's mother would be the death of me. You know I can scarcely hold myself still long enough to read a book."

"No, but do you not, my daughter, keep yourself still and staid to stitch and baste all the day long?"

"I do not *always* sit as I sew, Mamma. Sometimes I pace, if you must know. As for books, we haven't money to buy a single one."

"Nonsense! We could buy a book if we wanted. Mrs. Colthurst gives you a good wage. And the annuity your late uncle left us provides a bit of quarterly interest. We are not paupers."

Downstairs the clock on the hearth mantel had begun to chime the time: seven thirty (or very nearly seven thirty, for the clock ran fast). Maggie sprang from the bed. "Now I am late." She reached down and kissed her mother on the cheek and then pivoted on her heel to face the door, poised for swift retreat. Just as suddenly she bethought herself of that thing which often troubled her. "Oh. The palpitations that came again last night—have they now suspended?" Mrs. Barton nodded, smiling pleasantly. "This morning, my dear daughter, I am ticking as regularly as a newly wound clock. My vision is restored as well. It was so cloudy yesterday, but now it is clear."

"Was it the drops Dr. Osborne gave you?"

"Most assuredly! Molly's father is a veritable wonder. How fortunate for *me* that you and Molly are such good friends or I should never have known him—so skilled he is, and so kind and considerate. And I shouldn't even mention how very little he charges."

Maggie shook her head intemperately. "Dr. Osborne cannot charge much above what he does, Mamma, or word would get out that he is practising the medical arts without proper training or proper credentials. In truth, you and I both know he's a dentist-surgeon. He pulls teeth. Whatever facility he purports to have for healing the sick—and I shall be charitable—has been gained in a most haphazard and piecemeal fashion."

Mrs. Barton bristled. "*However* the gift has come to him, he is the best I have ever had, and I am quite on my way to a full recovery."

"And he drinks."

"I thought you were late."

"I should simply like to remind you that *Doctor* Osborne, as you have chosen to denominate him, drinks. He drinks gin. More gin than is prudent, according to Molly, who, I fancy, frets about him daily. If you are setting your cap for this doctor, who is not, in fact, a doctor in any proper *legal* sense, I would rather you not."

Mrs. Barton gaped in disgust. "What an inestimable privilege it is for me to be receiving such sauce and pepper from you, and at such an early hour!" Mrs. Barton folded her arms in a harlequinade of parental disapproval.

Maggie held her ground. "You are a widow, Mamma. And he is a wido*wer*, and I would rather not have him for a father, and that is that." She turned again to go.

"You know very well and good," said Mrs. Barton, addressing her daughter's back, "it was the death of Molly's mother and that baby which drove him to the spirits. But two years have passed and he drinks far less than he used to, for he has told me it is no longer necessary to apply such a heavy salve to his mourning heart, when the heart seems to be mending itself sufficiently without medicinal assistance."

"Medicinal indeed," mumbled Maggie.

"What was that you said?"

"No film or cloud has ever passed over *my* eyes, Mamma. What I see, and see quite clearly, is a woman who wishes to marry a certain dentist who would be a doctor, and if I am to place myself before this looking-glass..." Which Maggie did, taking the opportunity of reflection to adjust her bonnet. "...I would see, as well, a daughter who could not under any imaginable circumstances permit her mother to do so."

Mrs. Barton's voice became adamantine: "My darling dear! You are neither my keeper nor my turnkey. It is unavoidable illness that has placed me with frequent inconvenience upon this cot, but I am still free and unbound in thought and spirit; whatever control you feel you exercise over me is illusory."

"If you have done, Mamma, I will conclude this most uncomfortable interview by stating that if you marry Dr. Osborne, I shall very likely kill myself."

Mrs. Barton turned to look at nothing at all upon the bedroom wall. "Mind, just don't throw yourself down the well and pollute the town drinking water." Then, turning back to her daughter's dorsum with a sad moan of repentance: "You are so very fond of Molly. Would you not wish to have her for a stepsister?"

"You know that in a very real sense Molly is *already* my sister. Molly and Jane and Carrie and Ruth. We are, all of us, much more than mere friends. There is no need for you to marry a frequently intoxicated tooth-tugger to have what I, in point of fact, have already. Now I'm very late, Mamma, and I'm keeping the other girls. You know we walk together, and when one of us is late we are all late. Mrs. Colthurst doesn't like that."

"Maggie?"

"Yes?"

"Mr. Osborne has already put things into motion. He has asked me to marry him."

Maggie took a deep breath and exhaled slowly to steady herself. "I rather suspected."

"And now that it is become a very real thing, have you anything new to say in response?"

"Anything *new*? No, Mamma, I have not."

Maggie moved with a heavy tread to the door.

"Are you going to leave without kissing me?"

"I've kissed you already."

With that, Maggie Barton betook herself in great haste down the steps and then flew out the front door and down the lane, whilst her mother sate up in bed and bowed her head in silent lament.

Then Clara Barton raised her head and shook it, and shook her shoulders as if to wrest herself free of a tangible burden placed thereupon, whilst saying to herself, "I do not live only to satisfy the whims of my selfish, benighted daughter. And I *will not* have this special day spoilt!" Subsequently, she stretched out her arms and yawned and embraced the morning in a mood that was uplifted by calling to mind Osborne's visit the previous day under the pretext of administering drops to clarify his patient's vision. Yet the visit carried a far more consequential purpose: the bestowal of a formal proposal of marriage. This recollection was succeeded by a recurrence of the rapturous thought that Osborne was returning the next after noon—this very after noon—to hear her answer!

Clara Barton had deferred that answer to give herself the opportunity to talk the matter over with Maggie, but she had lost courage the evening before, and this morning woke feeling defiantly independent of her daughter's self-imposed jurisdiction. That assertion of maternal liberty was validated when, without even raising the matter with her, Maggie had expressed an opinion that was severally predictable, very much to the point, and altogether maddening.

But such thoughts were not without momentary repining: "I *should* have discussed the proposal of marriage with her at some length, for, yes, as my daughter, Maggie is entitled to some opinion in the matter. But what would it serve? Maggie is a stubborn, wilful girl, but she isn't the mistress of this house! If only she could find a husband of her own and set herself up elsewhere—someplace where she may decide things which have naught to do with *me*. Would that Mrs. Lumley's son Henry *did* ask her to be his wife, and then gave up the nautical profession and took up the vocation of his greengrocer father. Then she would be happy and *I* would be happy and there would be cabbages and radishes for everyone concerned."

Mrs. Barton's thoughts now turned to the girls who formed "We Five." "Each of those five garden flowers are at the height of bloom and blow, and yet attachments go wanting. Is there not a single man who durst intrude upon that circle of sisterly affinity? Perhaps a good many men *would* have them if they would only place themselves in situations of inviting eligibility. But how is such a thing possible when all they do is sit in that back room and sew and knit and squint in the darkness and cackle amongst themselves like old hens?"

Clara Barton glanced at the eye-wash cup set upon the table next to her bed. A feeling of warm affection overspread her. Then she smiled. She bethought her of the man she esteemed—a man who had taken such good care of her through her recent illness, though he was clearly not permitted by law to do so—a man who would take even better care of her in other places than simply *beside* the bed, and her smile broadened with *this* thought, and then a frisson of something very much like love shot through her body. She fell back against the mattress in the manner of a giddy schoolgirl, hugging her pillow to her chest as if it were a newly received valentine she should place close to her heart. In the next moment, a new thought suddenly intervened; she wondered if Maggie had put away whatever it was she had purchased from Mrs. Lumley (Clara had asked for broccoli sprouts), or had it all been left downstairs to wither without attendance?

Food was on her mind, for her appetite had returned. And it was all due to Dr. Osborne—attributable both to his physician's skills, which he had acquired through years of opportunistic study and informal apprenticeship, and to the healing wonders that naturally derive from a man's loving heart.

A heart the likes of which her daughter Maggie had yet to behold.

Chapter Two

San Francisco, California, U.S.A., April 1906

(*from* We Happy Five, *by Grady Larson*)

Molly swiveled full circle in her father's dental chair. Then she turned herself around in the opposite direction, giggling like a little girl. Attending the delight in his daughter's voice, Michael Osborne entered the dental parlor from the living quarters in the back of the flat, which the two shared. He was whipping up lather in his shaving cup with his brush. "If you aren't careful, you're going to auger that chair right down into Mrs. Dillingham's front parlor. And I'll leave you to contend with her wrath all by yourself."

Molly stopped the chair from revolving. She dizzily wagged a forefinger at her father. "Don't be silly. You *always* come to my rescue. That's what fathers are for: to love, protect, and defend their children, no matter how monstrous their behavior."

"Explain to me how you can be on the watch for Maggie when you're nowhere near the window."

Molly hopped out of the chair, grabbing one of the arms to stabilize herself. "To which window are you referring, Papa? The one in this parlor that is of absolutely no use? Perhaps you haven't noticed, but that big tooth blocks our view of nearly everything. I must go to the rear of the flat if I'm to see anything of Polk Street."

Osborne crossed to the window at issue and gazed proudly upon his recent purchase: a large ceramic sculpture in the shape of a tooth. It had the words "Osborne Dental Offices" painted on it in big black letters. The tooth hung from an iron rod projecting from the lintel of the window. The morning was breezy; the tooth rocked gently and squeaked.

"It *is* quite large, isn't it? Hum. Would it have been better for me to have bought myself a smaller one?"

Molly walked over to the window as well, some of the strands from the swirl of long blond hair that had been gathered atop her head escaping and flying off to one side. "Oh, I like it that size," she said, looking it over. "It's a real attention-grabber. And it's very funny. It's as if one day a fairytale giant came to you with a toothache and he let you keep the tooth after you'd pulled it."

"But will it get me more customers?" mulled Osborne aloud. "*That's* the question."

Osborne had to admit that Molly was right about the tooth impeding any view of the street below. All that could be seen beyond it was a sliver of the bright morning sky.

"Papa, I think it was a good investment. Didn't one of your patients say only last week that it was seeing the silly tooth which brought him to you?"

"Not exactly. He'd already heard about my practice, so it was actually the *toothache* that put him in that chair. Although my giant tooth did confirm he'd come to the right building."

Osborne grinned. It was a crooked grin, made even more obvious by the fact that it uplifted half of his thick black moustache. He dipped his head and squinted through the narrow dagger of light entering the room beneath the tooth. "As if there's anything else on this cluttered, woebegone street to take notice of. When my practice picks up, you have my promise: I'm going to move us out of this flat and away from this street forever. Even better: we'll leave San Francisco altogether. I'm thinking Sausalito. I'll find us a nice cottage there, with a handsome view of the Golden Gate. Someplace where you can plant violets and San Rafael roses, which were always your mother's favorites, behind whitewashed pickets. I'm sure people in Sausalito have just as much need for dentists as people in San Francisco do."

"Oh do be serious, Papa. How can we even *think* of leaving Frisco! My four best friends in the world live here. And besides, shouldn't we include Mrs. Barton in this decision, since she's going to be a member of this family?"

"*That* has yet to be decided, monkey." Michael Osborne was now on his way back to his sink in the rear bedroom.

Molly followed. "So you think there's the possibility she'll say no? Oh how *could* she, Papa? How could she possibly rob Mag and me of the chance to become *true* sisters?"

Osborne began to apply the foamy white lather to his accumulation of weekend whiskers. "I'm feeling *fairly* good about my chances with Clara. But I'm not sure your friend Maggie will be all that pleased to see the two of us wed."

Molly sighed. "I wish I could say you're wrong, Papa, but no, I'm afraid she won't like it at all." Molly sighed again. "Oh, I do wish you had let me talk to her yesterday. Her influence over her mother is strong, and I'm worried that even if Mrs. Barton *wanted* to marry you—"

"Oh, I know she *wants* to, monkey. No doubt about *that*."

"Yet Mag could still talk her out of it. Mag Barton is quite good at talking my heart-sisters and me out of—*and into*—all sorts of things. She's very persuasive."

The dentist pursed his lips in thought. "So just what do you think it is, Molly girl—the thing that makes our little Mag Barton dislike me so much?"

"I don't think she trusts you, Papa."

Osborne held his razor in temporary abeyance. "Trusts me to do what?"

"Well, to be a good husband to her mother, for one thing. I hope you don't mind me speaking frankly."

"Please, be as frank as you wish. I ought to know exactly where things stand with the girl."

"Well, there's also the other thing. She's told me already how uncomfortable she is with your practicing medicine without a license."

Molly's father laughed. "Oho! Wait until she finds out I'm also practicing *dentistry* without a license!"

"And one thing more," said Molly.

"Good God! You're making me sound like the most disreputable man in San Francisco. Is it the drinking?"

Molly nodded. "It was drink that killed her father, you know."

"To be accurate, it wasn't demon rum that killed Barton. It was a California Street cable car."

"Which he stumbled in front of because he was soused to the guards, Papa. You saw it happen from that dental parlor window— back before there was a gargantuan ceramic tooth blocking the view."

"Have you not informed my potential future stepdaughter Maggie that I drink far less than I used to?"

"Of course I have. She doesn't listen to me. None of my four heart-sisters listens to me. I'm like the youngest in the family who must sit all clammed up in the corner and hasn't the right to say anything about anything. Of course, that isn't completely true. It's only at work where I'm to know my place. At all other times I have license from my sisters to say whatever I please."

"You may be low girl on that department store's totem pole, but I'm happy and proud of you for getting yourself hired on."

"Though I would like to be more than a ribbon packer at three dollars a week, Papa. Mag and Jane and Carrie and Ruth have risen to salesclerks, and Jane has her eye on becoming a buyer someday, but I'm stuck in the stock loft above the shelves tying parcels all day—the little mouse in the attic: quiet and all but forgotten except when she peeps."

Osborne laughed. "Then you're hardly ever forgotten, Molly girl, because I've never known you to hold your tongue for more than a minute at a time. But you're right to set your sights on something better, and I'm very proud of you for signing up for stenographic classes. I only wish you'd let me pay for them. Generally speaking, girls your age who must seek employment to pay for their night classes are girls without papas to provide for them."

Molly smiled. "I like getting up and going to work each morning, Papa, and keeping myself out of your way. I also like spending time with my four sisters."

Osborne smiled. "Even though they sometimes treat you like a child?"

"Not a child. Just a new employee who is supposed to know her place."

"You mean up in the attic making her wee mousey bed out of a litter of excelsior?"

Molly knuckled her father playfully in the arm. "Ye Gods, Papa, you're so droll sometimes."

Molly put her arms around her father's waist and gave him a hug. He checked his wish to answer the gesture with a paternal pat on the head, since his hands were dappled with shaving lather.

"Only a few days ago Jane said I was flighty-brained and nearly useless. Of course, I *had* just dropped a roll of ribbon on her head."

"Everyone makes mistakes. But you shouldn't be too hard on Jane for these sudden bursts of exasperation. It cannot be easy living the way your friend Jane does, forced to care for that failure of a junkman brother of hers. I buy dross gold from him for fillings; I think sometimes I'm the only customer he has. I'm certain it's your Jane who brings most of the income into that sibling household. Alas, with her plain looks and unpredictable disposition, she's probably saddled to him *and* to near-impoverishment for the rest of her days."

"Jane will find someone, Papa—someone who will deliver her from her present circumstances. You'll see. She isn't pretty, but there are men who won't mind such a thing either on account of their own deficient looks or because she's smart and would be an asset in a certain kind of marriage—one built on mutual respect."

"You sound like a suffragette."

Michael Osborne pinched his daughter's nose affectionately, leaving a small dollop of white shaving lather there. As she was dabbing the spot away with her handkerchief, he toweled his face dry. "How do I look?"

"Perfectly shorn, Papa, and oh so handsome. Mrs. Barton will fall swooning into your arms, crying, '*I do! I will! I must!*'"

Osborne bellowed with laughter. He was a large man and his merriment sometimes came in Falstaffian expulsions. "Oh you think so? Say, is that Miss Maggie I see standing on the corner below? Do you think she knows?"

"Only if your heart-object has told her. I've kept my promise, Papa. I haven't breathed a word about your proposal. Of course, to judge by that severe look on her face, I'm to get an earful from her all the way to Carrie's, and I'm not sure if I can bear it. Everything expelled through those astringent lips will be against the marriage. Against your happiness—*my* happiness—the happiness of her very own mother. Doesn't she know we won't *always* occupy this dreary Polk Street flat? And yes, yes, yes, I know we can't move in with the two of them because their flat is even smaller than ours. But the point I'm trying to make is that things are bound to get better. I feel a turn of fortune is due all of us—long overdue."

Osborne smiled. He looked deeply into his daughter's wondering eyes. "When your face lights up like this, it reminds me so much of your mother. How dearly she loved life and all its possibilities."

"And she loved *you* too, Papa. I could see it in the way she looked at you. And I could hear it in those soft sweet sighs of hers when you held her close."

Osborne sighed too. It was not, however, the same sort of sigh to which his daughter was referring; his was filled with painful, aching remorse. "Had I only been home that day."

"A thousand times you've said this, Papa. I won't allow you ever to utter that sentence again. We will never know why she did what she did, but at all events, you are not to blame. Would you have forbidden her to take that walk? Of course not. She would have gone out had you been home or had you *not* been home. It makes no sense for you to continue blaming yourself."

Michael Osborne collapsed into the chair next to his bed. He dropped his face into the cradle of his palms. He took a couple of deep breaths. Molly watched as the tips of her father's fingers pressed into his forehead. Slowly, he raised his head to look at his daughter. "It is difficult for me to believe that all things happen for a reason. For what possible reason did your mother have to die? What was the purpose behind the death of that beautiful baby? For so very long I teetered between life and death myself."

"You say that, Papa, but I can never believe it. You wouldn't have left me. I know you wouldn't."

"Of course you're right. When I was lucid, when my thinking was unclouded, I knew that I *did* have something else to live for. Some*one*."

Molly's father, his eyes now filling with tears from memory and regret, looked deeply into his daughter's equally dewy eyes—eyes the very same shade of blue as her mother's.

"Papa, let's not talk about this—ever again."

Osborne nodded.

"Promise me now. Promise."

Osborne nodded again. His expression brightened bravely. "And have we not already moved miles and miles down the road in the journey of our lives? Though Mrs. Barton would never be a perfect replacement for your mother, she's a fine woman, given to only occasional bouts with hypochondria and dyspepsia. And she'll make a boon companion for you and a good wife for me. And—and she makes me laugh, and isn't that the best tonic there is for the affliction of widowerhood?"

Molly nodded. She touched her lips to her father's forehead. Then she turned her head to glance out the window. "It appears," she noted in an analytical tone, "that Mag has no interest in coming up the stairs to fetch me. Today she simply isn't going to exert herself. She *is* looking up, though." Molly raised the window sash. She waved. "Hello there, Mag! Top of the mornin' to ye!" An aside to her father: "Sometimes I pretend to be an Irish charwoman. She absolutely *hates* it!" Molly exaggerated her smile for Maggie, so as to rain morning cheer down upon her impatient friend. "I'll be right down!"

"Take all the time you need!" Maggie shouted back up to her. Maggie's smile was manufactured as well, but it was frigid, almost scornful. And then in an exasperated under-breath, she said to herself, "Oh Molly Osborne! How you absolutely *jar* me!"

Molly closed the window. "Good-bye, Papa. I'll be on pins and needles until this evening."

"Hopefully there'll be no prick at all," said Osborne. He watched his daughter hurry from the rear rooms of the flat and then listened as the dental parlor's front door, which opened upon the building's third-story landing, was unlatched and then slammed shut. He promptly crossed to the window of the room where he slept and shaved himself and read his paper in the evening. (There were two other rooms, which comprised the Osbornes' "living quarters": a kitchen, large enough for a small dining table, and Molly's cupboard-sized bedroom.) He looked down upon Maggie. She was shifting her weight, with obvious impatience, from leg to leg. She glanced up of a sudden and caught his gaze, then quickly turned away, the gesture constituting an undeniable cut.

"You will not win this day, you minx," said Osborne in apostrophe. "I am to be your stepfather, whether you like it or not. I've heard stories of how you've browbeaten your mother into abject subservience, but those days, little Maggie, are over. I won't command arbitrary allegiance from you. But I *will* command respect. I am a good dentist—even if I did learn my craft through itinerant apprenticeship. I am a good father—even if I've had to, of late, carry the burden of being mother as well. And I do not resemble your late father in any respect except that we were roughly the same age when he died. He was a drunkard all his life. I've been a drunkard for two years only, and only by circumstance—circumstances that are finally being put behind me. I will continue to mourn the deaths of my late wife and baby daughter until my last hour upon this earth, but I have ceased doing so from atop a saloon stool. Your mother, Miss Maggie, believes me when I say this. Perhaps in time you'll come to believe me too, and then things cannot help but improve between us."

Osborne observed Maggie and his daughter Molly as they exchanged perfunctory morning greetings on the sidewalk. He smiled as Molly, lifting her head, and, seeing him standing at the window, waved good-bye. He waved back, though Maggie refused to be witness to any of it, staring ahead, her face set and unemotive. Then the two girls moved along, Molly hooking both of her arms around Maggie's left arm to effect a lively bonhomie, whether the recipient chose to subscribe to it or not.

Michael Osborne had cleared his calendar of patients for that day. Today—the *entire* day was reserved for Clara Barton. Because she was certain to say yes. This he made himself believe. And he was certain they should spend the remainder of the day celebrating her acceptance of his proposal, perhaps by taking themselves to North Beach, where the pounding surf would applaud their decision to be together forever thereafter, and perhaps even replace at long last the mental picture of his late wife, in that very same spot, walking herself into a watery tomb.

Maggie Barton and Molly Osborne had just turned the corner into Bush Street when they were hailed by a bubbly young woman with singing eyes and a massive coil of black hair held upon her head by a superfluity of tortoise-shell hairpins. Whereas Maggie and Molly wore the sedate and understated "uniform" of the female department store salesclerk—starched skirt and soft-toned shirtwaist (the only permissible flash of color being found upon their nearly matching pink-dotted neckties)—the girl beckoning their attention was rigged in an ornately embroidered orange-and-gold men's Mandarin jacket and a fringed Chinese shawl that had been twisted and turned so as to become a nest for her bobbing head. "Do you like it?" she asked, modeling her rig with palms down and projecting out to the sides like those of a posing mannequin—especially one from ancient Egypt. "It's Reggie's jacket, but I made it my own. It's to grab people's attention so I can slip them a printed advertisement for his lecture Thursday night." The girl handed a piece of paper to Maggie. "You two must share it, because I haven't an inexhaustible supply. Do you think you'll be able to come?"

Molly looked up from the paper. "I'm sorry, but I have my stenography class at that hour."

The girl, whose name was Mirabella, was on friendly and familiar terms with both Maggie and Molly due to the fact that the three of them had attended grammar school together. She turned to Maggie with the same bright and hopeful look. "What about *you*, Mag?"

"I'll *try*," fibbed Maggie, "but I cannot imagine your new husband will have many others in attendance. 'The Extinction of the Human Race' is a very depressing topic for this month's 'Lecture for the Masses.'"

"And yet it's something to which we should all be giving serious thought. Futurists tell us that humankind may not survive this new century—that the tragedy of Galveston was only the first of many such devastating catastrophes that will, in the end, wipe all human life from the planet."

Maggie handed the paper announcement back to Mirabella. "You and your newlywed professor husband sound like those sandwich-board-wearing fanatics who stand on Market Street and preach the end of the world. You dismiss the fact that there are a good many others—like that Mr. Bellamy whom Ruth's been reading—who believe quite the opposite. By the way, Mirabella: what does your husband predict will be the nail in the coffin of our species—the one big, final event which will make all humankind disappear forever?"

Mirabella frowned. "Well, it sounds to me like you aren't coming, so I shouldn't tell you *anything*, but of course I will because we're friends. Reggie lists five different potential agents of permanent annihilation."

"Perhaps you should name them some other time, Mirabella," said Molly, uneasily. "Mag and I are both late for work."

"Then I'll walk with you. I should vacate this block anyway. The Salvationists are about to start caterwauling on that corner and they'll drown me out completely."

Maggie and Molly resumed their brisk walk along Bush with Mirabella falling into skip-step next to them. "First. *Water*. Reggie calls this the Noachial model—whatever that means. Then. *Fire*. Either by the hand of nature or by the hand of man. Oh, let me see. Slow down, will you? *Wind*. Tornadoes, hurricanes—we've seen a good deal of *that* already. Then earthquake, volcano—that sort of thing. 'Earth eructions,' my horned-rimmed honey calls them."

"Earth e*ruc*tions?" asked Molly.

"No. E*ruc*tions. Like big terrestrial belches. Isn't my new husband clever? He's such a wooz."

Maggie and Molly nodded as one, or rather like two kittens tracking a playfully dangled bit of twine with their whole heads.

"Anyway, don't we get a taste of *that* from time to time here in wambling ol' Frisco? Oh, do slow down just a smidge. I'm going to trip, I really am. Thank you. And the last one—hum, what *is* the last one?"

"Yes," sighed Maggie with only slightly masked annoyance, "what *is* the last one? Molly and I are dying to know."

"Well, if you're going to be like that, I won't tell you."

"Mag was just having fun," said Molly pacifically. "Please tell us the last one."

"Yes, I remember it now. It's the sun."

Maggie stopped. Her companions halted as well. Maggie glared at Mirabella. "You mean the human race could go extinct from too much sunshine? Would this apply to Eskimos and Santa Claus too?"

"Well, what do you think causes droughts, for Heaven's sake? *Moonbeams?*"

Maggie snorted. "Mirabella Hampton Prowse, *you* are a moonbeam. A true mooncalf."

"Of whom we are very, very fond," Molly hastily put in. She reached over and demonstrated her fondness for her former grammar school desk-mate by giving her a little buss on the cheek. Then she seized Maggie by the arm and the two dashed off. "Very late!" Molly tossed back. "Love and kisses to you and the professor!"

After Maggie and Molly had put themselves a good distance ahead of their gaped-mouth friend, they slowed their pace to a stroll. "I know it was mean to dash away like that," repined Molly, "but I also knew if I didn't do *something*, you were going to chew her up for breakfast. You *were*, weren't you?"

Maggie grinned and nodded. "But not breakfast. Dinner. A big plate of mooncalf's liver."

Chapter Three

(*from* Five Saints, Five Sinners, *by Gail Lowery*)

Since the two of them seemed, at least for the time being, to be getting along, Molly wanted so badly to speak to Maggie about the marriage proposal, and how, should Mrs. Barton accept it, a union between their two parents might redound to the benefit of all concerned. But she kept her ongoing promise to her father and scrupulously avoided the topic. Instead, the two friends, as they strode past the solid brick mansions and quaint wood-frame houses of oak-lined Ninth Street, turned their conversation to the day that lay ahead, one greatly anticipated by Maggie and Molly and their three circle-sisters.

The woman for whom the five worked, the famed female evangelist Lydia DeLash Comfort, had "come home." After several peripatetic years preaching the holy gospel in tents and auditoria throughout the country, money was raised (and was still being raised) to build a great Christian "tabernacle" in Zenith, the city of her birth and the place where her evangelizing career had begun. When construction of her "Tabernacle of the Sanctified Spirit" was completed in a couple of weeks, it would dwarf all other houses of worship in this middle-western metropolis, *and* be the envy of every pastor, priest, and rabbi in town.

The opening, the unveiling, the "Inaugural Service of Sanctified Celebration," was scheduled for a week from Sunday. Leading up to this day, Maggie and Molly, and their equally assiduous sisters, Carrie and Jane and Ruth, were pitching in alongside all the other employees of "Sister Lydia's Square Deal Ministries" to make ready the big day. We Five handed out circulars to spread the word about the tabernacle's jubilant opening. They answered telephones and prepared mailings in the tabernacle office. They also worked as factotal Christian soldiers in service to all the various auxiliary groups that were popping up like mushrooms in Sister Lydia's sacred garden, as the evangelist's ministry, which had once been popular only with Pentecostals and others who spoke in tongues and rolled around on the floor, was now becoming a transformative and very nearly respectable religious and cultural phenomenon of significant renown. There was still the little residual matter of the Sister's miraculous healing powers and whether these miracles would continue, with or without the reputed snake-oil operandi. But regardless, it was hard to deny that Sister Lydia's Square Deal Ministries had the potential to become veritably global in its scope and outreach.

Yes, Sister Lydia DeLash Comfort was doing the nearly inconceivable: she was becoming even more famous than Mary Pickford.

Today, though—*today* the saintly singing sisters were finally getting to sing. Under the leadership of choir director Vivian Colthurst, choir rehearsals in preparation for the inaugural celebration were finally getting underway. It was on this warm Monday in early July that We Five (lovingly named by Miss Comfort "Sister Lydia's Quintet of Songful Seraphim") joined the other fifteen women hired by Lydia on the basis of the mellifluity of their laryngeal pipes and their willingness to lead the congregation once daily (except Thursdays) and three times on Sunday in making the requisite joyful noise unto the Lord.

It was the best job the girls had ever had. It sure beat working as bookkeepers and file clerks in the cramped front mezzanine office of Ramfield Wholesale Drugs and Sundries from whence they were— *rescued* would be the best way to describe it—by none other than the Reverend Lydia DeLash Comfort herself, when, upon a visit to the offices of that venerable Zenith concern to extract a sizeable contribution to the tabernacle's building fund from the company's circumstantially devout and philanthropic owner, Sister Lydia overheard the five singing "I Don't Know Why I Love You But I Do" in the employee lunchroom and was struck statuary by the close harmonies wafting from the girls' sweet lilting voices, and then was commensurately struck euphoric over the idea of having the five youthful female songbirds join her permanent choir (which had replaced the itinerant berobed and somewhat bedraggled quartet that had tagged along with Sister Lydia throughout her traveling ministry).

From the flat shared by Molly and her father above his dentist offices, it wasn't too long a walk to the house in which Molly and Maggie's friend Carrie and her mother lived. But they were late.

Both Mother and Daughter Hale were taking their breakfast on the front verandah. The colored cook and maid, Vitula, was home with a head cold, and Sylvia Hale, an inefficient time manager, was behind the clock. Eyeing that clock, Carrie suggested the two eat on the porch so she could watch the street and then be able to dash off when her friends came to collect her.

"Well, we certainly made a good thing out of Vitula's unfortunate absence this morning," said Mrs. Hale, shaking out her lap napkin at the little wicker tea table. "This is *quite* lovely." Carrie agreed with a nod. For a moment, mother and daughter sat upon their marginally comfortable chintz chair cushions in silence and listened to the bright and chirpy sounds of their Floral Heights neighborhood as it rose and shone.

Finally, Sylvia said, "Finish your waffles, dear. You know what they say about breakfast being the most important meal of the day."

"No, Mother, what do they say?" Carrie grinned. "I respect you for trying, Mother, but your waffles taste nothing like Vitula's. But don't fret. There's always fresh fruit in the tabernacle offices. I'll just grab a peach or something before rehearsal starts."

"You have a smudge on your cheek," said Mrs. Hale, rising to wipe it away. "You look as if you've been sleeping in the coal bin." Out of the corner of her eye Sylvia Hale caught her neighbor, Mrs. Littlejohn, coming down the sidewalk, tethered to her Cairn Terrier, unimaginatively named Toto. Thinking Carrie's mother was being especially friendly by standing up to greet her, Mrs. Littlejohn waved with wriggling fingers and called out, "Good morning, Sylvia! Good morning, Carrie! There was such beautiful music coming from your front parlor last night. Was that the two of *you* or the phonograph?"

"It must have been us," returned Mrs. Hale. "I don't think we touched the Victrola last night."

"What a contrast to that perfectly awful jazz scritch-scratch that comes tumbling out of the Prowses' house every time you turn around." Mrs. Littlejohn's eyes went to the house in question, which she'd just passed. It belonged to Professor Reginald Prowse—head of the astronomy department of Winnemac Agricultural and Mechanical College—and his new baby bride, Mirabella (or Bella, to those who were close). "How you can live next door to all that racket and all those bohemian goings-on without pulling out all your hair, I cannot possibly imagine."

Mrs. Hale drew an index finger to her lips, and then, thinking the gesture required some buttressing, she said, "Keep your voice down, Deloria. It's still early."

"And wouldn't *that* be a tragedy: depriving the professor and his flip-flapper wife of their beauty sleep, when this is exactly what *they* do to all the rest of us two or three times a week!"

Mrs. Littlejohn interpreted Sylvia Hale's admonition as reason to come up the flag walk and address her neighbors on a more intimate basis upon the front steps. As the three spoke, the woman, who looked—it cannot be expressed otherwise—like a human-sized pear with legs, permitted, by slackened leash, her small terrier to trespass upon Mrs. Hale's flowerbed and dig its paws into the ground, still moist and friable from the heavy watering it had received the evening before. The scruffy dog was to do this more than once, and each time it did, Mrs. Littlejohn tightened the lead and yanked the dog cruelly back to heel, and Carrie, who was watching the multiple acts of this painful little drama from her seat, involuntarily grabbed at her own throat in sympathy.

"Mattie Parcher tells me you're starting your choir rehearsals today, Carrie. You must be so excited."

Carrie nodded. "I am. It should be such fun."

Mrs. Littlejohn gushed, "I've always known you Hales to be musical, but I thought the family talent was limited to the instrumental rather than the vocal. Sylvie, dear: wasn't your husband—the man who ran away and left you nearly destitute—wasn't he some sort of vaudeville musician?"

Mrs. Hale masked her displeasure over Mrs. Littlejohn's having brought up such a sore topic with the veneer of amiable froth: "Why, Deloria Littlejohn, you are the worst person I know for getting things completely jumbled up. My husband did *not* leave Caroline and me 'nearly destitute.' I have always had income from my father's real-estate holdings—never as much as I would like, but enough to keep the wolf far from the door. As for my husband's profession, yes, he was in vaudeville and, yes, he played all manner of musical instruments. But he was not a performer per se. He was an impresario."

Yank.

Carrie seized her throat. Was the little dog choking? Why was its tongue now protruding frog-like from its mouth?

Mrs. Hale proceeded: "Had Gordon remained in Zenith and retained all his wits, he would have been quite proud of Caroline.

Singing in Sister Lydia's choir! Just think of it. *Sister Lydia*! I understand she searched far and wide for every single member of that chorus of angels. Isn't that right, Caroline?"

Carrie removed her hand from her throat. "She *was* somewhat selective."

Mrs. Littlejohn hum-sighed. Then she rhapsodized, "Who knew that such a beautiful songbird lived right on this very street?"

Yank.

Mrs. Hale seconded Mrs. Littlejohn's observation with a knowing nod, her eyes closed, her fist gently thumping her equally proud maternal heart. "Well, I can't say I'd known all along that Caroline was *this* talented, but it wasn't as if I never entertained the possibility. My daughter excels at whatever she sets her mind to. Don't you, darling?"

"I don't know, Mother. I suppose I—"

Yank. Yelp.

Seizing her throat once more, Carrie said, "Molly and Maggie are late. They're hardly ever late."

"Perhaps they swung around to pick up Jane first," suggested Sylvia with a superfluous swirl of her fork through the air.

"Well, that wouldn't make any sense. Jane lives two blocks closer to the tabernacle. Coming for me *after* picking her up would require doubling back." Carrie succeeded in saying this without the use of any hand movement at all.

"Well, *I* should be getting back," said Mrs. Littlejohn with misfired relevance. "Home, that is. I have an early appointment at the salon. Mrs. Tubb is coming to pick me up. Do you know Mrs. Tubb—Hermione Tubb? She lives in that newer section of Floral Heights—she's taking me to her beauty salon for my very first violet-ray facial treatment, and then if all my pores close up properly we're having chop suey and seeing that new Betty Compson picture at the Grantham." Mrs. Littlejohn gave her little dog one great, decisive tug with the leash. "Something has been in this bed, it appears. Perhaps the squirrels have buried nuts here. Goodbye, Sylvia. Goodbye, Carrie, and congratulations. We're all so proud of you. I'm so fortunate to have the two of you for neighbors." Mrs. Littlejohn glanced at the house next door and narrowed her eyes into coin slits. "Not at all like *some* people, who taint this block with absolute cacaphonia and the most appalling African rhythms, and dare to call it music. Whatever happened to Franz Lehár and Victor Herbert?"

"I think they're still with us," said Carrie. "I mean, still alive."

"Well, I hope they're still writing music. Because what I'm hearing today by the Negroes and the Tin Pan Yids has no business even being *called* music." Mrs. Littlejohn waddled off without waiting for a response.

After she was safely out of earshot, Mrs. Hale said to her daughter, "I'm sure she means well."

"I'm sure she does," agreed Carrie, nibbling around the burnt part of a piece of toast.

Mrs. Hale looked both ways down the street (as if her daughter's friends might have taken leave of their attendance to practicality and created a new and even *longer* route by which to come and pick up Carrie). "Or maybe they *have* gone to fetch Jane first for some reason. How *is* Jane, by the way? You haven't spoken of her lately."

"She's fine. All of my sisters are doing well."

"I really wish you wouldn't call them your sisters. By proper definition, they really *aren't* your sisters, now are they? They are your friends. The only real family you have in the world is sitting right here, still wondering why you've hardly touched your waffles. And after I bought a brand new tin of Log Cabin syrup! Pure cane and maple syrup. Not that cheap Temtor Maple *Flavor* stuff. I don't know what's in that rot. It looks like motor oil."

"The waffles are soggy, Mother, and I haven't put *any* syrup on them, real or otherwise. I don't think you left them in the iron long enough."

"I wish Vitula weren't sick so often. I worry she has T.B.—that little cough she always has."

"I think she coughs because she smokes, Mother. I think she steals a puff or two when you aren't looking."

Mrs. Hale harrumphed. "It's so unbecoming—women who smoke. Like those wanton flappers. Drink your orange juice."

"There's a gnat in it."

"I don't know why we came out here." Mrs. Hale blotted the corners of her mouth (which, like her daughter's mouth, had welcomed very little food inside) and placed her crumpled napkin next to her plate. "Who knew we'd have to contend with Mrs. Littlejohn so early in the morning?"

"I like it out here, Mother. And I'm glad Maggie and Molly are late, because it gives me the chance to discuss something with you that's been on my mind for a couple of days now."

"What is it, dear? I so hate it when things trouble you, and you keep it all bottled up inside. It isn't healthy."

"It isn't something that's necessarily *troubling* me, Mother. It's just something that came up, which I've been meaning to talk to you about."

Sylvia Hale gave her daughter a look with which Carrie was quite familiar. It involved a rimpling of the lips and a slight bulging of the eyes and it said, "I don't believe any part of the statement you just made but will pretend otherwise through this fixed expression, certain to indicate full acceptance of whatever banana oil you might wish to peddle me." At the same time she gurgled, "And of course there should be nothing of any *substance* bothering you, my dear. For aren't things, on the whole, going quite well for us? You have that nice new job with Sister Lydia, and I have my charity work, and there is enough rental income from the properties your grandfather left me that we want for very little, so long as we don't become *too* extravagant in our tastes."

A pause. A breath. An opening.

"Well, you know, Mother, it's very interesting Mrs. Littlejohn should mention the Prowses. Because I just happened to bump into Bella Prowse at Blue Delft on Saturday."

An arched brow. "Oh, you're calling her *Bella,* now, are you?"

"Well, she *does* live next door to us, Mother. And I *do* happen to remember her from grammar school. Anyway, I was buying those nut-center chocolates you asked me to get for the piano candy dish, and I was standing in front of the Johnston's display."

"Yes, I noticed they were having a sale—the dollar boxes of the mixed chocolates were going for eighty cents to the pound. You are a savvy shopper for that to have caught your eye."

"I'd like to finish, Mother."

Receding, chastened, into her chair: "Please."

"Anyway, I look to my side and there she is—"

"Rolled-down stockings and her skirt up to here, and she was probably wearing a long enough rope of those ridiculous shell beads that you could slice it all up and have enough *normal*-length necklaces for half the women on this block."

"Mother, *please!*"

A pantomimic buttoned lip. A nod. A hand upon the teapot. A declining wave from her daughter.

"*So. Anyway.* We exchanged a polite greeting, and she asked me if the music from the party the night before had bothered us, and I could hardly keep from smiling, because I *do* remember how loud it was—the music and the sound of the motor cars coming and going—and, yes, there was drinking, and how does one defend something like that—well, of course you can't because it's against the law—I'm not saying anything you aren't already thinking, Mother, in big bold letters, but the way she said it, it was almost as if she were wishing I *had* come over and told her to soften the gramophone and make her raucous guests behave themselves."

"And why do you say this?"

"Because I think she was looking for an excuse to invite me to her party."

"And why ever would you say *that*? Oh dear, is that another smudge? Have you been playing Cinderella in the fireplace, sweet?"

Mrs. Hale licked a finger to saliva-dab away the offensive speck, but Carrie pulled herself out of reach, drew a handkerchief from her strap purse, and applied it to the cursed spot. "I'm sure it's cinders in the air. Zenith has dirty air from all of its factories. Or haven't you noticed? Sometimes I think *your* face looks smudged as well."

Mrs. Hale sighed. "I'd like us to move to California someday. I think you should be in pictures. I think you'd be *divine* in pictures."

"Thank you, Mother. That was very supportive. May I go on?"

"By all means."

"I say she might have wanted to ask me in the other night because I actually *did* get an invitation—to her *next* party. It came right after I smiled and said, 'No, your music never bothers us.'"

"Now why on earth would you say such a dishonest thing as— wait!—did I just hear you say you've been invited to the Prowses' next bacchanal? By that hell-kitten? By that baby-vamp the professor snatched for himself from the bassinet?"

"Oh Mother, sometimes you sound exactly like Mrs. Littlejohn."

"On *this* point, I shall take that as a compliment."

"The party is Friday night. Bella's birthday. And I want to go. She said I'm to invite my 'four girlfriends' as well, and I think I'd very much like to do that."

"I am absolutely flabber—"

"I've been giving it a lot of thought over the last two—"

"—gasted. You know exactly the sort of crowd that will be there: all the professor's long-hair friends, and, and all the local Bohemians, and every happy violator of the Volstead Act from here to Mohalis—"

Carrie, taking her mother literally for the moment, responded by shaking her head. "I don't think anyone's coming from Winnemac U.

She did say she's planning to invite some boys from the A&M here in town. And she told me with all candor the *reason* she's inviting those boys. It's because she thinks it's time for We Five to come out of our clamshells like Venus on the beach—but here's the part I *really* wanted to talk to you about, Mother."

"The invitation alone isn't sufficient to send me into apoplexy?"

"No, there's more—a little more that was said that day at the candy store which I need your opinion on. And this is about you too, Mother. She said—well, she said we're *boring*. She just came right out with it."

"Well I *never!*"

"She said you and I are the most drab, the most boring people on the block, and this even includes Mr. Gruber with his string collection. She said it's probably too late for *you*."

"To do what? To stop being boring?" Sylvia Hale's jaw was set. She could hardly get the words out.

"That's right. But maybe there was hope for *me*. I still had a chance to kick up my heels for a few years before the Grim Reaper came knocking—because wasn't that the purpose of life, after all: to make a little noise before we go quiet into the grave?"

"Good God."

"Well, I'm quoting her, of course. Like how *she* quoted Edna St. Vincent Millay—that little poem she wrote a couple of years ago."

Wearily: "What little poem?"

"'My candle burns at both ends; it will not last the night. But ah, my foes, and oh, my friends—it gives a lovely light!'"

"Oh sweet Jesus. She wants *you* to be like *her!*"

"No, Mother. She wants me to *live*."

"Live fast and die young. I'm faint. Hand me that *Town & Country*. I want to fan myself."

Carrie handed her mother the magazine, but Mrs. Hale didn't make a breeze with it. Instead, she pointed to the photograph on the cover and said, "Isn't that a pretty gazebo?"

"We *are* boring, Mother. You know we are."

Sylvia tossed the magazine aside with an indignant snort. "Well, we can't *all* drink from ankle flasks and dance on tables. Is that really something you'd like to do, darling?"

"I don't know just *what* I'd like to do, except sometimes I think I'd like to do a little more than sit at home nearly every night."

"Well, if you'll permit *me* to be candid, may I just say that your four friends aren't any more exciting than *I* am. Mark my words: you'll drag them to this orgy on Friday night and they'll just—why, they'll just recede into the upholstery."

"But that's my point. I have found friends—whom I love, please don't misunderstand me, Mother—who are just younger versions of—well—*you*."

"I may be mistaken, but I think you just insulted me."

"I love you so much, Mother. But let me kick up my heels just a *little* and see what it feels like." Carrie got up from her chair so she could put an arm around her mother's shoulder. Through the embrace she could feel her mother trembling slightly. "I promise not to write you out of my life."

"I don't believe it. That isn't how this scenario usually plays itself out. The daughter skips away and she forgets to write and she doesn't even remember to send her mother a wire on her birthday. Then one day she reappears. Out of the blue. Now she's pregnant with a Negro man's baby or shaking with delirium tremens or some other such ghastly thing. And she isn't the woman's loving daughter anymore."

"I'll always be your loving daughter, Mother. Whether I choose to bruise my heels on tabletops or not."

Mrs. Hale took a deep breath and smiled.

"What is it?"

"Something Reverend Mobry said in one of his sermons. He said, 'God doesn't wish us to embrace life with one finger.' Is this what we've been doing, dear? Have I held you too close? Do people laugh at the mother and daughter homebodies behind their backs?"

"If they're laughing, Mother, then they're rude not to be minding their own business. Because I happen to think I'm the luckiest daughter in the world. I have a mother whom I love and who I know loves me with all her heart."

"And when someday you find yourself a beau—"

"You *do* want that for me, don't you?"

"Of course I do. But the *right* boy. And you know you aren't likely to find 'the right boy' among a bunch of roughneck Aggies coaxed into attending one of Mirabella Prowse's wild parties with promises of contraband Canadian whiskey."

With a chuckle: "Yes, Mother. You are exactly one-hundred-percent right."

"Here come Molly and Maggie. And Jane isn't with them. So they are merely late. Hurry off now, or you'll all be even later than you already are and have that demanding Miss Colthurst in a ridiculous dither."

"Sometimes, Mother, you're as awful as Mrs. Littlejohn the way you talk about people."

Carrie bounced up from her seat and pecked her mother on the cheek. Mrs. Hale reciprocated. Then she pulled back and pointed. "There's a smudge."

"I'll wear it as a beauty mark. Good-bye, Mother."

"Good-bye, darling."

Mrs. Hale watched her daughter dash across the front lawn to join her friends on their delayed morning march to Sister Lydia's Tabernacle of the Sanctified Spirit. Maggie and Molly greeted Carrie's mother with a wave. Mrs. Hale waved back.

As the three friends moved at a quick clip down the sidewalk, Molly apologized for their tardiness. "Maggie was late and then it got even later when I didn't go down right away, because apparently *this* particular morning was one in which she just *wasn't* coming up to get me."

"Perhaps you don't remember, Molly," said Maggie, bridling, "that there was a snoring hobo blocking the stairs, and frankly, I didn't care to wake him. You should have been on the lookout for me."

"Can we please not hash this all out again?" said Molly. "It's such a beautiful day. Why ruin it?"

"As it so happens, Molly, it's already ruined." Pause. Importantly: "And it was your father who did it."

"Well, well, *well*! Now you've come out with it. And I should say it's about time."

Carrie looked puzzled. "Come out with *what*?"

Molly answered for both Maggie and herself. "My father has asked Maggie's mother to marry him. Maggie is opposed."

Carrie nodded contemplatively. "Well, Maggie, aren't you generally opposed to pretty much *everything*?"

Maggie stopped in her tracks and seized her hips with both hands. "I may be crabby from time to time, Carrie, but at least I don't go through life in an absolute *drowse* the way *you* do."

Carrie glowered. Then she took a deep breath and announced, "I have just the thing to wake us *all* up. Do either of you have plans for Friday night? Well, of course you don't. Now here it is…"

Chapter Four

(from Songs and Sirens, *by Daphne Rourke)*

Jane, keeping one eye on the shop window, beheld her brother lying splayed out on the couch with the torn upholstery, which mouldered in a neglected corner of the showroom. It was the couch he was supposed to have slip-covered a month ago, but had not. A few hours earlier, Lyle Higgins had collapsed in a drunken stupor not upon his own bed in the back rooms, but upon this very piece of furniture, which was merchandise, which some future customer would sit upon and expect not to be assaulted by the stench of alcohol or old sick. Jane thought about waking him and sending him to the relative comfort of his bed, but why bother? No matter where he dormez-voused, he'd still fail to open the shop at nine. She didn't know why he even pretended to have an interest in continuing to run the family business when it was all too obvious that all he *really* wanted to do was drink and play cards and sometimes carouse with members of the opposite sex, though it took a little effort on his part to be halfway charming to a lady and Jane knew he was averse to doing anything that required the expense of much effort. Why else had she spent all of the previous afternoon gathering up everything in the shop comprised of the least bit of aluminium for the scrap-metal campaign whilst he slumbered the day away like some hibernating creature in a cave?

Nobody wanted Lyle Higgins. Not any of the women—mostly tarts—whom he happened to meet. Not any of his mates, who weren't so much mates as opportunistic spongers *pretending* to be mates. Not the British Expeditionary Force, whose recruitment office physician said he'd seen few candidates for enlistment with so compromised a liver.

And most certainly not Jane, who had grown weary, since their father's death, of carrying Lyle on the family dole when he could not or would not support himself (let alone his unmarried sister). The two would most surely have lost the shop, which they'd inherited from their dad, were it not for the war effort and its need for dedicated labourers—both men *and* women—in the aeroplane works and Royal Ordnance factories.

No, Jane didn't want Lyle in her life at all. Yet a part of her suspected he could not help being shiftless and by all appearances bereft of any redeeming qualities whatsoever, for there seemed to be something missing from his brain from the start, and how could this be his fault? This was the charitable view that came to Jane every now and then (when she was feeling a little generous). Most days, however, she wanted to take a few of the cartridges she'd packed with gunpowder from the factory in which she worked on the outskirts of London (with her friends Maggie, Carrie, Ruth, and Molly), load them into a compatible machine-gun magazine, and then deliver them *ratta-tat-tat* into her brother in a way that would swiftly and conveniently end his life. Then one of the biggest worries of *her* life would be removed, evaporating in an effervescence of twinkling Walt Disney fairy dust.

Jane had always wanted to be a schoolteacher, but even before her father died, there wasn't money to pay for her education. She loved children and thought she might like to work as an evacuation officer for the London County Council, which relocated East Enders (and their large broods) to less dangerous parts of the country. But before she went into the offices to interview, she had a nightmare in which, during one of her assigned excursions outside of London, her brother fell asleep with a lit fag between his fingers and burnt himself to a crisp. She would have to keep a hand in the running of the shop (and in the running of Lyle) is what she would have to do, and as luck would have it, when the window slammed shut on a position with the Council, the door to factory work swung wide open. It was her friend Ruth who made the case that We Five should assert their independence in service to their country by helping to defeat Hitler, and they could do this by making bullets and bombs.

Lyle might still some day or night fall asleep with a lit Player's cig in hand and burn himself to a crisp, but at least now Jane could preserve what was left of her family's reputation by saying it was a German incendiary bomb what done it.

The phone bell rang.

"Yes?"

"Jane, it's Carrie. I'm at the call box in front of the Boots."

"What are you doing there? It's six fifteen. We'll never make the factory bus in time."

"That's why I rang you. You should go on. Go meet Ruth at the stage so at least the two of you can catch the six-thirty. The rest of us will have to go out on the *seven*-thirty."

"But you'll lose an hour's pay!"

"It won't be the end of the world."

"What's happened? Is anything the matter?"

"I'll tell you everything when I see you in assembly. In short: Molly's father. Maggie's mother. A marriage proposal. Everything hunky-dory except for Maggie, who has suddenly decided she'd rather be dead than have another soak for a father."

Jane shook her head. "Ain't *that* a bugger! And with the way things are right now... She really shouldn't say such things."

"Hurry along, Jane. Or you'll miss the bus."

Jane thought for a moment. "I'm going to wait and take the stragglers' bus with the three of you."

"But what about Ruth? She'll be waiting for all of us and I haven't another penny to put into this telephone."

"*I'll* ring her up. Oh, sometimes I could strangle Maggie—putting herself in the way of everyone's happiness like this."

"Then you know all about it."

"I know enough. And I don't agree with any of it."

"I should go and see if the two have come to blows. Goodbye, Jane. We'll see you later in the morning—*I hope.*"

After ringing off, Jane placed the call to Ruth. However, it was Miss Mobry, the Methodist minister's sister, who picked up the telephone. "Hallo, Miss Mobry. This is Jane Higgins. I wish to speak with Ruth."

"Oh yes, she's right here. Is anything wrong? Ruth was afraid that—well, last night's air raid—"

"Oh no, Miss Mobry. It isn't that, although a shop not too far from the emporium did take a nasty hit. Thank God no one was hurt. No, this isn't life and death, but it's really quite involved. I'll have to tell you about it some other time."

"Yes, do, my dear. And you should come to tea. Do you fancy loganberry tarts and seed cake? Who doesn't? Ah, two old maids taking tea together. Is there anything cozier?"

Jane didn't respond. She resented being called an old maid. First: she *wasn't* one. She was only twenty-three and still eminently marriageable. And although she hadn't any prospects at the moment, neither had any of her circle-sisters. Second: "old maid" was such a loathsome designation, especially for an unmarried woman who was not at all content with her present unaffiliated status.

Unlike her friend Ruth.

Ruth had let it be known that she did not plan to marry under any circumstance, that this was her choice, and furthermore, that she had the *right* to make her own choices. Jane respected Ruth, though Ruth always seemed out of step with her sisters.

"Jane?"

"Good morning, Ruth. There's been a hitch. You're to step out and catch the six-thirty and not wait for the rest of us. Maggie and Molly and Carrie are running quite late and won't be able to make it."

"What about *you*?"

"I've decided to wait for *them*."

"Then I'll wait as well."

"Then we shall *all* be late, and how will *that* look?"

"It will simply look as if we've all been detained together. Everyone knows we come to work in a clump, Jane. We are only as punctual as our weakest link allows us to be, and I take it the weak link this morning is Maggie."

"So you must know a little something about Maggie's mother's big decision."

"*Know* something? I received quite an earful from Maggie the evening we spent together in the A.R.P shelter. We shouldn't tie up this line into the parsonage; otherwise I'd tell you all about it."

"Maggie is being quite unfair."

"Well, of course she is."

"But you really should nip over to the factory bus kiosk, Ruth. 'Save yourself!' they always say in the movies."

"I haven't an overwhelming desire to wait for that bus alone."

"Why?"

"Must I tell you now? Miss Mobry is flitting in and out of the vestibule with little bits of unnecessary business. I know it's so she can eavesdrop on this conversation."

"Is this something you don't want her to know about?"

"Only that I shouldn't wish to make her worry," replied Ruth. "She's a nervous bundle of nerves after the recent raids. She gets so flurried sometimes when she thinks of the Luftwaffe dropping a bomb on our factory. I fancy she thinks she's my mother sometimes, or at the very least a doting gran or aunt. As it so happens, I've always been asked to call her 'aunt.'"

"Have you met with some trouble, Ruth?"

"It depends on how you define 'trouble.' I have nothing better to do. I'll come and tell you about it, and free up this instrument for those wishing to burden Mr. Mobry with matters of faith and conscience."

"Do I detect a bit of cheek in that statement?"

"None at all. I owe everything to Mr. Mobry and his sister. It is only a *small* inconvenience that they still consider me the same woebegone waif who arrived on their doorstep with little more than the clothes on her back."

Jane laughed. "They'd sing a different song if they ever clapped eyes on you working in the main shed. Dressed to the nines in your mob cap and your greasy brown overall!"

"Would that we could wear those shapeless overalls outside the factory. It might solve that little problem at the bus kiosk."

"What little problem?"

"I'll see you shortly."

Ruth left the house at that moment. A scant five minutes later she was standing next to her friend Jane in the showroom of Higgins' Emporium in Balham High Road. The name was Jane's father's idea; he thought it would entice a better breed of clientele for the junk shop (to little avail). The two young women were studying Jane's sleeping brother in the casual and detached manner of two visitors to the zoo observing a slumbering gorilla.

"Sometimes he'll be out like this for hours," said Jane with indifference. (This wasn't the first time she and Ruth had stood over Lyle, watching him sleep when the rest of London was up and about and being industrious and productive. And lately he'd been even more slumberous than usual, using the nightly air raids that kept him 'up for all hours' as convenient justification for dozing the entire day away. As if no one but Lyle Higgins was so terribly incommoded by the Blitz.)

Ruth shook her head slowly and evenly—a demonstration of both disgust and empathy: disgust for Jane's brother and empathy for Jane, whose burden it was to contend with such a sibling. "I don't see why you continue to live here. They'll soon be finished with the dormitories near the factory. You really should apply. Since you're a charge-hand now, I'm sure they'll put you at the top of the list."

"And then what? Move to the dormitory and have the death of this human sloth, what also happens to be my brother, on my conscience for the rest of my days? I'm not lying to you, Ruth, when I say that Lyle shouldn't even eat if it wasn't for me sliding the plate of food in front of him and then nudging him a few times out of his usual fog."

The two friends sat down at a little table close to the large plate-glass window, purposefully out of sight of Jane's snoring brother. The window, crisscrossed with sticky brown tape, had remained intact after several nearby bombings. (It was kept *un*-blacked out because from sundown to sunup lights in the showroom were never turned on.) Ruth was inspired on a previous visit to recite, with the obvious nod to Rudyard Kipling, "If you can keep your glass when all about you are losing theirs and blaming it on the Nazis, then you'll be one lucky bloke of a shopkeeper, my son—um—*daughter.*"

"Should I put on a pot of tea?" asked Jane. "I haven't any biscuits. All the ones I like have disappeared from the Sainsbury's."

"I just had my own cuppa; don't go to any trouble. I'm perfectly content sitting here gabbling with you and playing Nosey Parker to all the passersby in the street. I love this block, Jane, I do. Bustling, yes, but still rather quaint. It reminds me of Mrs. Gaskell's Cranford. And this shop—I remember when we were girls—do you remember how tidy your father kept it?"

Jane nodded and smiled. "Not a shilling in the till, but you'd think he was Mr. Selfridge himself, the pride he took in this place."

"Do you recall how he used to scold us for playing hide-and-seek behind all the old wardrobes and chest-of-drawers?"

Jane nodded. "Those were happy days. Even happier when Mum was alive. Now, you said something was the matter and you must tell me what it is."

Ruth nodded. She allowed her gaze to lose its focus as she composed her thoughts. "There are several men—*young* men I see in the early morning once, sometimes twice a week, when I'm waiting for the four of you at the kiosk. They go into the pub across the street—almost always at the same time."

"Cor! What public house opens so early in the morning?"

"Ones like the Fatted Pig that serve men who work through the night. Like those I mean to tell you about. They're part-time fire watchers with the A.F.S. and theirs is the midnight shift. I overhear some of their talk on the way to the pub. Their full-time daylight job is delivering coal for Mr. Matthews. I suppose you know about Mr. Matthews."

"You mean the fact that he only hires conchies?"

Ruth nodded. "After losing both of his sons at Dunkirk. Naturally, a father would be consumed with anger over his family being so cruelly singled out. And he's *very* bitter, *frightfully* angry. But rather than direct his anger at the ones really responsible for taking his boys from him, he's decided, instead, to abhor war in the abstract—*all war*, including the very one we're in the midst of fighting. And become a violent pacifist. I say violent because he fired all the men who'd been delivering coal for him who refused to join him in taking a stand against the war. He wanted them to sign statements of conscientious objection. Those who wouldn't, he sacked."

"How does this concern *you*?"

"Those five lads who go to the pub together—they look to be our age, maybe a little older. They are each of them *proud* conchies—happy to go to Mr. Matthews and present themselves as replacements. And they seem to have taken an interest in the five of *us*. They watch us from the pub windows as we wait together for the factory bus."

"There's no crime in that, Ruth."

"Of course not. Nor is there crime in whatever scheme they're devising to put themselves in our way."

Jane laughed. It was not a laugh of derision but only one of disbelief. "How do you know they are—as you put it—set to put themselves in our way?"

"I'll tell you. Mr. Andrews, the Scotsman who opens the pub so early in the morning—not only for these lads but for the other night workers who are known to pay a premium for their cock-crow pints—he came out to speak to me one morning last week, before your arrival. He said he'd overheard the five talking amongst themselves about their interest in the five of us. One of them said it was kismet the numbers should come out even and that we should all be in the same vicinity two or three mornings a week, and they were planning to divide us up amongst them, as if it were all some kind of game, to see who could get the farthest."

"The farthest. Now what exactly does *that* mean? I should hope it doesn't mean what you *think* it means, Ruth. I fancy it's about winning our favour—winning our *hearts*."

"Jane Higgins, you cannot be that naïve."

"Mr. Andrews knows their character, and if *he* believes the thing to be all quite innocent…"

"*Innocent*? Being pursued by men with conquest clearly on their minds?"

"To be pursued by *any* man, Ruth, when there are so many of *us* and so few of *them* round these days, should be taken as flattery at first pitch."

"*Flattery*. Are you potty? It's definitely sport, though. You have that much correct, at least."

"But isn't love in its early stages a kind of sport, Ruth? Pursuit and conquest. It *is* a game, rather. People don't just bump into each other at a Lyons Corner House, fall instantly in love, and then go skipping off to the vicar to marry."

Ruth's brow furrowed. "How can you make light of such a serious matter?"

"Because I ain't yet seen the *serious* part of it. These are, no doubt, five lads what spend their dismal days delivering coal to housewives and housemaids and grumpy old men in cardigan sweaters, and then spend half their nights freezing their bums off on draughty rooftops watching for incendiaries, and where and when, I ask you, are they ever to meet interesting girls—that is, girls what haven't had all the life crushed out of them by falling walls and timbers? You must admit, myself excepted, that the five of us are quite dishy to look at—and very much *alive*—and who *wouldn't* want to take us out for a whirl on the dance floor some night?"

"First, Jane, I so tire of hearing you denigrate yourself. You are pretty in your own way and let's have done with *that*! Second, these boys don't know a thing about us except for what we look like."

"But isn't that what the male species considers first? How a woman looks. Later a bloke will have himself the chance to discover if the girl who attracts him's got a charming personality or a sharp mind or find out if she be C of E or Presbyterian, or—or casts her vote for Labour or Tory, but not until later. I should be rather *pleased* if they're looking at us and talking about us and scheming over some way to meet us. There's only one chap in my life in the bloody here and now, and he is, according to all those who meet him, a worthless invertebrate. I will confess to you, Ruth, that sometimes I come to the parsonage pretending to drop in and visit with you, when it's really Mr. Mobry I most fancy seeing—not that I find him especially attractive or got himself any more personality than a goat, but what he *does* have to commend him is this: he's a *man*—and *not* a man what also happens to be my brother, and I should like to have the privilege, at this stage in my young life, to simply sit and exchange a fine how-do-you-do with any *man* who just happens to be halfway *male*. I've even given thought to darkening the door of that Fatted Pig myself, but I hesitate to do so, as I know the sort of woman who most often mooches into London pubs alone, and I'm not keen on being put in her league. Nevertheless, I hunger for the companionship. You do not. I know it. I've always known it. I don't judge you for it. But you shouldn't judge me for *craving* it."

Ruth sat quietly for a moment, digesting what her friend Jane had just said. "And does it not bother you," she finally said, "that these men, who've taken such a curious interest in us—that they're conscientious objectors? That they refuse to risk their lives for their country as so many other young men are doing these days?"

Jane shook her head. "There are those who don't think that war should be the cure for all the evils of the world. They believe God created man for a much higher purpose than slaughtering other members of his species."

Ruth nodded. "There *are* those conscientious objectors who believe exactly as you say. They have my respect, they do. But there are also conchies who are conchies for one reason only: cowardice. They won't take up arms because they're frightened witless by the possibility of getting themselves killed. They think they have a better chance of surviving this war if they can keep themselves off the battlefield and out of the Navy and R.A.F. altogether. These men I do *not* respect."

Jane tried not to laugh, but she simply couldn't help herself. "Of course, Ruth, any one of these conchie cowards could get hisself gassed to death or blown to bits in his very own bed by the Luftwaffe on any night of the week. They're dropping the most insidious bombs now. Some are timed not to go off until after the firemen and rescuers arrive! You can be just as dead here on the home front as you are in the trenches fighting for a cause. And then there's this, lovie: the fact of what it is that you and I and Maggie and Carrie and Molly do sixty hours a week: we help make the instruments of war. In the end, any of these five conchies might woo—and who knows?—perhaps even *win* the hand of a girl what helps Britain do that very thing he's supposed to be against!"

"Life is full of ironies," Ruth sighed. "*And* delusions. We could all be dead tomorrow, you know. And yet we go to bed each night expecting that fate will be kind to us for one night more—that we'll rise the next morning to gather ourselves together to take the six-thirty to the Filling Factory. Your brother passes out after his binges, assuming that he too will rise to drink another day. Life goes on—life beautiful, life ugly and unseemly, and most people can only follow the pattern of life most familiar to them and act upon the instincts that go along with it. But I am not 'most people.' I am not the instinctive creature you are, Jane. I fancy something different from my life, something that has nothing to do with the men I've told you about—something which I cannot put into words. There is something missing inside me, but I don't know how to fill the void."

"Friendship with the four of us ain't enough for you, Ruth—at least for now?"

Ruth patted the top of Jane's hand—sweetly, not condescendingly. "For the present, you're all *more* than enough, but it can't be that way forever."

"I understand. I do, Ruth. I understand because sometimes I feel the same way—about the five of us, that is. That we're all just circling and circling and waiting to land. But whilst *I'm* circling I can't help wondering if there just might be some fine-looking bloke inside the Fatted Pig Tavern what might like to get to know me a little better, seeing's how we're all just passing the time."

Ruth frowned. "Oh, I'm sure there is. I'm sure those five have already divided us all up like Christmas crackers."

"Don't talk about Christmas. It's just going to make me hungry. I scrambled some powdered eggs this morning, but I couldn't eat a bite. I detest powdered eggs, Ruth, I do." Jane sighed. She looked out the show window past the items Lyle had hung there, which seemed to make sense only to him: a small (and broken) Wilkinson Sword lawn mower, several rusty tools and other largely unidentifiable metallic oddments, and a broken pushchair without tyres. "It would be just our luck if we all ended up missing the six-thirty by only a minute or two. Then We Five would have to wait a full hour until the straggler bus comes along. Of course, I know a good place to *spend* that hour." Jane raised an eyebrow impishly.

"Jane Higgins, sometimes I think you're no better than your ne'er-do-well brother."

"That is absolutely the worst thing you've ever said about me!"

At that moment said brother rose, with a stretch and a groan, from his royal couch. He stumbled toward the front of the shop, blinking his eyes against the bright sunshine flooding in through the window and combing his fingers through his matted hair. Glancing at a clock on the wall—an antique Victorian clock diminished in value by its cracked glass cover—he declared, "It's getting on for six thirty and you're still here."

"That's right, Lyle, we're still here," replied Jane in a dull voice.

"Then you've missed your bus by my guess, and should have plenty of time to put on a pot of coffee."

"There's no coffee, Lyle," said Jane, still without any show of exasperation. "There was none at the market. We are apparently in the middle of a coffee shortage."

"Tea, then."

Ruth eyed her friend, wondering how she would respond.

"I'm rather engaged, Lyle. Be a love and make tea for all three of us if you would."

The novelty of this idea struck Jane's brother as something quite intriguing. "I could certainly do that. But you'll have to direct me to the proper cupboard."

"Shall I tell you first where you'll find the kitchen?"

"How can you be such a bloody lark so early in the morning?" he grumbled.

Ruth and Jane waited until he had left the room to collapse into hysterics.

Chapter Five

Bellevenue, Mississippi, February 1997

(from Five Came Running, *by Mark Dunn)*

Ruth heard a knock at the trailer door. She had been watching Katie Couric talking to a woman Ruth didn't recognize. There was no sound coming out of the television because the volume knob had fallen off when she hit the set with the closet door. It was an old Sylvania portable black-and-white the Mobrys had given her when she moved into the trailer.

Ruth had been living with the now-retired minister and his younger sister since she was fourteen. Before this, she'd been housed in two different orphanages and then parked with six different foster families. The Mobrys, Ruth's very last foster guardians (they couldn't be called foster *parents* because they weren't husband and wife), had been very kind to her, as had the congregation of the small non-denominational church the Reverend had shepherded. The Church of the Generous Spirit was unique among the Protestant churches of northern Mississippi. Not only had it been racially integrated from its inception—this in a part of the country in which integration, while the law of the land, wasn't always the law of the heart—the church had an unusual take on Christ himself. For Reverend Mobry's flock, Jesus was an unabashed, unapologetic liberal. Kind of like Hubert Humphrey, if Humphrey had been the son of God.

It was a small congregation, but a well-knit one, and in it Ruth had found the loving extended family she'd always wanted. She knew nothing of her blood family—only that her mother, a migrant worker thought to be from Appalachian Kentucky, had died in an automobile accident. The near-term baby she'd been carrying at the time was pulled from her corpse and saved, but circumstances— Ruth's mother had no traceable relatives—required that Ruth make her entrance into the world as a ward of the state.

Ruth had now reached the age at which she was no longer a ward of the state.

And she was no longer the responsibility of the Mobrys. And though she was very fond of the brother and sister who had taken such good care of her for the last seven years, Ruth was ready to spread her wings. She'd been the first of We Five to notice the ad placed in the local paper by Lucky Aces Casino, which was about to open up in Tunica County, right on the Mississippi River. (The Mississippi state legislature was very specific in crafting the 1990 law that permitted gambling in the state: its casinos had to be docked either along the Mississippi River or on the Gulf of Mexico.) Lucky Aces needed cocktail waitresses, and Ruth thought this was something she and her friends could do.

By choice, Ruth had never gone to college, choosing instead to pursue a path of "self-education." The term she used for herself, but which she never said aloud, since most people would think it had something to do with an interest in cars, was "autodidact." Whenever Ruth wasn't assisting Ms. Mobry around the parsonage (the house where the Mobrys lived was called the "parsonage," though it was owned by the siblings free and clear) or helping out at the church, Ruth read. She'd set out at the age of fifteen to read from cover to cover every book at the Bellevenue Library, as well as all the hundreds of other books which she'd bought at garage sales and second-hand book stores throughout Desoto County. (Except, that is, for the bodice-ripper romances; these she got for Ms. Mobry. It was a secret passion of Lucille's, which no one at the church was supposed to know about.)

Ruth hoped someday to write professionally. This was her dream.

Now that she was grown and Reverend Mobry had turned the pulpit over to a younger man, the waitressing job seemed a perfect fit for her. It would give her time to read. And write. Bringing drinks to people at their slot machines and gaming tables didn't sound like a very taxing kind of job; it was definitely one she wouldn't have to take home with her every day in the way of frets and regrets. Ruth would also have the chance to see more of her four friends from childhood, Maggie, Jane, Carrie, and Molly, both at the casino and during the free hours the five liked to spend together.

We Five applied for the waitressing jobs together and were all hired. The head of Human Resources, a Ms. Touliatis, liked it that her new applicants got along so well; they seemed much more like sisters than friends. "You're all so, so, so *cohesive!*" she had marveled. "And Lucky Aces Casino *needs* cocktail waitresses who are cohesive." Then Ms. Touliatis, who was forty-one and looked to Ruth as if she'd been twice run over by the ineluctably trundling steamroller of life, added through a wistful sigh: "I wish I had friends who were as dependable and devoted to one another as I see ya'll are. By way of contrast, I just last week caught my best friend Lawanda in bed with my husband Mack. Well, not just my husband, but also our Irish Setter, Dakota. Can you imagine that? Both my husband *and* my dog were cheating on me!"

"I don't think we can imagine that at all," replied Jane, who felt a response of some sort was required.

"And then," Ms. Touliatis went on, "there's my other good friend—*former* good friend, Heidi. Heidi once made fun of my lazy eye over the loudspeaker at Kmart." Ms. Touliatis pulled a tissue from the box on her desk and blew her nose. "A good and true friend is one of life's great treasures."

"That's a fact," said Jane.

The Mobrys had taken news of Ruth's new job very well. "How convenient," said the Reverend, "with the casino just down the road. And nowhere in the teachings of our socially progressive Lord and Savior do we find objections to cocktail waitressing in riverboat casinos, though the Southern Baptists would certainly have you think otherwise."

"But do be careful," Lucille Mobry added. "Men do get drunk in those places and try to take advantage when they can."

Ruth nodded. "Yes, the woman who's in charge of all the waitresses—Ms. Colthurst—she's gonna have us all watch a training film called 'How to Keep Their Mitts Off Your Tuches.' I think it was put out by the New Jersey Gaming Commission."

Lucille suddenly looked tristful. "Does this mean you won't be living with us anymore? Are you gonna be moving in with one of your girlfriends?"

"Well, she doesn't *have* to," suggested the Reverend. "She can have the trailer out back. You can be a real working woman, Ruth, with a place of your own, but you'll have us close at hand for whenever you need anything."

"That's very sweet, Uncle Herb," said Ruth. "But if I took you up on this, I'd want to pay you rent."

"We'll take a little somethin' from you if it makes you feel better," said Mobry. The retired minister was halted by a thought. "You know, Ruth, you've got an awful lot of books, and I'm not sure they'll all fit into that trailer. I might have to buy you one of those steel storage sheds and we can turn that into a little library for you."

Ruth smiled. "That would be a funny-looking library."

Lucille slapped the air with her hand. "Oh let's just keep the books in her old room. Whenever she wants one, she can come get it. Oh honey-girl, I guess you can tell how hard it's gonna be for us to let go of you. Just moving you outside into Lucius's old trailer is gonna feel like a huge separation."

"I'm sure everything will work out fine," said Ruth, as she stepped over to her "aunt" to give her a kiss on the cheek.

"Unless there's a tornado," fretted Lucille, "in which case we'll get to watch you fly away like Dorothy Gale."

Mobry nodded. "You two remember when the big one touched down about a mile up the road? You recollect how much trouble we had getting Lucius out of that trailer and down into the basement?"

"Well, you don't have to worry about *me*," said Ruth. "I'll be camped out in the basement long before the Weather Channel even puts up the Doppler radar. Me and my good friend, Little Debbie." Ruth moistened her lips, visions of Swiss Cake Rolls and Oatmeal Creme Pies now dancing impudently in her head.

The Lucius of above mention was Lucius Redder. He'd been CGS's building custodian since the church was founded by the Reverend and his sister in 1962. The siblings couldn't pay him much but allowed him to live rent-free in the house trailer, which Mobry had bought at an estate sale and which he'd docked permanently in the backyard. Lucius had died in his sleep about six months earlier—right before Mobry's retirement. No one knew how old he was, but Ruth guessed he'd reached at least ninety before he passed. Her friend Molly thought he was even older than that: "I think he was born into slavery."

Molly said this with a straight face and nobody corrected her. "Molly isn't stupid," Jane had once remarked to the others. "She just doesn't know very much."

"This'll work nicely," said Lucille Mobry a few days later. She was standing inside the old trailer and giving it a good looking-over the way interior decorators do. "It needs a *little* fixin' up, I'll give you that, but Herb and I have a lot of time on our hands now. He can wedge those bed legs so you don't roll off in your sleep, and I can sew you some nice new café curtains and re-cover this old couch. And I'll get you a bunch of lavender sachets that'll remove the old-man smell."

"Don't go to too much trouble, Aunt Lucille. I can do most of those things myself."

"But I *want* to, honey-girl. And just think: you can sit out here and read in peace and quiet. You won't have to listen to all those shows Herb and I watch now, which we never had time for before, like that funny Moesha, who looks like Stelloise's girl Jerline, or that show where Rob Petrie is a doctor who solves crimes, but his wife Laura is nowhere to be found."

"The television never bothered me," said Ruth simply, thinking distractedly of what she was going to do with the big armchair next to the door with the batting coming out of it.

Jane Higgins was standing on the concrete pad outside the door to Ruth's trailer. Ruth held the door open for her.

"Where are the others?" she asked, craning her neck to see around Jane.

"Mags' car went into a ditch."

"Is she all right? Was anybody with her?"

"She'd just picked up Molly and Carrie. It happened over by Carrie's house. Everybody's fine. The road had some ice on it and she just slid right in."

"What are they gonna do?"

"Well, Molly's daddy can't drive us to the casino because his car's in the shop with a distributor problem, and Mrs. Hale was already on her way up to Memphis for a doctor's appointment, so Mags got the idea of calling the casino to see if they could send over one of their courtesy vans to pick us up. And guess what? They said they would."

Ruth sighed. "Couldn't we just see the new insurance man some other day—like maybe one of the nights we're all waitressing?"

Jane shook her head. "The meeting is for *everybody*—that means *all* the employees of Lucky Aces. Ms. Touliatis isn't gonna make that insurance man drive all the way back down to make a second presentation for just five cocktail waitresses."

Ruth acquiesced with a nod. "Why do we even need medical insurance anyway?"

"Because one of these days Mags just might drive us all into the Mississippi River and we'll probably have to get our lungs pumped out." Jane looked around the trailer. "I like what you've done with this stinky ol' place."

"I haven't done half the things I *want* to. I did put up those curtains. Lucille helped me. I don't know anything about curtains. I should have asked Carrie to be my 'aesthetic advisor.'"

"Whatever the hell that is, I'm sure she would've been glad to do it. Carrie's so cultured. Do you know what Lyle said about Carrie? I don't go quoting my brother very often because most of what comes out of his mouth is drunken garbage, but this one was funny. He said Carrie and her mother had such high airs they probably shitted divinity."

Ruth's mouth wasn't doing what Jane's mouth was doing; only one of the two friends was smiling. "What does he mean: 'divinity'?"

"*Divinity*! Like pecan divinity. Like what you get at Stuckey's."

"Oh, you mean *candy*."

"But *divinity* candy. That's the joke. You know: divinity's white and shit is—oh, just forget it." Jane rolled her eyes and groaned. "It spoils everything when I have to explain jokes to you. You're getting as bad as Molly."

"Maybe it's because I've been living with a minister and his sister all these years. When I hear the word 'divinity' I don't usually think of candy."

"Well, thank you for letting me know I'll have to start tailoring my jokes to your personal life experience."

Ruth stared at her friend. "Why are you such a sourpuss this morning?"

"I'm not a sourpuss. On the other hand, I was in a slightly *better* mood before your Aunt Lucille made a crack about my handbag. You must have told her I got it from Second-Hand Roseanne."

"When was this? You mean just now?"

Jane nodded. "When I was coming through the house. Now why do I have to come through *their* house when I'm here to visit *you*? Can't I just come *around* the house without having to pass Go and collect two hundred insults?"

"Oh stop it, Jane. Whatever she said, I know she didn't mean it the way you heard it. Lucille wouldn't even know how to insult a person if she tried."

"She insults *me*. She calls me her 'sister-in-spinsterhood,' her 'bosom bachelorette.' Why does she think I'm never gonna get married? I'll tell you why she thinks that—because she thinks I'm ugly. That's what she thinks. That we're two 'sisters-in-ugliness.' Do you know how offensive that is? Especially since *you're* the one who never wanted a ticket on the marriage train."

Jane sat down on the couch.

"These shoes are hurting me already. They're new. I don't know what I was thinking." She kicked off one of the shoes and began to rub her foot.

"Do you want to wear one of *my* pairs?"

"What size do you wear? I can't remember."

"Eight."

"I'm a ten, but thanks anyway. Does Lucille know you're a lesbian?"

"I'm sure she's figured it out."

"But you've never told her? *Or* the Reverend?"

"No, but they have to know. They never ask me why I don't date. And they see some of the books I read. I'm sure they're okay with it. So, you're sure the courtesy van's gonna swing by to get *us* too?"

"That's what Mags said. Isn't it nice how things work out? Like the way Ms. Colthurst is letting us all work the day shift so we don't have to go all the way home and then have to come right back again tonight."

"It *would* be nice, Jane, except for the fact that we hardly ever get good tips on the day shift. From nine in the morning till five in the afternoon it's just a bunch of stingy old farts who hog the nickel slots and drink up as many free Diet Pepsis as their bladders'll hold."

"Whoo boy! There's a Ruth Thrasher I don't see very often." Jane ran her hand along the fabric of the couch. She sniffed the air. "Did somebody pee on this sofa?"

"I think Lucius had a dog for a while."

"Let's *hope* he had a dog. Aren't these colors *wild*? How old is this trailer house of yours?"

"Ancient. I didn't mean what I said about those old people. I like old people. I guess I just prefer old people like the ones who go to CGS—people who are trying to make the world a better place— not the ones who just sit at slot machines until all their organs shut down."

"I know that, honey. I also know that going to that church has given you a big ol' conscience. I depend on your conscience, since sometimes I can't find where I put mine. That comes from having a brother it's so easy to want dead. First tortured with acid and then dropped off a bridge."

"Jane, have you ever once thought something and then *not* said it?"

"All the time. Like all morning I've been thinking of how much I'm gonna enjoy getting the night off. Lyle's doing something with his friends tonight, and I'll have the apartment all to myself for a change. I plan to take a sudsy bubble bath with scented candles all around and sip white wine like somebody in the movies. And there'll be no Lyle to come banging on the door and tell me to please feed him, like he's a helpless baby chick waiting for his worms. I thought I might ask if I could move in with *you*, Ruth, since we're the only ones of the five of us who aren't abnormally attached to a parent."

"Because we don't *have* parents," Ruth superfluously interjected.

"Well, duh, *yeah*. But now that I've gotten myself a good look at this place, it's really small."

"You're right. It *is* pretty small. But I'd have you for a roommate in a New York minute if it wasn't. You know that Mags' mother and Molly's father might be getting married, right?"

"Yeah, I'd heard that. Mrs. Barton will be saving a ton on chiropractic services and all those holistic teas and things Doc Osborne sells. Do you have any coffee?"

"No. Do you want me to get you a cup from the house?"

"What? And give your opinionated Aunt Lucille a chance to say something *new* about how sucky my chances are of getting a husband? I don't know why she has it in for me."

"I think she means well, Jane. She just can't overlook those things the two of you have in common."

"*Excuse me, Ruth Thrasher, but I have absolutely nothing in common with your shriveled-up old Aunt Lucille!*"

"Now who's talking smack about old people?"

"Who's that guy walking up to the trailer?"

"By the look of his livery uniform, I'd say he's the courtesy van driver from Lucky Aces."

"That was fast."

"I think he must be picking us up first. Put your shoes on."

The man seemed more boy than man. He looked like a college kid. Very well groomed and nice-featured. Big lips, though. Mick Jagger lips. He introduced himself as Tom. Full name: Tom Katz.

In the van, Tom, now seated behind the wheel, said that his father had a sense of humor.

"Katz is a Jew name," said Jane, seating herself right behind their young, good-looking driver. "Are you Jewish?"

"First, Jews don't generally like it when you use the word 'Jew' as an adjective, although I don't think you meant anything by it."

"Oh I didn't mean anything at all. I *like* Jews. Especially the ones who give me the giggles like on *Seinfeld*."

"Well, as it so happens, I'm *not* Jewish. I mean, technically. Although my father's Jewish. Hence the name. But to be Jewish your mother has to be Jewish and my mother was a Pillsbury. Not one of the baking company Pillsburys, but the Greenville, Mississippi, Pillsburys. Though ironically, Mama did go to the Pillsbury bake-off one year before she married my father, but they wouldn't let her compete because they were afraid people would think things were rigged if she'd won. The good thing was that she got one hundred dollars anyway just for showing up and being a good sport, and everybody liked her cobbler and didn't even guess it had brandy in it."

"You're a good driver," said Jane. "You handled yourself on that ice patch in a very fruity way. You know: 'with a plum.'"

Ruth rolled her eyes.

"A plum?" asked Tom, addressing Jane through the rearview mirror.

"Jane only tells jokes that have to be explained," shouted Ruth from the rear of the van. "In my opinion, they stop being jokes at that point and just become a nuisance."

Jane emitted a low growl. "What I was *trying* to say, Ruth, is that I notice he hasn't spun us into a ditch like some people we know and love."

"Yeah," said Tom. "They did put us through a little mini training course. But it was mostly about how to treat our passengers—you know, how to lay the Southern hospitality on real thick, since a bunch of Lucky Aces employees are coming from other parts of the country where rudeness is the order of the day. My four buddies and me—as it happens: we're locals. We just graduated from Ole Miss last year, so we know all about Dixie manners."

Jane looked as if she was merely feigning interest, but she was actually genuinely engaged in what Tom was saying and couldn't help it that her face didn't register sincerity convincingly. "You graduated from college and now you're working for a casino?"

"Just till the end of the summer. We all thought it would be nice to get ourselves a taste of the real world before going on to law school."

"You're all going to be lawyers?"

"Well, four of us. Pardlow wants to be a legal historian. He wants to write about the law and go on Court TV and CNN and say shit like—sorry. Say *stuff* like, 'Well, you know, Wolf, this isn't the *first* time a man has been charged with killing his whole family with a fireplace poker. That would be the People of Ohio versus Billy Pokeman back in 1923.' Anyway, I mention my buddies because we've been watching the five of you since we started working at the casino a couple of weeks ago."

"Oh, you *have*?" Jane raised her eyebrows for the benefit of Ruth, the way people in sitcoms do to show wry, shared interest.

Tom nodded. "And we were wonderin' if any of you were seeing anybody. I mean, we haven't noticed any guys hanging out at the casino who looked like they might know you."

Jane laughed. "You mean since you don't see any guys who might be our boyfriends, that means we don't *have* any?"

"Yeah. Well, *yeah*."

"Well, we *don't* have any boyfriends," Ruth blurted. "And some of us aren't even in the *market* for boyfriends."

"Just one-night stands," Tom Katz let fly.

Jane mimed drumsticking a snare. "Ba-bum-bum! Does your Pillsbury Dough Mama know her little Jewboy talks like this?"

Tom locked eyes with Jane through the rearview mirror. "Not to get too P.C. on you here, but Jewish men don't generally like it when you put the word 'boy' after the word 'Jew.'"

"I was just funning you."

Ruth interjected sourly, "Why don't you *explain* to Mr. Katz just how that was funny?"

"Oh why don't you just hush up, Ruth?"

Tom tried to get the conversation back on track: "I guess what I'm tryin' to say is that we all—my four friends and me—we're gettin' a little hard up for some decent female companionship. And ya'll are the only ladies anywhere *near* our age in skuzzy Casino Land who don't look like they used to be strippers or drug addicts, or've been out there spreading STDs around since junior high school."

Jane's mouth fell open. Ruth rolled her eyes again and tried to find something distracting out the window to take her attention away from the conversation.

"You're awfully disgusting," replied Jane, with a casualness to her delivery that belied the harsh sentiment, "*and* awfully picky, considering you drive a courtesy van for a living." Jane punctuated her observation with a flirty wink directed toward the van's rearview mirror.

"Nothing wrong with being picky even while you're slummin'," replied Tom. "Anyway, if I can get all your phone numbers, then I'll divvy them up between the guys, and we'll all do something together. Some nice, safe, 'break-the-ice' group activity."

"Count me out," said Ruth, under her breath. She was looking at a cotton field, the plants not yet plowed under. Little white bolls polka-dotted the landscape like dandruff.

"I tell you what I'll do," said Jane, sounding like a used-car salesman. "I'll give you *my* phone number. You can probably get it easy anyway. It's in the book under 'Higgins Antiques.' And I'll talk to my friends—including Ruth here, who I'm sure would be up for anyplace where she can get fried catfish or hot tamales or ribs. Ain't that right, Ruth?"

"You act like I'm a shark that just has to eat all the time," said Ruth, still looking out the window.

Jane ignored this. "Anyway, Mr. Katz, I'll let you know how I did when you call."

"Sounds like a good plan," said Tom. "You'll like my friends."

"You mean even though they're clearly 'slummin' to be with us?"

"I shouldn't have said that. They're good guys. And they know you're good girls."

"What does that mean: 'good girls'? Maybe you haven't noticed, but we all work as cocktail waitresses in a casino."

Tom laughed. "We won't hold that against you."

Ruth groaned again, this time quite audibly.

Chapter Six

Tulleford, England, August 1859

Tom Catts and his four friends, all of whom worked at the Tulleford Cotton Mill, took their luncheon in the High Road. At six or seven minutes past the matutinal hour of eleven o'clock from Monday through Friday (luncheons were not taken on Saturday half-holidays), the five men placed themselves side-by-side upon the long bench which had been installed by Mr. Crawdon to accommodate those who came to have their shoes repaired in his shop. Sometimes there was a lady or gent waiting upon the bench for the heel of a top boot to be mended or a blucher to be revamped. But this person would not reside there for very long after the importunate arrival of Tom and his fellow millhands, for their intercourse was noisy and roistering, and their slovenly workingmen's dress—oily and cotton-fibre-dusted fustian—was equally difficult to bear, especially if one was not disposed to affiliate with those of ill-bred behaviour and disreputable appearance. As the men would laugh and jostle one another whilst clanking their lunch buckets and clinking their tin cups, the customer would be crowded and crushed to the point of removing him or herself to another precinct—perhaps the bench in front of the blacksmith's shed or the one before the linen-draper's concern, or even the fishmonger's shop (where the fragrance of fish was only slightly less insulting to the nostrils as that of working men bearing the stench of grease and metal-and-spindle-lubricating mineral oils about their persons).

And why was it was that Mr. Catts and his mill-mates should insist upon *this* particular bench and none other? The answer was a simple one: the spot where the bench was placed commanded the best view of Mrs. Colthurst's Fine Dress Shop, situated directly across the lane. Here the five young men partook daily of their forenoon refection (for unlike Mrs. Colthurst and her employees, who were not expected to begin work until eight o'clock, early-shift millworkers commenced their labours at half past six). Was there something architecturally interesting about the dress shop that drew the young men so close? Of course not. It was a rather drab and dingy building, only slightly redeemed by the charming colourful frocks hanging in its large street-side window. No, as the reader has, no doubt, already guessed, it was the young lasses who went thither to toil each day, and who, by fortunate coincidence, came *out* from it to take their bit of late-morning sun in fortuitous concurrence with the latter half of the young men's luncheon.

However, today was different. The weeks of male gawking begetting female blushing and bashful giggling had drawn to a close. A new epoch was dawning, ushered in by none other than Mr. Tom Catts himself, whose idea it was to move matters into a brand new sphere of engagement betwixt the sexes.

Tom, though informal leader of his group, was not its oldest member. This distinction belonged to Tom's lifelong friend Cain Pardlow, who, at three-and-twenty years of age, had watched his four companions wax from early childhood—their collective friendship cemented in the shabby and soot-begrimed side avenues of the Manchester neighbourhood of Hulme. It was from this city that the five had fled only two years earlier to seek employment in a different town—one that afforded fresh air and salubrious sunlight, at least during those hours spent away from the bronchiotoxic and Cimmerian cotton mill.

Cain was quite blind without his spectacles. He had dark brown hair and skin of perhaps a lighter tone than that of his companions, for as boilerman's apprentice, Cain worked in the mill year-round. The other four, who were engaged as spinners and weavers, slipped away with most of the other men of the town in early summer to make hay in the neighbouring fields, as was the long tradition of this parish. (It was a tradition that would soon be coming to an end with the anticipated demise of Lord Tulle, who had always wished his many tenanted acres kept under cultivation and the parish to maintain its historical bucolic character. His heir, on the other hand, was a majority stakeholder in one of the mills, and was eager to see Tulleford join the march to rapid industrialization, which was producing smoke-belching mills and factories from the Pennines to Liverpool Bay, whilst reducing the parish's cornfields to a state of permanent stubble. For an expenditure of only a few extra pence a week a farmhand could be enticed to abandon his plough and pitchfork and take up the operation of a mule spinner or a loom, which generated enormous profit for the mill owners.)

Cain Pardlow read. He read Lucretius and Epictetus and *The Meditations of Marcus Aurelius* and *The Six Enneads* of Plotinus, betwixt the alternate firings of the twin furnaces of the mill's new Lancashire boiler. He spoke sometimes to his chums of what he had learnt from his scholastic maunderings, but found little in their responses with which to fuel the flues of enlightened discourse, and therefore he largely confined his conversations with his mill-mates to more prosaic observations. It was axiomatic that most men (and women) in the mill town of Tulleford—with the exception of fireside dips into the Holy Bible and the occasional browse of a Manchester newspaper—did not read.

Cain was born a twin, and when his brother was brought forth into the world strangled by Cain's umbilical cord, his parents named the dead child Abel and its apparent fetal murderer the only logical companion-appellation. Though Cain was slender—almost scarecrowish in frame—yet he possessed nonetheless a gently rounded face, his cheeks deeply dimpled—the indentations becoming even more pronounced when he smiled—though this was not a common occurrence, for whilst Cain sometimes perceived the potential for levity in situations deriving from his daily intercourse, he was not inclined to acknowledge this fact upon his face, except when there should be missteps and pratfalls resulting from the impetuous blunderings of his mates. (For how could even the most inveterate stoic not laugh—or at the very least, *smile*—over such puerile behaviour?)

Next oldest by but a few weeks was the wittiest of the five, Jeremiah Castle. Jeremiah—familiarly called Jerry—was an orphan. He was, at a very young age, taken in by a benevolent cheesemonger and his equally benevolent wife, in whose company he grew to solid, strapping manhood (largely through the hoisting of heavy cheese wheels). Jerry was the strongest of the group, and though quick to put his opinions forward and to lose his temper with those who did not subscribe to them, yet he would never engage his fist unless it was absolutely necessary, and even then would apply it with measured restraint, lest the recipient of his displeasure incur permanent bodily injury.

Next came Tom Catts, who wore thick mustachios, in part to hide his plump, girlish lips, which were the object of ribald remarks by his companions, although he could certainly melt the heart of any member of the gentler sex who found soft blue-grey eyes, ruddy cheeks, and pouting, bristle-browed lips to be creditable aspects to the physiognomy of a young man. Unfortunately, Tom's character was blemished by a scheming, unscrupulous nature. Intrigue was mother's milk to him, and it pleased him to no end to get the best of others. He did not see himself dwelling forever in the company of his four mates, for there were mountains to be climbed and fortune to be chased, and most importantly, people—a good many people—to be bested.

The youngest-but-one of the group was William Holborne, called Will, whose ancestors came from someplace with fjords. He had a thick shock of straw-coloured hair, which grew even blonder in the radiant summer sun, and a baby caterpillar fixed above his upper lip, so lightly shaded as to be missed in bright illumination. He had bulging Viking arms and a buckler-like chest, and whereas Jerry was blessed with the kind of bodily strength that is marked by sinew and agility, Will's physical prowess was muscle-bound and all but enchained, save when it should be summoned in a burst of brute force, such as upon the occasion in which one of the looms came crashing down on its operator and Will was called upon to lift it single-handedly to the plaudits of all his co-workers and to the tearful, though largely moot, gratitude of the operator's widow (for the crush had unfortunately been too great for her frail and diminutive husband's body to survive).

The baby boy of the bunch—a lad of a mere nineteen years of age—was given the name Patrick Harrison at birth, though he was usually called Pat—that is, when he wasn't Runt, Scrunt, "Papist Paddy," and "Hairless-son," as pleased his four friends, who tolerated his tagging along with them in the beginning with only the greatest reluctance. Yet later, after he had grown out of knee-shorts, Pat's gaping ignorance and pop-eyed ingenuousness came to be regarded as almost endearing, and so he was welcomed into the manly society of the other four without regret. Pat became the willing pupil of his four teachers, who instructed him in the arts of manhood, sometimes with secretly cruel intent, but just as often with some measure of manfully masked compassion.

Pat was, in a word, stupid. He had a boyish face and a most handsome turn of the mouth, and mud-coloured hair that was long and fell with whimsical negligence over his roguish blue-eyes. He bore, in some aspects—such as the winsome cleft in the chin—a striking similarity in appearance to our comely young Molly. But unlike the youngest member of the five sewing circle sisters, who had a head upon her shoulders that would serve her well (whenever she took a mind to use it), Pat, on the other hand, was, and forever *would be*, an amusing dolt—a silly pup to be either kicked or snuggled as circumstance required.

Whether Tom or Pat should be deemed the best-looking of the five is entirely a matter of opinion. Tom's looks tended slightly to the feminine and Pat's to the fuzz-faced man-child, and neither of the two had any idea as to which of them was the better favoured, nor did they necessarily care, as most men generally do not, unless they be foppish and overbred. Yet there *was* one of the other three who was neither of these two things, and who, in fact, cared a great deal, for he was drawn to male pulchritude as part and parcel of his exceptional nature, this verity placing him in league with Ruth, who had a similar affinity for her own sex. For what it is worth, this young man, whose identity shall later be revealed, found Pat to be the better-looking of the two, and so treated him with demonstrably more fondness than he did his other mates.

"If you shilly-shally a moment longer, Tom Cat," bawled Holborne, "you will find yourself unveiling your brilliant scheme just as its intended recipients come trooping out to take their little turn in the fresh air. It should be an awkward moment, largely avoidable by any man with half a brain. Speak, sir!"

Tom Catts responded by placing a silencing finger to his lips. Then he said softly, "If you would kindly keep your *own* voice down to a chick-peep, Holborne, the gossiping wife of a certain shoemaker won't have opportunity to spread intelligence of my plan all the way from here to Manchester."

"Then let us discuss the matter elsewhere," offered Holborne, who belied his suggestion by moving not an inch from his spot whilst falling to his repast of crusty loaf and butter and cold loin of mutton as if it were the finest feast ever put before him.

"There's to be *no* discussion," pronounced Catts, "until I receive a sign from the modiste's front window. Without it, the plan will expire in the cradle."

"What manner of sign?" asked Pardlow, looking up from his book. Though the studied absorption of what he was reading generally proceeded apace without regard to where he was or how the world was spinning round him, Pardlow possessed a valuable facility for keeping himself peripherally attentive to anything being said within earshot that might redound either to his benefit or misfortune. For he was not the sort of young man to immerse himself so deeply in a book that he should be flattened in the lane by a runaway gig or have the wall of a house fall down upon him unawares until he be dead.

Catts replied: "A sign proffered by the delightful Miss Higgins."

"The delightfully *ill-favoured* Miss Higgins," croaked Castle with callous merriment. "Of the five, *this* is the one who has drawn your strongest interest? Powers above, Catts! Have you suddenly become struck with the same disease of acute myopia which afflicts our friend Pardlow?"

"I will have you know, sir," readily protested that very object, "that there are things I can see quite clearly without even need of my eye-glasses!"

"Things two inches from your peeps!" croaked Castle again.

This statement propelled Pardlow from his seat. He moved his own face to within two or three inches of Castle's, so the two men nearly touched noses. "What I see at this distance, Castle, is a boor who is constitutionally incapable of keeping his tongue inside his lip-flapping mouth. Miss Higgins may not possess so beautiful a countenance as her fellow seamstresses, but she is nevertheless wholly *un*deserving of your disapprobation."

"Duly noted," said Tom Catts, as he retrieved his bespectacled friend from the provocative vicinity of the group's most inflammatory member and eased him back down upon the bench. "Jerry means only that Miss Higgins isn't the loveliest flower in the spray. Yet to me she possesses charm and wit and there's a twinkle in her eye, which our friend might catch if he paid better attention to *all* the maidens in their daily promenade."

Castle wrinkled his lips in annoyance over having been so hastily confronted by the one among them least given to provocation (for Pardlow generally kept his own displeasure to an all-but-silent simmer). "I would not know, Catts, if Miss Higgins or any of the other maidens has charm or wit or just what their eyes do when one beholds them, with the singular exception of the bonny-faced Miss Barton who would command *my* attention from even the greatest distance."

Holborne laughed whilst interlocking his large arms across his expansive chest. The picture was one of near Michelangelic statuary (beclothed, of course). "So, Catts, you have yet to set forth the rules of the game to the others, and already at least one of them has selected his victim."

Castle cocked his head and looked queerly at Catts. "You've discussed the game with Holborne before the rest of us? What entitles our esteemed Norseman to this especial privilege?"

Catts shrugged. "I sought to put it to at least one of you in embryo to see if it was a proposition worthy of pursuit."

"And what, pray, was the all-wise Holborne's verdict?" asked Castle, grinning curiously. "Did it meet with his approval?"

Holborne grinned as well. "It did, sir. It did indeed. And it will meet with yours, depend on it. But let us suspend here, gentlemen. The scheme is too precarious at this early juncture to be exposed in such a public place as this." He turned to Catts. "Where is Miss Higgins? Do I take this as a sign that your opening gambit has been inadvertently checked?"

"Alas, it was all too good to be true," concurred Castle with a comically theatrical sigh, "*whatever* the gambit was."

"Patience, gentlemen," said Catts. "And do not fear. Miss Higgins is but momentarily delayed. Return to your book, Pardlow. And as for you, Master Harrison, feel free to proceed with your wonted woolgathering. Let no one disturb you."

"What is that you say?" asked Harrison, shaken from a reverie.

Castle laughed heartily. "Paddy, my boy, have you been deaf to every word spoken here this morning?"

Pat Harrison's face became a vacancy. "I was watching the shaping of the clouds. See the one just overhead? Don't it resemble a fluffy white rabbit? Can you not make out its floppy ears?"

Castle could not contain his mirth. "And here are *your* ears—" He pinched at both of Harrison's ears, as the latter emitted a boyish yelp. "And if there is aught betwixt them but sawdust, *I'll* play the monkey for the next fortnight."

"And how should that be any different from your present simian-like behaviour?" mumbled Pardlow without raising his eyes from his book.

Catts whistled to summon the attention of his mill-mates. Then he pointed in the direction of the dressmaker's shop. "Lord love her! Miss Higgins now appears."

Jane Higgins did not present herself in the shop window as had been arranged, but came instead to the street door, where she now stood upon its threshold. However, rather than signing anything to Catts from that spot, she began to walk *toward* him and the other men, who sate and stood in a picture of slovenliness and slouch on the opposing side of the lane. However, it took no more than five or six steps before Catts straightened himself to full erection, and the ever-courteous Pardlow scrambled quickly to his feet and sleeked down his hair with his free palm in an effort to make himself more presentable. In contrast, their three companions did nothing with themselves whatsoever. In fact, Castle shrunk a little more upon the bench in bodily contempt for the young woman who deserved no especial treatment in his estimation, given her far-from-prepossessing features.

"Good morning, gentlemen," said Jane in pleasant but formal tones, and in spite of the imbalanced reception. "How are things at the mill? I see that all your fingers and noses remain intact, so that is a blessing, eh?"

Pardlow nodded his approval of Jane's wit.

"My dear Miss Higgins," said Catts, "you have completely forgotten the terms of our agreement. You were simply to *sign* acceptance of the proposal. It wasn't necessary for you to—"

"But my dear Mr. Pussy—pardon me, Mr. *Catts*—"

Here, Pardlow dropped his book in shock to hear a woman speak with such easy frivolity.

"—I have not raised the matter with my sisters, for there are still three of us who have yet to arrive this morning."

"Nothing serious detains them, I trust," said Catts, with the requisite lineaments of concern.

Jane shook her head. "It is nothing with which you gentlemen need trouble yourselves. There *is*, however, a matter at hand which demands an immediate resolution. Miss Barton and Miss Osborne have tramped off into the woods for the purpose of effecting an amicable agreement, with Miss Hale as mediatrix. Mrs. Colthurst has received word that she is not to expect them until early this afternoon. At such time, I will communicate your proposal of a Sunday outing. I shared your invitation with Miss Thrasher a short time ago. She is opposed to un-chaperoned picnics as a matter of principle and refuses to come along without strict attendance to propriety."

"Meaning which thing?" sought Castle. "That we are to be one chit short for our woodsy romp *or* that we must endure the odious presence of chaperons?"

"The latter, of course. We Five are never only We Four, unless it cannot be helped. And such an instance has never before occurred. What is your name?"

"Jerry Castle."

"Mr. Catts didn't give me all your names. I know you only as faces that gape and gawk at us when we come out for our morning stroll, as if we are prizes at the county fair."

"Prizes at the fair, oho!" bleated Pardlow.

"And you are—?"

"Cain Pardlow, madam." The reply was accompanied by the respectful suggestion of a bow.

"Like Cain of the Bible, who killed his brother?"

"Yes, Miss Higgins. For it is said I killed my own twin brother in the womb."

"It is also said," offered Castle with a mischievous gleam, "that it was the wrong brother what popped off." This statement was greeted with immodest laughter by all the men save Cain, who lowered at Castle. Even Catts could not contain his dark delight over the remark, though he made an earnest effort to conceal it.

Jane shook her head with disrelish. "If this is a demonstration of the level of respect with which the five of you uphold one another, I should think my sisters and I would do better to have naught to do with the whole lot of you."

Holborne bounded to his feet. "We are not at all as you perceive us, Miss Higgins." Surlily addressing the two men still residing upon the bench on either side of him: "To your feet, boobies. Can't you see there's a lady present?"

As Castle and Harrison were reluctantly accommodating their friend's husky-voiced directive, Holborne exchanged a glance with Catts. The latter placed a finger aside his nose, the gesture going unobserved by Jane.

"Madam," said Catts, "I give you the undeniably disreputable but occasionally charming Messrs. Holborne and Harrison. And now you know us all, and I would ask that you extend our invitation to your 'sisters' when at last the contingent should appear, and perhaps you will let us know your answer at this hour on the morrow."

Jane nodded. "And you are amenable to our request for chaperons?"

"If such a thing is absolutely necessary."

"It *is*, Mr. Catts. Otherwise, Miss Thrasher will refuse to come along." Jane tossed a glance at Pardlow. "And I think you should like Miss Thrasher, Mr. Pardlow. She *also* very much loves to read."

Pardlow nodded and smiled. He coloured a bit, as well, to have his favourite pastime so deferentially acknowledged.

"We shall bring along Mrs. Colthurst on our side," Jane went on. "And you gentlemen must find a man of impeccable character to accompany the five of *you*."

Castle roared merrily. "*We*? Know of a gentleman of 'impeccable character'? Whoo! I dare say we'll be hard put to conjure up a man of even *middling* character. I put it to you, Miss Higgins, that we are lowly millworkers and haymakers who do not generally fraternise with men not of our own ilk."

"Then if you cannot find even a single man who will vouch for your reputations and who will warrant behaviour beyond reproach when in the company of my sisters and me, we shan't be taking an excursion on this coming Sunday or *any other* Sunday."

Jane turned as if to take her departure.

"But my *dear* Miss Higgins!" This ejaculation came in a most desperate tone from Tom Catts. "Mayhap the vicar will agree to join us. He's a jovial sort and would no doubt enjoy an after noon out of surplice."

Jane Higgins shook her head. "Miss Barton will not have the vicar because he drinks. I won't brook disagreement on this point, because I have seen it for myself. I would suggest, instead, should you gentlemen not be too averse to having a Dissenting minister superintend our outing, that Mr. Mobry come along. He is a good and kind man, and you must know how strongly he has advocated for the rights of labour in this and well nigh every mill town in

Lancashire. In other words, he is a friend to the working man and thus would be a good friend to you gentlemen as well."

"He is already a friend to *me*," said Pardlow, "for I have attended services at his church on several occasions."

"Then you must *already* know my circle-sister Miss Thrasher."

"I have seen her at services there, but we have yet to be properly introduced."

"Then we should fix that straightaway! Ruth—rather Miss Thrasher—will be delighted to know that you are also an inveterate votary of books and such like."

Castle made a funny face with his eyes and lips. "Love among the literate! Someone should write a book!"

Jane ignored this remark (or at least *pretended* to ignore it). "So we are all agreed. I shall deliver our reply to your kind invitation about this time to-morrow. Should it fall out that Misses Barton, Osborne, and Hale are unable to come in today, We Five will have ample opportunity to discuss your offer on our walk to work in the morning."

"You are so very kind, Miss Higgins," said Tom Catts, "and on behalf of myself and my four friends—Mr. Pardlow and Mr. Holborne, and young Mr. Harrison and the habitually churlish Mr. Castle—allow me to say that we eagerly await your answer."

With that, Tom Catts bowed to bid Miss Higgins good morning. And all his mates did the same, young Mr. Harrison's bow being ridiculously deep and quite formal (for he had attended two classes in etiquette from a woman of breeding who had come to town to uplift and enlighten its youth, but left quickly thereafter when she discovered that Tulleford had neither iced champagne nor a vol-au-vent or timbale which wasn't rancid to the taste and pasty in its constituency).

Ruth was waiting for Jane just inside the door to the shop. "Jane, you must know that Mrs. Colthurst is quite worried that the lilac-coloured muslin gowns for the five Misses Cuthwaite won't be ready for that family's trip to London on Saturday. Unless, that is, you and I work doubly hard in the absence of the others."

"I shall work late into the night if need be," replied Jane. "I'll tell her not to worry."

Ruth elevated her eyebrows with anticipation. "And so what was made of my request for chaperons? Is the whole thing now scotched?"

"On the contrary, Ruth. To their credit, the young men expressed a decided willingness to accommodate you."

Upon Ruth's look of surprise, Jane drew her friend into the rear workroom, so as to avoid Mrs. Colthurst's curious gaze. Still, she spoke no louder than a whisper: "I should like to wait a day or two before asking Mrs. Colthurst to accompany us. Her mind is, at present, much too occupied with the Cuthwaite gowns."

Jane and Ruth settled behind their sewing tables.

Ruth sighed with discontent. "Even with chaperons, I'm not certain—"

"It is a *picnic*, Ruth," Jane snapped, "and nothing more. And I must say that the young men have had their eye on us for some time. So the invitation was a natural consequence of their long-lived interest."

Ruth remonstrated with a slow and negatory turn of the head. "Had their *eye*? I should say 'their *ogling* eye' would be the better way to put it."

"Still, you do not fully know a man until you've had opportunity to see him at his leisure out-of-doors, capering through a fragrant meadow, taking a gentle hand to guide a young maiden over the slippery stones of a murmuring brook."

Ruth whistled. "How you fancy this alfresco holiday which you and your cohort Mr. Catts have devised for us! I should like to see how the others take to it—especially Carrie, who hasn't exchanged so much as two words with any of our town lads since she was a chattering child of four."

"You may very well be wrong about Carrie. She told me only two days ago that she fears her life has lost its savour."

A smile now curled Ruth's lips. "There may be some *literal* truth to that, when one remembers that her mother cannot bake a muffin which isn't burnt to indigestibility."

"Yet she tries," laughed Jane indelicately. "Oh bless the woman, she does try!"

The two stitched for a moment without speaking. Then Ruth said, "Oh Jane, you won't hate me *too* much if I don't join you on Sunday."

"*Too* much? I shall hate you more than it is possible to hate another. Now there are five of them and there are five of us, and if you do not come, there shall only be *four* of us and that would put the whole thing out of balance."

"But the young men will come to know I haven't any interest in a connexion of any sort. It will be like the parlour game of musical chairs in which one chair is removed and then someone is left without a seat when the music stops."

"But why do you impute this picnic with such serious purpose? It is merely the means by which ten young people who are seldom placed in the way of one another other than as unacquainted passers-by may enjoy a few hours of leisurely and inconsequential companionship. The good Lord knows I have sought to have the four of you accompany me to the village dances where we may meet some interesting young men, but each of you does not agree to it for all your various reasons: Carrie fears her mother will sit at home alone and pluck and plink and weep and burn things in the kitchen. Molly's father desires to keep her close at hand. Maggie's mother has no control over *her*, but Maggie is nonetheless motivated by her desire to avoid the society of farm boys who will reek of hay and manure and perturb her digestion. And you—it cannot be said too strongly—you haven't use for boy *or* man in this or any other life you shall ever live. So...we do not dance. We do nothing all day but stitch and sew and net and chitter, and when we are *not* in harness we may shop and sup a little together, but 'tis always within our own circle, and the one time we took the train to Manchester for a girls' holiday, if you will recall, we shopped and supped and chittered and met no young man of any consequence whatsoever, and it constituted no startling surprise, I must tell you. These five young men from the mill may not be men at whom we may wish to set our caps, my dear Ruth, but I have no doubt their company will at least constitute a pleasant diversion."

"I don't believe you. I don't believe you and Molly and Maggie and Carrie won't be seeking husbands in this bargain. And, by the by, what if either Dr. Osborne or Mrs. Barton opposes this venture?"

"Then someone should blow the horn of hypocrisy and blow it loudly! For how can it be fair for either of them in the midst of their own autumnal courtship to deprive their respective daughters of similar romantic fulfilment?"

Ruth shook her head, her face darkened by fearful concern. "What I see withal is calamity and disaster, for we do not know just what these men are up to."

"I choose to give them the benefit of the drought."

"What is that?"

"I said that I *choose* to give them the benefit of the doubt."

"That isn't what you said."

"It very well is."

"It isn't. You said *drought*. You said 'benefit of the *drought*.' And *I* say that this sums things up perfectly."

Maggie sate upon a stile. Molly paced. Carrie shook her head anxiously.

"There can be no resolution," asserted Carrie, "if neither of you is willing to speak another word to the other. This is why we stand here apart from town, where none shall hear us but the errant cow. So talk. The both of you. Or I shall find things to chuck at you for inducement?"

"There's nothing else to be said," answered Molly sulkily. "Every word that flies from her mouth casts aspersions upon my father, for Maggie cannot draw a difference between her deceased father, who was a disreputable toper, and my perfectly *alive* and *happy* and *loving* father who wants only for his new wife (and by obvious association both his residual daughter and his prospective daughter) to be blissful and contented with this impending union."

"*Impending?*" muttered Maggie. "I should say not. For I will stop the marriage by all means available to me."

"You most certainly will not."

Maggie amplified her voice to match the intensity of her manner. "I *will* and I *must*. Mamma has suffered far too much already. Shall I name her woes and throes? Her many years of ill health. The terrible loss of two of her daughters. And then the dissipated decline of a husband whose useless life ended when he stepped, stupefied by the spirits, into the path of a fully-stoked L&NWR 2-2-2 Number 3020 Cornwall locomotive." Maggie took a moment to fetch her breath. "I will not subject this poor mother of mine to the possibility of yet another heavy dose of sorrow and regret."

"As for your mother's health, Maggie," said Molly, who was no longer pacing, so that she should hold one spot and stare at her friend with a piercing gaze, "most of her troubles are self-inflected. I suspect she makes herself sick for the sole purpose of sending for my father. But he never minds it. Perhaps you haven't noticed it, Maggie, *but they are in love.*"

"I will not dispute the fact that my mother is the occasional hypochondriac."

"And it is a terrible thing, as well, to lose one's sisters. You know I too lost my own sister only two years ago."

Maggie dipped her eyes in melancholy memory. "They say that I may have lost a brother as well—that my sister Octavia had a twin. Once when Mamma was delirious with fever, she muttered something to this effect. But then she later disavowed it."

"Whether it be two siblings or three, the sadness is the same, Maggie. It is a sadness that wants to be overcome by the joy of my father's ascendance in your mother's heart and in your heart too, if you will but allow it. And as for my father, I cannot tell you how it stabs my own heart for you to say the things you say about him."

Now Carrie, the peacemaker, interceded: "Maggie isn't saying she loathes your father, Molly. Only that there are aspects to his character to which she cannot comfortably reconcile herself."

"Being a quack and a fraud," jerked out Maggie, "is not an 'aspect of character.' It is a crime."

"He is *not* a quack and a fraud!" cried Molly. "He is merely uncredentialed."

Maggie replied in a sulky under voice: "I would rather he *not* be uncredentialed. For without the proper documents, he will never make enough money to provide for my mother as she deserves."

Molly's mouth fell into a gape. "Then *that* is what this boils down to. That my father isn't *rich* enough for your mother."

"Not precisely," replied Maggie. "But it would certainly help matters if he *were* more prosperous. It would counter a number of deficiencies on his side."

Carrie wasn't certain if it was Molly whose fingers went first to pull Maggie's hair, or Maggie who clawed at Molly's in defensive anticipation. But the outcome was the same.

And it was all rather appalling.

Chapter Seven

San Francisco, April 1906

Miss Colthurst looked up at the clock on the wall and tutted.

11:20.

She summoned her head salesclerk in ribbons, Jane Higgins, and addressed her fretfully: "Any sign of them?"

Jane shook her head.

"It's nearly lunch," said the harried floor-walker. "I've had to pull two girls from Hosiery and another from Misses' Ready-to-Wear. This leaves us short in both of those departments. But that isn't my greatest concern. I'm worried something serious might have happened to them."

Jane was looking at the clock herself. It hung over the pass-through to Men's Furnishings and carried the name of the department store in bold script: Pemberton, Day & Co. "I'm a little worried myself, Miss Colthurst. When Mag telephoned to me this morning, she said they didn't anticipate being *too* late, but that was over two hours ago."

"Surely there's some logical explanation, though I must say that this just isn't like them—and all three at the same time!"

Jane glanced at the counter directly behind her. There was a customer standing there looking around for someone to wait on her.
Her hat was so ridiculously aigretted that Jane could not stop herself
from saying, "Let me help this woman with the private aviary, and
then I'll tell you what I think is going on."

Miss Colthurst shook her head. "You needn't bother. Miss
Thrasher has given me *her* theory, which will probably be the same
as yours. See to the customer. Miss Thrasher! Miss Thrasher, come
over here! I'd like a private word, my dear."

Ruth, who was working behind the Gloves counter nearby,
pushed open the little gate next to her and was at her supervisor's side
in that next instant. Vivian Colthurst was standing in the middle of
the Ladies' Apparel showroom. Cash girls were flying by on their
roller skates and giving the room the feeling of a festive roller rink.
"Yes, Miss Colthurst?"

"I was going to—why, that's a lovely lavender tie. Did you get
it here?"

Ruth smiled. "I did. Thank you for noticing, Miss C."

Miss Colthurst winked. "When it's only the two of us, Ruth,
you may call me by my Christian name."

"Yes, of course, *Vivian*," said Ruth, as Miss Colthurst straightened
her favorite shop girl's necktie with solicitous hands. "Carrie—Miss
Hale—saw it on the bargain table and thought it would go very
nicely with this shirtwaist."

"It does indeed. Our Miss Hale has impeccable taste. With the
lavender and the pink, Ruth, you are looking quite hydrangeaish
today."

Ruth blushed. "I never know exactly *how* I look unless somebody
tells me. I don't have that feminine knack for the harmonizing of
apparel that most of my female co-workers have."

"Which is why I keep you in Gloves where you can do the least
harm!" teased the floor-walker, winking again, this time more
playfully.

"You wished to see me about something?"

"Oh yes." Miss Colthurst patted her slightly unraveling pompadour into submission. "Ruth, oh my good Lord, this is absolutely the worst possible day for any act of truancy on the part of your three friends. You see, I hadn't wished to spread it about because it was only a select number of you girls whom I intended to recommend, but circumstances now require me to make a clean breast of it."

"A clean breast of what?"

"Oh bother, you have a customer."

"Oh, it's only Mrs. Withers. *I'll be with you in a moment, Mrs. Withers.*"

"Hum. Mrs. Withers." Miss Colthurst nodded pregnantly while pursing her lips.

Ruth drew closer for the purpose of conveying a confidence: "Nearly every other morning I have to contend with that fool woman for longer than I can stand it. She tries on the black lisles and then she tries on the imitation suedes and then she tries on the dogskins, and then just as I'm ready to scream, she ambles off without buying a single pair. I think shopping without buying is her favorite pastime."

Miss Colthurst shook her head. "It isn't her pastime, Ruth. It's her job. She's a private shopper for I. Magnin's."

"A pri—?"

"A *spy*! She thinks she's clever and has been able to hide this fact from us. But everybody knows. Everybody except, apparently, *you*, Ruth. And so now so do *you*. So let's just make her wait until Satan puts on woolens, shall we?" Ruth noted a mischievous twinkle in her supervisor's eye; she smiled and nodded conspiratorially.

Now Miss Colthurst sighed…rather noisily.

"I have had much better mornings. My toothache has returned, which always puts me in a dreadful mood." Miss Colthurst took a deep breath. "Here's the situation: there are five men due here early this afternoon from the Katz Advertising Agency. Mr. Pemberton has fired the somnolent Mr. Leeds, our advertising manager, and given the wide-awake Katz agency our account. That's the way things are being done with the big stores these days—even stores *without* advertising managers who've been known to fall asleep while standing fully erect. There is to be no more internal advertising, but there *will* be advertising, and a great deal of it, thanks to the vigorous efforts of the smart young men who run that enterprising concern. Well, the agency wants to start things off with a big bang. It wants to place photo advertisements in the *Chronicle* and the *Call* and the *Examiner*, and in several magazines that have a large readership throughout northern California. It's quite an outlay of money for the store, but Mr. Pemberton is convinced it will be worth it, since sales have been in such a terrible slump lately. *You there! Mrs. Withers! You cannot be putting your hands behind the counter like that.* The absolute nerve of that woman. *Miss Guinter, would you please wait on Miss Withers…*before I lose the last ounce of my sanity right here in the middle of—what was I saying?"

"Something about the new advertising agency doing photo—"

"Yes, thank you. Photo advertisements. So, these young men— and they're all quite new to the advertising firm—including Mr. Katz Junior, who is the son of the owner…"

"Who, I take it, is named Mr. Katz Senior."

"Yes, of course. Now don't play on my last nerve, Ruth dear."

"I won't. Go on."

"All of them, hired on fresh out of Stanford only a few months ago to bring pep and youthful ideas to that firm—they'll choose five young women from among the ten female salesclerks whom I have chosen for their consideration, and the girls will be escorted to Golden Gate Park on Friday to have their plein-air photographs taken, as it were."

"All five men are needed for the one photographic session?"

"Oh yes, oh yes. They are each of them responsible for a different aspect of the whole operation. One will work with Miss Dowell and me in selecting the clothes—obviously we'll want to promote our summer lines—another to photograph, another to write the copy as he is so inspired, and so forth. I've never seen anything like it. I understand this represents the future: these scrubbed-face advertising agents pulling out all the stops to make a 'campaign,' as they call it—it's quite *like* a little military operation, isn't it?"

Ruth nodded. "So, Miss Colthurst, I take it from the look of disappointment on your face that you'd selected my friends Mag and Molly and Carrie as candidates."

"Naturally. And you and Jane as well."

"*Jane?*"

"My goodness, Ruth—how you say it! And Jane being one of your dearest friends."

"No, no, no. It's not that I think Jane isn't—"

"Oh, it most certainly is." Lowering her voice: "And why *shouldn't* a person think such a thing? Jane is a dear, and smart as a whip, and I know that someday she'll be one of the best buyers this store has ever had, but she is no Gibson girl, and we both know it. Even so, it was she who first spoke to young Mr. Katz when he came to the store last Thursday while I was at the doctor's having my knee looked at. And there was apparently something about her which the young man deemed 'photogenic,' and so when the two of us had our meeting on Friday, he asked that Jane be included in the ten finalists he'll present to his fellow account men. And it wasn't my place to dispute the request. I asked Mr. Pemberton later that afternoon how he would feel if Miss Higgins happened to end up in photo ads for his store and he said he'd be perfectly fine with it. I was quite surprised at first, but then I came quickly to realize just *why* he should be fine with it. Our employer, as you probably know, is the father of a daughter with a harelip. I believe it's the reason our store mascot has been that damned little bunny rabbit for the last ten years. I think the bunny reminds him of her. Well, of course, that would make him inordinately accommodating when it comes to matters of outward *and* inward beauty. And he did tell me—to put a topper on things—that plain-looking women have just as much right to look at a Pemberton, Day & Company store advertisement and picture themselves wearing the garments we sell as women who are more prettily disposed."

"Well, he does have a point, I guess."

"So the gentlemen will be here at two o'clock and I will cross my fingers we'll have Maggie and Molly and Carrie with us at that time, because they are so very beautiful, each one of them, and it should be such a credit to the store to have them presenting its merchandise in artful photography."

"Should I go look for them?"

"I had considered asking you. But I haven't another clerk to spare. Oh, fiddlesticks! I can take over Gloves for you if you aren't gone too terribly long."

"Then I'll go."

"Yes, yes. Go. Skiddoo."

Ruth found her friends exactly where she thought they'd be: Maggie's uncle's drugstore on California Street. To be accurate, Maggie's "Uncle" Whit was *no longer* Maggie's uncle-in-actuality, since her aunt—Maggie's mother's older sister—had divorced him a couple of years earlier. But Maggie still claimed him as such, since he'd never lost his fondness for her, nor had he ever suspended his willingness to treat Maggie and her friends to free strawberry ice cream sodas or fruit-flavored phosphates or Coca-Colas at his fountain. Today it was lemon and orange phosphates Maggie and Molly and Carrie were drinking at one of the fountain's little café tables.

Seeing Ruth first, Carrie proclaimed with welcoming silliness, "Behold! The search party has officially arrived!"

"It didn't take much searching," admitted Ruth, while pulling a whitewashed wrought-iron chair over to the table. "What's the *opposite* of a wild goose chase?"

"I don't know," said Molly, in a sullen tone. "Would you like something to drink, Ruth? Mr. Whitten has a new root beer on tap and wants opinions as to whether it's worth keeping."

Ruth shook her head. "What I'd *like* is for the three of you to get yourselves out of these chairs and right down to the store before you lose your jobs. I cannot believe it! Sitting here like ladies of leisure and putting Miss Colthurst in such a terrible fix. She had to bring over Miss Grable from Misses' Ready-to-Wear—Jeanna Grable, who doesn't know the first thing about ribbons, and Miss Shields is making a terrible muddle out of measuring and packing in *your* absence, Molly."

Molly frowned. "Is that my fault? Any other girl could learn the job in five minutes."

"And just look at your faces," Ruth grumbled on. "I've never seen such a study in glumitude. Honestly. You all look as if somebody just died owing each of you a very large sum of money."

"Ha ha and hee hee," returned Molly with a sneer and a flounce. "You may take your little vaudeville funny act elsewhere, Ruth."

Ruth turned to Carrie, who was wearing a frothy lemon-phosphate mustache. "Carrie, can you not make them see reason? Nothing is going to get settled this morning and you're all needed at the store. And today most especially."

"And what makes today more special than any other day?" queried Carrie.

"If you must know, the new advertising agency that has been given Pemberton, Day's account is going to photograph several lucky shop girls at Golden Gate Park on Friday, and each of you is in the running."

"What do you mean, 'photograph'?" asked Carrie.

Ruth sighed with exasperation. "*Photograph*. With a camera. A *professional* camera—not a Brownie. Five of Mr. Pemberton's salesclerks are going to become photography models for the entire day and they'll appear in Pemberton, Day advertisements all over town—you've heard of advertisements?"

Molly's face lighted up, while Carrie mumbled petulantly that of course, she'd heard of advertisements.

Ruth went on: "Miss Colthurst has picked ten of us who will be looked over by the agency men. And from those ten they'll select five for the job."

"Will we be paid?" Maggie, having finally decided to join the conversation, did so without the slightest suspension of her dark mood.

"Of course you'll be paid," replied Ruth. "If you're selected." Ruth's expression suddenly changed; she grinned slyly. "My goodness, but aren't we being a wee bit presumptuous about our chances?"

Maggie sucked up the remaining puddle of phosphate at the bottom of her fountain glass. Unlike her friend Carrie, who liked to slurp from a spoon, Maggie used a straw. "Not at all. We four are the prettiest salesclerks in the store. Of course, I have no idea who will occupy that fifth spot."

"*I* do," said Ruth. "Jane."

Maggie's look of surprise replicated that of her friend Carrie. Molly registered her own astonishment with nothing more telling than a slight clearing of the throat.

"*Jane?*" said Maggie. "And just how is this possible?"

"Oh do be kind!" ejaculated Molly in a burst of magnanimity for her absent friend. "We've had all we can take of your monstrous behavior, Mag. It is common knowledge that Miss Colthurst is very fond of Ruth, and it's probably a very simple thing for Ruth to ask her to exert her influence with these agency men to win Jane that fifth spot. And then it shouldn't be far-fetched at all for the five of us—including Jane—to model those clothes together as we do nearly everything else together—even though Jane probably *is* ill-suited for the modeling profession."

Ruth groaned. Withholding the fact that she had nothing to do with Jane being seriously considered for the advertisements, Ruth glared at Molly as she acerbically observed, "As far as I can tell, Mag isn't the *only* one here today who has taken sudden leave of her generally kind and gentle nature."

Carrie nodded. "It's true. Both Mag and Molly have had a peach of a grouch with each other since they got up this morning, and now they've taken to lashing out at people who've done nothing but wandered innocently into their presence. Mag, I don't believe, for example, that you ever thanked your uncle for these refreshing beverages."

Maggie snorted. "Didn't I?" She shrugged. "Well, I don't remember one way or the other. My mind, as you already know, has been elsewhere. Besides, Uncle Whit probably didn't even notice. He generally preoccupies himself during our visits from behind his pharmacy-office window-blind, peering and leering at us as if we're the original Floradora girls."

"*Mag!*" exclaimed Carrie, her hand quickly flying to her mouth in reaction to this low insult.

"It's true," Maggie resumed. "And don't—none of you!—turn around and look at him. He'll know we're talking about him. Ruth Thrasher, did you make all that up about the photography outing just so we'll hustle ourselves over to the store?"

"Absolutely not. The agency men *are* coming. They'll be there at two. But whether they're coming or not, you've been most derelict and irresponsible—all three of you—in letting this spat keep you from your work."

Maggie made as if she would contest this rebuke, but then surrendered and nodded with obvious contrition. "You'll be happy to know, Ruth, that Molly and I have come to terms. We've smoked the pipe of peace. I remain unhappy with this deuced marriage, but I've promised no longer to actively oppose it."

Ruth turned to Molly for confirmation. Molly nodded.

Then Ruth exchanged a look with Carrie. "And what was it that *Molly* brought to the armistice table?"

Molly spoke for herself: "A willingness to speak to Papa and ask if he might postpone the marriage for a while. Perhaps for a couple of years. Mag is right about one thing—"

"One very *big* thing," put in Maggie.

"However you may wish to characterize it, Mag. Our parents *are* rushing into this marriage. They've planned nothing. They're like Romeo and Juliet making googly eyes at each from opposite sides of the ballroom. The postponement works very much to my father's benefit, because it gives Mag time to come around—to see that Papa *has* changed, that he isn't at all the man he used to be."

Ruth curdled her forehead into a frown. "This doesn't smell right."

Carrie laughed. She had tried to suppress it, but it came out none the less.

Ruth pointed at Carrie with an accusatory finger. "You *know*! Out with it! What's the *real* reason Molly's agreed to these previously unthinkable terms?"

Carrie laughed again. Her laughter was blubbery: little puffs of merriment escaping from behind wobbly, loosely compressed lips. "You should sit down, Ruth. Molly, go and get Ruth a sarsaparilla."

"I don't want a sarsaparilla. I want the truth, and right this very moment, if you please."

Carrie reached out and took Ruth's hand. "Ruth, dear. You are to go to Miss Colthurst who, as it has been said before, is immoderately fond of you, and who will do anything you ask, and you are to tell Miss Colthurst that Molly can't take another minute in that stuffy packer's warren above the ribbon shelves doing the work of a galley slave. She's to come down behind the counters and join the civilized world. It's the only decent thing to do."

"But who will—"

Maggie answered the question Ruth wasn't given time to ask: "The cash girls are all being let go next week with the installation of all those bizarre and perfectly futuristic pneumatic tubes. Any one of those poor young things will be more than happy to take over Molly's job as packer in the ribbon department to keep herself on the Pemberton payroll."

Ruth thought about this. "It's a lot to ask."

Maggie shook her head, smiling pleasantly. (The very first smile of the morning from her.) "Is it too much to ask for such a helpful employee as yourself, Ruth, who knew exactly where her missing fellow salesclerks would be found loafing, and who will have heroically brought them back and saved the day for Pemberton, Day? Miss Colthurst cannot help but be exceedingly grateful—not that she isn't already—"

"—*immoderately fond of me.* The next one of you who utters this phrase will get a crowning with whatever I can find nearby that is hard and heavy and bound to crack the skull!"

"Why *is* she so fond of you?" asked Molly, setting her empty glass on the tray with the others.

"It beats me," said Ruth. "Perhaps she likes orphans." Ruth rose from the table along with her three sisters. "Well, of course I'll ask her. I've always hated it that Molly has to spend the whole day toiling away up in that stuffy, cramped little loft."

Molly could not help herself. She got up from her chair and planted a kiss upon Ruth's soon-to-be-blushing cheek.

"Isn't it nice how things sometimes work out?" Molly asked. "And on top of it all, we're going to be fashion models! I've always wanted to be a fashion model."

"Only if we're selected," cautioned Ruth. "There are other pretty girls working at Pemberton, Day who are also to be considered."

"Pretty, yes, but not nearly as pretty as *we* are," said Molly. "It's what Mag said earlier. And you'll get no argument from any of those agency men. Look at how Mag's uncle gawps at us. Like we're the most beautiful girls he's ever seen."

"It's unnerving. Creepy," commented Ruth, catching the pharmacist out of the corner of her eye. Maggie's Uncle Whit was indeed looking in their direction—and quite absorbedly.

"Yes," said Maggie. "But he really *is* harmless. It wasn't a roving eye that broke up his marriage to my aunt. It was his addiction to Heroin-Hydrochloride cough elixir. Which reminds me that I really *should* thank him for opening the fountain to us before hours. I'll only be a moment."

Maggie strode back to her uncle's office at the rear of the drugstore. Observing her approach through its little window, he flung open the door to admit her before she'd even had opportunity to knock.

"Uncle Whit, we want to thank you so much for all your hospitality this morning. We must be going along to work now, but you were such a peach to let us sit here for nearly an hour."

Uncle Whit had a ready smile on his round, almost cherubic face. His eyes were veined and red with bloodshot from his various addictions, most of which robbed him of consistent (and restorative) sleep; but otherwise his noxious habits took little noticeable toll upon his body or countenance. (And Maggie had always been astonished by how much energy he seemed to have.) "Have you worked things out with your friend Molly?" he asked with warm solicitude. "I couldn't help overhearing bits and pieces. Does this mean your mother *won't* be marrying Molly's father?"

"Not for the time being, at least. We're going to convince them to delay the nuptials."

"Perhaps 'no nuptials at all' would be the better course. Are you aware that Dr. Osborne practices both the medical and dental arts without a proper license?"

"I knew he wasn't a qualified physician. I *didn't* know that he shouldn't be practicing dentistry either. That's an intriguing discovery."

"*And* he drinks. I've never met a hard-drinking man who didn't come to a bad end."

"Nor have I, Uncle. Including my own father. But you already know everything there is to know about *that*."

Uncle Whit nodded. "Before you go, Niece, I have something to give you. One of my fountain customers accidentally left it behind yesterday. I don't know a thing about her, except that she said she was on her way to Oakland to catch a train for someplace in the East. Since I don't know where to send it, or whether she should ever be back here to collect it, I wanted *you* to have it."

"What is it?"

"A book. She was reading it at the counter." Uncle Whit opened a drawer to his desk and took out the book of mention.

Maggie accepted the volume from her uncle. "You are very kind to me, Uncle. In so many different ways."

"I consider you my niece still. And do come back and see me again when you have the chance."

"I will." Maggie squeezed her uncle's hand.

"And bring all your pretty friends with you."

"Yes, well, of course. Good morning, Uncle Whit."

Once outside the drugstore, Maggie put the book into Ruth's hands without looking at it. "Uncle Whit knows a lot about me," she said, "but he's apparently forgotten that I don't read for pleasure. You may have this—whatever it is."

"Thank you, Mag," said Ruth. As the four friends walked along California Street, Ruth opened the book to look at its title page. It was a novel with which Ruth was familiar, and she told this to Maggie.

"*A Florida Enchantment*," said Molly, peering over Ruth's shoulder. "But you haven't read it yet?"

"No. But Miss Colthurst strongly recommended it," replied Ruth, now leafing through its pages.

"What's it about?" asked Molly.

"A magic seed that when eaten changes a woman into a man and vice versa. Not outwardly, but inside."

Maggie snorted. "Yes, I can see why Miss Colthurst would 'strongly' recommend such a book."

At that moment a cable car trundled noisily past. Ruth was given to think, as she sometimes did, of Maggie's father stepping in front of it and ending his life in an instant. Today she pictured Maggie in her father's place.

And didn't feel guilty at all.

Chapter Eight

Zenith, Winnemac, July 1923

Cain Pardlow was always the first to arrive at Dodsworth Hall on that one morning a week in which he and his four college pals were able to grab a late breakfast together. Only on Monday mornings did their various lecture and lab schedules open up for long enough (from ten to noon to be precise) to afford the five longtime friends the chance to graze coevally in Winnemac Agricultural and Mechanical College's revamped dining hall. (This semester marked the first time W A&M tried the relatively new "cafeteria dining concept," which had been growing in popularity since the war.) Seated at their favorite table, they would trade stories from the week past, argue politics—national, state, and campus—and generally shoot a great deal of bull before being called away to afternoon classes covering such esoteric subjects as Cost Accounting, Mechanics of Trade, Machine Drawing, Agricultural Survey and Drainage, and Efficacies of Farm Manure.

Cain, the agricultural history student, had his unvarying "usual": two cups of black coffee (Monarch—"Quality Seldom Equaled; Never Excelled") and a bowl of Kellogg's Shredded Krumbles with strawberries and cream.

Pat Harrison, who was usually the next to show up—Pat, the science education major (at least this was the degree path that interested him *this* particular semester)—ate cereal, as well: Quaker Quakies corn flakes. And because they looked appealingly plump and succulent this morning, Pat also topped his cereal with strawberries and cream. Having always been taught by his father that caffein frayed the nerves and impaired the digestion, Pat drank Postum, and, to the amazement of his friends, was able to do so with little facial indication of his absolute revulsion for the gritty, pulpy beverage.

Today it was Tom Catts who arrived next. Tom appeared slightly bleary-eyed from an evening of getting himself stewed, if not to the eyebrows, then perhaps to a point just below the cheekbones. Tom had a fried egg sandwich—or at least he *bought* a fried egg sandwich—but because of the condition of his stomach, he was destined to spend most of the time just staring at it, occasionally peeling back the toast to see if the eggs had turned into anything remotely palatable. Tom was working toward a degree in the relatively new field of agricultural economics.

Next came Will (a.k.a. "William," "Willy," and "Willy-Boy," but never "Billy") Holborne, who was in the mood for bacon, and was provisioned that morning with a tall glass of orange juice and a plate piled high with nothing but crispy rashers of the aforementioned. There was a logical explanation for this beyond the fact that Will was terminally hungry. He was presently taking a class in pork production. Perhaps no further elaboration is necessary.

And making his wonted straggling appearance sometime around 10:30 was Jerry Castle, who was studying for a degree in Business and Industry. Jerry had his customary king's breakfast of cinnamon toast, corned beef hash with poached egg on top, a side of fried ham, a bowl of fruit-in-season (today it was those mouth-watering strawberries), and a short stack of Aggie flapjacks (which were just your garden-variety pancakes, with the chance of a little embedded ash from one of "Chef" Shemp's ubiquitous Lucky Strikes).

Castle spoke for the others as he flumped down with his tray: "Tom Catts—you look like somebody the eponymous dragged in, you bedraggled ol' whisker-licker. What kind of hootch did you get your little snub-snout into last night?"

"It wasn't the *quality* of the beverage so much as the *quantity*. I'm a pushover for Golden Wedding, and the Gamma Delts were serving up quarts and quarts of it. Worse thing of it, I missed my co-operative marketing class this morning, and that's my third absence. I'm going to have to throw myself on Prof's mercy or take a deficiency. This one's a must-have for graduation."

Will threw his arm around Tom's shoulder. "I got all my drinking out of the way at Saturday night's game. You should know better, Catman, than to get yourself stinko on a Sunday night. What were *you* doing on Saturday when you should have been root-root-rooting for the home team?"

"I was at the pictures."

"What picture?" asked Pat, who still hadn't gotten out of his boyhood habit of seeing a new movie every weekend (or gotten himself out of any of his other boyhood habits, for that matter).

"The Lon Chaney thing. That Hunchback movie."

"*The Hunchback of Notre Dame*," said Cain. "I didn't see it. I didn't *want* to see it, although I've heard all about it. I also happened to have read the book. Victor Hugo wouldn't have been very pleased with what they did to his story."

"*I* enjoyed it," countered Tom defensively.

At the same time Jerry said, "Since that frog's probably long dead, I wouldn't think he'd give two damns *what* was done with his story."

"What's wrong with the movie?" asked Pat.

"Twisted the thing all around," replied Cain. "Turned it into preposterous melodrama. Although, admittedly, the novel's a little melodramatic on its own merits—don't know if maybe that was the fault of the translator—but I still don't think the movie serves the original very well. And they made the archdeacon, Dom Claude Frollo, into one of the heroes of the thing."

"He was a villain in the book?" asked Pat.

Cain nodded. "You see, in the book—"

Cain was silenced by a loud *thwack*—the result of Jerry slamming both palms flat and quite jarringly upon the table. "Can we just once, Pardlow, get through one of these breakfasts without you opening up the top of your egg-head and letting every fact and figure you've packed away in there just tumble out, until all of our eyes glaze over from boredom? You're worse than all five of my profs put together."

Pat jumped to Cain's defense: "I thought what he was saying was interesting."

"Of course *you'd* think that, Patty-Cake. You're six. The rest of us have more important, grown-up things to chin about here. Tommy, as it has now been established, didn't go to the game on Saturday night because he went to the flicks, but something happened *after* the flicks that's worth telling. Tell them who you met, Tommy. Tell them everything you told me yesterday."

"Well, I came out of the movie house and there she was—"

"*She,* brothers," interrupted Jerry. "See, now we've reached a topic worthy of serious consideration."

Cain settled back in his seat, folding his arms into a bodily pout.

"Go on," said Jerry, looking at Tom, who sat directly across the table from him. "We're all ears. Especially Holborne, with his pachyderm mud flaps."

Will wriggled both of his large ears with the help of his index fingers to show that he was comfortable with Jerry's (nearly accurate) observation.

Tom took his time. He smiled mysteriously. He even managed a little nibble of his fried egg sandwich to get his think-pistons greased. "Her name is Jane. She runs that antiques store down the block from the Grantham, where they're playing the Hunchback picture. Well, she *and* her brother, rather—they own it together. I

see her standing in front of the store and there's this fellow with
her. He's giving her a first-class bawl-out. I mean, he's raking and
razzing her at the top of his lungs. And you known the chivalrous
way I was brought up, gentlemen. I'm not going to let some gutter-
mouth swosher get away with treating a lady like that, so I step in
and deliver the business, not knowing, you see, that it's one of those
'family-only' kind of fallouts—the guy, turns out, *is* the brother,
and they both live over the store and she's trying to get him to go
up for the night, but he's not ready for the hay just yet, even though
a couple of minutes later, he's out like a light—oozes right down
to the sidewalk like a blob of quicksilver and goes beddy-bye right
then and there. So I make the suggestion that maybe the young lady
might like me to lend a hand—help tuck her brother into a *real* bed.
And she's very grateful. This has become a nightly ritual for her, you
see, and it's wearing her down. So we get him up to his room, get
him undressed and deposited beneath the sheets, and then she asks if
I'd like to stay for a cup of coffee. And I say, sure, and there we are
sitting at her kitchen table until nearly one in the morning."

"Doing what?" asked Will, enrapt.

"Just talking."

"That's *it*?" Will's face fell. "I thought this story was going
somewhere."

"It is," said Jerry. "Finish the story, Tommy. It has an interesting
twist."

"Okay," said Tom. "Here's the twist. It turns out she's one of
those five girls who showed up on campus a couple of weeks ago
handing out circulars for the big shindig that's supposed to open
up that behemothic brick cathedral they're building downtown—
the one the evangelist, Sister Lydia, will be preachifying at. Do you
remember those girls?"

All four of Tom's companions nodded. Of course, they remembered them...but only as a group. "Now which one was Jane?"
asked Pat.

"Yeah," put in Jerry, "you neglected to say the other night. Was she the hotsy-totsy blonde with the Marion Davies eyes?"

Tom shook his head. "Jane's the tall one."

"Oh. The *tall* one," said Will, rolling his eyes.

"Oh yes. The *tall* one," chimed in Jerry, opening his own eyes wide in a parody of great interest.

"That's right," said Tom, growing noticeably annoyed. "It turns out Jane and her friends don't just pass out circulars for Sister Lydia. They're in the choir. And because they're church girls, I'd give you some pretty good odds they don't have all that much experience..." Tom's look suddenly became soiled. "...in the ways of love."

"*Love?*" Jerry hooted.

"Shut up, Jerry," snapped Cain. "Tommy, I think I know what it is you're leading up to."

Jerry grinned. "My dear Mr. Pardlow, you only know the half of it. Things are about to take themselves a nice little turn. I'll pick up the ball here, Tommy, ol' chap, because you talk too slow. So Tommy, he asks Jane what she's doing on Friday night and she says she and her fellow canaries—they're not doing nothing. But of course they *are* doing something Friday night—only at this point none of us knows it. See, Professor Prowse is throwing a big ol' wingding birthday party for his brand-new wife on Friday and we're all invited—all five of us *and* the songbirds, who, as it so happens, went to grammar school with bella Bella. Tommy just got *our* voice-vite from the missiz yesterday."

"And the girls—just how do you know *they'll* come?" asked Cain.

"Oh, they'll fly their chancel cage, all right. Bella says one of them lives next door to her in the Heights, and she says she'll flush her and the whole covey right over if she has to. Now, with our stage properly set...*let the show begin.*"

"Show? What show?" asked Pat, the perpetual literalist.

"Now wait just a minute," said Cain, holding up his hand like a traffic cop. "We're not doing *anything* that has *anything* to do with those girls."

Jerry tossed a strawberry at Cain's upheld hand. He batted it away. "The rules say Tommy can come up with any kind of challenge he pleases," Jerry gustily bayed. "And I've been waiting a long time at this stag institution for one of these silly intramural contests of ours to finally put me into a nice torso-lock with somebody that smells of Djer-Kiss lady talc. After all this time whiffing bay rum, gentlemen, don't you think we're *due*?"

Pat looked puzzled. "Are you *sure* it's Tommy's turn to make the challenge?"

"Positive, Patty-Cake," replied Jerry, pinching Pat's nose playfully. The pinch hurt and Pat yowled. "And Tommy can make us do whatever he likes—so long as there's no threat to the health and safety of the participants. That's the rule we all agreed to. And we *all* have to play. No exceptions allowed."

"What if we seriously, sincerely do not *want* to play?" asked Cain, the lines of his face set in stone-faced severity—like Buster Keaton—a dramatic contrast to the looks of animated mischief to be found upon the fizzes of his table companions.

Tom took the floor again: "You want to know what happens, Cain? You get ostracized from the group, that's what happens. Not to mention, we sneak into your dormitory room some night and douse you with a bucket of ice water in your sleep. Now we played *your* stupid game last semester and we all thought it couldn't have been any more painful to our self-respecting manhood if we'd all been hung up in the middle of the quad by our BVDs. But we did it. We picked a damned Shakespearean character and we showed up at Mr. Herzer's Shakespearean class dutifully dressed as that character—"

"I was Puck," said Pat, beaming.

"Yes, Master Fauntleroy," laughed Tom. "How could we ever forget?"

Tom, who was sitting next to Pat, reached behind him to create tiny horns over Pat's head with two fingers. Pat flicked the fingers away as if they were pestering insects.

"And I speak for everybody but Puck here," Tom swept on, "when I say there is no challenge I could ever put forth as humiliating as *that* one. So I dare you, Mr. Pardlow, to try to pull yourself out of *this* particular competition—I dare you in the name of fair play and common decency and the preservation of your warm, dry little dormitory cot."

"So just what is it?" asked Cain, with a weary sigh. "Winner is the first to wheedle a kiss from one of these choir-girl innocents?"

Tom shook his head. A diabolical grin settled upon his lips. "Move farther around the bases, my friend. And send me a wire when you get to home plate."

Cain dropped his cereal spoon. It struck the now empty ceramic bowl in front of him with a noticeable ping.

"*Absolutely n*—"

"One night of carnal passion. Just like what Captain Phoebus wanted from Esmeralda. See, I've read the damned Hunchback book too, Pardlow. The difference is that Phoebus, perverse little piece of work that he was, invited Frollo to sit himself right down there at the fifty-yard line to witness the seedy mechanics of his conquest— Cracker Jacks and all. But *we* aren't going to play it that way—not going to turn this into a spectator sport, gentlemen. We're going to take each other at his word. But that word is important. Because it's going to tell everything. And the conquest that wins will be the one that takes one of these five virginal lasses farthest down the road of depraved carnality."

Cain glared at Tom. "I don't know *exactly* what that means, but I'm guessing application of the word 'rape' wouldn't be that far off base."

Tom and Jerry spoke at the same time. Tom said, "Now hold on there!" while Jerry said, "Nothing of the kind, Pardlow. Seduction! *That* is the word. Seduction isn't rape. Seduction is, well, *seduction*. It's in all of your favorite petticoat novels. It's in *The Hunchback of Notre Dame*, for crying out loud."

Tom nodded. "Esmeralda wanted it. She begged for it. So that's our mission—to make our five maidens want it just like oversexed Esmeralda."

"What's the prize?" asked Jerry, unaware that he was, at that moment, actually licking his lips like the villain in a Victorian melodrama.

Tom answered breathlessly: "My roommate Gill—you know, Gill of the 'My dad may have more money than all the Rockefellers and the Mellons put together, but I'm for the good ol' A&M!'—just got himself a new Stutz. And I can get him to lend it to me for a week. Winner gets to caress the wheel of an honest-to-God fire-engine-red 1923 model Stutz Bearcat for a whole damned week."

"And what do you get if *you* win, Tom-Cat?" asked Holborne, his head tilted in canine-like anticipation.

"A sawbuck from each of you will suffice. Forty bucks in my pocket and a week with a Stutz—I'll be the happiest one of us all."

Three of Tom's auditors smiled. The fourth stared out the window.

"I know what you're thinking, Pardlow," said Tom, his eyes narrowing on Cain. "You think you can get away with *pretending* to play the game and none of us will be any the wiser. Your shyness around women is, after all, legendary. But it isn't going to work that way. We're going to keep tabs. *Close* tabs. And if you don't play, we're all going to know about it."

"I'll tell you right now: I don't want to play."

"Then you know what this means, Pardlow."

"Do whatever you're going to do to me. It will be worth an ice-water bath to see at least one of these girls escape your contemptible designs."

Tom was about to speak, but Jerry preempted him: "How do you know these five sheltered nuns-in-training won't end up *liking* what it is they've never tried? There's always *that* possibility, you know."

"And you're totally off your nut, Castle." Cain stood up from the table. "You know, fellows, some of these challenges have been silly, and yes, I'll admit my Shakespeare stunt was pretty punk, but we've never done anything before that could end up hurting somebody. This new challenge takes us to a place we have no business going. It's something I can't go along with, and I would hope the rest of you will come to your senses and reject it too."

"Sit down, Pardlow," said Will with sudden severity.

The two men looked at one another. Something passed between them, unknowable to the other young men at the table. Cain dropped obediently into his seat.

Will continued to look squarely at Cain, as if there were no one else present at the table. "You're going to play the game, Pardlow. Or I'm going to tell what it is I know. And what it is I know, if it gets known by certain other people, could put you in a bad spot."

"Why are you doing this, Will?"

"For your own good. You know exactly what I'm talking about."

"Somebody mind telling us what's going on here?" asked Jerry. Tom and Pat nodded, all three now caught off guard by this inexplicable turn in the conversation.

Will looked at Jerry and shook his head. "This is between Cain and me. And Cain—I intend to keep my promise, but only if you play. If you don't play, all bets are off."

Cain closed his eyes. His voice softened to near whisper. "I still don't understand, Will. I don't understand why this is so important to you."

"If you don't know why, then you're worse off than I thought."

Cain's eyes popped open. He rose to stand next to his chair. One by one, he looked into the faces of the four young men whom he'd considered his friends. He wasn't sure how to define his relationship with them now, but he knew in any event he'd have to play the game. The consequences for *not* playing were simply too serious to be ignored.

"I'll do it," he finally said, his words almost inaudible. And then he walked away without taking his tray.

Diners were supposed to dispose of their trays. This was one rule Cain felt he could break *without* consequence. For someone like Cain Pardlow, rules like this one—rules one *could* disregard—didn't come along very often.

After he left, Jerry turned to Holborne and said simply, "Okay. Now tell us."

And Will replied just as simply, "No. I keep my word."

And then he left the dining hall as well.

Chapter Nine

London, England, October 1940

"It's very pretty, Mum."

"No, love, come look at it in the light. See how it sparkles."

"I'm surprised he could afford to buy you a ring."

"Did you not tell me you've decided to be a good girl about this?"

Maggie took the last bite of her broiled plaice. It wasn't her favourite fish, but she indulged her mother by eating it with *some* demonstration of appreciation. After all, Clara *had* stood in a forty-minute queue outside the fish shop to buy it. "I *am* being a good girl. But I've still held on to that wee bit of hope that—well, now it just seems inevitable."

"Nothing is inevitable, Maggie, dear. But this comes close. And you're going to continue to be a good girl, because you told me that putting off this marriage was just what you and Molly wanted."

"What *I* wanted—and still want—is for you not to get married at all. But I've agreed to this compromise."

"Then start being nice. It will be very wearing on me if you intend to continue with this moping and moaning until the end of the war."

Maggie got up from the table. She picked up her plate and cup to carry into the kitchen.

"No dessert?" asked Clara, over her shoulder. "I made orange whip and gingerbread."

"I'll have a slice of gingerbread later," answered Maggie from the kitchen. A moment later she returned to clear away more of the tea dishes. "I'd rather not be the last to arrive at Jane's. After being the one largely responsible for Molly and Carrie and me being so late to work on Monday, I am now called—and I don't think this is an *affectionate* jest—'the late and not-so-great Maggie Barton.'"

Mrs. Barton's harrumph was clearly audible. "Well, you didn't spend the morning arguing with a lamp post, dear. Molly played her part as well. Never you mind about the dishes tonight, dear. I'll wash them." Clara sighed. "But I do wish you'd wait just a *few* minutes to say something sweet and congratulatory to Dr. Osborne. I'm expecting him at any moment."

"If I'm still here when he comes I'll be polite."

It took two more trips for Maggie to take away the rest of the dishes from tea. Clara sat thinking whilst Maggie ran hot water into the kitchen basin to give things a soak. "I must say, Maggie," said Clara, raising her voice to be heard through the doorway, "that the begrudging way you've been *accommodating* me is just as unpleasant as if you were still standing squarely against the marriage for all time. You really should be more like Chamberlain and appease me with a fixed smile."

"Which you would see straight through," rebutted Maggie, her own words amplified for carriage into the dining room. "The fact is: I'm hanged if I do and hanged if I don't. What do you fancy, Mum? That my feelings about this marriage should change with the snap of a finger?"

"What I *fancy*, to be perfectly honest, is a different daughter."

"I'm sorry, old woman, but it looks like you're stuck with me. And I'm stuck with you. Even if I marry. Because I don't intend to be one of those unhappy children that blots her mum out of her life forever."

"I suppose I should thank you for that." Clara sighed again. Sometimes her sighs had a way of working themselves into yawns. This one seemed of that variety. "What are you girls getting together for, anyway? I asked Dr. Osborne if Molly—"

"You don't have to keep calling him 'Dr. Osborne.' First, he isn't a doctor. And second, he's the man you plan to marry. Will you still be calling him 'Dr. Osborne' on your rose-petal-strewn honeymoon bed?"

"I haven't decided. And don't be vulgar." Clara smiled privately. "I must say that part of me has grown rather accustomed to it— calling him that—not that it's any of your business how the doctor and I choose to refer to one another."

"You asked him *what* about Molly? Finish your sentence. I don't have all night."

"Then stop pottering with those dishes! I told you I'd wash them."

"Oh, and then have you telling my future stepfather when he shows up tonight what a terrible daughter I am to do no chores round the house—even though I bring in most of the money we have, thanks to my job at the factory, and even though every time you climb into bed with one of your dizzy spells, it is *I* who must do all the marketing and cooking and scouring and pushing of the bloody Hoover from one dirty carpet to another until you're up and about again. But you won't tell him *that*, will you? You'll say I'm lazy and a perfectly beastly excuse for a daughter because that's what comes easiest to your tongue."

"I never said anything of the sort to anyone! I appreciate every little thing you do for me."

"Of course you do," said Maggie dryly to herself. She stopped chinking plates and saucers. Then she said, "You asked him what?"

"What's that?"

"You asked Mr. Osborne what? You just said—"

"Stop shouting at me." Mrs. Barton left the table and stepped into the kitchen. She sat down at the little breakfast table snuggled against the wall. "Now would you listen to us? We sound like a couple of Newham ironmongers' wives." Clara took a deep breath to calm herself. "I was going to say that I had asked *Michael* if Molly was coming along with him tonight and he said no, she was going to Jane's house with the rest of you. So now I am asking *you*: what is it that requires the five of you to gather yourselves together tonight when you've already seen one another for eleven full hours at the factory? I ask because Michael is bringing a bottle of port, which he'd put by for a special occasion. We're going to raise a glass to our future happiness. And it would be nice if—"

"There's an unopened bottle of port in the Osborne flat? Forgive me, Mum, but I'm feeling rather faint…from *shock*."

"You stop it! 'Tisn't funny. And after you said you've changed. You haven't changed one bit. You're going to make the three of us miserable. Here I was finally allowing myself to start looking forward to things—to the marriage, to the move to Burnham, to things turning round for all of us, but this doesn't matter to you in the least, does it? Because you've set your mind to spoiling everything, and spoiling everything is precisely what you'll do!"

Maggie dried her hands on the tea towel hanging from the wall. Then she went to her mother and took both of her hands into her own. "Don't cry, Mummy. I'll be good. Burnham is quite lovely with the woods so close by, and I'm very happy you and Dr. Osborne will be moving there after the war—moving there as husband and wife. And your health will improve, and Molly and I will come to visit you as often as we can—along with our new husbands and our bouncing little poppets for you to dandle upon your palsied knees."

"You're being silly now, but I appreciate the sentiment…*if* it's sincere."

"Quite sincere, Mumsy."

"Mr. Forrest predicts the war will be over by Christmas. He says Hitler will see that the air raids are having no effect on our morale and he'll just have to be content with what he has already, and there will be the end to it."

"Mr. Forrest is dotty, of course, just like his wife."

"There's so little to be hopeful about these days; I'm happy to listen to anything Mr. Forrest has to say. Did he not predict there'd be no invasion, and *has* there been an invasion?"

Maggie shook her head. "There's been no invasion, Mum. Only nightly bombing raids that are turning London into smoking piles of rubble and turning all our nerves to marmalade. And so many killed, and so many lives left in shambles. You and I—we've been lucky, though our time—if this goes on long enough—will certainly come. So many nights, Mum, I don't sleep at all, waiting for the sirens."

"If that's the way it's supposed to be, then doesn't it make more sense to stay at home and die in the arms of your dear old mum? Tell me why you must go to Jane's tonight. Has she engaged you all to carry her worthless brother to the East End docks and chuck him into the Thames with all the rest of the city rubbish?"

Maggie sat down next to her mother. "There's something We Five must discuss and we can't very well do it at the factory. As it turns out, we're going dancing on Saturday night. At the Hammersmith Palais."

"Goodness."

"I've never been there. None of us has. We've never been *anywhere*, for that matter, that Jane has asked us to go, and we thought it would be a good turn for all of us to be nice to her for a change."

Clara Barton shook her head with only slightly masked sadness. "That is to your credit, but mind, you'll *arrive* as wallflowers and *depart* as wallflowers. In the time in between, you'll cling to one another whilst casting longing glances at the dance floor. Are you sure you wouldn't rather go to the Hales' flat and play cards and listen to George Formby on the wireless?"

"The last time we got together to play cards, Mum, we got caught in an air raid and had to spend the rest of the evening sitting in Jane's wee Anderson shelter behind the shop. It was made ever the more pleasant when it began to drizzle and Jane's brother Lyle's fine workmanship afforded us a lovely bathe. I'd much rather go to a public shelter in the company of a hundred other people my age, each one of them gay and festive and decked out in Saturday night finery, thank you."

"Well then, don't say I didn't warn you."

Maggie frowned. "I wasn't going to tell you, Mum, but it so happens that we will most assuredly *not* be clinging to one another on Saturday. We intend to be dancing. There are five lads very close to us in age who are also coming, *and* who just happen to be coming for the sole purpose of seeing *us*."

Clara's eyes grew big. "I'm so glad you *have* told me. Are they are R.A.F. pilots?"

Maggie shook her head.

"Soldiers? Sailors? Submariners?"

"No. None of the above."

"Then they are young men who work with you at the factory?"

"They don't work at the factory. They deliver coal. When they aren't on fire watch for the A.F.S."

"What's wrong with these boys that they aren't serving their country in uniform?"

"They're conscientious objectors."

"Good God."

"I won't permit it!"

Molly wheeled upon her father. "What is that?"

Michael Osborne had been sitting at his worktable, polishing his dental instruments, but now he was on his feet and glaring at his daughter. "I *said* I will not permit my daughter to socialise with a bloody conchie, let alone *five* of them."

"May I remind you that the days of your permitting or *not* permitting me to do anything are over? You agreed to my full emancipation quite some time ago."

"This is different. To preserve your good reputation, I'll not have you associating with men who won't fight."

"All five of these lads are serving their country in their own way. Don't make me argue this with you. It's a waste of breath. I probably won't find a single one of them worth my time anyway, so this whole discussion is pointless."

"Just promise me this: if you happen to meet a *different* chap there tonight—one who just happens to be wearing a uniform and who just happens to show some interest in you, you'll give him more than passing notice. I should like someday to have a son-in-law who *is* willing to do his duty by his country."

Molly smiled. "Be careful what you wish for, Daddy dearest. Tommies can't *always* be trusted to do their country proud. They come to the canteens and dance halls really quite ravenous. And I'm not just talking about food. And what if I *were* to fall in love with one of them? And he were to ask me to marry him? What if it turned out that he was an Aussie or a Kiwi? How would you fancy traveling halfway round the world to visit your only child? Or to see your grandchildren? Wouldn't you rather I fall for a London coalman who'll—"

Michael Osborne did not give his daughter leave to finish. "Enough!" he roared. At the same time he flung the tempered steel excavator, which he'd been gripping tightly in his hand, down onto the table. It struck the porcelain top with a loud clack. "It's all tommyrot, if you ask me—this whole business of fathers being forced to give over their daughters to bleeding blokes with only one thing on their minds. Would that you were more like your friend Ruth, who chooses to have nothing to do with the opposite sex."

"It isn't fair to compare me to Ruth."

Osborne sat back down. He massaged his temples as if in doing so he might succeed in getting the veins protruding there to draw themselves back. He took a couple of deep breaths. "I'm curious. How did you get Ruth to agree to come along on this little escapade?"

Molly smiled. It was a sincere smile, though it had the ulterior purpose of calming and quieting her father after his outburst.

"It was really quite easy. The Hammersmith Palais tries to keep its guests well fed. And we all know how much Ruth loves to eat."

"Take the rest of my Spam," said Lucille Mobry. "I can't eat another bite."

"Only if you're truly full," said Ruth, whose fork was already making its way over to Lucille's plate to spear the last few bites of the battered meat.

"Did you know that when you first showed up on our doorstep like—oh Bert, who was it that walked for days and nights to his aunt's house in Dover—was it Oliver Twist or David Copperfield?"

"It was David Copperfield, I think. I'm picturing Freddie Bartholomew and that horsey-looking actress—Edna something."

"Anyway," Lucille resumed, "you were just skin and bones. Wasn't Ruth just skin and bones, Bert?"

"Skin and bones and a stomach that hasn't stopped borbarigging ever since." Mr. Mobry winked at Ruth, who returned the wink, along with a smile.

Lucille continued: "Those old beldames you'd run away from had been starving you for certain. We should have had them arrested."

"Well, everything worked out for the best," said Ruth, reaching across the table to requisition one of Lucille's boiled potatoes as well. Lucille assented with a nod. "And look at me now, Auntie: I weigh eight hundred pounds. In truth, I *should* reduce. There's a chart that hangs in the cloakroom at the factory; it says how much a woman should weigh at such-and-such a height."

"And how did you measure up to that ideal woman in the chart?"

Ruth shook her head with resignation. "I cannot say the two of us will ever be mistaken for one another." Ruth laughed ruefully. "I suppose that's the only silver lining to this ghastly war; most of what's being rationed or is absolutely unavailable isn't good for the figure anyway. I have to get ready. We're all getting together tonight at Jane's to make plans for Saturday night."

Herbert Mobry nodded and smiled. "It's good you're going out—good that Londoners as a whole aren't giving in to these damned raids."

Lucille's hand flew to her mouth. "Dear brother, you just said a foul word."

"*Raids?*"

"You know exactly the word I'm referring to."

"First, Sister, my career as a minister is over, so I needn't watch my tongue as closely as I used to. Second: it was a perfectly appropriate use of the word. The Nazis and their air raids *are* to be damned."

"*Still—*" Lucille returned her attention to Ruth. "I assume there's an A.R.P. shelter near the Palais, if one should be needed."

"Of course there is, Auntie. And if the sirens sound tonight, I'll just follow all the others right down into it. You needn't worry."

"It cannot be avoided," Mobry contributed. "I must tell you, though, Ruth, that we do worry less—Sister and me—when you're close by and safe—well, as safe as any Londoner can be these days. But then again, it's good to have friends who understand you as Sister and I do."

"*Do* you understand me, Uncle? I *am* rather a complication."

"All of God's children are complications, child. We're entangled bundles of nerves and sinew and twisted-up brain matter. Who can probe *any* mind with success, let alone the mind of, say, an Adolf Hitler who each day conceives new horrors to unleash upon the world? Of course, invoking the Fuehrer doesn't make my point at all. I suspect he is the exception to the rule. There *are* exceptions to be found now and then—these men of diseased consciences and cankered souls. Our loving Lord and Savior implants a soul in each of His children, but sometimes that soul withers or festers. Hitler and the men who willingly serve him—men responsible for the kind of atrocities that stagger the mind—these men have a sickness that robs them of every ounce of their humanity."

"Or perhaps they were defective to begin with," offered Lucille. "Perhaps God dozed off a bit, and Hitler and Goering and Goebbels slipped off the assembly line ill-formed."

"I would not dismiss that possibility," said the former pastor, just finishing his postprandial spot of tea. "On the other hand, God—we have been taught—doesn't make mistakes. So it is a conundrum. But then again, there are a good many mysteries to this world that won't be solved until after we're gone on to our reward—and perhaps not even then."

"Here's another mystery, Ruth," said Lucille Mobry, pushing herself away from the table. "It was left on our doorstep this afternoon." Lucille went to the sideboard to retrieve the parcel she'd placed there earlier. "Your name is on it, but nothing else. It feels like a book."

"Thank you, Auntie," said Ruth, taking it. She turned it over in her hand.

"Should we avert our eyes?" asked Mobry, with a grin. "Perhaps it's from a secret admirer who wishes to go on being 'secret.'"

"I have no admirers," shot back Ruth, "secret or otherwise."

But Ruth knew that she did. And for this reason she went to her room to open the package in private.

Lucille had guessed correctly; it *was* a book. And one Ruth didn't have. It was a very special book, in fact, and had come all the way from the United States. Ruth knew this because she knew all about the novel's troubled history. *The Well of Loneliness* had come up in conversation between Ruth and her forewoman, Miss Colthurst, at the filling factory. The book had been ordered destroyed by the British courts several months after its publication in 1928. Copies occasionally made their way into the country from France, where it was still being published, and from the United States, where its American publisher was successful in winning a court ruling declaring that the book *wasn't* obscene, though it depicted an unambiguous romantic relationship between two women. The conversation between Ruth and Vivien Colthurst orbited round both the story and the curious name of its author, Radclyffe Hall. "She sounds rather like the name of a building, doesn't she?" asked Miss Colthurst, who put the question to Ruth with a look that indicated an intense interest in knowing just how much Ruth was enjoying their private chat.

Ruth could not believe that Vivien had obtained a copy of the American edition. She looked forward to thanking her friend for going to so much trouble (for surely it wasn't an easy thing to put one's hands on such a book). But she looked forward even more to the chance to actually read it.

As Lucille cleared away the tea dishes, Bert Mobry browsed through his copy of *Radio Times* in his easy chair. With his recent retirement from the pulpit, Mobry was indulging himself in all the radio programmes he'd missed over the last few years. During his many busy seasons in ministerial cassock there had only been time for the news broadcasts, but now he could listen to anything he pleased, although there was much that *dis*pleased him. He adamantly refused, for example, to twiddle the dial for the broadcasts of the German propagandist Lord Haw-Haw, who set many a Briton's teeth on edge, though his programmes were popular; with the continuing clamp down of information on British air and sea misadventures, this was sometimes the fastest way for British citizens to learn the outcome of engagements that did not go so well.

Lucille came into the parlour and stood next to her brother's chair. "Would you like me to turn on the wireless?"

"If you don't mind. Once I'm settled into this upholstered marshmallow my poor old back doesn't allow me to get up without complaint."

But Lucille remained for a moment longer just where she stood. "Do you think our Ruth might have herself a follower? Perhaps someone who loves to read as much as she does?"

Bert shrugged. "Ruth is an enigma. I cannot say."

"I'm surprised that she's going dancing with her friends on Saturday night. But I'm happy for her."

Bert turned his head to look up at his sister. "Your troubled expression tells me otherwise."

Lucille fabricated a smile as if to contradict her brother. "I'm happy *and* I worry. Isn't that the way it is for everyone these days? Even our most pleasant moments are never without their dark edges of care and fear. It does make me sad to think of Ruth and those four special friends of hers. What a terrible time to be young and so full of life—only to have all the verve and spirit drained out of you by all the retched things men have shown themselves capable of doing to one another."

"Do you mean men as representatives of mankind, Sister, or men as—well—*men*?"

"Both, I fancy." Lucille sat down upon the fat arm of the chair and placed her hand lovingly upon its occupant's shoulder. "You spoke of men like Hitler earlier—those with a sickness that robs them of their humanity. Might there be men of similar infirmity— men right here in London of whom Ruth and her friends must take careful heed? I'm thinking of the girls in our congregation who found themselves—need I say it?"

"You needn't say it," said Mr. Mobry, patting his sister on the hand. "I'm rather glad I've retired from the ministry. 'Tisn't a good time to be a shepherd among men. Far too many black sheep in the flock these days."

"And what else is on the agenda for the evening?" asked Mrs. Hale. "I mean, besides approving which frocks you'll be wearing Saturday night—which, may I just say, makes absolutely no sense unless you're all hoping to go there looking like a colour-matched, fully-grown version of the Dionne quintuplets?"

"Mother, you're a panic," said Carrie. Mother and Daughter were sitting on Daughter's bed amongst all the various pleated skirts and panelled skirts and straight skirts Carrie had been trying on. At present, Carrie was decked out in a pale green silk dress (her nicest one) for which the matching fabric-covered belt could not be found, and which, as it was, fitted much too tightly just below its sweetheart neckline. A long interval had passed since she'd last put it on, and during this time her breasts—which had already made Carrie the most mammarily blessed of We Five—had expanded to even greater proportions. "It's really the entire *package* which we want to carefully put forward, Mother, and clothes are only a part of it. This is what Jane says. She says we should be careful when we make our appearance at the ballroom not to appear as either Bow's Belles *or* Mayfair slummers. Jane would like us to stake out some spot in the cautious middle: girls without too terribly much money, but girls who are still capable of comporting themselves with taste and decorum. It's not an easy thing to put over, Mother, so we'll need to work at it."

Carrie's mother clasped her hands together in a show of cheery confidence. "You'll be a credit to all those middling girls just like you. Why should only the very rich and the very poor have all the fun?"

"And you *do* want me to have fun, don't you, Mother? Even though you'll have to sit at home, rocking and knitting away with only the voices of the BBC for company?"

Sylvia Hale shook her head. "Do you fancy I'll be lucky enough to spend the entire evening so indulgently? More than likely it will be me and Mr. Whiskers in the staircase cupboard. And if I'm *very* lucky, I'll have Deloria Littlejohn crawling in beside me, so I'll be treated to her unkind opinions of all the neighbours until blessed 'All Clear.'"

"Why doesn't she use her Anderson? I've seen the inside of it. It's very nice the way she's fixed it up."

"Mrs. Littlejohn said she'd rather take rat poison than spend even an hour in such close quarters with *Mr.* Littlejohn. They don't get on, or didn't you know? At any rate, don't go fidgeting yourself over me. You said on Monday that you and I—that we may have got a bit dull, even in the midst of this terrible war. And I've thought about it, and I have come to fancy there *is* some truth to it. We go round like lifeless twin automatons until the bombs fall, when we run all about like frightened children. And then when the sirens shut off and those nasty Messerschmitts disappear for the night, we're back to tea and yawns and languid violin sonatas by Austrians, which we aren't even supposed to be playing since the Anschluss. I want you to be happy, Carrie. You're a beautiful girl and it's time you met a young man who will appreciate you for your beauty—but also one who'll be drawn to your cleverness and your winning personality."

"You left out my various musical talents and my ability to stand on my head. You're being a dear, Mother, but you're being far too generous. Next you'll say you're troubled not in the least by the possibility that I may fall in love with a conscientious objector."

"But it's true, pet! If you love the lad—who*ever* the lad may be—I intend to respect your choice, because I'm confident my daughter will choose wisely. And by the way, conscientious objectors stand a far better chance of surviving this war than their counterparts in the service; it's a simple fact. I'm being selfish, I know it, but I don't want a young war widow for a daughter. I remember the last war, dear. Almost a million of our young men killed. Why else do you think I was forced to settle on your horrid father? You go to that ballroom on Saturday, my darling, and you bedazzle every young man there, conchie or not, and you come home and tell me every little thing about it. I'll be your housebound girlfriend who lives vicariously through your breathless adventures."

"Mother, one of these days you're going to slip up and actually treat me like a daughter and not like your best friend in the world— and you'll have to go looking for the sal volatile to revive me."

Carrie got up, smoothed herself, and started to put all the skirts away.

"Let *me* do that," said Sylvia. "You run along. The dress isn't too tight?"

"A little, but we have until Saturday night to let it out, and I do want my sisters to see it tonight. Thank you, Mother."

"Caroline?"

"Yes, Mother?"

"You don't think—for just this coming Saturday night—that We Five might not become, well, *We Six*?"

Carrie regarded her mother with surprise. "You'd like to *join* us?"

Sylvia Hale nodded.

Carrie smiled. She went up to her mother and kissed her on the forehead. "Don't be silly. You know you can't come."

Sylvia's look of excited anticipation over what could be Carrie's answer vanished without a trace.

Carrie appended: "But I promise to rush right home and tell you every niggling detail. *Breathlessly!*"

This wasn't much of a consolation to Carrie's best friend in the world, but it would have to do.

———

Jane stared at Lyle and Lyle stared back at Jane from across the kitchen table. Lyle had a blackened eye, for which he couldn't account. "I fancy you won't be going out tonight with an eye like that," said Jane.

Lyle, having finished his tea, licked his fingers like a hungry man in a bad play. "It might stop me. It might not. I haven't made up me mind yet."

"Perhaps if you retrace your steps from last night, you'll recall how you got it."

"My guess is that I rattled some bloke's cage and he punched me lights out." Lyle grinned mischievously. "Oh I have it now. You want me out of the way so's you can have the chickies here. I heard you talking to one of them on the Ameche earlier."

"Maybe they *are* coming tonight. But I'll not let you get anywhere near them. If you so much as wink or blink in their direction whilst they're here, you'll have to fend for your own bloody self for all of next week. You'll have to take all your meals at the Fatted Pig, and just how easy will that be, when I don't intend to give you a brass farthing to pay for them?"

"You wouldn't do that to me after how badly things have been going for me lately."

"Everything what's happened to you I wager has been of your own making. Now what is it? Will you be going to your room and mind yourself like a good lad, or will you be going out and trying not to get yourself another black eye? It's all one to me. Either way, you're out of *my* way for the evening."

Lyle thought about this. "I'm completely stonkered. I think I'll go to my room and sleep for twelve hours."

Jane nodded.

A moment passed. Then Jane said, "Now that you've made up your mind, I'd like to say, speaking honestly, mind, that I was *hoping* you wouldn't go out. Generally speaking, I *don't* care, but today I was almost proud of you—the way you ran the shop like some creature what was very nearly human. Mrs. Meeker just rang me up to say that you were such a good-hearted gent to give her the discount on the mahogany dressing table with the missing leg. And, wonder of wonders! the money you got from the sale was still sitting in the cash drawer when I came home this evening."

"Mrs. Meeker was friends with Mum and Dad. It seemed the right thing to do."

"I wish you was that person all the *other* days of the week."

Lyle didn't look at his sister. "I wish I was that person too. Apparently, it isn't in me nature."

"Run along to your room, now. I want to tidy up a bit before the girls get here."

Lyle nodded. He rose from the table. He reached out his hand to touch one of Jane's folded arms. She didn't pull away. She allowed his fingers to rest for a long moment upon the crook of her arm. Then he removed the hand, turned away, and moved slowly and heavily from the room.

It was a single tear that escaped Jane's left eye and she quickly brushed it into nothingness.

Chapter Ten

Bellevenue, Mississippi, February 1997

It was after two in the morning and only one of We Five was asleep.

Molly had been dropped off at nearly 1:40, had walked around to the back alley and climbed the outdoor stairs to the small apartment she shared with her father over his chiropractic and holistic dentistry office. She'd seen the blue glow of the television through the street-front windows of the den. (The Osbornes had no living room.) After letting herself in, she'd wordlessly crossed the thick, faded-green shag carpeting and sat down next to her father on the sofa. He patted her hand but kept his eyes focused on the television screen, where the boxer George Foreman was demonstrating his popular tabletop grill.

After a moment, Michael turned to his daughter and said, "Now *there's* somebody I'd buy a product from. You'd never know from that Pillsbury Doughboy face of his that he still climbs into the ring to take power punches at people."

A silent moment passed. Then Molly said, "He looks like Mr. Biggers. You remember the crossing guard at the elementary school? He once saved a woman who was choking to death on a peanut shell."

"Right in the middle of the crosswalk?"

"No. When he was off duty. I think it was at the Big Star. In the produce section."

Silence.

"What was she doing—just popping peanuts into her mouth without paying for them?"

"Apparently."

"Oh."

Another silence passed. Then Michael Osborne said matter-of-factly, "The infomercial before this one was for something called 'Mick's Club.' It looks like a golf club, but it isn't. It's a hollow tube a golfer can pee into whenever he has the need to go."

Molly thought about this for a moment. "*Male* golfer, obviously."

"Obviously."

Molly thought some more. "But couldn't he just find a tree or a bush or something to do his business on?"

Molly's father shook his head. "You're not supposed to go peeing all over golf courses. They generally frown on that." Michael Osborne turned down the sound on the television so they couldn't hear what George Foreman was saying about all the grease he was drawing off his hamburger meat. "How was it?"

"The place was kind of touristy, but the music was good. And the food. I had the fried catfish. It was 'all-you-can-eat night.' I just kept eating."

"Did they act like gentlemen or like those boys in that *Animal House* movie?"

"They were pretty well behaved. Although one of them had too much to drink and got a little handsy with Mags. But she put him in his place."

"So nobody got fresh with *you*?"

Molly shook her head. "Somebody told me that George Foreman has four sons and they're all named George."

"Somebody told you correctly." Michael sniff-laughed to himself. "I suppose *Mrs.* Foreman isn't complaining. She just has to shout 'George!' and the whole family shows up for dinner."

Michael turned the volume back up. Then almost immediately he muted the television again.

"So did you all kind of pair off like you thought you might?"

"Yes and no. I mean, we were pretty much coupled up, but we were all still sitting at the same table."

"That must have been a big table. Did you like the boy *you* were paired up with?"

"I did. He was nice. I think we wound up together because we're both the youngest, but it worked out okay. He's pretty cute, I'd have to say. He looks kind of like Nick Carter of the Backstreet Boys—I mean, like if Nick Carter was a little bit older and didn't have his teeth whitened so much. But I don't think he's all that smart—even though he just graduated from Ole Miss."

"Why do you say that?"

"I don't know. He just seems like one of those guys who doesn't pay much attention to things if he doesn't have to."

"You mean things in the news and such like?"

Molly nodded.

"Did he pay attention to *you?*"

"He did, Daddy. He paid a lot of attention to me. He wants to see me again."

"Oh. Really?"

"I told him I'd think about it. I should probably go to bed. I'm really sleepy." Molly got up from the sofa.

"Which shift do you girls have tomorrow?"

"Primetime. Five to one. You know we always get five to one on Friday and Saturday nights because that's when they need the most waitresses. Daddy, don't fall asleep on the couch. I'm home. I'm safe. Go to bed."

"This boy—what's his name?"

"Pat Harrison. He's from Hattiesburg. I think he really likes me, Daddy."

"I could give him a good whitening treatment if he wanted it. What does he plan to do with his life?"

"He's pre-law."

"Pre-law. Hmm." Michael grinned. "I guess he wouldn't be the first dimwitted lawyer practicing in the state of Mississippi."

"You're terrible, Daddy." Molly tossed a throw pillow at her father. He tried to dodge, but it still made contact with his head.

"You sure you don't want to watch a little of Dionne Warwick and her Psychic Friends Network? I think George Foreman's just about said everything he's gonna say."

"Let me get into my P.J.s first."

Fifteen minutes later, Molly Osborne—dressed in warm flannel pajamas, her hair and teeth brushed—was curled up at the end of the sofa. Within a couple of minutes, though, she was fast asleep, her head cushioned upon a throw pillow on the armrest. Michael Osborne, who often fell asleep in front of the TV himself, drifted off shortly thereafter.

At eight minutes past two father and daughter were both slumbering away, even though the woman on the television was being stridently giddy over having just been informed that she was about to come into a large sum of money.

It was her psychic friend who told her this.

At this same time, four blocks away, Carrie lay in bed not even the least bit sleepy. She stared into the enveloping darkness of her bedroom while stroking the family tabby, which was scrunched into a furry oval next to her. Over and over again she replayed the sequence of events from one of the most enjoyable nights of her life.

Her mother had wanted details. She had summoned Carrie to her bedroom upon her return to hear whatever interesting tidbits Carrie might wish to share with her. And Carrie *did* tell her things—a good many things—just not *everything*.

Because how on Earth *could* she? On this seemingly ordinary Thursday night, Carrie Hale's ordinary life had *stopped* being ordinary, and it was hard for her to even put into words how she felt about this sudden turn of events.

It frightened her. It excited her. It actually made her feel a little woozy.

What she *did* tell her mother was this: that she really liked the one named Will. The one with the dreamy hazel eyes. The tall one. The one with the linebacker's build and the overdeveloped biceps, which seemed close to bursting right through the fabric of his button-down shirt, like Bruce Banner's shirt did while he was transforming into the Hulk. Even better: Will really seemed to like *her* from the second she'd climbed into the courtesy van.

The seat next to him had been empty. It was almost as if he'd been holding it for her. Carrie wondered if the five former fraternity brothers had already put in their dibs based on Tom's descriptions, which had obviously been supplied by Jane when the two of them set things up. Carrie meant to ask Jane about this—how it was decided who got who—but she never got the chance. Things had moved so fast. Tom had gotten the fleet boss's permission to borrow one of the casino's vans for the night. It wasn't a problem; Thursday was always a slow night for Lucky Aces. Tom, with his four buddies already on board, had picked up each of the girls at their respective homes and then, this time, instead of dropping everyone off at the Lucky Aces Casino as he had done on Monday morning, he took himself and his nine passengers all the way down Highway 61 to Clarksdale, to a blues club he'd been to there.

Tom Katz, a student of the Mississippi Delta, knew all about its rich musical heritage. He'd grown up in Greenville, farther south. Tom had shown the others the exact spot where the blues singer Bessie Smith had met her tragic vehicular fate, and pointed out the crossroads where Robert Johnson—as legend had it—sold his soul to the devil.

This in spite of the fact that Jerry Castle, born in the exclusive white suburb of Memphis called Germantown, had crowed right in the middle of Tom's commentary that he'd "had enough nigger history for one night," so would Tommy please shut his "blabby-mouthed Jew pie-hole?" Maggie had cringed to hear such a string of filth belched from her date for the evening. Carrie was pleased, though, that Will had been the first to dress down his friend for it. She squeezed Will's arm to demonstrate her approval.

When it was Carrie's turn to be dropped off, Will walked her to the door of the 1960s-era brick ranch-style she shared with her mother on the north side of Bellevenue (where the second and third–generation middle-class white families lived). Carrie wondered if he was going to kiss her goodnight.

He'd wasted no time in satisfying her curiosity. They'd hardly reached the concrete porch before he pulled her against him and gave her a deep, hungry kiss, his powerful hands clamping her upper arms firmly, almost painfully. After releasing her, he'd whispered with incongruous tenderness, "I want you."

She didn't know quite how to respond.

He pushed on: "When can I see you again?"

"Call me," she said.

He had nodded and clumped back to the shuttle van, planting each foot carefully upon the concrete walk to the driveway so as not to slip on the slick ice.

Carrie didn't tell her mother about the kiss, or about Will seeming to really like her. But she was honest in admitting she was very interested in him, and yes, she'd probably be seeing him again.

Then she talked about the catfish and the ribs and the "crawdads." She knew her mother, herself a child of the Delta (Greenwood), also loved crayfish. Carrie conveniently neglected to mention that there had also been some drinking on the order of two Lemon Drops

(Molly), one Fuzzy Navel each (Jane and Carrie), two Sea Breezes (Ruth), and a Diet Coke, plus refill, for non-imbiber Maggie. And why shouldn't she leave this out? None of the girls had overindulged. Ruth had left the club a little buzzed, but it had worn off long before she'd gotten home.

Of course, Sylvia knew. She smelled the peach schnapps on her daughter's breath. After all, Sylvia Hale wasn't born yesterday.

She let it pass. She only wished she'd been there too. She would have ordered a strawberry daiquiri.

Jane noticed upon her return to the rooms she shared with her brother at the back of the antique store that several lights had been left on. She turned them off while grumbling to herself that he could have thought a little about their electric bill before going out for the night. Or *had* he gone out? The previous night, when We Five had gotten together to eat Domino's pepperoni and talk about what they were going to wear on their group date, he'd been in his room (and never once ventured out, just as he'd promised). More than likely, thought Jane, Lyle would make up for it tonight. He'd be off with his buddies till all hours, either blowing money he couldn't afford to blow at one of the nearby casinos or drinking himself cross-eyed at some titty bar fifteen miles up the road in Southaven. (Also something he couldn't afford to do, but which he did anyway once or twice a week.)

She opened the door to his room nonetheless, and discovered she'd been mistaken in her first assumption. He was there. He was awake. And he was doing something she'd never seen him do before.

Startled, he threw himself involuntarily over the sketchpad which had been resting on his knees. There was a book next to him, propped open. He'd been working with colored pencils, copying one of the images from the book; Jane couldn't quite make it out from where she stood in the doorway.

"What are you doin'?" she asked.

"Why do you just barge in here like that?"

"The door was unlocked. If you were in here with your girly magazines you'd have it locked and I'd mind my own business. Are you *drawing*?"

"So it appears."

"Why?"

"What do you mean: *why*?"

"I don't know. I just—Lyle, I never knew you liked to draw."

Lyle closed the sketchpad so Jane, who was craning her neck to get a better look, wouldn't have any idea as to what he'd been sketching. The open book gave her a clue, though. Stepping closer, she was able to glimpse a pastoral scene—a verdant grassy hill with a flock of sheep on it—before he slammed that shut too.

"I thought you'd still be out," Jane said, "or conked out in front of the television with a can of Budweiser balanced on your knee. I found you like *that* one night. I almost took a picture. I can't believe you don't even have the radio on."

"I like silence when I draw. Total quiet."

Jane sat down on the bed. Lyle was sitting Indian-style at the end, his back pushed against the wall, his cluttered side table pulled over so he'd have a place to prop up the book he was sketching from.

"How long have you been doin' this?"

Lyle shrugged. "I don't know. A while."

"Can I see your sketchbook?"

"I don't think so."

"I think it's great."

"Thanks, but your approval don't make no difference to me."

Lyle got up. He tucked his sketchpad and the art book into his bookcase. It was mostly an open junk cabinet, but it did have a few books there. Jane hadn't noticed before, but almost all the books were art-related.

"I mean seriously, Lyle. How long have you been sketching?"

"You really interested? Five, six months."

"Wow." The word was nearly inaudible, as if Jane had intended to keep her amazement to herself.

"Isn't it way past your bedtime?" he asked.

"I know it's late, but I'm keyed up. Now I know what you mean when you sometimes say you're too wired to sleep."

"Did you let him in your pants?"

"Don't be gross. We all had a nice time."

"Does he want to see you again?"

Jane smiled. She tried not to, but she couldn't help herself. "I think so."

"What's he look like? Is he mule-faced like us?"

Jane got up. "Why do you do this? Why do you assume the only man who'd ever want to take me out would have to look like Beavis or or or or Butthead? Which one's the ugly one?"

"They're both pretty fucking ugly. I'm sorry. Sit down."

Jane sat back down.

"Do you want a beer?"

"Okay."

Lyle went to the little mini fridge he kept in his room and got a frosty can of Bud for each of them. He popped the cap on both before he sat down.

Then he said, "You know those paintings of the countryside the old woman brought in a few weeks ago?"

"You mean the ones we took for the frames? You were gonna toss the pictures into the incinerator."

"Well, I never did."

"They were pretty awful, Lyle."

"Of course they were. But the more I looked at 'em, the more they got me to thinkin'—Dad was a good artist, I mean, back when he was young. And I liked to draw when I was kid, remember?"

Jane nodded.

"So it's kind of in the genes. Well, I kept lookin' at those crappy paintings the woman brought in and I started sayin' to myself: 'Hell, *I* could paint better than *that*. I mean, if I worked at it.'"

"I like it you're tryin' something different." Jane touched her brother's hand, taking a swig of her beer.

"Don't talk down to me."

"I don't know any other way to talk to you, Lyle."

"You're funny. My life is a shit pit. This ain't no big news bulletin. Both of our lives are shit. You're workin' as a cocktail waitress at a casino. And when I *do* have the store open, the people who come in—they know the stuff we're sellin' here ain't antiques, even though that's what the sign says. They know it's all junk. Crap. And I'm tired of trying to sell it to them. I wanna do somethin' different. So that's what I'm doing: I'm trying somethin' different. Like you meeting that Katz guy and all of a sudden you're walkin' around here with a kind of smile on your face I ain't never seen before."

"I made a New Year's resolution, Lyle: that I was gonna shake up *my* life this year."

Lyle smiled. "It looks like you're shaking up *everybody's* lives in the bargain. I mean, you and your four gal pals. Never thought I'd see the five of you going out on a what—a quadruple—"

"Quintuple, I think it is."

"—date. It's like I'm in some kind of alternate reality where everybody's almost normal."

Jane play-glowered. "I'm glad you're happy for me. Show me your sketchbook."

"Why?"

"I wanna see your work. Please."

Lyle went to the bookcase to retrieve the pad. "I'm just starting out," he hedged.

"I won't judge you."

The sketches, each taken from famous landscape paintings and rendered in colored pencil, were good. *Very* good. Jane didn't say a word. She just shook her head in undisguised amazement. And for the next twenty minutes, she didn't think of Tom Katz at all.

However, later, alone in her bedroom, she allowed her thoughts to return to the young man who had made her laugh and think quite differently about herself. Sleep wouldn't be coming any time soon for Jane Higgins.

Maggie stood in the doorway watching her mother sleep. Clara Barton didn't snore per se, but because of constantly clogged sinuses, she often breathed through her mouth when she slept. Someone once told Maggie the word for it; her mother *chuffled*.

Part of Maggie wished her mother had been awake when she got home so she could tell her all about the night she'd just spent. In spite of her pair-up for the night being a first-class dick, she'd still had a great time. It was fun seeing her sisters let their hair down and get silly and flirty—showing sides to themselves Maggie hadn't thought existed.

But how the hell did she get Jerry Castle? He wasn't even all that good-looking—that is, compared to Carrie's Will and Molly's Pat, and Jane's Tom, who looked like a particular rock star whose name she couldn't quite conjure up. Jerry had a high forehead, which came partly from the fact that there was simply a lot of head above his eyebrows. But, as it turned out, his hair was also receding. An "early receder." Just like Maggie's father. She guessed Jerry would be totally bald by the time he was thirty.

And it would serve him right. Jerry Castle had a Mack truck– sized ego and a real mouth on him; he was brash and smart-assed in a way that could never be considered attractive. Plus, he kept grabbing her leg to the point where she had to tell him off. In front of everybody. Maggie wondered why his friends put up with him. In the ladies' room, she asked Jane if *she* knew. Jane guessed it was because Jerry had had to overcome a pretty sucky childhood.

According to Tom, Jerry's father had been a real tightwad. He was assistant manager of a Hickory Farms store and Jerry grew up eating mostly castoff cheese and nitrite-embalmed summer sausage. Jerry's buddies probably felt sorry for him.

"Just because you had bad breaks when you were a kid is no reason to act like an asshole when you grow up," Maggie had replied, checking her teeth in the mirror to make sure some of the rib meat hadn't gotten stuck in a way that would be unsightly when she opened her large Julia Roberts–esque mouth to laugh or talk. "Look at Ruth," Maggie pushed her point with Jane, who was applying a little of Molly's Tommy Girl perfume to the back of her ears. "Ruth had the very same messed-up childhood and she's as nice as can be."

"Did you just wake up from a *coma*?" retorted Jane. "Ruth has an edge you could use for a Weed Wacker. I've seen it. You have too."

"But she doesn't talk over people and blabber her opinion all the time and use the 'F' word for all the different parts of speech."

Jane snickered. "He *does* have one big ol' gutter mouth on him, don't he?" Jane turned to Maggie, her look suddenly sympathetic. "Oh, you really *don't* like him, do you? I'm so sorry, Mags. I tried to match everybody up right, but it looks like you got the short straw, didn't you? You're not gonna hold that against me, are you? I mean, you don't have to ever see him again."

"I won't hold it against you, if you do me a favor."

"What?"

"Talk me up to…" She pointed to the word 'Tommy' on the perfume bottle. "I think I like him."

Jane sucked in her lips. Then, dourly: "You can't have Tommy. Tommy is spoken for."

"*Really*, Jane?" said Maggie, not even trying to hide her annoyance. "You and Tommy? You're *serious*?"

"Mags, you can be such a bitch. Yes, I'm serious. As it so happens, he's already said he wants to see me again. Without his entourage. And I said yes."

Maggie's bead-eyed stare said she still didn't believe her.

"You'll just have to make do with Jerry or nobody at all," said Jane, now in a full-fledged huff. "I'm sure he don't act like that much of an asshole when his buddies aren't around. He's just a showoff, is all."

"He makes my flesh crawl."

"I'm sorry. I'm really sorry, but that's the breaks, Mags. You're very pretty. You can have anybody you want—I mean, if you actually opened yourself up to possibilities. It ain't my fault you haven't put yourself out there."

"I don't like any of the boys in Bellevenue. They talk like hicks and have dirt under their fingernails."

"Then, honey, you should go someplace else. Especially now that your mother and Molly's father are gettin' married and you don't have to look after her no more."

Maggie nodded. "I just might. Even though you'll all miss me. At least I *hope* you'll all miss me."

Jane reached over and pulled Maggie to her so the two could hug. "Of course we'll miss you. You know how much we love you."

"If you really loved me, you'd let me have Tommy and *you* can take Jerry."

"He won't want me. I'm ugly, remember? Besides which, he makes my skin crawl too." Jane pulled back so she could brush a strand of hair from her friend's eyes. "Honey, just get yourself through tonight. It'll all be over real quick."

Maggie appreciated the thought, even though she didn't say so. She forced herself to smile in a way that didn't look forced. "I hope you and Carrie and Molly don't schedule your three weddings *too* close together. The 'always a bridesmaid' thing—well, it's gonna get very old for me very fast."

"You *funny* lady," said Jane, imitating the impatiently indulgent immigrant waitress at the Chinese restaurant We Five sometimes went to in Bellevenue. "*Now what you ordah?*"

No. Maggie couldn't talk to her mother about any of this. She let her sleep. Maggie got ready for bed, but she knew she wouldn't be able to turn off her brain. *Was* there a little something there— between Jerry and her? A little something about that gauche, foul-mouthed, all-but-certainly racist and anti-Semitic and xenophobic Jerry Castle that redeemed him just the teensiest little bit? Maybe he had a secret life in which he nuzzled kittens and puppies, and took meals to shut-ins and taught Sunday school to five-year-olds when nobody was looking. Maybe he was a good lover, or at the very least a good kisser. Of course, Maggie lost her chance to find *that* out when she'd refused to let him even walk her to her front door.

She wished he'd acted just a *little bit* disappointed over the brush-off.

At around this time Ruth was also lying awake in bed and thinking. She was wondering if she wanted to see Cain again. Although she *had* said yes to his suggestion that the two of them get together the next week when they were both off work at the same time, still she wondered. He'd made it *fairly* clear it wouldn't be a date. They would just go for coffee somewhere and talk without all the noise that made conversation so difficult in the blues club.

Still…

There was a new combination bookstore/coffeehouse on the square in Bellevenue she'd been wanting to visit. Bellevenue, with its antebellum courthouse, quaint post-bellum shops, Victorian-era frame houses and stately antiquarian oak trees, had a certain Southern charm to it that hadn't been entirely erased by the arrival of all the new casinos and fancy destination-hotels down the road. Movie companies liked Bellevenue. Several films had recently been shot there. But also recently, the native Mississippi residents who called the town home had come to want some of the same things other American towns—not so "local-colorful," and much more hip and progressive—were enjoying. Like combination bookstore/

coffeehouses where you could sit and sip tea while flipping through the latest issue of your favorite magazine.

But if there was a chance this was a ploy by Cain to get his romantic foot in the door, it wasn't going to work. Ruth didn't want a serious relationship with Cain, or *any* man for that matter.

In spite of this, Ruth liked Cain. He was bright and aridly funny and nothing at all like his buddies. But she liked him as a potential friend. Eventually, she'd have to let him know this.

Ruth didn't know that at that very moment, Cain Pardlow was lying awake thinking the very same thing, in spite of the bet. In spite of Will's threat to expose him—to tell what he'd walked in on in the men's room at the casino. Cain didn't really care whether he lost the casino job or not, but he didn't want it to get out there—to screw up his admission to law school, to find its way to his father's ears, to the ears of all the people his father worked with as district attorney in Cottondale. Isaiah Pardlow didn't need a scandal like this right after announcing his decision to run for another term.

Cain had been with girls before. He could be with Ruth in that way if he had to, but he'd certainly be leading her on, lying to her while compromising himself.

Cain, like Ruth, had had a nice time that evening. Unfortunately, he was now back to feeling like shit.

Chapter Eleven

Tulleford, England, August 1859

Mrs. Colthurst sighed contentedly. "It is done. And I commend each of you for your care and diligence in completing the task. The gowns are quite beautiful and Mrs. Cuthwaite will be most pleased. I warrant the five charming Misses Cuthwaite, when transformed by our singular creations, will catch the appreciative eye of every eligible young man at the Starlight Ball."

Mrs. Colthurst's five seamstresses, situated behind their five identical worktables, looked equally proud and rather satisfied with themselves. However, none seemed more pleased with the accomplishment than Jane and Ruth, who had toiled at Mrs. Colthurst's side long past the setting of the previous workday sun. It was not required that the gowns be delivered to Mrs. Cuthwaite until Saturday morning, but Mrs. Colthurst, sensing interest from her best customer in the work of a different seamstress—one who had recently opened her own shop in Warrington only five miles away—thought it would be to her advantage to complete the job one day early in an attempt to secure the wealthy woman's continuing favour and patronage.

"Jane and Ruth were so very helpful to me, that I must charge *you*, Maggie, with the task of delivering the finished gowns to Mrs. Cuthwaite. I've arranged for Bob, the hostler at South Haven Inn, to come along at half past ten to take you in Mr. Lincoln's fly. At the same time, Molly, I will ask *you* to take Mrs. Dowell the frock I've just mended for her. She isn't far, as you know. I'm certain you'll manage sufficiently by dint of your own two good legs."

"Without doubt," said Molly with a compliant nod.

"Carrie is the lucky one today, but in no time at all I'm sure I'll have something for *you* to do, my dear, to even the ledger with your diligent circle-sisters." Mrs. Colthurst looked about the room, nodding complacently. "Now *this* is how a business should be run—each contributing a part to make a success of the whole. It is as if each of us was a different leg of the hard-working dung beetle, who pushes his dung ball hither and thither in happy and productive industry."

"Have you been looking at that book again, Mrs. Colthurst?" asked Jane, with a wag of the finger.

Mrs. Colthurst coloured. "The illustrations are really quite remarkable, and I must confess I take great inspiration from the assiduity of the superfamily *Scarabaeoidea*. Every one of us should apply ourselves to our tasks in the manner of our insect friends, the hard-working beetles."

After Molly and Maggie had left on their appointed morning errands and Mrs. Colthurst had returned to her little office alcove to balance the accounts, Ruth and Jane and Carrie smiled amongst themselves. Jane rolled back her eyes with especial delight. "I cannot say I fault the woman for her love of curious books, but it is her enthusiastic admiration for dung beetles which I cannot completely fathom."

Ruth defended the honour and worth of her employeress. "The comparison is a fair one, Jane. Let us not be uncharitable, simply because the insect happens to be coprophagous."

Carrie bridled up. She tossed aside the black bombazeen cloak she was making for Mrs. Evers, who had asked for mourning weeds in anticipation of her husband's demise. (Mrs. Colthurst had well nigh refused to accept the commission; Mr. Evers seemed in robust health, but Mrs. Evers, having received a premonition of her husband's premature passing in a dream, insisted it would serve for her to be sartorially provident.) "I must say, Ruth, that it is a burden to be the constant recipient of so many words which cannot be understood except by the one who has just said them."

Jane threw up a hand to silence her friend and co-worker. "We're fortunate to have Ruth here to improve our vocabularies, Carrie. Now if you'd been paying the least bit of attention you would *know* the meaning of the word from the context in which Ruth used it."

Carrie picked up the cloak and resumed her work. "It is too much with which to tax the brain so early in the day."

"My word, Carrie!" protested Ruth in a tone of playfully contending vexation, "you tax your brain each and every time you visit a new piece of music upon the page. You are no sloth. What I wager you *are* at this moment is tetchy and irritable, and I should like to know the reason why."

"Then I shall *tell* you why," replied Carrie, setting the cloak aside to look at Ruth with a flashing eye. "You are like the cat that cannot decide if it wishes to go inside or out. You have now changed your mind *three* times about whether you will be coming along with us on the picnic on Sunday. Or is it four? I cannot keep track of which side of the door you are clawing at any given moment."

Jane spoke before Ruth had opportunity. "She is *in*. She will remain in. Won't you, Ruth?"

"I'll go," said Ruth with a bland sigh. But almost instantly her voice stirred, the colour returning to her face. "Though may I ask, Carrie, why it should be any concern of yours? Must the five of us always do *everything* together? Except, of course, for those things *you* do not wish to do. May I remind you that last night it was Jane and me who stopped here for four hours more whilst you and Maggie and Molly skipped merrily home?"

"That isn't the same at all," returned Carrie in slightly puling rebuttal. "The three of *us* have parents who would fidget and worry if we were abroad past dusk. Neither you nor Jane has a mother or father whose feelings must be considered."

Ruth did not pursue her side of the argument, which would have put to Carrie that Mr. Mobry and his sister treated her as their own child and that Jane's brother, for all his defects of character, was *still* her brother, and must by definition care if she be gone too long without an appropriate explanation (although truth be told, Jane had said that upon her return to their apartments the previous night, Higgins was nowhere to be found, and perhaps had no idea she'd even been delayed).

Jane signed to Ruth that she would speak now and she did so in a soft and conciliatory tone. "Dear, sweet Carrie: you must tell Ruth and me what has *really* put you in such a state of distemper this morning. It cannot *only* be the fact of Ruth's vexing indecision. It simply isn't like you to be so petulant and difficult."

Carrie nodded. She closed her eyes to gather her thoughts and then opened them fully to convey the following: "Yesterday after I was left at my doorstep by Molly and Maggie, and as I was fumbling for my latchkey, who should I discover coming out from behind the poplar tree next to the house but one of the young men with whom we will be picnicking on Sunday! His name is Holborne. I was startled that he would take such liberties to introduce himself since we had not, as of yet, been properly presented to one another, but he made bold not only to present himself to me but also to insinuate an intimacy with me, which I will not portray. In fine, he was quite rude and disrespecting of all propriety and I could not understand why he would accost me in such a manner until that moment in which he finally chose to explain himself."

Jane and Ruth both stood as one, and, as if the movement had been rehearsed beforehand, lifted their chairs and brought them round to Carrie's table with great alacrity and immoderate anticipation of the next paragraph of their friend's intriguing unbosoming.

Carrie lowered her voice, with Jane and Ruth now situated in close proximity. "He said it was decided that he and his fellow millhands—the ones with whom we will be spending Sunday after noon—should each select one of us to affix himself. But it so fell out that there was some disagreement as to which would have *me,* for, apparently, both Holborne and one of his mill-mates had heard my singing voice one after noon as we were walking home, and were quite taken with it, and he found it incumbent upon his interest in both me *and* my tuneful voice to obviate any unpleasant rivalry between the two come Sunday. For this reason he said he was forced to make a preemptive sally, and though he sought my forgiveness for the impropriety, it could not be helped. He desired, beyond anything else, to possess my *exclusive* attention and companionable society this coming Sunday."

"And what did you say to *that?*" sought Jane, her voice quavering with excitement.

"He is a very good-looking fellow. I have seen the others as they take their luncheon before the shoe shop. I must say it is *his* looks which appeal to me the most. And here is something that pleases me, as well: that he should wish to break every rule of propriety to have me."

"And *does* he 'have' you?" asked Ruth. Her interest in the upshot to Carrie's story was equal to Jane's, but fraught with far less passion of feeling. Jane, for her part, had observably placed herself vicariously (and palpitatingly) into Carrie's shoes, whereas Ruth's investment was largely academic.

"He *does* have me!" ejaculated Carrie. "He does! I was all but overcome by his impertinent ministrations. Subsequently, I acceded without hesitation to his terms of engagement on Sunday."

"Setting aside the indiscretion of his loutish behaviour," said Ruth, "I have yet to glean, then, how this can be construed as anything but a *good* thing for you."

Carrie's elation was now supplanted by a look of sudden trepidation. "Oh, but what if the other fellow will not be satisfied by my choice? What if he means to contend for me? Perhaps blows will be exchanged, grievous injury inflicted!"

Ruth emitted a loud groan, which sounded as if her throat were being scoured. "Carrie Hale, sometimes the things you say make the inanities our friend Molly occasionally spouts sound like pearls of wisdom. *This* is what troubles you? That two men may fight over you? You, who hasn't spoken a single syllable to any man who wasn't transacting business with you from behind a shop counter or asking you courteously to mind the *dung* his horse had just deposited in your path within the lane!"

Jane sought to stay her friend with a fluttering hand. "Do be kind, Ruth. This is all quite new to Carrie." Then, turning to the recipient of Ruth's uncharitable remarks, Jane said with softer accents, "Carrie, it is the dream of every girl to be pursued by multiple suitors. If it so happens during Sunday's outing that these two men end up fighting over you, rejoice! Be glad for the attention, regardless of how much blood may be spilt."

Carrie relaxed into a half smile, which quickly transformed itself into a smile in full, accompanied by carefree, girlish, giggling laughter.

Ruth lifted herself—and then her chair—and returned surlily to her own worktable. Jane and Carrie, who bethought themselves at first that Ruth would apply herself wordlessly to her work, were mistaken. Ruth *did* speak. She said, "You aren't the only one of us who can sing, Carrie. We *all* sing. And quite beautifully, I might add."

"That is certainly true," replied Carrie, who, with Jane still sitting hard-by, returned her attention to her eagerly receptive friend to disclose: "His body is quite well-formed, Jane. His look reminds me of that picture of Hercules in *Bulfinch's*."

"Bull *cods*!" expostulated Ruth in a rude voice, making certain to scrape her chair loudly upon the slate floor to keep the oath from a precise audit by her two companions.

But even though there was no guessing from Carrie and Jane about Ruth's tenor or her present state of ill humour, they purposefully ignored it.

Molly Osborne delivered Mrs. Dowell's grey satin pelisse into the hands of the woman's maid-of-all-work. She was upon her return to Mrs. Colthurst's dress shop when she was hailed in the High Road by her cousin, Jemma Spalding. Though Jemma, who was the child of Mr. Osborne's sister Cecily Spalding, was only one year older than Molly, yet the two had not been close since childhood, for as Jemma grew older she began to display a capricious nature that removed common sense altogether from the equation of her life, and became unpredictable and erratic in her behaviour, once taking it to mind to have a bathe in the stream that meandered behind the church she attended, and to do so right after morning services and whilst still dressed in all her Sunday finery. There were some who thought her mad. Molly did not. To Molly, her cousin was merely maddeningly eccentric.

Having completed her marketing for the morning, Jemma was bending her steps to the home of an old woman she knew who lived in a crooked house on the apron of town—a woman who, Jemma explained to Molly as they walked along, was of gipsy stock, but no longer roamed the countryside to sell gispy jewellery and colourful hand-knitted scarves and shawls, but was now settled upon a little piece of tenant land, where she raised poultry and grew parsnips and did only one thing that she confessed was a residual indulgence from her former life: she told fortunes.

"I have my fortune told once a fortnight," said Jemma, with a look that conveyed a great eagerness to see the woman again. "Then I hurry home and tell Mamma and Papa all that Madame Louisa has told to *me*. Alas, they never believe me—not even when those things which were predicted come true. Yet I know that the Madame has a rare gift, and I cannot help wishing I had leave and means to tell a good many others about it."

Molly smiled with genial indulgence. "That is all very interesting, Jemma, but I must go back to work now. The dress shop is just round the corner."

"Yes, I know, but won't you come with me for just a few minutes to see my fortune-telling friend? I have nearly half a shilling left from my marketing and will be happy to pay to have *your* cards read for a change. Aren't you the least bit curious to know what *your* future holds?"

"Who isn't curious to know such a thing?" returned Molly. "But I cannot spare another moment. Mrs. Colthurst will wonder what has become of me."

"I will tell her you were helping me—that I sprained my foot and my basket was so heavily laden with vegetables and eggs that I simply could not hobble home without assistance."

"And that would be a falsehood. I do not tell falsehoods, Jemma—as a rule."

"As a rule, *no*. But as an exception, you have been known to dissemble without the tiniest scruple—such as the time when we were girls and found the kittens and their mother in my father's barn and made a nice nest for them and brought little kitchen scraps for the mother each morning before school, because we knew she could not be both a successful mother *and* a successful mouser under the circumstances. We kept the secret together, did we not? For we both knew that Papa would drown the little ones if he should ever find out about them."

"That was an exceptional situation, Jemma. The lives of five kittens hung in the balance."

"But this is *equally* exceptional. My last reading was quite disconcerting."

"What do you mean?"

"I cannot say. Not until we hear what the future holds for *you* by way of comparison."

Molly sighed cheerlessly. "Jemma, you've become tiresome."

"Do come. It's very important."

"Yet you will not tell me why."

"I cannot. Not just yet."

Molly thought for a moment, her brow knitted in annoyance. "My dear cousin, there is a reason the children in our town make up little rhymes about you."

"I am different, I'll admit. But this hardly resembles the times I climb the roof of my father's cottage wearing wings fabricated from chicken feathers to fly myself off and away to London for the season."

"When did you do this?"

"I'd rather not say," replied Jemma, whilst brushing a chicken feather from the left gigot of her frock.

"I will warrant, Jemma, that there are extremes to your behaviour, and by comparison this request *does* seem very nearly reasonable." Molly sighed. "So let us go quickly to hear what the gispy woman says, and I should hope very much that she will not foretell how I am to be cashiered by Mrs. Colthurst for shirking my responsibilities at the shop."

Molly had never seen a woman so burdened by troubled thoughts as the scarf-headed Madame Louisa. Jemma responded to the old woman's expression of worry by delivering soothing pats to her shawl-draped shoulders. Madame Louisa answered Jemma's thoughtful enterprise by producing an appreciative glimmer of a near-toothless smile, which showed bravery in the face of apparent desolation.

"It has happened again," confided the old gipsy in a low tone. "Three times, in fact, since your last visit, Jemma."

"Three times out of how many?" asked Jemma. She was now patting the old woman with a much stronger hand, for it seemed required.

"Out of three," the woman answered glumly. "For after these I shut my door and locked it tight. I only admitted the two of you this morning for I have decided that I must have *someone* to whom to confess my fears. And they are dark and terrible fears, indeed."

"And how did the three react when they heard what the stars foretold for them?"

"I confess—I could not bring myself to speak the truth as the cards conveyed it to me." Madame Louisa took pause to blow her nose into her handkerchief and to dab at her tear-glistening eyes (and in that order, although a different order would have been tidier). "I told each of the three that which came most conveniently to mind, for if I had said what I actually saw upon the cards—what they had to say about the town at large—I should send them into a similar state of despondency, and I did not wish to be so cruel."

"And what did these new readings reveal?" asked Jemma, cringing in anticipation of the answer.

"The same as was revealed for you, dear girl. The same, no doubt, as we should see if I were to lay out the cards for your young cousin. Which is why I will not do it, for this would make five, and what is already a certainty will only be a superfluity."

Jemma thought this over, whilst Molly sate quiet and confused and not wishing to intrude, for the look on the warty face of the old gipsy was frighteningly wretched, and she knew not what she *could* say to contribute aught of value to the interview. Finally, Jemma spoke: "Yet, perhaps, Madame Louisa, there is still the glimmer of a chance that if you will but deal the cards for Molly, they may speak only to her *own* circumstances and not to the fate of the town at large. Could that not be possible?"

Madame Louisa considered the prospect as she drew a slice of apple from a plate set before her and popped it into her mouth. "Apple slice?" she said, proffering the plate to the two cousins.

As the gipsy looked too much like the crone in the fairy story who offered the poison apple to Snow White, Molly declined with a shake of the head, though Jemma took a slice and bit into it appreciatively. Molly noted that Jemma was quite carefree and casual in her society with the gispy. Perhaps, thought Molly, the woman served as a preferential surrogate for Jemma's mother, as Molly's aunt was severe and uncommunicative and demonstrative of so little affection for her oldest daughter. And Jemma's father was not very different in this respect from his wife. It was a home with little love within—or at least the kind of love with which Molly was most familiar: one which dwelt in sweet union betwixt her father and herself. In that moment, Molly felt a little sorry for Jemma. And who could not also feel sorry for the miserable Madame Louisa who wore pain upon her face in every corner and wrinkle?

Subsequently, Molly was compelled to say, "Whether the reading should apply to me alone *or* to the town of Tulleford, I should like to know what the future holds. Perhaps we will be lucky and the spell will be broken and all will come out well in the end."

Madame Louisa turned to Jemma, her lips compressed with censorious displeasure. "What is this fool girl saying?"

"She's saying that she'd very much like to have her fortune told."

"Very well, then. We will all rue it. Yet I will do it."

The fortune was told through the laying down of the gnarled, colour-faded, dog-eared cards upon the rickety-legged deal table.

And it was not good. Not good at all.

But there was a small compensation. "Ah, this is most interesting," said the gipsy, as she closely examined the cards she'd put down before her in the configuration of a cross. "At least we know now roughly *when* the tragedy will occur: in two weeks' time. Or sometime thereabout."

"A tragedy? What manner of tragedy?" asked Molly, leaning forward in her chair.

Madame Louisa did not lift her eyes from the cards. "We do not know the *nature* of that dire thing which is in store for the townspeople of Tulleford. We know only *that* it will occur. Many will be touched by it. Some—perhaps many—will die. This is the death card, you see—this centre card. Its propinquity to the cards above and below magnifies the portent. You will note that *this* aspect of the cards' configuration has not changed in each of the five readings. It is the *calendrical* cards, which now appear—it is these which give us a fixed time frame for supposition."

Jemma shook her head with regret. "I should never have pushed you to read for Molly. You knew what to expect and I didn't believe you."

Madame Louisa reached out first to stroke Jemma's hand and then to give her another apple slice in consolation. "It is good that we've given the cards leave to speak once more, for as it turns out, they *did* have something else to say."

"Perhaps," said Molly, wishing to be helpful, "if we were to read the cards yet again, further intelligence pertaining to the forthcoming tragedy—as you have put it—may be gleaned, and this would help us to better prepare for it."

The gipsy woman shook her head dismissively. "The cards have said all they intend to say. With the passage of a fortnight something most dreadful will befall the town of Tulleford and everyone who lives herein. I advise the both of you to *leave* this place—go abroad for a period—to save yourselves from it. This I intend to do myself at my earliest convenience. That will be six pence, Jemma, and I should also like one of those stalks of celery from your basket, if you are willing."

It took not five minutes for Molly to change her thinking about what she had just heard and observed, and to change it in a most drastic fashion.

"A fine thing," bolted out Molly, as her cousin Jemma walked along with her to the dress shop, "having a laugh at *my* expense!"

"What do you mean? Did you see either of us laughing?"

"I detected a smirk on that old hag's face as we left."

Jemma shook her head. "It was no smirk. She has a mouth tic. It cannot be helped."

"Stuff and nonsense! The two of you set all of this up to make the fool of me. I'm fortunate to have come to my senses as quickly as I did."

"It is *no one's* good fortune that you have changed your mind about it," said Jemma with a fretful look. "The thing was neither a joke nor a lark, for I should never be so heartless. You did at one point believe it; I saw it in your face. What *I* find difficult to contemplate, dear cousin, is the fact that you now do not."

"I will own she was good. *Quite* good—the both of you. Then when I stepped out into the bright light of day, I came straightaway to see through your comical scheme, as if I were waking from a terrible dream."

Jemma grew quiet as the two cousins walked along. Finally, she said, "Oh, Molly, I don't think I should be able to bear it alone, knowing there isn't a single person here in Tulleford—once Madame Louisa has fled—who knows what I know and dreads what I dread. The next two weeks will be so frightfully lonely and so frightfully *frightening.*"

Molly stopped upon the spot. She put her hands together and applauded her cousin for what she perceived to be a fine performance. "Brava! Brava! But I cannot commend the little play entirely, cousin Jemma, for you have left out an important point of plot. Just what *is* supposed to happen? On this point the cards fall conveniently silent. At any rate, the curtain has come down, you've had your bit of fun for the morning, and there's the end to it. Run along now, Jemma, and leave me to my terrible fate. You may go, if you wish, and climb once more to the roof of your family cottage and become a flying chicken. Mind you don't forget to send me a letter upon your aerial arrival in London."

With that, Molly Osborne resumed her march, quickened her step, and left Jemma standing silent and quite unhappy on the side of the road.

Molly was determined to think no more of all the nonsense that had delayed her return to the dress shop.

Except that she could not help herself. After the curtains had been drawn, the candles snuffed out, and the darkness of the night had settled upon her bedchambers, she thought of it so much, in fact, that she did not sleep a wink. She pondered over what it might be—that most horrible thing from which she, like Madame Louisa, should flee in wild-eyed panic. And *if* she fled, what would become of her circle-sisters? What would be *their* fate?

Nonsense! Nonsense!

And yet.

Chapter Twelve

San Francisco, April 1906

To Tom Katz, the agency account manager responsible for Pemberton, Day & Co.'s summer advertising campaign, fell the enjoyable task of deciding which of the most picturesque spots in Golden Gate Park would make the best backdrops for the full-page advertisement he wished to present in the guise of a photographic essay: "Tramping in Taffeta; Aestivating in Lace." More to the point, it fell to Mr. Katz, assisted by his agency colleague Will Holborne, the delectable duty of deciding where the five young women who had won the modeling lottery might best show off Pemberton's summer lines while showing *themselves* off to the five young men whose responsibility it was to shepherd and/or superintend them.

To that end, both men, equipped with "slide in 'n' shoot" Hawkeye cameras, had visited the park a few days before. They had selected three sites for the all-day Friday photography session: the Dutch windmill, Sweeney Observatory at the top of Strawberry Hill, and the Japanese Tea Garden, with permission granted by the Stow Lake boathouse proprietor for use of one of its rooms for costume changing.

The day of the "shoot" having now arrived, a casual bonhomie quickly developed between We Five and the ad-men, who either furtively or manifestly could not take their eyes off them. Miss Colthurst was pleased to see the day proceeding so smoothly and everyone getting along so well. Miss Dowell had remarked that the models had been chosen wisely. The manager of the Ladies' Departments had agreed with her assistant, whom she had brought along with her to the photography session, and dismissed the murmuring plaints of the five rejected finalists back at the store that "something didn't smell right." (Although there was, to be sure, *some* truth behind this suspicion, since Miss Colthurst had made it clear to Katz whom *her* particular preferences had been, "for whatever my suggestions are worth." A great deal, as it turned out.) During those periods in which Katz and Holborne went about setting stops and focal lengths, posing their subjects this way and that, and waiting for those moments that offered the most aesthetically illuminative marriages of sun and cloud, Molly found herself in comfortable colloquy with the youngest Katz agency ad-man, Pat Harrison. It was Harrison's job to escort the models to and from the boathouse—but only after Miss Dowell, as dresser, gave each of We Five a last-minute prink and primp and "spin-around-once-more-for-me-dearie-thankyoueversomuch."

As for Carrie, she had spent a good part of the morning avoiding the interested gaze of Mr. Holborne, who, as often as not, was framing her most particularly in his photographic sights. He knew what she was doing and she knew what *he* was doing, and it became an amusing little game of wordless cat-and-mouse until Katz, taking notice, ordered his photographer to "knock it off."

Maggie, in the meantime, while changing from a blue and white shirtwaist and golf skirt into a pink, lace-sleeved tea gown, made a confession to her friend Jane, who was changing from striped shirtwaist and cloth skirt into a lavender silk house dress.

She admitted that she very much liked the look of the one named Castle, whose job it was to keep onlookers out of camera range, which he did with such commanding and nearly martial authority that Maggie was given to tingle, admiringly, in his presence. "You may have your Mr. Castle," confided Jane. "I'm far more interested in Mr. Katz, and *have* been since we first met last week. He's quite the gentle general. Did you notice how deftly he arranged each of us upon the bridge above the waterfall—adjusting our arms and heads this way and that with such tender attentiveness?"

"All *I* noticed," returned Maggie with a sly smirk, "was a modern-day Pygmalion falling in love with his statue. But as for the rest of us, we were merely items of still life to be shifted and shoved about, with little show of respect at all."

"You're being quite ridiculous, Mag. Although I'll admit that Katz does seem just a little more interested in me than he is the rest of you." Jane leaned in, addressing Maggie through the sheer fabric of her chemise, which she was in the process of lowering over her head and shoulders. "In fact, only moments ago he asked me to have dinner with him next week."

"And what did you say? Will you go?"

"Of course I'll go. A girl's got to eat, doesn't she? And I can't think of any finer company—I mean, of course, company of a different gender." Having answered Maggie's question frankly, Jane turned to Miss Dowell, who was serving as human clotheshorse, Jane's silk dress draped at the ready over her arm. "Miss Dowell, these clothes reek of benzine!"

"It cannot be helped, Miss Higgins. The agency wanted them crisp and clean for the photography session. But I sympathize fully, my dear. I am nearly to the point of asphyxiation myself."

The tall, spectacled member of the Katz contingent wandered through the morning accoutered with pencil and pad, taking notes from which he would draw inspiration for the advertising copy that would accompany the photographs. Ruth followed him about at what she thought was a safe and respectful distance until that point at which he finally decided to engage her, and in doing so discovered she too was a writer (of sorts—hence her fascination with his peripatetic scribbling) and took the opportunity to solicit her opinion as to what in the world could be said about five young women standing before a very Low Country–looking windmill, themselves looking not very Low Country at all in their tasteful drawing-room lounging garments—looking, in point of fact, like the very young women they could not help being: five modern female residents of the very modern American city of San Francisco.

"It's certainly a conundrum," admitted Ruth. "I thought the same thing while Mr. Katz was posing me—that a bucolic windmill was an incongruous thing to place within a city park. To my knowledge, Central Park in New York hasn't a single one."

Cain Pardlow nodded. "If Katz had been smart, he would have jettisoned the windmill and jettisoned Strawberry Hill—everyone's so tired of pictures from that blasted hill—as if San Francisco hasn't got hills and lovely scenic views in dozens of other places—and limited our pictorial presentation to the Japanese garden alone."

Ruth smiled. "But wouldn't we have found ourselves in a similar fix? I mean similar to our situation with the windmill. My fellow models and I don't look very Dutch, but then again, we don't look all that Oriental either."

"True," said Cain. "But Miss Colthurst has an idea which Katz also subscribes to, of putting the five of you—at least for one of the photographs—into summer kimonos. She says that Mr. Pemberton really wants to push the store's new line of silk kimono-style wrappers, and the setting is perfect for that purpose."

"Yes, that may very well work, so long as we don't look as if we just tumbled out of bed. I've never seen a woman in a kimono who didn't appear a little, well, *frowzy.*"

Cain smiled. He pulled his watch from his fob pocket. "It's almost time for lunch," he said, closing the watch with one hand while patting his stomach with the other. "And the agency has quite outdone itself in the way of provisioning our palates."

"I thought the *store* was footing the bill for our lunch."

"Of course it is. But Mr. Pemberton won't know until he gets our invoice of expenses how very well we ate on this day." Cain winked as Ruth laughed. "There's a nice picnic area over by the children's quarters. What would you say to the two of us having lunch together—that is, if you don't have other plans?"

"I haven't any other plans," said Ruth. "And I'd like to hear if there are other things you enjoy writing besides advertising copy."

"Only if you tell me what kind of writing interests *you.*"

"Yes, of course," said Ruth shyly.

The photography at the windmill now having been completed, Holborne was in the process of gathering up his equipment and returning it to one of the two rented carriages that transported the dozen from one end of the long park to the other and everywhere in between. It was up to Harrison, as chief wrangler, to round up all the other members of the photography party, but first someone had to round up Mr. Harrison, who could not at that moment be located.

"What do you mean you don't know where he is?" sputtered Katz to Castle.

Castle responded with equal irritation: "Just what I said."

"Check the beach. You'll probably find him splashing around like a two-year-old. Then remind me why my father hasn't fired him yet."

"Because he's your cousin," shouted Castle over his shoulder as he loped off.

Castle didn't find Harrison on the beach. But, playing a hunch, he walked the four blocks up the Great Highway which overlooked the ocean, and confirmed his suspicion that his agency colleague had ambled up to the Sutro Baths.

And quickly learned that Harrison hadn't ambled up there alone.

Pat and Molly—Molly still dressed in her stylish mustard-colored lawn dress from the windmill session—were standing on the Sutro Heights promenade watching an ambulance pull up in front of the street entrance to the baths. From the knot of onlookers also milling about, they learned the reason for the ambulance's sudden appearance: one of the tobogganing bathers inside hadn't cleared away quickly enough from the spot where the chute deposited its wet merrymakers into the pool, and he was knocked in the head beneath the surface of the water. The woman next to Molly, cloaked in a dripping wrapper which covered her bathing costume, surmised that the young man was probably dead. Her male companion disagreed. He argued that the poor bather had more than likely merely been struck unconscious, and once all the water was pumped from his lungs he "would be back to his old self in no time."

Castle, who had sidled up next to his fugitive ad-man and the fashion model with whom he was playing hooky, said, by way of announcing his presence, "No time to find out how this little drama turns out, children. Your carriage awaits."

Maggie sat in one of the two horse-drawn carriages, wondering when Jeremy Castle would return. In the other carriage, Jane conferred with Miss Colthurst and Miss Dowell over how the remainder of the day would proceed.

Carrie climbed in next to Maggie. "Do you see that woman over there on the bridge?"

"No," replied Maggie. "All I see is those buffalo."

Carrie turned Maggie's head with a light application of palm to chin. "Over *there*. See her now?"

Maggie nodded. "What about her?"

"She was watching our photography session. We started talking to one another. She thinks she knows you."

Maggie squinted in the bright sunshine. "The woman's too far away for me to know whether I know *her* or not. Why doesn't she just come over here?"

Carrie shook her head. "She isn't dressed very well. I think she's in service. You know that maids can be timid."

"Are you suggesting I walk over to the bridge and talk to *her*?"

"Only if you're interested. There's certainly time for you to at least say hello."

Maggie sighed. "Of course, now you *have* piqued my curiosity."

Maggie drew herself up and out of her cushioned seat, steadying herself with a hand upon the side of the open-topped landau, which generally took visitors through the park on day excursions but was now being put to a different form of commercial use. The woman, seeing that Maggie was now traversing the open field which separated the windmill from one of the little ponds where the park's anachronistic buffalo herd came to drink, cut the distance short by meeting her halfway.

Even before the two came together, Maggie could see that the woman was someone she indeed *did* know. It was Mary Grace, the live-in housemaid who had worked for the Bartons when Maggie was a girl and then had to be let go when Mr. Barton could no longer afford her.

The two embraced like old friends. "I *thought* that was you!" exclaimed Mary Grace, holding Maggie apart from her with straight arms so as to get a better look at her. "Come up in the world, have you—posing all pretty and proper for that man's camera."

Maggie smiled warmly. "I work for Pemberton, Day. They're putting advertisements in all the papers to promote the new summer fashions."

"You always was a beautiful little girl, and now I see that you've blossomed into a fine and lovely young lady." Mary Grace reached out and gingerly touched Maggie's cheek. "And hardly any trace of the pox at all."

"Oh, the magic of modern cosmetics! Although it helps that the pock marks don't go *too* deep."

"I thought we was going to lose you too, just like your sister Octavia. And after your poor sister Eleanor died of consumption. Some families get all the hard luck, it seems."

"The deaths of two of their three daughters wasn't something my father and mother bore very easily," Maggie said with a sad nod of concurrence. "I know that it contributed to my father's downward slide into dissolution, and turned my mother into such a terrible hypochondriac. I wish there were somewhere we could sit." Maggie looked around for a convenient bench, but the only one she could spot was presently occupied by two young women sitting back to back like bookends while having their double-caricature sketched by one of the park's roving lightning artists. "I'd so love to catch up with you. Mama's getting remarried. Can you believe it? To a dentist. I'm not very fond of him but my opinion doesn't seem to count for much. I know, I know! Come sit with me in the carriage. I'll introduce you to my friend Carrie. She and her mother have a maid who reminds me a little of you—but only a little. She's colored."

Maggie introduced her family's former maid to Carrie.

Carrie offered Mary Grace a boiled egg. Carrie had, only moments before, successfully sniffed out the three baskets of lunchtime provisions gathered for the photography party. "It's an absolute feast!" she marveled, flipping back the hinged top to one of the wicker baskets. Mary Grace whistled her own amazement in the presence of such an excess of culinary riches. Carrie excitedly itemized the contents, as if her two companions hadn't eyes of their own: "Eggs, crab salad—what are these—ham sandwiches—the devilish kind, it appears—and one—two—three—four different kinds of fruit." Carrie plucked up a banana. "I just adore bananas. I'm a regular monkey. Oh, is this beer? Bottles of beer, oh my goodness!"

"Are you quite finished, Carrie?" asked Maggie through a scowl. "Because I'd like to talk to Mary Grace. I haven't seen her in years."

"Don't let me stop you," said Carrie, unpeeling a perfectly ripe banana.

As Mary Grace was undressing her hard-boiled egg and letting the pieces of shell drop daintily into the napkin Maggie had spread upon her lap, she said, "Miss Maggie, you spoke of you three girls. But you made no mention of your brother. Why is that?"

"Because I'm not sure there ever *was* a brother. Do you know something I don't know?"

"Your mother never said nothing about him?"

"She mentioned a son when she was talking out of her head one night with a high fever. I asked her about it later and she denied having said any such thing. Either she was imagining a boy she never had, or—I sometimes thought—perhaps there *was* a child who died at birth, and to lessen the heartbreak my mother and father agreed that each of them would simply pretend he'd never been."

Mary Grace neither nodded nor shook her head. Instead, she chewed her egg in enigmatic silence.

After a long and trying moment, Maggie could no longer contain herself and erupted, "Well, is it true or not, Mary Grace? Because if there has been something deliberately kept from me for all these years, I would very much appreciate your setting the record straight. *Did* Octavia have a twin brother—as my mother mumbled that feverish night—and *did* he die shortly after birth?"

"Are those Uneedas? I do love Uneeda soda crackers and cheese."

"Here. Take the whole damned box. Tell me what you know."

Mary Grace, to Carrie's surprise, did not quail in the face of Maggie's sudden burst of temper—evidence of years of exposure on Mary Grace's part to employers and their families who attacked their servants either purposefully or collaterally without care or cause. "You are right, child. There was a baby boy. I was there at his birth. He came several minutes after his sister. The healthiest little newborn you ever saw. Could you open this package? I have arthritis of the fingers. Thank you. Squalling and kicking his little legs like he was eager to take on the entire world."

"But then he died?"

"*Died*? That baby didn't die, Miss Maggie. It was sent away."

"*Sent away?*"

Mary Grace nodded. Carrie produced a saltshaker. Mary Grace shook her head. "I have these salty crackers now. And this salty cheese. I'm well set."

Some of the color had escaped from Maggie's cheeks. "I don't understand."

"Your mother didn't want it. *Him*. They never named him but it was a healthy little boy, all right, all right. He came at the time when your father had taken to drinking so much after the death of the oldest one. I heard your mother say it to your father late of a night when the little babe was but a few days old. She said she didn't want a boy-child raised in the house what would only grow up to follow in his father's drunken footsteps. She said it was hard enough to watch what had become of your father; she didn't want to see it happen with a son. I surely would have thought that some day one of them two would have told you the truth about it all."

Maggie didn't speak. Carrie did. She said, "May I say, Mary Grace, that what you just said is absolutely outrageous. You should apologize to Maggie this very instant for fabricating such a preposterous story."

Mary Grace shook her head with casual indifference. "Wish I could." She crunched a Uneeda Biscuit soda cracker. "It is every word of it the truth. It isn't in me nature to tell falsehoods."

Maggie could scarcely release the words from her mouth: "So my parents just *gave* my sister's twin brother away? A snap of the fingers and he was gone forever?"

"There was a family your minister knew about who'd been wanting a child. They couldn't have none of their own. They was mighty grateful over it, and there's the end to *that* story."

Carrie shook her head slowly in disbelief. She looked at her friend Maggie, who was doing the same, although Maggie's look was deeply contemplative and inscrutable.

Carrie took a deep breath and said, "This doesn't sound at all like the Clara Barton *I* know. She has a kind and loving heart, just like the famous nurse who shares her name. I simply cannot conceive it: that she would give away her very own son, and for such a ridiculous reason."

Maggie found her voice: "If you'd truly known my father during all those terrible years before he died, Carrie, you could half understand what would drive my mother to do such a thing, especially if she knew there was a good family in great need of a child. I don't excuse her, but perhaps I could find it in my heart to forgive her. Just as important, though: I must speak to the Reverend Mobry and find out if he knows anything of the family that raised my brother. I suppose they moved from San Francisco many years ago, or I would have heard *something* about them from someone before now."

Mary Grace looked contrite, even as her hand reached for a jar of pickled pigs' feet she spied in the open basket. "I hope I haven't upset you *too* much, miss."

"No, no, no, Mary Grace," said Maggie, clasping the woman's hand, which seemed filled out and strong and hardly arthritic at all. "It was more than proper that I should know the truth, and I apologize for kicking the messenger in the shins."

"Then we're all squared. That's fine. And that bottle you'd be holding, Miss Hale—may I have a wee swallow? I'm a bit dry in the throat."

Mary Grace finished the entire bottle of beer in five or six pulls, while Maggie gazed absently at the browsing buffalo and thought about the possibility of meeting the brother she never knew, and Carrie meanwhile set off to find Mr. Holborne, for no other reason than his quiet company.

On their walk along sandy Ocean Beach to the join the others at the carriages, Pat noted how upset Molly had become after seeing the ambulance which was to take the unfortunate young man either to the hospital or to the morgue. "If I'd known that's what was in store for us once we'd reached the baths, I wouldn't have suggested we go up there," he said apologetically. "But you said you'd never been to the baths, so I just figured we'd give it a look-see."

Molly smiled. "It was very sweet of you to take me, and the view of the ocean from the Heights was just as lovely as you said it would be."

The two walked on in silence for a moment, several paces behind Castle. Then Pat said, "Would you like some oysters?"

"When? Right now?"

"No. Some night when you're free. I know a place near Fisherman's Wharf where you can get the best fried oysters and boiled shrimps in town. Do your mom and dad let you drink beer?"

"I have no mother, and my dad hasn't a thing to say about anything I might want to do," answered Molly with slight indignation.

"Corkers!" Pat exclaimed. "An *independent woman!*"

Castle turned. "Pick it up, little ones—everyone's waiting."

Pat hurled back in full voice, "You give me the cramp, Castle. Why are you hustling us just for lunch? What say Molly and me skip the picnic and spend the next hour on our own little stroll back to the boathouse? For eats, we'll just filch a tamale or something along the way. I saw a Dago's cart over by the paddock."

"Suit yourself," Castle shouted back, "but have Miss Osborne at the boathouse and in costume by one fifteen prompt, or don't come at all, because you'll be out of a job."

"Yeah, yeah, yeah," answered Harrison, uncowed. "You—you got me all aquiver, you mush-headed gazabo!"

Molly's hand flew to her mouth in surprise.

As Castle quickened his step, Molly and Pat could see his shoulders bouncing—an obvious indicator of immoderate laughter over the juvenile insult. Pat Harrison wasn't the best deliverer of put-downs among the clever ad-men with whom he worked (brash young men who had raised masculine verbal abuse to an art form). In fact, he was, as evinced by the aforementioned—which entailed being so obviously laughed *at* rather than laughed *with*—quite dreadful at it.

Pat halted up and Molly stopped alongside him. Pat turned to Molly, his face flushed with anger. "When they talk to me like that—like I'm some snot-nosed *inconvenience*—I'd like to knock their blocks off."

"I know the feeling," said Molly with a sympathetic smile.

"Maybe I shouldn't have suggested that— Would you rather—"

"I love tamales. I also love oysters."

Pat smiled. "Swell."

Molly glanced over her shoulder in the direction from which they'd come. A shadow of worry crossed her face. "Gee, I hope he's all right."

"You hope *who's* all right?"

"The man at the baths who went down the slide and didn't pop up again. They really should be more careful."

"Accidents happen, I suppose. Some people just have the bad luck to be in the wrong place at the wrong time."

"I'd like to tell you something, something I haven't told a single soul—not even my father. I want him to think I'm brave and strong, but sometimes I'm not. Sometimes I worry dreadfully about things."

"What are you worrying about right now, Miss Osborne?"

"It's a silly thing, really, and I shouldn't have done it, but there's a woman in my neighborhood—she lives up the street from my father and me—a Mrs. Froda. She and her husband run a confectionery. Well, they *used* to. They just moved back east. To New York. That's where her husband's from. We've become friends over the last few years—Mrs. Froda and me—and I agreed to help her pack up her things in exchange for some candy. I do love candy, and I suspected she had great lashings to give away before she and Mr. Froda shuttered up their shop."

Pat grinned. "And *did* you get candy?"

A smile peeped out from Molly's worry-darkened countenance. "Boxes of chocolates and caramels and nougats and bags of lemon drops and candied cranberries and orange slices. My father took one look at all my loot and accused me of planning to drum up business for him by distributing free candy to all the children of Polk Street!"

"Your father must be a dentist," laughed Pat.

Molly nodded. She stopped walking and dipped her head. Pat stopped as well. "I had the opportunity to ask her about their move while we were packing things into boxes—she remarked how good I was and I said this is exactly what I'd been doing for the last six months at Pemberton, Day, which, thankfully, I'll not have to do again, thanks to my promotion—I asked her why she and her husband were leaving San Francisco. You see, they had been doing quite well with the confectionery, and it didn't make a great deal of sense to me why they'd want to go."

"And the look on your face, Miss Osborne—it tells me the reason for their leaving is the thing that's upsetting you."

"Of course, I *shouldn't* be upset by it. It's really quite silly. Mrs. Froda doesn't think it's silly, obviously, but I do. And *Mr.* Froda takes his wife seriously—seriously enough, in fact, to go along with her wishes."

"You've now got me quite curious, Miss Osborne. You'll have to tell me."

"I intend to. There's the tamale man, and I'm suddenly famished. It's about dreams, Mr. Harrison. Terrible, frightening dreams. She's been having them nearly every night for quite some time."

"The same dreams or different ones?"

"The same. Always the same. About—about the end of the world. Well, at least the end of San Francisco."

"Earthquake? Fire? Some comet shooting down from the sky?"

Molly shrugged. "She doesn't know the agent. She only knows the outcome. And it makes her wake up each night in a cold sweat. *Two* tamales, if you please. I'm very hungry."

Chapter Thirteen

Zenith, Winnemac, July 1923

Bella's birthday bash was in full swing, but for the present, Molly Osborne and Pat Harrison had chosen to limit their own swinging to the gentle and decidedly more intimate sway of the Prowse porch swing.

"And how is it you can just stand there and and lissem to all that ma—larkey?"

"I can't pull myself away. She's right there on that street corner every day—ruh—right in front of Sister Lydia's new tabernacle. If you squa—squint and stand back far enough she—" Molly cupped her hand to convey a confidence in the manner of a back-fence gossip out of the funny pages. "—she looks just like Sister Lydia herself." Molly giggled. She removed her hand. "Funny to think, that's exactly how the good sister started her ministry: evan-guh-lizing on the street corners. Although this woman—she isn't evan-guh-loozing. She's—she's—she's *what?*"

"She's doom-glooming."

Molly nodded exaggeratedly. "That's it! *Doom-glooming.*"

"Say, did anyone ever tell you your eyelashes are the cats? Like they belong to some kind of—*hiccough*—storybook princess?"

Pat handed the silver flask to Molly. He utilized the hand that wasn't fixed proprietarily to Molly's shoulder. She snuggled up closer to this young man whom she'd met only two hours before—the young man who, within moments of their meeting, had begun to ply her with hootch from his private stock, even though there was an ample supply of unadulterated smuggled Canadian import inside. She noticed through the fuzzy, alcohol-sotted gauze of her semi-consciousness that the similarly cleft-chinned, blue-eyed, blond-haired (albeit of the dirty variety) young boy-man presently clutching her where no man or boy had ever clutched her before seemed halfway interested in her story, and so she resumed: "She stands on the street corner and talks about the end of the world, to be brought about by Sister Lydia—the false—the false prophet— the puh—puh—personal handmaiden, she says, of Satan himself."

"She don't very much like Sister Lydia, now do she?" *Hiccough.*

"No, she don't." Molly curled the ends of her lips down into a clown's frown to embroider her point. "Which isn't fair. Not fair at all. Sister Lydia, as evanjaleens go—why, she's the snake's hips! (No, no, let's leave snakes out of this.) She's the real deal!"

Molly took a gulp from the flask and handed it back.

"No, you keep it," said Pat, waving it away in a wozzle-limbed flail of the hands. "There's more where *that* came from."

Molly's head was tilted back. She was studying the cloudless night sky. Suddenly, she squealed, "Ooh! Is that a shooting star?"

Pat didn't turn to either confirm or deny the observation. His gaze was fixed on the face next to his. He moved closer and whispered, "Must be your lucky night, Molly Olly. Wish on that star and as your fateful servant, I'll make it all come true."

Breathlessly: "Are you my genie in a bottle?"

"I *am* your genie, and if you want we should have a bottle, I'll get us a bottle. Scotch whisky or Canadian rye?"

Molly sniggered. She had never been lit before. She didn't understand why she felt *so* good and why everything—*everything* she'd said to the good-looking Aggie named Pat had been so well received. "You may please me most, sir," she drawled, "by not nibbling my earlobe like that. It tickles. Here. Nibble my neck instead." Molly lowered the scoop-neck collar of her purple crepe de Chine with two hooked fingers to give Pat even more of her neck to explore.

Pat moved his osculatory attention to Molly's soft, supple neck as she tried valiantly to keep the conversation aloft.

"Still, I wah—wonder—what if there's some truth to what this strange woman on the street corner is saying? What if—*giggle, giggle*—she has the gift of—oh you're tickling me there *too*, you bad boy! What if something terrible really *is* about to happen?"

"Horse hooey! You think too much. Say, lessskidoo. Come for a walk with me."

"*Can* I walk? My legs feel like Jell-O."

"You'lldofine. Come on. This porchtoocrowded." The equally inebriated Pat Harrison squinted at the porch's other occupants, all coupled up, clinging to one another like human barnacles. "Lesstroll. I'll carry you if I have to."

"You'll carry me where?"

"To my car." Correcting himself: "To my friend *Jerry's* car. He won't mind. And I know he ain't using it 'cuz I can see him standing right there at the door. Upsy-daisy."

Molly allowed Pat to raise her up onto her wobbly legs and then to walk her off the porch.

They did this under the nervous, watchful gaze of Carrie and Ruth, who stood at the front picture window.

"Where's he taking her?" asked Ruth, her voice registering alarm.

Carrie grimaced. "Right down the sidewalk and right past that awful Mrs. Littlejohn's house, and you better believe our neighborhood busybody is going to have *volumes* to say about this to my mother in the morning."

Ruth exchanged a worried look with Carrie. "Molly's drunk," she said. "She doesn't know what she's doing. Carrie, somebody needs to stop that boy before he gets her into his car. You know what happens when boys get girls into cars at parties like these. Now it was your idea we come here tonight, so you're responsible."

"I merely suggested it, Ruth. It was Jane who put it all together."

"Well, I don't know where Jane is right now, so it's up to you, since it was *your* neighbor Bella who invited that baby sheik and his fellow frat-house muckers to this party."

Carrie's eyes grew large. "You're asking me to wrest her away from him?"

"To preserve her virtue and her good reputation while there's still time, yes, indeed. Don't worry. I'll be right there next to you, lending moral support."

Carrie stared at Ruth. "You sound as potted as Molly. It looks to me like we're *all* doing a good job of making total nits out of ourselves tonight."

Ruth ignored this. She gave her friend a tug, though Carrie's feet were set in place by something akin to abject fear. Confrontation was not one of Carrie Hale's strong suits.

Cain Pardlow, having successfully threaded his way through a room filled with slightly-squiffed to sloppily-stinko one-steppers, each attempting to foxtrot to Ted Lewis's effervescent rendition of "Runnin' Wild," reached his intended: Misses Thrasher and Hale, the two highballs held protectively above his head relatively intact.

"Why the worried pusses, ladies?"

Carrie replied: "It looks like our circle-sister Molly is being dragged right off to the lion's den."

"*Wolf's* den would be a better description," put in Ruth, peering into the semi-darkness beyond the Prowses' front lawn. "Or from all appearances, the wolf's Ford Roadster. That *is* the car he came in, isn't it?"

Cain nodded. He pushed the two highball glasses at the two women, some of the gin sloshing out. "Can't have that. No sirree." And then with a second, more deferential nod: "If you'll excuse me—"

Cain did a quick about-face and left the way he came, crossing once more the crowded, tangle-legged parlor floor and stepping on one of Bella Prowse's slippered feet in the process (though the tipsy-topsy flapper didn't even seem to register the injury). Reaching the front vestibule, Cain was about to make his hurried exit to introduce chivalry and male gallantry into the demonstrably *unchiv*alrous and *un*gallant 1920s, when his arm was roughly seized by Jerry Castle, who had been poking his head out the front door in search of the currently elusive Maggie Barton.

"Where are *you* going, pardner?"

"To your car. To rescue a damsel in distress."

Jerry lowered his voice, though it wasn't entirely necessary with the sound of music and the clamor of human merriment dinning all ears. "You can't change the rules in midstream, Pardlow, even if Master Paddy *does* appear to be putting himself several furlongs ahead."

Cain tried to shake Jerry off, without success. "Pat isn't going to make any kind of conquest tonight, Castle—and especially not with those two looking on in horror." He nodded in the direction of Carrie and Ruth, who remained at the window, effecting a tableau of "nail-nibbling apprehension" that even Cecil B. DeMille would have approvingly put to celluloid.

Jerry tightened his vise grip on Cain's arm. "To my knowledge we've placed no restrictions on the means and manner of conquest, Pardlow, so back the hell off and let nature take its course. I, for one, think the young lady will come quickly to her senses and put a stop to things before he gets too far. At least that's what I hope. I'd hate to think bootleg booze and dumb luck are going to win the whole shebang for our little Baby Skeezix."

Jerry and Cain discovered in that next moment they weren't alone. Will Holborne had dropped in to make his own observation. "Gentlemen, you forget that the winner isn't the one who rounds all the bases first. It's he who slides into home with all the pennants flying. And I, for one, see little brilliance or panache in Patty Cake's playing five-and-dime Casanova in the dusty backseat of a broken-down 1917 Lizzie. Been done far too many times before."

"Then how about I go and tell him he's wasting his time?" sought Cain.

Jerry grinned. "Say, maybe Paddy isn't even thinking about the game. Maybe he actually does like her. There's *that* possibility too, you know."

"How about I go talk to him and find out?" Cain persisted, finally freeing himself from Jerry Castle's meat hooks.

"Suit yourself," said Jerry, "but if Pat isn't jake, you mind your business and keep right on walking." Holborne concurred with a nod.

"Since when do you give a rat's rump about Pat Harrison?" Cain tossed to Jerry on his way out the door.

"Since you turned Paddy into the little brother you never had," responded Jerry with a half sneer/half grin.

"Among other things," added Will, pregnantly.

Lover-boy was preoccupied. "Castle—he always leaves his keys in the car for a quick getaway, but damned if I can find where he's gone and stashed 'em."

Molly made a baby face. "We can't cuddle and coo right here in the moonlight?"

Pat shook his head. "Nothing doing. I got a much better spot in mind—nice little hidey-hole sort of joint on the other side of town where the darkies go. They got hot jazz and all the liquor you can hold and there's dark little booths in the back where nobody'll come poking their heads into your business."

As if to prove his point, Pat nudged Molly's attention in the direction of the man now standing just outside the car on Molly's side. Molly turned and started.

"What the hell are you doing poking your head in my business, Pardlow?" barked Pat (the bark being more pinnipedian than canine).

"I just came to tell Miss Osborne that her friends are asking for her."

Molly smiled. "They *are*? Oh, they worry too much. Tell them I'm perfectly fine. Mr. Harrison and me are going for a nye-slettle-drive." Then, her hand cupped as if to deliver a secret—this *particular* secret broadcast with enough volume to cause at least one neighborhood dog to start sentry-yapping: "He's taking me to a speakeasy—my veerfirst."

Cain responded by shaking his head and opening the passenger door. He had to seize Molly to keep her from tumbling out onto the grass between the curb and the sidewalk. "First, Miss Osborne, I'd like to draw your attention to the fact that Mr. Harrison doesn't actually *know* of any speakeasies—or at least where they *are*, although I don't doubt he's heard the rest of us talking about them. Second, Mr. Harrison is in no condition to drive. Third, this isn't even his car, and the gentleman whose car this *is* isn't going to take too kindly to the two of you joyriding around in it, sideswiping mailboxes and mowing down fire hydrants, all in a fruitless quest for some blind pig that—even if you should get so lucky as to *find* it—probably won't admit you because you both happen to look twelve."

Molly laughed noisily and gustily. "You're a funny one, Mr. Parloom. Pat, your friend Mr. Pardrew is a very funny man. I like him."

Pat stared straight ahead, chewing his lower lip with unmitigated anger.

"And fourth—"

"There's a *fourth*?" Pat snarled.

Reason Number Four was delivered in a whisper for Molly's consumption only.

"Have you given any thought, Miss Osborne, to what Sister Lydia will say—let alone *do*—were she to find out how one of her choir girls spent the latter part of this evening?"

A look of terror suddenly overspread Molly's face. "Oh no!" she exclaimed. "She wouldn't be very pleased at all, would she?" Tears sprang to Molly's rheumy eyes. "Oh, what will she say to what I've done *already*? I've danced like a wicked wild woman and said things I shouldn't have said and I've drunk things I've had no business drinking and, and—"

Words suddenly failed Molly, to be replaced by an aberrant bodily function, which carried an equivalent amount of information. Cain assisted her as best he could by holding her head while removing his patent leathers from the vicinity of deposit, as Pat huffed and snorted and flung daggers of hatred at his friend for the crime of his intrusion.

"It's for your own good, Pat," Cain calmly explained, his look lovingly placatory. "In terms of our game, this stunt wouldn't have even won you the consolation prize."

"I had plans for something much more adventurish than simple vee—vehicular *petting!*" delivered the petulant baby sheik through partially gritted teeth.

"The word is adventur*ous*, Paddy, and if your idea of adventurous seduction is to drive this poor girl to a speakeasy and drink until the two of you pass out under the table, then you have no business playing the game. You'll know where to find me tomorrow when you want to thank me."

Cain took out his handkerchief, wiped some of the sick from Molly's lips, set her aright in her seat and started off. A moment later he stopped, wheeled himself around and returned to the car, this time putting himself on the driver's side. "This performance of yours, Pat, makes your Puck in our little Shakespeare festival look like Hamlet by comparison. You're far better than this." Cain held his gaze for a moment longer than he could have gotten away with if Pat had been sober. With tender fingers he brushed back a lock of tumbled hair from Pat's forehead, then left.

The music was louder now, the partiers singing along with the record, "I'm Just Wild About Harry," except that William Holborne was putting it a bit differently. "I'm Just Wild About *Carrie*" was what he warbled right into the ear of its most appropriate recipient, in the process spraying one side of Carrie's face with atomized droplets of gin-scented saliva.

"You, sir, are absolutely *disgusting!*" she cried, locking arms with Ruth, who was still looking out the window, still waiting for the denouement to the little drama being played out a half block away. "And it's time for us to go. Let's gather up the girls, Ruth, before Deloria Littlejohn or my mother or *someone* on this block who values their sleep 'phones the police."

"Yet the evening is young and you are—I do not exaggerate, madam—the most beautiful woman I've ever met!" Will said all this without slurring a single word. He was soon joined by Jerry Castle and Tom Catts.

"They're leaving," announced Will with a display of exaggerated dejection. "The evening has hardly gotten started and these choir babies are 'much skidoo about nothing'—nothing at all."

"Well, we can't have *that!*" boomed Jerry thickly. "Not to mention that, practically speaking, we seem to have lost all trace of Miss Barton."

Carrie and Ruth looked about the room in hopes of proving Jerry wrong.

Jerry cheerfully elaborated: "We were having ourselves a nice cozy gas in the kitchen while I was helping the little lady prowl around for something ice-cold and zero-proof, and in marches this flannel-tongued hunkie or—or wop or some such species of Ellis Island gorilla, who starts to muscle in on my territory, and while

I'm fending *him* off, I got a couple of thirsty professorial Yid butt-inskies stealing in behind me from the back porch, and now they're buzz-buzzing around the flame of luscious Lady M, and before I can get her hustled away to safety, two la-di-dah lizzie boys with Theda Bara eye-paint flounce in and give me the puke-belly from the stinking reality of their very *existence*, and while I'm contemplating which of these disturbers of my very own peace is going to get the knuckle sandwich, I see my Lady Fair duck out and disappear into the night, and now I feel cheated and wholly maligned by cruel circumstance."

Will grinned. "You could have spared us the silly-quee, Jerry. She just walked in. See her over there by the clodhopper in the glee-club boater? Go tell her goodnight."

Jerry stiff-armed his way across the crowded dance floor to reintroduce himself to Maggie, as if such a thing were necessary. At the same time, Maggie was swimming in a different direction, over to Bella Prowse, who lay sprawled upon the carpet next to the Victrola, surrounded by a cluttered imbrication of phonograph records from the Prowses' prodigious music collection. Reaching Bella, Maggie went down on her knees to put herself at eye level with her hostess.

"Hey, *you*," said Jerry, now towering over Maggie. "Do you remember me?"

"Of course I remember you," replied Maggie, looking up for an eye-blink and then returning her attention to the record she'd casually plucked up to inspect.

"*Struttin' the Blues Away*," offered the blissfully bleary-eyed Bella Prowse. "That's one of Reggie's favorites." (Not that Bella's husband Professor Reginald Prowse would be in any condition to enjoy the selection. He had, quite some time earlier, entered alcohol-abetted dreamland in his favorite easy chair in a relatively isolated corner of the room.) "I love that one too. It's the Atlantic Dance Orchestra. Do you know them?" The question was directed to Maggie, though it was repeated for Jerry's benefit. "Do *you* know them?"

"I don't know nothing except that I have to see this chickie"—
pointing at Maggie—"before she flies the coop."

"See me about what? Am I leaving?" Maggie looked up to see
Ruth and Carrie, with Molly propped unsteadily between them,
stationed near the front door. Ruth and Carrie were nodding exaggeratedly and making broad hand gestures indicative of departure.

"There's something I want to give you—in parting," said Jerry.
His voice now sounded poised and friendly, although there was the
hint of something else there: a childlike wishfulness, which couldn't
be easily dismissed.

Maggie's resistance dissolved. "I'll take it. What is it?" Maggie
held out her hand, palm up. The hand wobbled.

"Not here. In private."

Maggie was now sitting with her legs tucked delicately beneath
her like a sleepy fawn in a glade. She gave Jerry her hand. He lifted
her gently to her feet.

He led her to one of the bedrooms. He flung open the door. Inside was a young woman and man in a bunny hug, she seated in his
lap on a chair.

"Beat it!" Jerry rumbled.

The command was speedily obeyed, the door slammed shut
upon exit. And then, without a moment's hesitation, Jerry Castle
bestowed his "gift": a kiss for Maggie to remember him by.

"You drive me wild. I gotta have you," he said, after their lips
had parted.

"I—I'm flattered you need me," inhaled Maggie, while trying to
catch her breath, "but I hardly know you."

"Then find out about me. Let's see each other. You say when. I'll
say where. Or versa vicea."

"I don't know. The room's spinning."

"I'm sweeping you off your feet."

"No. I think I'm drunk. I think you put something in my lemonade."

Jerry looked away in an attempt to conceal his smirk.

"Answer me! Look at me! Did you do something to my glass of lemonade?"

"I cannot tell a lie. I adulterated your lemonade."

"You—"

"—turned your lemonade into *adult* lemonade."

"Why?"

"I thought you needed a little loosening—"

Maggie's hand met Jerry's face before he could even complete his answer. He responded by pulling her roughly toward him and kissing her again. This kiss was delivered without affection or even passion. It represented only the brute desire to thoroughly control her in that assailing moment.

It was answered by yet another slap.

Followed, finally, by the emergence of a sly, devilish grin on the face of the victim, and the panting declaration: "*I. Will. Have. You.*"

"*In. Hell,*" returned Maggie, who then flailed blindly for the door, yanked it open, and half-marched, half-fled down the hallway to the parlor in a show of frazzled, trembling indignation.

The phonograph wasn't playing "Strutting the Blues Away." Instead, its speaker was blasting out the comical song "Yes, We Have No Bananas," while Bella Prowse was eating a banana in contradiction of the lyrics, and Jane Higgins was being roused from slumber upon the sofa by three of her friends, each with one eye on the front door, and each looking conversely regretful over having to skidoo from the most interesting night of their young lives.

Chapter Fourteen

London, England, October 1940

The sign in the grocer's window read:

Yes, We Have no Bananas
Nor onions nor oranges, sultanas, currants,
dried fruit of any kind, spaghetti, kippers & herring.
So please don't bleeding ask.

Jane laughed; Molly, Ruth, and Carrie smiled. Maggie registered nothing. As We Five hurried along to take shelter, Maggie Barton was red-faced, brow-cinched, and broodingly silent. Once the public ARP shelter was reached and the friends settled inside, Maggie persisted in closing herself off from communication with everyone round her—both those she didn't know and those four young women whom she did. Maggie was too busy recalling with revulsion exactly what Jerry Castle had said to her, had *done* to her outside the Hammersmith Palais.

And after the two had been getting on so well.

Jane had seen it. She'd been saying her own goodnights to Tom Katz and had noticed out of the corner of her eye the outlines of the ugly exchange: the vulgar overture, the harsh rejoinder. She'd then watched, now with her eyes targeted like a huff-duff antenna, as Jerry, taking drunken offense to the rebuff, pushed and then penned Maggie against the wall, where he took liberties in full view of other couples emerging from the ballroom. Jane was prepared to go and assist Maggie in removing herself from the man's vile clutches when Maggie succeeded in doing that very thing on her own, but not without delivering retributive justice in the form of a hard slap to Jerry's face.

It was a slap, which, curiously, prompted a smile, as if this—her expression of instantaneous hatred for him—was what he'd been after all along.

Jane had thought at the time: if this is how the bloke thinks he can win the affections of Maggie Barton, he'd best look elsewhere. Of We Five only Jane would have fallen for such brutish, caveman tactics, and only then because Jane would have given back as she got: cudgel-wielding caveman, meet cudgel-wielding cavewoman. But Maggie, and Jane's other circle-sisters, weren't cudgel-carriers. They hadn't the leathery hide of the scrabbling London East Ender like Jane. They were much too staid and naïve to desire the attention of anyone but a gentleman—with special emphasis on the "gentle." From what she'd observed outside the Hammersmith, Jane did have to admit, though, that modesty and girlish innocence hadn't prevented her friend Maggie from asserting herself when need arose.

Thought Jane: "Huzzah for my friend Maggie Barton for standing up to the bloody lout!"

Up to then—up until this display of most deplorably bad behaviour on the part of Mr. Castle, behaviour which reminded Jane in retrospection of some beastly belch from the pulpit after a particularly inspirational sermon—the evening had proceeded quite swimmingly. It was such a night as none of the five had ever before experienced. Over the course of the three and a half hours spent in the company of the five young men who'd sought them there,

Maggie and Jane and Carrie and Molly and Ruth had learned things about themselves, about their needs and their natures, which could not have been predicted only a few hours before.

And best of all: they learned how to have fun—the kind of fun for which the Hammersmith Palais was nationally famous.

Carrie and the hulking young Scandinavian named Holborne had taken to one another like ducks to a cool summer pond. Carrie's love of music propelled her out onto the dance floor without a moment's hesitation, and Will did a yeoman's job of keeping in good step with her. They sat out only three or four dances through the long evening. Slowly and soulfully they gyred and dipped to both of the celestial serenades made famous by Glenn Miller. Elsetimes they jitter-jived like seasoned Lindy Hoppers to the more energetic numbers like "Woodchopper's Ball." This particular song was played as loudly as possible to cover the sound of the evening's first Luftwaffe air attack. (Maggie had guessed wrong; it was the Hammersmith Palais's custom never to evacuate its ballroom in the midst of a bombing raid. Regular customers knew when they entered the palace each evening that this might very well be their last night on Earth, but, by Jove, at least they'd die happy!)

Whilst they were dancing, Carrie and Will, both of whom seemed to know the lyrics to every popular song, sang along with the orchestra, Carrie demonstrating her inarguable lyrical gift, Holborne's own voice generally on-key and perfectly serviceable as amateur voices go. They concluded their tuneful tête-à-têtes with the antepenultimate number of the evening, "The Breeze and I" ("...they know you have departed without me, and we wonder why...") Even more moving than this was the song which came next (which they listened to in respectful silence)—the movingly valedictory "We'll Meet Again," sung not by its famous interpreter, Miss Vera Lynn, who was presently abroad performing for the troops, but by a woman who looked and sounded very much *like* the U.K.'s beloved Miss Lynn, and who capitalized on this fact by calling herself *Deirdre* Lynn.

Molly, like many others in the crowd, could not keep herself from tearing up during the poignant "We'll Meet Again," though the song lost all of its personal relevance given that Molly was saying goodnight (and not goodbye) to a conscientious objector, who had a very good chance of meeting Molly not only on some sunny day but for that matter *any* day of the week, irrespective of the weather. Molly also wept when the band struck up for its last number of the evening, the patriotic "There'll Always Be an England," though in a very large room (the Palais was a great converted tram shed) with a very large number of men in uniform, We Five's beaux for the evening stood out quite conspicuously in their civvies. As a result, they became recipients of judgemental stares and glares during both this song and the earlier rendition of "Bless 'Em All," and specifically during the song's pointed lyric, "You'll get no promotion this side of the ocean."

Molly was comforted through her tears by the tender ministrations of her demonstrably Molly-ravenous new boyfriend Pat, the two calling into serious question through their intermittent gaiety and unfettered physical familiarity with one another on the dance floor their assertion that they had only just met.

Neither Ruth nor Cain danced, but kept up a lively marathon rag-chew over topics ranging from the recently discovered Paleolithic cave paintings in southwestern France to whether or not the popular radio comedian Tom Handley was brilliantly funny or annoyingly overrated. Their relaxed and friendly chat was marred only by a look of passing indictment from Holborne—one totally lost on Ruth—which came when the band struck up the droll "Kiss Me Goodnight, Sergeant Major," sung, as it always was, by a male vocalist.

The first kiss of the night—and one which met the approval of both participants—was shared by Jane and Tom and elicited the following exchange:

Jane: I don't think I've ever been kissed by a Jew before.

Tom: My dear Miss Higgins, I would hazard a guess that you've never been kissed by an Anglican or a Catholic before either. Excepting, of course, your mother and father.

Jane: To tell you the truth, you'd be correct. But why don't you be a gentleman and not spread this fact about?

Tom: I spread very little about these days, Miss Higgins. We Children of David try our best to keep our heads down as much as possible. That way Herr Hitler's troops will have a little more trouble finding us when it comes time to cart us all away.

Jane: If Ruth were standing here she'd ask why, with other members of your faith quarantined behind fences in those bloody camps they're talking about—why you don't put on a uniform and join the fight to set them free.

To which Tom replied with a simper: "Oh, it's only your friend *Ruth* who wonders this, is it? Then do be sure to relay my answer to her: 'Tom Katz is a coward—a "fraidy cat," as the Yanks say. He takes no pride in it, but it cannot be helped.' Now, enough of this empty jawing. Give us another kiss and be quick about it."

Which Jane did, enjoying the kiss terribly, though it troubled her that Tom had come to such comfortable terms with all the glaring defects to his character.

And as for Maggie and Jerry, the two had jollied and jousted with one another through most of the evening, each finding in the other one who fancied jesting with a hard edge but a soft wink... until that moment when Jerry Castle stopped winking and beheld his companion for the night with a suddenly predatory eye, this moment arriving without any warning whatsoever.

Of the five couples, only Maggie and Jerry had made no plans for seeing each other under decidedly more intimate circumstances later in the week. Or rather, Maggie and Jerry *might* have made plans, but the chance of this happening was dashed in an instant by Jerry's sledgehammer approach to romantic conquest.

Inside the Hammersmith Palais de Danse (the original name given to this, London's most popular nocturnal gathering spot, by the two enterprising Americans who opened it in 1919), one could almost forget from time to time that there was a war going on, or that London was being subjected to a series of nightly bombings, "the Blitz," which was originally purposed to tear the heart out of the proud city and destroy the will of its armed forces to keep fighting and its citizens to keep stiffening their collective upper lip. But reminders did abound: not only did the walls and floor of the hall frequently judder and tremble and the nearby air raid sirens sing out in notes discordant with those being produced by the performing dance bands; and not only was the Palais clotted with young men in R.A.F., Royal Navy, Royal Marines, and British Army uniforms, but unfortunately, the refreshments offered up were also sadly indicative of this time of economy and sacrifice. Here at the Hammersmith Palais could be found the very same restrictions and shortages experienced in other places throughout the kingdom, where people were required to be as creative as possible in the preparation of meals. In the kitchen of the ballroom that meant marge and Marmite sandwiches, and Spam on crisps, and "finger foods," dominated by the flavor-deficient root vegetables, which all of England was planting and digging up in their backyards and public allotment plots.

Which was why Ruth was disappointed. And hungry. Even more hungry than usual. *And* hardly able to bear the intrusive redolence of the flaky, perfectly browned meat pie that was presently being devoured by the inexplicably well-provisioned middle-aged woman sitting next to her in the shelter.

Ruth wasn't alone.

"You could have at least waited until the rest of us had nodded off," said the man sitting beside her, "you *cow*." The last was said under his breath, but the woman heard it nonetheless. Everyone seemed to have heard it. Someone said, "Hear, hear."

"We'll have no such talk as that," said the shelter warden reprovingly. He was a lean, pinched-face man in his late sixties, and if he had not been a schoolmaster in his productive younger years, he could certainly have played the part convincingly in pictures.

We Five had been lucky to find seats in the shelter. The air raid siren had gone off just as they were haring off to catch the last train of the night. Assuming there wouldn't be sufficient time to make it on foot to the station, they ducked into a public shelter and found they had a lot of company. Some of those huddled inside had arrived long before the latest cautionary wail and had brought with them blankets and Thermos flasks and decks of cards, intending to spend the whole night there, as many Londoners were doing these days.

Indeed, underground spaces of every size and description and degree of suitability were being converted into public shelters during that deadly autumn. Even tube stations throughout the city—especially those dug deep into the ground—were being commandeered, first without the approval of Underground administrators and later with their full cooperation, and turned into circumstantial safe havens, especially by those who lived in the vulnerable East End and by the thousands of other Londoners who did not trust their own basements and backyard shelters to offer adequate protection.

Carrie looked all about. No one seemed to be carrying a gas mask. After months and months of the "Phoney War," in which Germany had been thought to be planning a full-scale poisonous gas attack on British civilians, people had started to leave their masks at home. We Five had done just that, concluding that the oblong, fawn-coloured cardboard boxes wouldn't prove too fetching an accessory for a night of sparkle and glamour upon the dance floor.

Carrie had a strong desire to pinch her nose to prevent the foetid assault upon her nostrils which came from the dishevelment of unshod feet and the discourtesy of underwashed bodies. She closed her eyes and vowed to simply endure her travails until the All Clear sounded.

But Jane's spirits remained inflated and gay. "Except for what happened to Maggie," she said to Molly, who sat next to her, "I'd say the evening was a topping success."

Molly agreed with a nod whilst rolling her eyes with regard to those near her, none of whom, it seemed upon cursory inspection, came from the Hammersmith Palais ballroom. "I especially like the fine way it all ended up," she answered sarcastically.

"Better to be here and to be safe, Molly," retorted Ruth, who sat across from the two, "than to be roaming the streets only to be sliced up by flying bomb shrapnel, or perhaps even more buggery than that: take a direct hit to your person."

As if on cue, there came the sound of an explosion quite close by. One of the women in the shelter emitted an abortive scream, which elicited a whisper-chorus of "there there"s from the concerned women who sat round her.

Another woman, who sat next to Ruth, turned to her and said severely, "I wish you wouldn't talk that way with the children here." She pointed to the children of reference. "It frightens them so."

Ruth was about to observe that it certainly was a topsy-turvy world in which *talking* about bombs should be found more frightening than the actual *sound* of their nearby detonation, when a tweedy old man sitting within earshot said, "If you ask me, that boy and girl should have been sent away from London along with half the other children of the city. This is no place for a child, with them Nazi bombs raining down on us every bloody night."

Now it was the children's mother's turn to speak. She did so as she embraced her little ones, one on either side: "From what *I've* heard, London is only slightly more dangerous than all them other places the little ones been shipped off to. So why don't you just sod off?"

It was time, once again, for the shelter marshal to intercede: "Ladies and gentlemen, there is a proper and respectful way to speak to one another in such close quarters as this, and I am not hearing it.

Has anyone a mouth organ to play or a music hall song to sing—
mind, one appropriate for young ears?"

"Oh good God," muttered Carrie. She kept her eyes squeezed
tight and feigned sleep, lest any of her four sisters commit the un-
pardonable atrocity of informing the other sardines in this tight
little underground tin that there was one among them who had a
voice to put even Deanna Durbin to shame. Carrie conjured up a
picture of Will and the way he had held her during "A Nightingale
Sang in Berkeley Square," taking care not to squeeze her too tightly. She liked that. It seemed such a contrast to the way the evening
had ended for poor Maggie. Carrie peeped at her friend. In the
dim lantern light she could almost swear Maggie was crying, but
she wasn't close enough to ask her outright, nor would Maggie
much fancy it if she did.

Carrie thought of how similarly the two of them had been
brought up—each enduring early years with a father who wasn't
fit to be a father at all. Although Carrie's dad was still out there,
perhaps even going about the business of redeeming his putrid character by offering his showman talents to the Entertainments National Service Association (ENSA, to most), and Maggie's father was
gone entirely from this earth, both of the young women had been
required by circumstance to reside in more recent years in homes
in which the bond between mother and daughter was, by necessity,
crucially important to the survival of what was left of their attritive
families.

But Carrie could not help thinking there was something even
more special about how much *she* and *her* mother loved one another.
They got on very well together (everyone said so), and was this fact
not best demonstrated by Sylvia's willingness to gently nudge her
daughter fully fledged from the nest? Carrie could not contain the
frisson of bliss that ran through her in this paradoxically unhappy
and revolting place. Will Holborne's edges were deckled, his per-

sonality gruff, his intellect adequate but far from remarkable; yet there was something that commended him to her heart.

And yet.

First loves are anomalies, they always say. They cannot be completely trusted. Carrie knew this. Each of her sisters would be quick to tell her this. But the feeling of joy that came from knowing—or, in the very least, *guessing*—how Will felt about her was hard to ignore.

Carrie Hale couldn't wait to get home to tell her mother all she was able about the night at the Hammersmith Palais and about the man who made her sing—both from her lips and from her heart. She asked the time and was told it was nearing midnight. There had been one raid already, and then an hour later the All Clear. Now another raid was underway. She could hear it and feel it. She could see the fear imprinted upon the faces of her fellow Londoners, who never got used to it, never stopped wondering if this particular night would be their last. Perhaps if they were lucky, Carrie and her sisters wouldn't have to spend the rest of the night in this terrible place, like rats in a sewer. In the meantime, she would hum her way through this durance vile: "They know you have departed without me and we wonder why, the breeze and I."

Was Will safe?

You see, she was already worrying about him. When, if there was worrying to be done (and most will tell you that worrying is never productive), it was her mother who should have occupied her deepest, most fretful thoughts.

For at that very moment, in Elmfield Road not far from Balham High Road, a bomb—not one that shatters and rends and pulverizes and deforms, but one that only burns—a diabolical incendiary bomb—fell with a seemingly innocent thud upon the roof of the Hale row house and tumbled down the steeply pitched roof, coming finally to rest upon a loosely tied stack of paper rubbish Mrs. Hale had been gathering for the next paper drive. Its sputtering sparks ignited the paper and then the grass beneath it and within moments the sideboards of the house whilst Carrie's mother slept in the cupboard beneath the stairs, where she and Carrie would always go, having been told that staircases offered the best protection from falling bombs—at least the kind of bombs that destroy on detonative contact. And so the house began to burn as Sylvia slept (for she had just dozed off, having fought sleep for hours in hopes of being awake for Carrie's return) and the family cat, awake and motivated by an instinct for survival, fled through the cat flap in the kitchen door.

It wasn't until the house was nearly engulfed that a fireman fighting a blaze at the end of the lane spotted the curls of smoke coming from inside and rushed over to discover if there was anyone within. What happened to her mother Carrie would not learn for another four and one half hours: she was not dead, but she had been badly burnt in her attempt to escape the house upon waking to the acrid smell of smoke, and by only the most clinical definition could Carrie's mother and best friend in the world be called alive.

The house and nearly everything inside—the musical instruments, the sheet music, the books—were lost.

There was even a biscuit sheet of slightly scorched muffins, freshly baked, waiting for Carrie on the top of the stove, now burnt to a point that even Sylvia Hale had never taken them.

Chapter Fifteen

Bellevenue, Mississippi, February 1997

It was two and a half days before Carrie was finally able to make it
to the blackened shell which had been the house she shared with her
mother. In the meantime Carrie's next-door neighbors, the Prowses, had kept careful watch over what was left of the structure (in
addition to giving a temporary home to the now homeless Frisky
McWhiskers); Mira Prowse had even pulled a few things from the
less-damaged rooms that she felt her friend Carrie might want to
have—although everything she'd carried out was either singed or
smoke- or water-damaged. Mira's Samaritan salvage operation was
not without incident. At one point she was confronted by Ms. Littlejohn, the neighborhood busybody, who demanded to know "what
in God's name" she was up to. Mira's harried response: "What *you*
should have been doing yourself, if you were any kind of thoughtful
neighbor, you nasty old bitch!"

Since Sunday night when Carrie had been taken off the gaming
floor and told by Ms. Colthurst that "oh honey, darlin', something
just awful's happened and you need to go straight to the hospital,"
Carrie had cried so much that she no longer even resembled herself.
Molly insisted on keeping her friend's eyes periodically Visined to

get at least some of the redness and puffiness down. Molly had been right by Carrie's side ever since it happened. Carrie's other sisters had also remained in close orbit, but it was Molly who put everything in her life on hold to give around-the-clock attention to her devastated friend.

Neither of the girls had had more than a cat nap. They had spent all of the previous two nights in the I.C.U. waiting room as Carrie received continuous updates on her mother's precarious condition. Sylvia Hale had suffered burns over fifty percent of her body, and the doctors had thought it best to induce medical coma to spare her from excruciating pain. What the doctors *hadn't* been able to do was offer any kind of assurance that Carrie's mother would recover. It is always impossible to know such a thing in those critical first few days. Every patient is different, the doctors had said, and every patient's immune response to severe bodily trauma unique.

What was additionally difficult for Carrie to bear was that she'd been denied the chance to see her. "Oh goodness mercy! Why would you even *want* to, child?" was what one of the I.C.U. nurses had said to her (somewhat callously, though the harshness of the statement was softened somewhat by the woman's honey-sweet Delta drawl). "She won't know you're there and she'll be a fright to look at. Spare yourself, sweetie."

It was almost as if her mother were already dead.

Molly didn't know what to say that would be of any comfort to her friend. She only knew that Carrie needed her. And she'd be there for Carrie for as long as was necessary. Mr. Osborne had also made it clear that Carrie could stay with Molly and him if she liked, an offer repeated by three of her sisters. Ruth would have asked her too, but Ruth hadn't room in her tiny trailer to, as Jane had colorfully put it, "swing a dead cat."

The two young women wandered in silent head-shaking bewilderment through the remains of the house, its destruction caused by a short in its aging electrical wiring. When Carrie finally found her voice, she mused aloud, "In times like these it does make you wonder why people collect so much stuff. Although I hate it that we've lost all the photo albums and the scrapbooks." Then Carrie turned to Molly and said, "But I'd gladly give up everything I own to have Mama back the way she was."

Molly nodded, though she was having a little trouble understanding the logic behind such a hypothetical tradeoff. At that moment her eyes fell on the black carcass of Carrie's violin. "Oh, your fiddle!" she announced sadly.

"Oh, I can always buy another one when I want to start playing again. It's not like it came from Cremona."

Molly didn't get the Stradivarius reference, but she nodded and smiled nonetheless.

Carrie picked up a few things for Molly to take home and keep for her, and then the two left.

As Molly was driving them back to the hospital, Carrie said, seemingly out of the blue, "Do you know if Will's been asking about me?"

Molly gave Carrie a curious look. "You know I haven't been back to the casino, Carrie."

"But you talk to Jane and Ruth and Mags. Did he say anything to *them*?"

"If he did, they didn't tell me about it."

"Oh," said Carrie, staring contemplatively into space. Then she said, as if to herself, "I liked him."

"Will Holborne should be the last thing on your mind right now, Car."

Carrie shook her head. "He's the only nice thing I have left to hold on to."

Molly gripped the steering wheel tightly. "First, that isn't true. You have your four sisters. We're always gonna be there for you. Second, you need to stop thinkin' about Will. He's just like the others. We were just fun little pieces of ass to them."

"You sound just like Ruth," said Carrie, swiping a handkerchief across her swollen eyes. She half groaned/half sighed. "I could sleep for days." She slumped down in her seat. "I wish the doctors would put *me* in a coma. And if I'm lucky I'll never wake up again."

"You stop talking like that."

"Will is different," said Carrie groggily, her eyes now closed.

"Uh-uh. They're all the same," responded Molly, giving no ground. She took a deep breath. Then softly—so softly, in fact, that she didn't think Carrie in her present, half-somnolent state could even hear her, she said, "Except for Pat. He's the only exception."

Coincidentally, at that very moment Pat was very much the outlier—but only in the sense of physical proximity to his four Ole Miss frat buddies. Because while he was helping to hose out the casino's parking garage (not in his job description, but who respects job descriptions in the non-unionized American South?), Pat Harrison's four friends were all waiting together on the arrivals pick-up deck of Memphis International Airport, each man having driven one of Lucky Aces' four courtesy vans. They were waiting for the appearance of a large party (four entire vans' worth) of Atlanta Woman's Club members, who were treating themselves to three days of gambling and one night of the Jordanaires at their favorite Mississippi River casino. The plane was late. The four men had gotten tired of automotive circling, and one of the airport cops had eventually given them permission to stand.

"I hate this fucking job," said Jerry Castle through a cloud of cigarette smoke.

"It was supposed to build character," said Tom Katz, "although in *your* case, Castle, I always knew *that* was gonna be a nonstarter." Tom turned to Will. "So, are you gonna call her or what?"

"What do *you* care?"

"You *don't* care?"

"Course I care. But just how am I supposed to do this? Her phone's probably a glob of molten plastic."

"Then go see her at the hospital. Ms. Colthurst said they've got her mother in the Baptist in Southaven."

Will, who was also sucking smoke, exhaled his own thick cloud and shook his head. "Eh—I don't think so."

Cain unfolded his arms. He'd been leaning against the UNLOAD-ING ZONE sign cemented into the sidewalk, counting the number of times the same woman in the same blue Dodge Colt was making the "loop" while waiting to pick up whoever it was that was supposed to be flying in around this time. Cain wanted to tell the woman it would be much better for the environment if she'd just park the damned thing, eat the two dollars it would cost to leave the car in the short-term lot, and go inside.

Seeing no need for preamble, Cain said, "I think it's time to end the game, y'all. Now that Will's decided to remove himself from competition—"

"Who said Will's removing himself from competition?" hurled Will, straightening up. After flicking his butt to the ground and then mashing it with the tip of his shoe—it was a black cowboy boot, actually, the closest thing Will could find to go with the livery provided by Lucky Aces—he took a couple of steps in Cain's direc-tion. "Where's the rule that says I gotta be stuck with 'The Warbler'? Besides, I've already made big plans for my weekend with Tommy's friend's Maserati, and if any of you even *tries* to blow this for me, I'll fuck you over real good."

Jerry Castle hooted. "Being awfully cocky about your chances, ain't ya, Willy-Boy? Seeing's as how the girl *you* wound up with doesn't have much time for *anybody* these days 'cept her medi-um-to-well-done mawmaw." Castle cawed with laughter.

Cain looked him coldly in the eye and said, "Why do you talk shit like that? After what happened to that woman. And maybe you haven't noticed, Castle, but until this *did* happen, you were the only one of us who didn't have a date lined up for this week. In fact, you left such a favorable impression on Mags, you'd probably be lucky to get her inside the same county with you."

The fingers that comprised Jerry's right hand curled into a tight fist.

Noticing this, Cain said, "Wouldn't you rather wait and beat the crap out of me somewhere more private?"

"It's Tommy's game," Jerry shot back. "He's the one who gets to decide whether we keep playing or not."

Tom "the Kat" Cheshire-grinned. "Well, *that's* an easy one. We keep playing. Because I could easily wrap this whole thing up by Friday. Jane's as horny as a junkyard bitch in heat. She all but went down on me in the parking lot of the blues club last week."

Will and Jerry burst out laughing. Will said, "You really think you can win the game based on a pity fuck?"

Jerry added: "Bless the bestiality and the chilrens!"

Cain retreated to his van. After climbing into the driver's seat, he slammed the door with force sufficient to get across, unequivocally, his absolute disgust for the topic at hand.

Cain Pardlow wondered, as he often did, why he continued to associate with three men whose every word and deed turned his stomach into a roiling acid pit. But the answer always came quick and easy, and it was always the same: Cain hung out with Will and Tom and Jerry, as much as he had grown to despise them, as the price he had to pay for being with Pat.

Pat. The man he loved. The man to whom he was affectionately and dutifully devoted. Cain had tried to reroute these feelings—had tried to make himself think of Pat in that fraternal, protective way older brothers sometimes feel about younger brothers. But he never succeeded. The physical desire was too strong. There was nothing remotely fraternal or even platonic about Cain's feelings for Pat Harrison—feelings he knew *would* never and *could* never be returned. Not that this mattered. Because at this point he'd pretty much reconciled himself to circumstances. And if just being around Pat was the best it was going to get, then he would exercise his private devotion by helping to shepherd the boyishly adorable Pat Harrison safely and happily through these early formative chapters of his life.

Cain Pardlow had become, in his own mind, the self-sacrificing heroine of a schmaltzy Douglas Sirk soaper.

"*So,*" said Will Holborne, lighting up another Marlboro, "all things being fair in love and shit, and there being no rules in the game against poaching, I shall find myself another victim. So good luck, *suckahs.*"

Tom Katz couldn't help laughing. You had to admire Will's chutzpah. Jerry might be your garden-variety, old-fashioned Mississippi anti-Semite, but Will Holborne, when he wanted to be, could top them all: the aggressive, the assertive, the brawny Quicker-Picker-Upper Nordic über-man Nazi right down to his hollow core.

The next day, conveniently a day off from the casino for both Cain and Ruth, the two found themselves sipping caffé mochas (called, with a soupçon of pretension, "mocaccinos" on the menu) at Harvey Joe's, Bellevenue's popular new combination bookstore/coffeehouse on the town square. Although it wasn't, nor could it ever be thought of as a "date," their afternoon meeting didn't go to the other extreme either. Neither the gay man nor the lesbian felt like the kind of awkward stranger that circumstances required them to be in this early, exploratory stage in their friendship. In fact, the ease with which they settled into conversation was a first for both; Cain had never had a female friend with whom he felt comfortable enough to open up, and the same could be said for Ruth (with the required gender flip). Even though the Reverend Mobry had dropped many a hint that he would be receptive to anything Ruth wished to share with him, she'd never felt the desire to take him up on the offer. It would have been, for Ruth, a little like a daughter disrobing in front of her father.

"When did you know—or at least suspect?" asked Ruth.

"Maybe it was that night at the blues club. The way you kept checking out the waitress with the big—well—"

"You can say it. *Tits*. It's a great word. I love the word. I love the tits."

"You seem really close to your four friends—"

"Yeah, we've been like that since childhood."

Someone had left a promo postcard on the table for a local barbecue restaurant. Cain speared it with his index finger and spun it absently around. "You never had a, like, inconvenient crush on any of them?"

Ruth laughed. "To be totally honest, if Molly suddenly came out to me—not that Molly's budged from the zero mark on my gaydar in all the years I've known her—but if, miracle of miracles, she did happen to someday come out as the cute, pixyish little dyke of my dreams, I would, without the slightest hesitation, dive right into the sack with her. But I'm a realist who doesn't dwell on things that shall never be."

"Hmm."

Ruth cocked her head. "Which one?"

Cain grinned self-consciously. "Pat. The kid."

Ruth nodded. "He's cute."

"And as straight as your Molly. Probably straighter."

Ruth smirked. "*Probably straighter*. Now what the hell, Mr. Pardlow, does *that* mean?"

"I don't know. Isn't it common knowledge that women have a little more wiggle room in this area than men do?"

Ruth laughed out loud. "Well, that's certainly what the straight male media wants you to think—all the better to feed those fantasies about two hot women going at it with each other under the sheets.

No. There's never been much wiggle room with any of the girls *I've* known. Especially my four sisters."

"Has there—if you don't mind me asking—has there been anybody you've—?"

"Not really. Viv at work—*Ms. Colthurst*—you know, who supervises all the gaming-floor waitresses—she's been sending me a few not-*too*-subtle signals she might be interested in me."

"Do you like her?"

Ruth shrugged her eyes. "She's—I don't know. Maybe I could *grow* to like her."

"You don't have to settle, you know."

"Ain't you sweet."

"Ruth, I have to tell you something." Cain downed the rest of his mocha as if for fortification.

"You're gonna tell me about the bet, aren't you?"

"So you know about the bet."

Ruth nodded.

"It's more like a game, though, really—one of the twisted little games the guys and I play with each other. I hate most of them—this one more than all the rest put together."

"Then why do you go along with it?"

"Blackmail would be the best way to put it. Will walked into the john one day when one of the busboys from the buffet restaurant had me in a—I'll just say, a *compromised* position. Will's using this to force me to play the game. If word gets out, then it could turn into a big scandal that would probably keep my dad from getting re-elected. He's the district attorney down in Arkabutla County."

"This isn't 1950. What you do is nobody's business—not your father's, not any of the people who may or may not be voting for him down at the other end of the state."

"But maybe you haven't noticed: people in Mississippi still *act* like it's 1950, and they get off on being affronted and appalled. How'd you figure out the game?"

"There wasn't a lot of *figuring* required. I overheard two of your 'brothers' talking about it during our little field trip last week. They couldn't have been any more forthcoming if they'd deliberately set out to tell me everything I needed to know."

It took Cain a moment to recompose himself. "Have you told the others?"

"Not yet. But I think I probably should, especially after the way that asshole treated Mags. I'm afraid he's gonna start stalking her."

"I could see him doing just that. But I'd like to ask a favor of you."

"Okay."

"Do you want another mocha?"

"Maybe. Tell me your favor first."

Cain leaned over and lowered his voice. "I want you to hold off telling Mags and the rest of them what's going on—for just a little while longer. Jerry and Will and Tommy—even though they wouldn't have proof it came from me, they'd still pin it on me and then I'd be royally screwed. But that's just *part* of the favor."

Ruth sat up in her seat. "I'm not gonna sleep with you, Cain, to help you win your game."

"I wouldn't ask you to. I just need you to *pretend* like we did."

"Now *that* sounds like something straight out of the Archie comic books—*Millennium* edition."

"I'm not looking to win the game. Screw the game. I just want to come out of this whole thing in one piece."

"Well, I'm not so sure you could have won if you'd tried. Even with Mags and now Carrie off the field, you've still got Jane and Molly. Jane's bat-shit crazy about Tommy—go figure—and Molly seems to be *very* fond of your friend Pat. And neither of those two, I predict, will be losing their virginity in a quiet way. I see champagne, fireworks, and a real circus atmosphere to the proceedings."

"How do you know they're virgins?"

Ruth smiled. "We Five have lived disturbingly sheltered lives. *Your* four friends showed up just as *my* four friends decided it was time to pack up and sneak out of the convent."

Cain took a deep breath. "All right, then, we're gonna have to really put our heads together to come up with something comparably convincing."

Ruth nodded. Cain and Ruth looked at one another for a moment without speaking. Then Cain burst into laughter. He shook his head and said, "This is such bullshit."

Ruth grinned. "Do you *think*?"

"But I appreciate that you were willing to help me out."

"You're welcome." Ruth finished off the rest of her caffé mocha. "So what are you gonna do?"

Cain shook his head. "I don't know yet. But this shouldn't be *your* problem. It was wrong for me to even think of lassoing you into it."

Ruth was still smiling. "I wouldn't have done it for free, Mr. Pardlow. You would have been required to buy me a generous number of mocaccinos and cranberry scones. Don't those scones look good?"

"I'll be right back."

"Oh, and get something for yourself. I hate to eat alone."

That night, Carrie and Molly sat in the I.C.U. waiting room watching television in the company of a large family whose father had just undergone triple bypass surgery. Even though most of the country was tuned to *Suddenly Susan*, which had the good fortune to come on after the very popular *Friends*, Carrie and Molly and the Coombes family of Coldwater, Mississippi, were tuned into a different network—and specifically to a program called *Living Single*, largely because the character played by Queen Latifah reminded the younger members of the family of their ambitious and outspoken Aunt Vertice.

It was Carrie who saw him first: standing in the doorway, peering into the room and looking like somebody who wasn't sure if he was in the right place. She touched Molly on the arm and pointed.

Molly and Pat made eye contact. He smiled and walked over to where Molly and Carrie were sitting. "Real sorry to hear about your mother," he said to Carrie, keeping his voice low so as not to disturb the rest of the group parked in front of the television.

Carrie managed a small, appreciative smile.

"Is the cafeteria downstairs still open? I wanna buy you both a cup of coffee."

"You two go on," said Carrie, making a gentle shooing gesture toward the door. "I should probably stay here." With a nod to the television: "I think Régine's mother is about to give her baby the business for being such a terrible snitch."

"You got *that* right, girl!" confirmed Mama Coombes, her eyes never leaving the screen.

Chapter Sixteen

Tulleford, England, August 1859

Lucile Mobry smiled, and in doing so presented seven very bright white teeth and one that was brown and wanted looking after. "Your timing, my dear Maggie, is most impeccable, for only yesterday my brother opened the doors of this house to all the members of our church—did your mother not tell you?—in a long delayed fete of welcome for the new minister. These rooms were filled with such resounding joy and unity of the spirit, and very nearly everything I could seize from the shelves of both our town baker and confectioner to offer as refreshing collation were put to plate. So please, my dear, take another sponge biscuit. We've plenty left over, and happily, Ruth is not here to contend with you, for she loves everything that is spongy and clotted and savoury and sweet. But you knew that already, didn't you?"

Maggie nodded, whilst effecting a look that was the living portrait of "The Girl Who Tried Very Hard to Look as if She Were Smiling."

"By the way," said Mobry, "where *is* our inveterately famished niece? Was she detained by Mrs. Colthurst when all the rest of you were released at noon?"

"Do you not know?" asked Maggie, and then with a tease, "Should *I* be the one to tell?"

"I can very well guess it, Maggie," said Miss Mobry. "She's seeing that young gentleman, isn't she? The one with whom she had such a lovely visit at the South Haven Tea Room only two days ago."

Maggie nodded.

Lucile Mobry continued, "He seems like a most agreeable young man—some name which begins with 'P,' and we are eager to meet him, especially if Ruth is considering the possibility of a lasting attachment."

"As for lasting attachment, Miss Mobry, I cannot answer. But you have nonetheless guessed his identity. It is Mr. Pardlow, who works in the mill." Maggie subsided into her chair and took a nibble upon the proffered sponge biscuit of earlier mention.

Mr. Mobry cleared his throat and said, "I'm certain our friend Maggie here has numerous things to which she must attend on this Saturday half-holiday, so we shouldn't long detain her, though your visits to this house, Maggie—with or without Ruth—are always welcome."

"Thank you," said Maggie, nodding and colouring slightly from the generous compliment.

"You've nearly finished your biscuit," observed Lucile Mobry. "Have a damson tart."

Maggie took a damson tart.

Mobry clasped his hands together, and, in the composed manner of a solicitor with intelligence of some import to convey to his client, he said, "*Now.* I've looked into the matter you brought before me and wish to report that I've succeeded in learning a bit of what it is you wish to know."

Maggie's eyelids uplifted in eager anticipation.

Mobry went on: "I consulted my diary for that period during which the baby—your sister's twin brother—was put out. Is there any other way to say it? For I do not wish to cast aspersions on your mother. It is no business of mine the reason she and your father could not keep the child."

"Mr. Mobry, you may cast all the aspersions you wish, for you would not be alone in questioning why my parents did such a thing. *I* know the reason, and I forgive my mother for it to the extent to which I'm able, but I would certainly understand if the liberality of my feelings for her, which comes from my having lived with her for so long and observed her in all her moods and dispositions, wasn't shared by others."

"'Put out.' There it is, Herbert; the phrase is acceptable. Now, move along." Lucile seemed at that moment as eager to hear what her brother had to say as was Maggie, and for very good reason: Herbert Mobry had kept Lucile purposefully uninformed about the matter due to a tendency on her part to speak broadly of things out of turn and without her brother's leave.

"Yes, yes," said Mobry. "The family's name was Caster. Well, it still is, as a matter of fact. Not a family of any great means, but Caster has always been a man of aspiration and promise. An apprentice cheesemonger here in Tulleford, he was set adrift when the cheese-man under whom he worked decided upon retirement to hand the shop over to his daughter."

Lucile Mobry shook her head and narrowed her eyes depreciatingly. "To think! A *woman* selling cheese! Carrying that offensive smell of Stilton and Double Gloucester upon her person like a lunatic's perfume. Maggie, dearest, do take the almond cake. Your hand seems to want it, the way it's suspended above the serving plate."

Maggie obligingly took the little almond cake and placed it on her own plate next to the little squares of half-nibbled pound cake and cocoa-nut cake.

"My sister," said Mobry, in an apologetic tone, "carries her distaste for fragrant cheeses into every possible conversation. As it turned out, the cheesemonger's daughter died only two years after taking over her father's shop—which is why she isn't there still."

"She had an abscess of the stomach," struck in Lucile, "no doubt from consuming mildewed food, which is exactly what I believe strongly fragrant cheeses to be."

"Sister, dear—pray may I proceed? Maggie is waiting to hear what I have learnt."

"I will remain silent," replied Lucile, pouting a little from the upbraid. "Please, my dear, take a sweet seedcake and gooseberry tart."

Herbert Mobry soldiered on. "The husband—your brother's new father—took employment here in town wherever he could find it, but then was required by unrelenting near impecuniousness to remove himself and his wife and adopted son to Manchester, where prospects were far better. In fact, he wasn't there for very long at all before he secured a most promising apprenticeship with a successful Mancunian cheesemonger, and eventually, as I understand it, became a top-sawyer cheeseman himself."

"And whatever became of the son?" asked Maggie. "I should so like some day to meet my brother."

"I have no doubt you will, dear girl," said Mobry. "Caster was very prompt in responding to my letter of enquiry, once I was able to learn of his precise whereabouts. He did not give me the name of his grown son, nor where *he* may be at present, but I warrant it is only a matter of my asking. I have business in Manchester next week, and I will make a point of paying a visit to Mr. and Mrs. Caster to learn these very things."

"Thank you ever so much, Mr. Mobry. Up until the point of my discovering the existence of my brother, Jane was the only one of us to have a brother, although she's hardly taken pride in the family affiliation. The thought that I too should have a brother, and that he should have been raised far removed from the venomous influence of my morally bankrupt father, is a most propitious development. I can scarcely believe it."

Miss Mobry took Maggie's hand and held it firmly. "Do not raise your hopes *too* high, my darling girl, for there are few brothers who are as exemplary in temperament and disposition as is *my* brother," and then with a mischievous wink in that very gentleman's direction, she codicilled, "except when he should be domineering and officious. But thankfully, such misbehaviour manifests itself infrequently. Please, have another——"

"I cannot endure another bite," interrupted Maggie, placing her hand upon her stomach in demonstration of the pain of overindulgence that was more than likely to strike her if she didn't suspend her bolting of everything Ruth's aunt was putting before her. Maggie uprose from her chair. "You've both been most kind, and I'm quite eager to find out everything there is to know about my brother. Perhaps, if the Casters are willing, I'll go thither myself."

"I would not advise it," Mobry cautioned. "Allow me first to lay the proper groundwork. It's a delicate matter to reunite brother and sister when the brother, perhaps just like you, never knew there was a sibling in the picture."

Maggie nodded. She departed after accepting compliments on behalf of her mother (in spite of the historical fact of the woman having given away to total strangers the fruit of her maternal loins) and after a promise was made by Mobry to report to Maggie every little tiddle and jot of what he gleaned from his impending trip to Manchester.

An hour later, having betaken herself to the town common where the fresh air helped her to think more clearly, Maggie came to rue her accommodating subscription to Mobry's proposal that his visit to Manchester should precede hers. "After all, he's *my* brother!" she proclaimed to the grass and to the shrubberies, "and I have every right to find things out for myself without need of an intermediary. Moreover, if I am to betake myself with all dispatch to that city not so very distant, the trip will prevent me from exchanging harsh words with my mother over why she would ever do such a fell and cruel thing as to give up my brother, and why, once she'd done it, she'd never found need to tell me about it."

Whereupon, Maggie rushed home and filled her little hand-portmanteau with a few overnight necessaries, and drew out a sovereign and some silver from the jewellery drawer in her bedroom bureau, and, not wishing to wait for her mother's return from her after noon visit with Mrs. Forrest, lest she miss the last train to Manchester, Maggie dashed off a note to Mrs. Barton, which said she was going away for the night. Maggie could not keep herself from adding, "to ascertain facts pertaining to my brother, which you should have named years ago, you blatant banisher of boy babies!" But then, thinking the last phrase superfluously hateful and not entirely accurate (there having been only *one* boy baby at issue, and the blatancy of its banishing having yet to be confirmed), she struck it through.

At the same time, Carrie could be found at the infirmary, standing next to the bed of her own mother and assisting the doctor and nurse in making the patient as comfortable as possible, for with burns as severe as those sustained by Mrs. Hale, not much more could be done other than the application of ointments and salves and the imposing of the salutary delirium of laudanum to put the sufferer into a state of anesthetic insensibility.

And where was Molly at this same time? Young Molly, having been released by her friend Carrie with strong words to the effect that she must go home and rest, was now in that very place and doing that very thing.

As it so happened, several other characters in our story found themselves, by either coincidence or design, in a different place still: the Fatted Pig Public House.

Here sate Jane Higgins and the man who sought that very after noon to win her favour, and decisively so: the outwardly charming and prepossessing Mr. Tom Catts, who was funny, and demonstrably endearing, and eager to see their two bumpers of old Madeira refilled until Jane's head was a-swim in a swirling pool of compliments and blandishments the likes of which she'd never heard in all her three-and-twenty years upon this earth. Close by and watching the two with the studied intensity of a drowsy infant was Jane's brother, a warm pint of porter clapped between two moist palms. As the room had become mist and haze for the increasingly alcohol-fuddled Jane, it was all that, as well, for Lyle Higgins, although, having grown used to living with his senses dulled and degraded, he had a stronger impression than did his sister of what was up and what was down, and what was up was this and no mistake: his sister Jane was become recipient of the most concerted form of love-making by a man who, unbeknownst to Jane, oozed dishonour and ill purpose from every pore.

And whatever was Higgins to do about it? Catts had been the first man ever to pay Jane more than casual notice. And were not disreputable overtures better than no overtures at all? It was a puzzlement, and he would sit with his porter and puzzle it out even after the two left the pub, directed for someplace he knew not.

Lyle Higgins would sit for upwards of a full minute. And then…

"Begging your pardon, lads," said Higgins, after decamping from his chair and tottering with tangled steps to the table next to that previously occupied by his sister and her spurious admirer. "Did you happen to overhear any of what was said by the two what was just here?"

"Aye," said the older and slightly more sober of the two young men. "What is it you'd be wanting to know?"

"Whither he was taking her. That's the thing."

"And why, pray, would you be wanting to know such a thing as that? Have you a claim upon the girl?"

"It depends on how you mean the question. She's my sister."

"Ah. Now that is a horse of a very different colour," said the older man. "So I'll tell ye. There was mention of the emporium. Would you know the place?"

"Indeed I would."

"Is the man up to no good?"

"I don't know it for a fact. I only know that I've crossed paths with his like afore."

"Then join us for one last pint as be a send-off to rescue your sister from a fate unknown."

Higgins bethought himself of the merits of the proposition and concluded that one drink more—strictly for the purpose of lubricating his steps in service to his mission of potential rescue—could do little harm, and perhaps very much good.

Jane Higgins and Tom Catts walked in the High Road with slow, careful steps to mask their having just spent the last two hours drinking intoxicating beverages at a public house (though Jane's incapacitation was far greater than her companion's). "You say you have a brother?" asked Catts, as Jane placed her hand upon his arm to steady herself.

"I have a brother, yes."

"And he lives with you in the back of the family shop?"

Jane nodded.

"Yet you know with certainty he won't be there at this hour."

"With certainty I know this."

"And how is it, Miss Higgins, that you are so confident in this belief?"

Jane stopped in her place. She looked at Catts with a mischievous twinkle in her eye. "Because that was him sitting at the table by the old clock—the one drinking alone and slipping into his wonted state of daily hibernation. He'll not show up until all the chickens have gone to roost, he being the one confused cockerel that sometimes forgets where it even lives."

Catts laughed hardily. "Miss Higgins, you are perhaps the most delightfully clever young woman I have ever met."

"And is cleverness my *only* attribute?"

"Not by any measure, my dear woman. Allow me to enumerate your other fine traits when we are finally alone."

The two went along thusly. But unbeknownst to Jane, they did not go along unobserved. For Jane was, in fact, being most closely watched by her friend Ruth through the window of a mutton pie shop. Only moments before, Ruth had slipped guiltily inside that establishment after bidding adieu to her friend Pardlow following their after noon tea. Though she had imbibed three cups of the tasty beverage, yet it was a most gastronomically unsatisfying hour and a quarter, for there was naught to be had of a victual nature—not even a fragment of a caraway-seed biscuit or a crumble of an old gooseberry scone. Thus a much-famished Ruth now stood alone in a dark corner of the shop gobbling a crusty meat pie with ravenous shame, and being glad the proprietor was nearly blind and did not identify her, until such point as that familiar gait, that instantaneously recognisable tall and gangly presence abroad, caught her eye.

Ruth betook herself to the window to get a better look, and therethrough saw the thing for what it was: her friend Jane being led away by one who appeared to revel in her lurching debility. In that frightful moment Ruth knew there could be nothing propitious to be gleaned from their companioned procession in the lane. On the contrary, Ruth believed Jane to be careening down the path to dire consequence.

The well-being of her friend being more important to Ruth than the last three or four bites of mutton pie, she fled the shop with all due haste and bent her hurried steps to the doctor's infirmary to enrol Carrie in her mission of rescue (for any confrontation effected by Ruth singly would be misinterpreted by its recipient as officious intrusion in the customary Ruth Thrasher manner).

There was one other familiar to the reader who was at the Fatted Pig. This one sate drinking grog and a great deal of it, which was not a good thing, since the man of reference was one who had pledged himself to absolute temperance: Molly's father, Michael Osborne. Osborne was drinking to steal himself away from thoughts of Sylvia Hale and from his ineffective attempts to minister to her in the wake of the tragedy of her house catching fire from a toppled candelabra. It was right in his mind that he should do so, for not only did he know the good woman and felt her to be his friend, he also considered himself to be a legitimate member of the healing profession. Yet when he attempted to offer assistance to her through the herbs and other unconventional treatments he had learnt during his years of itinerate practise, he was insolently driven from the premises by the town doctor and made to feel small and unworthy in his adopted line of work.

And as Osborne took stock of his life and tallied the *reputable* paths he might have taken, which had eluded him, and faced the sad verity that he was in fine neither healer *nor* the best provider for a wife and child who had died in his deficient custody, and was not by any means the best claimant upon the heart of anyone, let alone the woman he now wished to marry, and was not nearly the prosperous and sober-headed father he should have been for his daughter Molly, he sank into a pit of despair and self-doubt, and then, by and by, into a state of wretched self-loathing, which caused him to drink ever the more and to lose all sense of himself.

In her dream Molly found herself in the middle of a field of daisies, or was it pennywinkles or marigolds or sunflowers? Yes, it was great sunflowers, bent like genuflecting Mussulmans from the weight of their Brobdingnagian seeds. She wandered amongst the flowers and did not know if she should be happy in their crowding presence or affrighted, for there were a good many of them and they choked her path and rose up to her own height. And there seemed traces of something lurking behind them—creatures of some mysterious sort. Lurking, Molly wondered, or merely abiding? Was there a human form to the creatures? If so, were they known to her? Dreams are never unambiguously revelatory, and sometimes they are not revelatory at all. So Molly was happy to have done with this one when into the field intruded the sound of a hand rapping upon a door. There being no doors in the out-of-doors, Molly found in this incongruity reason to waken herself. Once she had come fully to herself and realised the knocking had not suspended, it became incumbent upon her to rise and discover the identity of the visitor to the rooms she shared with her father over the stationer's and prints-seller's shop (for there was no maid or footman to do it, and of her father's whereabouts at the moment she had not the faintest idea).

With no need to dress, for she had lain down upon her bed without bothering to take anything off or to put anything on which was more appropriate for retirement, Molly plodded sleepy-eyed to the door that communicated with the public corridor and found, when she opened it, the young man who had touched her heart as no man had ever done before.

The two fell into one another's arms without the exchange of a single word. The door was shut, and all the world that had no place or claim on this moment was shut out with it.

Chapter Seventeen

San Francisco, April 1906

The waiter swept his arm before him—silent indication that Cain and Ruth had their pick of all the tables in the empty tearoom.

"That sunny spot over there," suggested Ruth, "right next to the door to the balcony."

The waiter nodded and led the couple to the table Ruth had selected. But Ruth didn't sit down. Instead, she stepped through the open door. The balcony commanded a generous view of Dupont Street all the way down to Bush. Cain joined her.

"How did you find this place?" Ruth asked, her gaze drawn to a fish stand and the two men haggling stridently in front of it. This being a Saturday afternoon, Chinatown's main thoroughfare was bustling with boisterous, clamorous activity.

"I come here now and then. It's popular with some friends of mine."

"The men with whom you work at the advertising agency, or a different set?"

"A very different set. The proprietor of this place is happy to entertain the patronage of Occidentals for whatever their purpose might be. The Plague's been over for some time now, but non-

Asians—as a rule—still can't find the nerve to venture back into this part of town."

Ruth stepped back into the room and sat down. Her eyes wandered about the room. She counted herself among those who seldom came to Chinatown, though she'd heard that it had many interesting restaurants and tasty noodle shops. The room was gaudily ornamented in the Oriental style. The walls were painted bright blue and adorned with vertical Cantonese legends in silver and red. The tables were partitioned off from each other by large screens of elaborately gilded ebony, a material echoed in the tables and stools themselves, each stool inlaid with a slab of speckled marble. The gas chandelier suspended from the ceiling in the center of the room was strung with tinsel, which glittered even in the suffused light of its subdued gas jets.

"It seems to me," said Ruth, running her palm along the contour of the smoothly polished table, "that this is one of those places where San Franciscans come who want very much to be left alone."

The waiter handed Cain a menu and took a few steps back. "And you'd be totally correct in that assumption," said Cain, his eyes now lowered upon the menu.

"What happens in those curtained-off rooms over there?" asked Ruth with casual curiosity.

Cain glanced up. "Opium smoking, for the most part, but other things take place there too—human activities that aren't much spoken about in polite company. Do you mind if I order for the both of us?"

"Not at all."

Cain signed to the waiter that he was ready to place his order. "A pot of Black Dragon, if you please. And we'll have a platter of the pickled watermelon rinds and candied quince." Turning to Ruth: "Do you like dried almonds?"

"More than pickled watermelon rinds, I think."

Cain laughed. "Today you are being adventurous, whether you like it or not." To the waiter: "And the dried almonds. Thank you very much."

As the waiter receded from the room, two young Occidental men retreated on his heel. They had just emerged from one of the curtained rooms. Both were dressed in bright and unconventional colors, the more pavonine of the two fumbling with the tying off of a large purple cravat, which had apparently been removed and was now being restored to his ensemble.

Ruth arched an eyebrow. "Do you come here often?"

"Not as often as some."

"Well, Mr. Pardlow, your secret is safe with me, as is anything else you may wish to tell me this afternoon—including whatever it is that has necessitated our coming to your hideaway in the first place."

Cain, who had been distracted by the sudden emergence of the two young men, now purposefully returned his gaze to the woman seated across from him. "I've made a decision, Miss Thrasher—one which obviates the need for the two of us to do or *pretend* to do anything."

"Have you arranged with a few of your Barbary Coast associates to have certain individuals we know *shanghaied*? I hear there's a lot of that going on these days, and it could prove very advantageous in our present situation."

Cain hooted with laughter. "Now just what do *you* know about shanghaiing?"

"I *read*, Mr. Pardlow."

"*That*, Miss Thrasher, is undeniable fact." Cain settled back in his chair and laced his fingers. "My decision has to do with *me*, Miss Thrasher. I'm leaving San Francisco—moving to New York. I've come to the conclusion that it's only been my fondness for Pat Harrison that's kept me here for so long. But it's sheer lunacy for me to continue to maintain a professional and fraternal association with three men who utterly repel me, all for the, the, the tenuous privilege of sustaining a friendship with Mr. Harrison that is—if I may be honest—one-sided and totally unfulfilling. So I will fly, Miss Thrasher, and I will start my life anew. And you'll be happy to know that I require nothing from you but your valedictory good wishes."

"Which I'm most happy to give you. But what about Will Holborne's threats to expose you if you don't play out that diabolical game of theirs?"

"If he should follow up with those threats out of some diseased form of vindictiveness—if he, to be more specific, intends to divulge certain of my proclivities to my father's opponents in his race for state senate—then so be it. Dad's given me nothing in all these years that I couldn't have just as easily received in one of the city's most miserly orphanages. 'Everyone by his own bootstraps!' That's been the precept his four children were expected to live by. So what I now do with my own bootstraps should be of no relevance to him whatsoever. I can't believe it's taken me this long to come to such a simple conclusion."

"So just as we're becoming good friends, you take yourself three thousand miles away." Ruth made a comical moue with her mouth. "What arrant inconstancy!"

"Then come with me."

Ruth's eyes grew big.

"*You* want to write," he elaborated. "*I* want to write. So let's the two of us move to New York City and see if we can make a go of it."

Ruth didn't respond. She was thinking the proposition over. She was, in fact, giving it very serious thought while trying with all her might to tame the feeling of sudden, bursting euphoria that accompanied it.

She was thinking of it still when, after saying good-bye to Cain and upon her walk home, she spied her friend Jane and the advertising man named Katz headed in the direction of Higgins' Emporium. Both seemed drunk, and Ruth didn't like at all the way he was touching her in the bright light of day. Not wishing to face the situation by herself, Ruth quickly turned herself around and headed in the opposite direction—hurrying in a near trot to nearby St. Francis Hospital, where Carrie could be found attending her mother.

"Now this place is the real goods!" pronounced Tom as he followed Jane into the Higgins' back parlor. "Homey, but with a personal stamp. *Say*, nice touch: that floor vase with the what's-it grass and the gilded cattails."

"It's pampas grass. Thank you. My mother was very fond of cattails."

Tom resumed his impromptu appraisal of the room: "The only thing missing is a wheezy old parlor organ and a lumpy old easy chair for Papa Bear to smoke his pipe and browse the *Examiner*."

"We *had* an easy chair—*Dad's* easy chair, but we decided to sell it after he died." Jane trailed her finger through the layer of dust that had collected on the surface of a side table. "Lyle and I don't come into this room very often. There are just too many memories of him in here."

Tom, ignoring the opening Jane had created for him to say something appositely consolatory about her late father, threw himself with bodily irreverence upon the plush rose-colored upholstery of the sofa that was Jane and her brother's pride—a Victorian construction of beautiful, unblemished mahogany, marked by delicately carved swirls and scrolls. The sofa easily dominated the cramped little room. If Tom had shown even a passing nod of respect for it, Jane would have shared that it had also been her father's pride; indeed, he had bought it at an estate sale and could have slapped a high price tag on it, but preferred, instead, to keep it in the family parlor and out of the showroom altogether.

Tom stretched out his arms expansively to each side and began to trace the carved curls with lazy fingertips. Then his fingers flexed themselves into an unambiguous "come hither" gesture. Though she felt flattered to be so keenly beckoned, Jane didn't budge from her spot. Because this was the most advantageous place from which to fully absorb the picture put before her: the handsome Tom Katz, guest in her very own home, laughing and lounging in complacent manhood, his expression of desire for her careless and unambiguous, his legs spread ridiculously apart as men are prone to do when they wish to make statements about themselves which cannot be said aloud.

"Should I put on the percolator?" asked Jane. "My head is spinning from the wine. Yours is too, I'm sure."

"Damn the coffee! It isn't coffee I want. It's you. Come sit in my lap."

Jane sniggered in an unintended parody of a coquette. This response to Tom's request made her seem both girlish and absolutely ridiculous, for she *wasn't* a girl, nor was she some blushing geisha. "Your lap? No, Mr. Katz, I think not."

"Then come sit *next* to me." Tom patted the cushion and slid to one side to make a little more room for her.

"I'll do *that*, but only if you promise to be a gentleman."

"What a bughouse proposition!" remonstrated Katz. "I will do no such thing! Because it isn't a gentleman you want right now, Jane. It's *me*. And I want *you*, so let's end all the pussyfooting and get down to cases."

Jane took a tentative step toward the sofa. "I wouldn't know how to get down to cases if I tried."

"Have you never even been kissed?"

Jane shook her head.

"Then let me redress that egregious wrong right at the outset." Katz reached out in a move that was both imperiously demanding and somewhat suggestive of the clawing "gimme-gimme" of a spoiled, importunate child.

Jane, overcome by his hungry attention, took the necessary steps to place herself directly before him. He responded by depositing her ham-handedly into his lap.

"I will not—" Jane squirmed, scarcely able to get out the words. "I will *not* let you take the kind of brazen ad—advantage of me that your friend Mr. Castle took with Miss Barton last week."

Tom looked up at Jane, stretching his neck to meet her eyes because of how tall she sat upon his thighs. "What the deuce are you talking about? At Golden Gate Park?"

"Yes, at Golden Gate Park. In the Japanese gardens."

"None of this rings a bell."

"He didn't tell you? I'd assumed he would have bragged about it all over town."

"Honest, I don't know a thing about it," lied Tom with a look of feigned conviction.

Jane rolled her eyes, her own look one of feigned petulance. "Well, I'm certainly not going to give you all the contemptible details. Suffice it to say, your friend Jerry Castle was an absolute orangutan, and that isn't being very kind to orangutans."

"Well, that does sum the duck up perfectly." Tom pointed to the space next to him, and Jane took her cue to remove herself from his lap.

However, once detached from him, reattachment in a different manner was quickly achieved, as Tom pushed her backward into the curve of the sofa. To anyone in casual, slightly squinting observance of this picture it would look as if the two were being devoured by a great puckered roseate mouth. Jane could feel his weight upon her, his hot breath upon her neck.

"When I look at you," he cooed softly, his lips close to her ear, "I see a woman unlike any I've ever met."

"In what way do you mean?" said Jane, pushing the heels of her palms ever so slightly against his chest to signal her need for breathing room.

"So many *different* ways."

Jane reached up and, surprising herself with her boldness, began to thread her fingers through his tousled hair.

"But one way most especially. You're a woman who is needful of something she's never experienced before, or more than likely will ever experience again."

Jane now permitted her maundering fingers to move down his temples to his cheeks, to caress each with lambent fingertips. Then after pronating her wrists with the balletic litheness of the sylphic romance-novel heroine whom she imagined herself at this moment to be, she tenderly stroked his face with the backs of her hands. "You've misspoken, Tom. You mean 'more than likely experience' with any other man but *you*." She smiled at the thought that was forming inside her still cloudy head. "Because once you are mine and I am yours, I intend to be faithful and true—to never seek intimacy with anyone else."

"Nicely put, Jane, but that isn't what I meant at all." Tom caught Jane's right hand and brought it to his lips.

He kissed her knuckles. She closed her eyes in silent rapture, but then just as suddenly opened them and asked him point-blank: "What *do* you mean?" Her look now registered undisguised confusion.

"That I have no intention of spending the rest of my life with you."

"I don't understand."

"It isn't difficult. You are, as I've often said, a very bright girl. Probably the smartest of your set. Smart enough to know there'd be nothing dottier for me to do than to be married to you for even ten minutes, let alone for the remainder of my days. Posi*to*rily bughouse."

Jane wanted up. Tom released his hold on her. She slipped out from under him and sat straight up and patted her pompadour back into place and made adjustments to her calico skirt and blue linen blouse (both purchased from Pemberton, Day & Co. with her shopgirl discount, though it still took a bite out of her small salary). Finally, she said between pursed, angry lips, "Is this the person you become when you drink, Mr. Katz? A repellent one-night roué?"

"I sobered up a good while ago."

"Then you'll have no trouble understanding me clearly when I say that it's time for you to go. If your pursuit of me has only been for the purpose of a single night of debauched conquest, which you'll either conveniently deny any memory of to your friends or, or blame on all those Manhattan cocktails we had at the Fatted Pig, then let me serve notice here and now: I won't go along with even a minute more of it."

Calmly: "You'll go along with it."

"What did I just say?"

Tom got up from the sofa. "Get up."

Jane remained seated on the sofa.

"Get up. I want to show you something." Jane rose slowly, warily. Tom reached out and took Jane—not by the hand, but by the wrist, as one leads a recalcitrant child who will not come otherwise—over to the mirror on the wall. He positioned her before it. "Take a good look at yourself. What do you see?"

Jane looked at her reflection in the glass. The gaslight was low. She hadn't bothered to turn up the flame when they'd first entered the room, thinking that Tom would appreciate the romantic mood created by the muted lighting. Now he did the unthinkable. He reached over and turned up the jet himself—all the way to its limit. It flared obscenely, flooding the room with harsh bright light. In that unforgiving illumination, every flawed feature which lived upon Jane's face stood out in exaggerated relief: the "horsey" nose, eye sockets set so deeply into her face that the dark brown of her globes seemed to disappear almost entirely in their retreat, a chin that jutted protuberantly like a witch's in a children's fairy story.

"That's what I look like," said Jane to herself, mesmerized by the starkness of the image before her. "A witch."

Yet Tom was not content with her only *thinking* about the way she looked. "Say what you see," he said, his voice steely, cold. "It's just you and me. No one but us is listening."

"I see a—a hideous woman."

Tom shook his head. "I wouldn't use the word 'hideous.' That's not being very kind to yourself, now, is it? I would use the less punishing word, 'unattractive.' But hideous, or unattractive, or just plain ugly or just plain *plain*, it's all the same, isn't it?" Tom gestured with a casual hand toward the image in the mirror. "No man wants to make love to a woman who looks like this."

Jane took a moment to reply. The words were freighted with such pain that she could hardly bring them to voice. "Then why do *you?*"

Tom smiled. "Because, my dippy darling, I and I alone have the capacity to ignore your repulsiveness in my mission of mercy. This is what I've always sought to do—from that first afternoon at Pemberton, Day when we discussed the photography session in Miss Colthurst's absence. I felt pity for you, working among all those pretty young women, and looking the way you did—the way you *do.*" Standing behind her, he moved his head slightly to the side to better see the reflected image Jane was beholding with a mixture of sadness and absolute horror. "I wanted to give you that thing you'll never have otherwise, because, speaking as a man, even ugly men have no use for ugly women. We men—let me speak frankly here— we know *our* worth is gauged not by the way we look, but by what we are capable of *doing*—the things we make of our lives. A woman's worth, on the other hand, is measured largely by her looks, her shape and carriage, by that sparkle in her eye—all of these things appealing to a man in a primal sort of way. This desire in the human male to seek out an ideal—it's the way we've evolved, how biology tells a man to be. A man doesn't go looking for a Jane. He seeks out a Molly or a Carrie. You know exactly what I mean. This is the quest. This is the game. The plain Janes of the world play no part in this game, in this 'chase,' unless, of course, they get lucky. But I doubt you are ever going to get lucky, Jane. Look at yourself."

Jane turned away. "I don't want to look at myself anymore."

Tom turned Jane around so she was forced to look at *him*. "I wanted to give you something tonight, Jane. I wanted to show you what it was like to be with a man, so you'll have that one special memory to sustain you."

The room was spinning, whirling about her. Jane was still very drunk and not used to this feeling; it had been a sort of twirling, pinwheel kind of dream, but now it had transmogrified itself into a terrible, ugly, formless nightmare. Yet as Tom was speaking to her in a soft and confiding voice, the ragged edges of the nightmare were being smoothed away. In their place was a form of tortuous, perverted kindness. Jane had a sense of the distortion. She had the feeling that what there was left of respect for self was being whittled away by the man who stood next to her, gauging her worth by his own selfish measure, leaving her a hollow reflection of who she used to be. And she was too weak to fight it. And she hated herself for it. She hated herself for submitting to him based on that singular desire to know what it would feel like in those next moments *to be loved*, even if the love wasn't real.

And in the end she became a helpless victim to that need, regardless of the price it cruelly exacted from her dignity.

Tom ran the back of his hand across Jane's wet cheek in a gesture which replicated what she had done only moments before to him. The act *represented* great tenderness of feeling, whether or not there was any sincerity behind it.

He dropped his voice to a seductive whisper. "I'm giving you the chance to see what the world would be like if you had been born beautiful. This is my gift to you, Jane."

Jane's eyes brightened. Then in the next moment all the light went out. "But it would only be pretend."

"Of course it would only be pretend. But won't we have fun with it all the same?"

Tom Katz took Jane to the sofa and undressed her and made carnal love to her. And all the while, he did not look at her. But she looked at him and imagined in those moments all the things she had imagined in all the hundreds, the thousands of moments of longing for an intimacy that had been denied to her.

And *then* when it was over...

But then when it was over...

A most horrible thing: the thing he made her do.

After the two had dressed, or at least after she had covered her nakedness with her pretty pink silk chemise (purchased from the damaged-goods table in the basement of Pemberton, Day, because there was a long snag in it that could not be repaired), he stood up. He asked her to kneel before him.

She obeyed.

"Now look up at me. Look up at me, Jane. We aren't finished yet. There. That's a girl. I want you to thank me."

It took a moment for her to form the words. "Thank you," she mumbled. Her eyes had strayed. He snapped his fingers to return them to his face.

"Say it as if you mean it."

"Thank you," said Jane in a stronger voice. "Please go."

"First, you must tell me that you'll always be grateful for what I've done for you today."

Jane shook her head. "I'm not grateful. I want to die."

"You'll be grateful once your head is clear and you've had time to think about it. I'm going now. You don't have to see me out. In fact, I'd rather you not. I'd like to remember you in parting—there on the floor, wanting more—begging me with your eyes for more."

Jane shook her head again. The word was all but inaudible: "Go."

Tom left. Jane did not move. She remained on her knees for several minutes, even as her kneecaps began to ache from the hardness of the oak floorboards. And then she lay herself down, lay on her side, pulling her knees up tight against her stomach. She closed her eyes. The room was no longer spinning. The cloud was lifting. She was thinking more cogently. She was thinking about what she'd just done—what she had *allowed* herself to do, what she had intentionally surrendered herself to.

This is how Ruth and Carrie found her. They went to her and knelt next to her, Ruth taking her carefully into her arms like the Madonna in the *Carracci Pietà*.

"What did he do to you?" Carrie asked in a terrified whisper.

Jane didn't answer.

"Tell us what he did," said Ruth. "Tell us, Jane. Did he do the thing we think he did?"

"Walk me to my bed, sisters. My legs are weak."

Having tucked Jane into bed, Ruth put the question to her again. Jane smiled and said, "You're so sweet to come."

"But we came too late," said Carrie softly. "If only Lyle had been here."

"I'm here now," said a voice at the door. Ruth and Carrie turned. Lyle was standing in the hallway just outside Jane's bedroom, his face hidden in shadow.

"Where were you?" snapped Ruth.

"I came as fast as I could. I saw her leave from the Fatted Pig saloon, and I came."

"Did you *crawl*, you useless bastard?" cried Ruth. She had been running her hand through Jane's perspiration-drenched hair. Now her hand stopped so she could point accusingly at Jane's brother.

Carrie had begun to cry. "Oh stop it, Ruth. Just stop it. He cares about her. He's here. He came. He's here."

Ruth turned back to Jane. "Tell us what happened."

"I'll tell you, yes."

Jane swallowed.

Lyle stepped into the room. His head was half bowed and he was holding his cap at his waist with both hands, with respect and reverence, as if he were visiting a deathbed or a body upon a bier.

Jane formed her words with great difficulty: "He raped me."

"I thought so," said Ruth, speaking for Carrie and Lyle as well.

"But it isn't what you think," said Jane.

"What do you mean?"

"He—"

"Yes?"

"Raped—"

"Yes?"

"My heart, Ruth. He raped my *heart.*"

The blows came fast and furious, but they were clumsy and generally missed their mark. Pat was dodging them with some success, even as he snatched up his clothes and tried to find a way around the drunken, enraged man who looked at him with flaming, murderous eyes. Molly screamed at her father to stop. She screamed that she *wanted* Pat there, that she loved Pat and wanted to be with him.

Michael Osborne heard none of this. There was a fire in his head and it would not be put out until he had killed the young man who had come to his flat to take his daughter's heart away from him—to steal the only thing left of the family he once possessed in full.

And so he swung and largely missed, and picked up a railback chair and pitched it in Pat's direction, but it struck nothing but the wall, where it splintered into pieces. Molly didn't suspend her screams. Pat made it past the madman and into the front parlor (where Osborne saw his dental patients), and he very nearly made a clean escape with both life and limb intact when Molly's father overcame him, and with the kind of bodily strength that comes only to those for whom strength is sought to do the most incredible kind of good or the most incredible kind of bad, Michael Osborne shoved Pat toward the window with such terrific force that Molly's young lover was propelled through the shattering panes of glass and the brittle framework of the sash and out the window and directly into the smooth ceramic enamel of the enormous tooth, which swung wildly from the impact, and, though fixed to the projecting wrought-iron rod above, did not prevent Pat's plunge to the concrete sidewalk three floors below.

Where he lay.

Motionless.

Chapter Eighteen

Zenith, Winnemac, July 1923

Maggie was the last to hear what had happened. Ruth had tried to reach her by telephone all through the night, but she wasn't home. Maggie wasn't even in Zenith. The previous morning, and in spite of her mother's vociferous opposition, she'd put herself on the train to the Winnemac state capital, Galop de Vache, for the purpose of meeting Mr. and Mrs. Caster, the adoptive parents of the brother whose existence she'd only recently discovered. Maggie had done this even though Herbert Mobry had asked her to wait until after he'd had the chance to pay his own visit of inquiry to the Casters.

Herbert and Lucile Mobry hadn't known she'd gone—that is, not until Clara Barton told them. She told them over late-morning Denver sandwiches at Lily's Lunch Box on Chaloosa Street.

"The girl certainly has a mind of her own!" Lucile had marveled aloud.

"Oh, she's every bit as stubborn and willful as her father," Clara exasperatedly agreed. "But what was I to do? Block the door with my body? She was put into such a foul mood when I confirmed it all. Yes, I could have told her years ago. But I never saw any purpose to it. Why should I give her one more reason to hate me?"

"Maggie doesn't hate you, not at all," said Herbert, shaking his head in his wonted display of pastoral, avuncular understanding.

"There, there," Lucile Mobry contributed. Clara had been a longstanding member of the congregation Herbert Mobry used to shepherd, and the Mobrys continued to feel responsible both for Clara's spiritual health and for her general sense of well-being.

"But traveling to Galop all alone—" Clara shook her head.

"Maggie's a big girl," Herbert concluded. "One night alone in Galop will do her no harm. And once she's had the chance to talk to the Casters about her brother, she'll return to Zenith in amazingly good spirits. You'll see."

Maggie didn't return in good spirits. Neither Mr. Caster nor Mrs. Caster happened to be in Galop de Vache during the brief period of her stay. From one of the Casters' forthcoming neighbors, Maggie discovered that her brother's adoptive parents were 330 miles away in Madison, Wisconsin, attending a convention of the Midwestern Association of Cheese Purveyors.

Even worse: Maggie had come home to discover the following note stick-pinned to the kitchen Hoosier cabinet:

> *Maggie,*
> *In your absence a terrible thing has happened. Talk to one of your sisters and they will tell you all about it. I have gone to look for Mr. Osborne and pray that I can find him.*
> *Your mother*

Maggie telephoned the Tabernacle offices and was told by Miss Colthurst's assistant Miss Dowell that none of her friends would be coming in for choir rehearsal that day.

"Why?"

"You don't *know* why?"

"If I knew why, would I ask you why? Where's Miss Colthurst? May I speak with her?"

"Sister Vivian left not five minutes ago. She and Sister Lydia are on their way to Zenith General."

"Who's in the hospital?" asked Maggie, now thrown into a panic.

"I don't know the young man. Someone is knocking on the door and I'm all alone this morning. Goodbye."

As Maggie was hurrying to the door to catch the streetcar that would take her straight to Zenith General Hospital, the jingle of the telephone bell summoned her back to the instrument. Ruth was on the other end of the wire. "It's Pat Harrison, Maggie. He's badly hurt. I'll tell you all about it when you get here."

"My mother left me a note. She said she was out looking for Mr. Osborne."

There was a brief silence. Then Ruth said, "She might start by checking the city jail."

Maggie found her four sisters on the fifth floor of Zenith General Hospital in the "Family and Friends Waiting Room." There was now someone else besides Carrie's mother who had taken up residence on that floor. Pat had been brought in the night before with multiple broken bones, facial contusions, and internal hemorrhaging. The prognosis was dismal.

Carrie and Molly were blanch-faced and baggy-eyed, though both had been partially revived by carry-cups of coffee, which Ruth had brought up from Dunker's, an around-the-clock luncheon across the street.

Ruth was sitting next to Jane, holding her hand. Jane looked nearly as haggard as Carrie and Molly. Her other hand—the one not clasped by Ruth—was shaking with an almost palsy-like tremor. Maggie looked over the young women in the room as one surveys a field of battle in its aftermath. She had never seen her sisters so broken and battered. Especially Jane. In moments of crisis, it was the oldest of We Five who usually stepped forward to take the reins. It was Jane Higgins who devised the best course of action, Jane who rallied the troops, Jane who annealed resilience through her emotional strength and her unwavering affection for her sisters.

But on this day it was a very different Jane who sat before Maggie. She was shell-shocked, frighteningly uncommunicative. Jane seemed to be locked inside her own head, running a terrible scene over and over again through the movie projector in her mind.

Carrie told Maggie what had happened to Pat. Ruth told Maggie what had happened to Jane.

Maggie was overwhelmed. She sat down. She put her hand to her mouth as if to hold back a scream.

Ruth got up and went to Maggie. "Where's Molly's father right now?" Maggie asked.

"Still at large. Everyone seems to be at large this morning, though we now have *you* back. *And* Cain. He's the only one of that bunch to show up this morning." Ruth added acidly, "Apparently, the other three can't spare a single moment from their busy class schedules to look in on their dying friend."

The phrase "dying friend" educed fresh tears from Molly, and Ruth found it necessary to offer a hurried apology for her callousness as Carrie descended upon Molly anew to deliver hugs and pats of sororal sympathy.

"Cain came," said Jane, nodding. "I always knew he wasn't like the others."

Ruth was about to respond, but Molly preempted her: "Pat was good too. *Is* good. He isn't like the others either!"

"Anyway, the two 'good' ones are down the hall in the men's ward," said Ruth. "Cain's with Pat. He's been with him since before I got here."

Ruth took a deep breath preparatory to saying something that very much needed to be said. "Now that the five of us are all together, there's something we have to talk about—something I need to tell you about our Aggie friends." With the word "friends," Ruth's

tone shifted from flat and reportorial to unambiguously contemptu-
ous. "It wasn't by coincidence they came after us the way they did.
It was all planned. They planned it together."

It was Molly and Jane who reacted the strongest to this statement. Jane, who had returned her gaze to her lap, now bolted up, her
eyes flashing with sudden painful interest. Likewise, Molly, who'd
always assumed her budding relationship with Pat to be engendered
by nothing but the pure Ivory Soap attraction of their two hearts,
tossed a hard and suspicious look in Ruth's direction.

Ruth was ready to explain, but she was silenced by the sudden appearance of Vivian Colthurst and Sister Lydia DeLash Comfort, who
had come to offer prayer and comfort to the young man who had
been brutally defenestrated not four blocks from her beautiful, nearly completed Tabernacle of the Sanctified Spirit. Sister Lydia went
straight to Molly. "I understand, Miss Osborne," said the evangelist,
"that you're quite fond of Mr. Harrison and he's quite fond of you."

Molly nodded.

"Then by all means you must come along with me to the men's
ward. Together we shall offer up a fervent prayer of entreaty, that
he will survive his injuries and live to love you even more than he
does now."

Molly wept. She nodded in full concert. Then she said faltering-
ly, "But you need to know—you *have* to know, Sister Lydia—that it
was my father who did this terrible thing to him."

"Yes, I know that already, little darling," Sister Lydia answered
softly. "And I've been praying for your unfortunate father as well."

Sister Lydia held out her hand for Molly to take.

"Please wait," interposed Carrie.

Sister Lydia turned and smiled benignly at Carrie. "Don't worry, child. We intend to visit your poor mother next."

"That isn't—thank you, Sister, but—Ruth—she was going to
tell us something. It's something I think we all need to hear. It's
something that, perhaps, *you* should hear too."

Ruth confirmed this statement with a nod.

"It's about those boys you were telling me about, isn't it, Ruth?" asked Miss Colthurst.

Ruth nodded. And then Ruth told everything Cain had told *her*. She left out details particular to Cain's unique status among his friends, but she didn't hold herself back in describing each aspect of the game that was to have used We Five as pawns...or worse. Ruth couldn't avoid including what had happened to Jane, even though in doing so Jane was forced to relive the vile memory.

After Ruth had finished, Sister Lydia placed a hand upon Ruth's arm and said, "Thank you so much for sharing this with me. But it's over now, thank God. These men can't hurt any of you ever again now that their plans have been exposed."

Sister Lydia was thinking, mulling the whole matter over in her head. Whenever Sister Lydia DeLash Comfort thought—especially when she worked on her sermons late into the night—she paced. We Five gave her a wide berth.

"No. As a matter of fact, I don't think we can close the door on all this just yet. 'Vengeance is mine,' sayeth the Lord. But the Bible *also* tells us that the Lord helps those who help themselves. And not a one of you girls is helping yourself by walking away from men like this without making them come to terms with what they've done. I'm concerned, as well, about what happens in the future when they decide to play this filthy game again—this time with a different group of girls."

Sister Lydia continued to pace as she cogitated.

"I know the president of the A&M. He's one of my biggest financial supporters. And he's a friend of your brother's too, isn't he, Sister Vivian?"

Miss Colthurst nodded.

"Then I see no reason these men shouldn't be held to account for their actions and expelled from the college, and the sooner the better. This very afternoon, in fact. Monstrous behavior like this shouldn't go unaddressed and unpunished." Sister Lydia checked a smile. "I'm afraid my Old Testament is showing."

"But you can't mean *Pat*," said Molly in a quiet but urgent voice.

"No, darling. We won't expel your Mr. Harrison, of course not. Sister Ruth, I assume you'd like to make the same appeal on behalf of your Mr. Pardlow?"

Ruth nodded. "He can't have that kind of blemish on his school record. You see, Cain's decided to leave Zenith and enroll in the U. of W. in the fall."

"I see," said Sister Lydia, the suggestion of a sly grin now breaking through. "It seems that 'Old Gang' of theirs is breaking up six ways from Sunday. And it's all for the best, girls. Now, Molly, let's go see your Mr. Harrison. And as for the rest of my Quintet of Songful Seraphim, Sister Vivian has told me she can get along without you for the next couple of days. But then I need the five of you back among the angels. Our inaugural service, in which you will all play so vital a part, is only a few days away."

As Sister Lydia began making her rounds (word of her impromptu appearance at Zenith General had now begun to circulate, and the renowned faith-healing evangelist simply could not, in good conscience, confine her bedside visits to only Pat Harrison and Sylvia Hale), Ruth Thrasher and Vivian Colthurst excused themselves from the company of Maggie, Carrie, and Jane, and went down to Dunker's for doughnuts and coffee.

"There's something I didn't say upstairs that you should know, Vivian," Ruth eventually worked herself up to saying.

"Yes?"

"Cain's asked if I might move to Mohalis with him. He proposed that we attend the university together."

Vivian nodded. "I've always *wondered* why a girl of your intelligence and with your obvious gift for words—why you never considered going to college."

Ruth waited to answer until after the waitress had set down the plate of doughnuts and cups of coffee. Then she said, "I never thought there was much need for it. There are plenty of writers who've made important careers for themselves without an advanced education. But Cain said that given the opportunity, I should take it."

"And *this* is that opportunity. Ruth, dear, do you love this man?"

"Not in the way I'm expected to. But he and I are becoming very good friends—*close* friends."

Vivian Colthurst nodded as she dunked. She tapped the doughnut on the rim of her cup to keep it from dripping on its way to her mouth. She thought for a moment and then asked, "Won't he be disappointed when he finds out you aren't the kind of woman he *thinks* you are?"

Ruth smiled and shook her head. "He knows how I am. And I know how *he* is. It's the kind of arrangement a lot of people like us are making these days. Society dictates that we must hide who we are, so if we find someone we're fond of with whom to do our hiding, why shouldn't we be with that person?" Ruth touched Vivian's hand. There was nothing in the gesture that one might not see on any given day between two female friends. But the touch meant something very special for *these* two friends.

Vivian Colthurst spoke softly and without smiling. "Why shouldn't you be with that person, you ask. Because you should be with *this* person—the person sitting right across from you."

Ruth shook her head. "I don't want a Boston marriage, Vivian. I want a *Winnemac* marriage. I think Cain does too, or he wouldn't have asked me to go with him. Besides, Mohalis is only a short interurban ride from Zenith. You'll continue to see me and I'll continue to see you. And there will be a nice advantage to your seeing me *there*: we'll be removed from the curious looks and the outright scowls of all those men and women of the 'Sanctified Spirit,' who are quick to judge in the name of their blessed Jesus." Ruth laughed. "Good gracious God, Vivian, leave it to *you* to pick a profession which offers no romantic flexibility whatsoever. You might as well give up your job as choir director for Sister Lydia and, and join a convent!"

Vivian tried to hold back, but Ruth had gotten the better of her and she acknowledged the comical irony in her situation with a shrug and a grin. "Your Mr. Pardlow—" said Vivian when the feeling of merriment had somewhat subsided, "—he's been sitting in that ward right next to his friend all this time?"

Ruth nodded. "He told me he thinks somebody should be there for those moments when Pat wakes up—so one of the nurses can be called to give him another shot of morphine to put him back to sleep again."

"Is Pat talking? Does he say anything during those moments when he's awake?"

"Not much. Cain says that once or twice he asked for his mother."

"And where *is* his mother?"

"She's dead. But in his delirium he doesn't seem to know this."

"And the boy's father?"

"In Hollywood. He's a carpenter. He works in pictures. But I don't think anyone's been able to reach him."

"Then it's good that Cain is there."

Ruth nodded.

Cain had moved his chair away from the bed and put it against the wall to give Sister Lydia more room. She spoke a few words to Pat, who could not hear her; the latest dose of morphine having placed him into a deep, almost coma-like sleep. Then she knelt next to the bed and clasped her hands prayerfully. "Kneel with me, Molly," she entreated. "You too," she said to Cain, over her shoulder. The three knelt together as Sister Lydia DeLash Comfort prayed first for Pat's speedy recovery and then for the redemption of his soul, should God decide instead to take him home. Molly nodded and amened as tears coursed down her cheeks. Next to her, Cain also nodded, his own eyes moist, his throat constricting as he fought the urge to blubber unmanfully in the presence of these two women and all the men bedded in the crowded ward.

That night Maggie and Molly telephoned all over Zenith in search of their missing parents. Molly was sure the two middle-aged lovers— one a fugitive and the other a very likely accessory after the fact—had found one another and were now hiding somewhere in town. Maggie wondered if they'd blown town altogether. She wondered this because Clara had failed to come home. When Maggie returned from the hospital that night, she found their house un- changed from the state it had been in earlier in the day. She also found no new hurriedly scrawled missive pinned to the Hoosier.

Nor had Molly's father left his daughter a single word as to *his* whereabouts. Molly knew why. Once he surfaced, he'd be nabbed by the police right away, a hot warrant for his arrest having been issued shortly after the incident.

As Molly sat on the edge of Maggie's bed, fighting sleep, Maggie made mention of her Uncle Whit's cabin in the northern woods of Minnesota. "He doesn't go there anymore, but he never sold it. He once told Mama and me we could use it whenever we liked."

"You think that's where they might have gone?" asked Mol- ly, holding her white muslin nightgown bunched in her hand. She had quickly packed up this and a few other night things from the apartment she shared with her father, which now sat empty and tomb-like, the shattered window a jagged reminder of what had happened there, the concrete ledge outside still littered with splin- ters of broken glass.

Maggie nodded. "The police would have no knowledge of the place. Mama's had hardly any contact with Uncle Whit since his divorce from my aunt. It would be the perfect spot for the two of them to hide out."

"But for how long?" asked Molly.

"Long enough for us to go there and help them figure out what they should do. If it were me, I'd leave the country altogether and go to Canada."

Molly got up. Her look had turned dark and angry. "Why would I even *want* to help Dad after what he's done? And your mother is nothing like the M-O-T-H-E-R in that disgustingly saccharine Eva Tanguay song."

"Let's respect a rule here, Molly. *You* may vilify your father and *I* may vilify my mother but we aren't permitted to *cross*-vilify."

Molly laughed sardonically. "Even though that's all *you've* been doing since those two discovered they had feelings for one another?"

Maggie took the bait. "And how right I was. I *knew* your father wasn't over his drinking. I just didn't realize how dangerous he became when he got himself *totally* sozzled."

Molly shot daggers at Maggie, and Maggie shot daggers back. "Do you want me to go?" Molly finally asked between clenched teeth.

"Only if you want to. Let it not be said I turned my back on you in your time of need."

A silence passed. Then Molly began to think aloud. "I probably *should* go. I'm not a baby. I am quite capable of spending the night in my own apartment alone. Besides, if Dad's going to be sitting in a jail cell for the next twenty or thirty years, I should probably start getting used to being by myself."

"Oh, I wouldn't think they'd keep him in that jail cell for anywhere near that long."

"Why do you say that?"

"Because Pat's probably going to die, so your dad will more than likely get the noose."

"I hate you so much right now, Maggie, I can't even see straight."

"Then by all means rid yourself of me by leaving. Don't let me stop you."

"I'm going to 'phone for a taxi, if it's all right with you. I'll leave a nickel on the table."

"You do whatever you like," said Maggie, quickly turning away. Then just as quickly she swung back around. "You know, none of this would have happened if you hadn't fallen for Pat—if you hadn't done the very thing that sinister game *expected* you to do."

"Pat wasn't playing the game like the others. I just know it."

"And just *how* do you know this, Molly?"

Molly brought herself to within a few inches of Maggie's face. "Because Pat's too *stupid* to play a game that thorny. There. I said it. I fell in love with a good-looking idiot. And I'll deal with the consequences without any help from *you*."

And with that, Molly, along with her night bag and her wad of nightgown, fled into the night.

At the hospital the clock in the corridor struck two. The men's ward was dark and quiet save for the sound of a couple of patients snoring lightly and another man moaning, but not too loudly, in response to his nocturnal pain. Cain, sitting in his stiff, upright chair, dozed off. It was only for the briefest moment, but was still long enough to nearly topple him headlong from his chair. One of the nurses had asked earlier if he might not be more comfortable at home, or at least stretched out upon one of the divans in the solarium, which was often used to billet those who wished to spend the night close by.

"Maybe later," he'd replied. "I'm fine right here for now."

"Well, I'll be at the nurse's desk just outside if you need any-thing." She smiled pleasantly. "You're a good and devoted friend to sit up with Mr. Harrison like this."

Cain nodded. Circumstances did not permit him to give an even more revelatory response to the nurse's thoughtful observation.

At a couple of minutes past two, Pat Harrison woke from his mor-phine induced sleep of the dead. But he was hardly awake. Like each of the three other awakenings Cain had witnessed, Pat asked only for his mother, wondering in fractured words interposed between strug-gles for breath when she would come to see him. Each time, and not even knowing if Pat had understood a single word of his reply, Cain told his friend that he shouldn't worry; she was on her way. Cain hadn't the heart to divulge the hard truth: that Pat's mother had died several years earlier after a lengthy bout with tuberculosis.

Cain supposed he could say the same thing he'd said before. And yet, something about the disconsolate way Pat asked the question—as if, in spite of his jumbled cognition, he was getting the strong sense that she *wouldn't* be coming—motivated Cain to say some-thing quite different this time.

At that instant, Cain's mind flashed on a movie he'd seen a few years earlier. It was a D. W. Griffith picture starring Lillian Gish, *The Greatest Thing in Life*. There was a scene in the movie that had always haunted him. It took place during the Great War and in-volved a white officer and a mortally wounded Negro soldier. As the Negro was slipping away, he asked for *his* mother, and the officer hadn't known what to say. He did know, though, that the soldier under his command would die easier if he thought his mother was at his side, easing him lovingly through the dark passage into death. Cain remembered vividly what happened in that next moment: the officer, pretending to be the dying soldier's mother, reaching over and kissing the young soldier.

The scene touched Cain deeply, the image of that kiss resonating for him long after he'd left the theatre.

Cain raised himself up from his chair. He placed a cool hand on Pat's feverish forehead. Pat, his eyes swollen tight from lacerations to his face, asked again if his mother was there. Had she finally come? The hand that touched him: was it hers?

Cain answered yes.

And then Cain placed himself halfway upon the bed so he could embrace Pat as a mother would embrace a child—holding him close and protectively in his arms. And then Cain, playing the part of Pat's mother, kissed him on the lips.

Pat accepted the kiss. He held the kiss tightly upon his lips as Cain slid back from the bed and into the chair.

And then, most remarkably, the cloud lifted from Pat's face and he smiled.

And then he spoke.

"Cain?"

Cain leaned in. "What is it, Paddy?"

With labored breath: "Tell my mother she needs a shave."

And in that next moment the rising and falling of Pat's chest, his attempts to breathe through lungs that were crushed and nearly useless, stopped.

Pat Harrison was dead.

Cain stared at Pat's lifeless body for a moment. Then he got up and went out to the nurse's desk to tell her what had happened. She telephoned the doctor who was on night duty, and went into the ward to confirm what Cain had reported. Cain stood next to the nurse's desk. He watched the night doctor and one of the other night nurses racing down the corridor, listened to their shoes clicking isolate upon the linoleum. He watched them disappear into the ward. Cain walked over to the swinging doors and observed attempts to revive the patient. Then came a shake of the head and mumbled instructions to the nurses from the somber doctor.

Cain walked down the silent corridor to a room he'd looked into earlier that day—the one with the locked glass cabinets lining the walls—the cabinets that had bottles and vials and ampoules inside. He looked for one with skull and crossbones on the label. He was set to break the glass and take something from inside which he could ingest to end the overwhelming agony of loss he was feeling in that moment—to remove himself to either a state of absolute nothingness or to some beautiful Afterworld where he might get lucky and find Pat among the angels.

But in that next moment he recalled from his chemistry class at the college that there were few medicines in modern times—even those Victorian holdovers, the mercury and arsenic compounds— that healed and killed with equal efficacy, few chemical substances to be found in a hospital medicine cabinet that could be depended upon to induce an instantaneous and relatively painless death.

Which is why Cain Pardlow withdrew from the hospital's medicine supply room without breaking a single pane of glass—why, still unseen by anyone in his quest for infinite peace, he found himself in an unoccupied room, its window left temptingly half open. He smiled over how perfectly condign it seemed for him to take himself out of the world he now abhorred in the very same manner in which he'd been robbed of the only person he'd ever truly loved.

And with that smile still pasted upon his lips, and with no thought of Ruth and the plans they had been making together, Cain Pardlow threw himself from the window. He died a convenient eight seconds later from a severely fractured skull.

Chapter Nineteen

London, England, October 1940

Three days later Carrie's mother died. Carrie was with her. And Jane had been with Carrie.

The two had grown very close during Sylvia Hale's final hours and in the wake of the senseless deaths of Pat and Cain. The week past had been a particularly hard one for residents of the nearby London neighbourhoods that were being bombed night after night, filling the beds of the venerable St. Bartholomew's Hospital with the injured until there wasn't a single mattress left unoccupied. (This in spite of a good many of the victims having been removed to hospitals elsewhere in the city, and even outside of the city altogether, any place that offered some modicum of safety in a land in which no one—not even the already severely injured—was really all that safe.)

During their leave of absence from the factory, Carrie and Jane were conscripted by the Sisters of St. Bart's to help tend to the Blitz's most recent casualties. The two had worked very hard. Their assistance to the many men, women, and children who, like Carrie, had lost both their homes and close family members to the air raids kept Carrie from thinking too obsessively about her own trials, and prevented Jane from reliving in her every waking moment what Tom Katz had done to her.

During their few hours of rest, the two had lain in Jane's bed, even when air raid sirens ordered them to retreat to the hollowed-out Higgins backyard Anderson shelter. As exhausted as they were, there were still times—a good many times—when the jarring, concussive sound of the bombs falling nearby and the AA guns noisily acking the night sky kept sleep beyond reach. During nights like these they whiled the time away by sharing whispered reminiscences of the happiest and funniest moments of their closely linked childhoods.

Tonight played out much as had the several nights preceding it. The only difference was that earlier in the day there had been a funeral. Carrie had watched her mother's coffin being lowered into the ground, and had wept upon the shoulders of her friends Jane and Maggie and Ruth.

Molly, as it turned out, was in Worcester, doggedly determined in the face of wartime travel obstacles to attend the funeral of her beloved Pat Harrison—even though the journey took twice as long as expected, even though she was booted from one particular train when all the civilian passengers were forced to give up their seats to soldiers in transit, even though she spent one long leg of her journey with a screaming, soiled child having been thrust into her lap, even though she was hungry and thirsty and very nearly knocked unconscious when the train came to a sudden halt and someone's hat box fell down on her head, and even though her trip required at journey's end a frank conversation with Pat's father about how he'd died. It was the most difficult conversation she'd ever had, but Mr. Harrison had shown her only kindness in spite of his overwhelming grief. He had even placed her in Pat's old room, where she cried herself to sleep for each of the two nights of her visit, a pair of her dead lover's boyhood pyjama trousers swaddling one side of her face.

The Prowses had also gone to Sylvia Hale's funeral. As had factory forewoman Vivien Colthurst and one of the other assembly workers, Miss Dowell.

"Don't you come back to work, love, until you feel up to it," Miss Colthurst had said to Carrie, smiling sympathetically.

"I'll be back tomorrow," Carrie adamantly responded. Jane, who was standing next to her, said that she also intended to come into work the next day.

That night Carrie and Jane drifted off early only to be awakened by the wail of the air raid siren. "I refuse to move from this bed," Carrie dissented wearily.

"I'll keep you company," said Jane.

A moment later Lyle stumbled into the bedroom and sought to know, in a harried tone, why the two of them were just lying there and not getting their "blooming arses out to the Andy."

"*Because*, little brother," Jane calmly replied, "we're waiting for the bomb that has both of our names stamped on it—the one that'll deliver us from this *blooming* vale of blood, toil, tears, and sweat."

"You go right ahead and bodge up Mr. Churchill's words like that. He can't hear you. But still it ain't very patriotic."

Jane chortled. "Since when have *you* got yourself all Hope-and-Glory patriotic, little brother?"

"Since I went down to enlist yesterday."

Jane sat up in bed, nonplussed. "You *didn't*!"

"I did."

"And they *took* you? Even though the first time you get shot you'll be bleeding Guinness all over the battlefield?"

"Have your bit of a laugh. They took me this time. By the way, that Peter Pan git what tried to fly himself out of that St. Bart's window—the recruitment officer was asking if I knew him, since I must have said something about knowing every bloke what ever set a toe in the Fatted Pig. He hadn't heard what happened to him and didn't know why he never came back in to finish filling out his enlistment papers."

Now it was Carrie who registered surprise on behalf of both herself and her bed companion. "Cain Pardlow had decided to enlist?"

Lyle nodded. "Even the most cowardly of conchies can sometimes come to see the light."

"Did *you* know this, Jane?"

Jane nodded. "Ruth told me. The two of them had made a pact. He was going into the army and she was joining the A.T.S."

"Now that Cain's gone, is that what she still wants to do—leave the factory and go into the Auxiliary?"

Jane shrugged with her neck. "I don't think she's decided." Jane became ruminative. "I didn't know Ruth was so fond of Cain."

"Oi! Ladies! It seems to *me*—if I may interrupt—that if we're all going to be buried under a pile of bricks by the bleeding Luftwaffe tonight, I should at least have the pleasure of a last supper."

Jane sighed. "Do you fancy a meal, brother? Are you saying you want me to get up and make you something?"

Lyle nodded. Then with a nod in Carrie's direction, he said, "Whilst I talk to this one here."

"Why didn't you just say you wanted me out of the way so you could have a chin-wag with Carrie? And maybe whilst you're wagging, you could do it in the Anderson shelter." At that moment the All Clear sounded. Jane laughed. "Or right here in my bedroom would be lovely too."

Jane got up from the bed.

"I've got two eggs. I didn't tell you because I was saving them for a special occasion. You deserve those eggs for your decision to enlist. I'm very proud of you." Jane delivered a kiss to her brother's forehead before leaving the room.

Lyle sat down on the bed facing Carrie. He waited until the sound of Jane's retreating footsteps died away. Then he said, "Do you know where he is? The bleeding bugger what did that to her?"

"You mean where he lives? No, Lyle. I don't. What are you thinking about doing?"

"He's a fire watcher with the A.F.S, ain't he? At night, I mean. And then in the daytime I've clocked him delivering coal for Mr. Matthews."

"*What are you going to do, Lyle?*"

"What do you fancy I'm going to do?"

"Be in for the high jump would be my guess. They'll either hang you straightaway or you'll end up spending the rest of your life in prison."

Lyle thought about this for a moment. "What difference does it make?"

"I thought you were joining the army."

"I *am*. If the police don't nick me. And maybe they won't, because I intend to do this smart—not leave behind any trace it was me. *And* I'll be cold sober. That was Osborne's problem. He went after that stupid little sod whilst his head was only halfway screwed on."

"Sober or drunk, Lyle, Molly's dad shouldn't have done *anything* to Pat."

"Says yourself. I never held with any of them buggers—not from what Jane said about 'em. And then after what that Katz did to her—"

"Miss Colthurst at the factory—her family's been friends with the Matthewses going back years. She told me at the funeral this afternoon she was going to pay a visit to Mr. Matthews on her way back to the factory—tell him everything she knew about the three men he still had working for him. She thinks he'll give them the sack right on the spot."

Lyle shook his head. "That ain't enough. There are jobs for conchies opening up everywhere. They'll just plant themselves someplace else and go right back in business. I know all about buggers like these. You see, I used to be one myself."

"You never were, Lyle. Don't put yourself in their camp."

Lyle looked away to avoid making eye contact with Carrie.

Carrie went on: "Mr. Matthews doesn't keep things to himself, Miss Colthurst says. Word will get around about what they did. People will find out about their game. They'll be forced to move away. And isn't that the best thing, Lyle? That they should be gone forever?"

"I still think the bleeder should be made to pay for what he did to my sister."

Carrie got quiet for a moment. Then she said, "You've changed, Lyle. You didn't used to be this way."

"You're right. I didn't used to be this way. I didn't used to care. Well, about Jane at any rate. Seeing her like that—*that way*—it, it changes things. You fancy my eggs? Poached on toast. You'll like the way Jane makes 'em."

There was great tenderness in Carrie's smile. "Eat your poached, Lyle. We both want you to have them."

Earlier that day, Vivien Colthurst had stood next to the table in the factory canteen where Maggie and Ruth sat sipping from their smoking cups of tea and not speaking. "I knew I shouldn't have brought the two of you in for the rest of the day shift. Your minds clearly aren't on your work."

"I'm fine, I'm fine," Maggie answered reflexively. Then she added, "Work helps. It keeps me from thinking too much about my missing mother, who went from being amusingly barmy to certifiably mental all in one week."

Vivien grabbed a chair and sat down in it back-forward the way men sometimes do. "First, Maggie—your mother isn't mentally insane. She's *romantically* insane, like one of those Thomas Hardy heroines—like, like *Tess of the Dubers.*"

Ruth rolled her eyes. "For love of heaven, Vivien! Mrs. Barton isn't at all like a Thomas Hardy heroine. I wish for once you'd read a whole book and not just the jacket description. What was the second thing you were going to say?"

"That if Maggie can't concentrate on her work—that goes for you too, Ruth—there's going to be an accident. She might die. *You* might die. This being a munitions factory, dearies, we could *all* die. I wish I'd left the two of you back at the cemetery." Ruth and Vivien rose together. "If you'd like to use my Riley to go back to the city, my three ride-alongs and I can manage with the seven-thirty bus."

"You're very kind, as always," said Ruth. "Perhaps we will. You're right. Maggie and I do have a lot on our minds right now."

Vivien touched Ruth on the shoulder. "I know you'll make the right decision, love. About whether to join the A.T.S. And it will be *your* decision."

"Yes, I know," said Ruth, trying to smile. Through brimming eyes she added, "We—Cain and I—we were good friends, but we were just friends."

The colour in Maggie's face had suddenly changed. It had nothing to do with the factory's mercury vapour lighting, which tended to make everyone look a little like the witch in *The Wizard of Oz*. There was a lighter cast to it. "I think I'm going to be sick," she announced. "I think my bloody mother has turned my entire digestive tract into a warzone."

"I'll fetch you a bromide, love," said Vivien.

After Vivien Colthurst dashed off, Ruth sat down next to Maggie, who was staring with an empty gaze. "She said she hated me," said Maggie.

"Who?"

"Molly. I remember her exact words: 'I hate you so much right now, Maggie, I can't even see straight.'"

"She didn't mean it. I know she didn't."

"What if something happens to her in Worcester and I don't get to tell her how sorry I am for provoking her?"

Ruth touched Maggie comfortingly. "Nothing will happen to her. She'll come back and you two will patch this thing up in no time. Good God, Maggie, you've had tizzes with every one of us at one time or another. They always blow over."

Maggie nodded and tried to smile. "I don't *enjoy* being a bitch."

"Of course you don't, pussy. Of course you don't."

Mr. Matthews wasted no time in sacking all three men. He told them he had been fully informed about what they had been up to and he had no doubt that all this business had contributed to the ghastly deaths of the other two young men who'd been in his employ. "I don't want to see the bloody lot of you ever again. I thought you was all good lads. I find out instead that you're a bunch of sodding buggery reprobates who stick your bleeding pecker spanners in the works of everything you do. And I never held with your cack-handed way of delivering my coal neither—skimming and overcharging and keeping the difference for yourselves. Don't look at me that way. I've been on to you blighters for some time. I've been against this war since both my boys was killed, but I'd like to say something you'll never hear me say to another soul: *Go and bloody enlist.* Now get out of my sight."

Holborne and Castle and Katz got out of Matthews' sight. First they went to Funland, which wasn't far from Matthews' warehouse, where they played the noisy pin-tables and a couple of games of Radio Billiards. Hardly a word was exchanged in the hour they were there, as if each needed some private time to recover from the shock of what had just happened. Even after Holborne lost half a bob trying to scoop up a cigarette case he fancied with the electric crane, and gave up, muttering to himself that the game was rigged, not a word was said in either agreement or commiseration.

However, they more than made up for their reticence once they reached the Fatted Pig.

Though its publican, Mr. Andrews, looked at them suspiciously when they showed up at a time when they should have been busy making deliveries for Matthews, he served them beer nonetheless and took their money.

"I wager it was Pardlow," said Will. "He told Ruth and then *she* told Matthews."

"Blooming pity we can't ask him," said Tom. "The poofter's gone and made that just a little difficult."

"Or it could have been Ruth it came from," suggested Will. "She told somebody else and *they* told Matthews."

"All I know is that *someone's* going to pay," grumbled Tom.

"Cor!" cried Jerry Castle, tipping backward on two legs of his chair. "Will you give a listen to yourselves? Cain and Pat are dead— *dead*. We just had our jobs terminated by that human tin of stinking pilchards, who only hired us in the first place because we were happy to sit the war out on our arses—this whole escapade one bloody disaster—and then the two of you *still* refusing to surrender the football and exeunt the bloody field. *I'm* exeunting the field, lads. I'm joining the army and kill me some sons-of-Huns. But first I'm going to the one I wronged and set things to rights, so I don't have *that* on my conscience."

"You have a conscience, Castle?" laughed Katz. "What'd you do? Dig one out of the shilling bin at Woolworths?"

"You're right. I've got no conscience. I never *had* a conscience. My kind is expendable, gentlemen. But here's the difference between me and the two of you: I *know* I'm a worthless placeholder in this world gone crackers. The two of you—you're both too daft or just too full-blooming deranged to see it in yourselves."

Will made as if to push Jerry backward, toppling him to the floor, but Jerry quickly righted himself. "So *they* win," said Will with a sardonic smile.

"The girls? Okay, they win. Ask me if I care a rap one way or another."

"Pat is dead," pressed Tom. "And that girl's father killed him."

"I'm not like Cain," said Jerry. "I never fancied putting a wig on the lad and taking him for a twirl round the dance floor at the Palais. In fact, if you want the truth, I always found Pat to be a bloody nuisance and Cain a sexual miscreant, and I know you won't deny it, Holborne, because you once saw the man in action. Why else did he always turn pansy yellow every time you went at him? I don't care to avenge *anyone's* death. I just want to break up this miserable little society of ours and let each of us go our bloody way."

Jerry got up.

"Where are you going?" asked Katz.

"If I'm lucky, someplace I can avoid the two of you whilst waiting to go wynken and blynken with the eternal poppies."

Jerry drifted out of the pub.

Will looked at Tom and Tom looked at Will with reflective gazes that revealed nothing. Then Will turned to the bar. His eyes clapped on the large ceramic pig sitting on the top shelf and looking very much like an oversized piggy bank. The pig's expression matched that of the pig on the sign which swung over the door to the tavern—self-pleased, blissfully unaware that he might at a moment's notice be converted into a tasty loin of pork or piping hot pork pie.

"She treated us like pigs," said Will to himself, though his statement could not help being audited by his increasingly besotted and equally belligerent companion.

"Who?"

"Who what?"

"Who treated us like pigs?" asked Katz. "I thought they *all* did."

"Ruth. The one who wouldn't have anything to do with us. I remember that sour look she gave me when Carrie and me were crooning like cats at the Palais."

Katz laughed. "We *all* looked at you like you were dotty. You were making a bleeding disturbance."

"She gave *you* that look too, Tom. She gave it to all of us. Like she was some bloody toff—*better* than the whole lot of us."

Katz took a pull on his beer. "Maybe she is."

"Bollocks."

Will sank deeper and deeper into vengeful thoughts—thoughts of how he might right things in a very different way than that sought by his now foolishly forgiving former friend Jerry Castle.

Night and darkness came quickly. Maggie had been home for several hours and didn't quite know what to do with herself. She'd yet to hear anything from her mother, but held to a shred of hope that some valuable piece of information might *somehow* find its way to her—perhaps from a go-between of some sort. With the mandatory blackout now drawing down upon both Maggie and all her fellow Londoners, she thought she might walk over to the Balham Underground station.

Maggie had got quite good at negotiating the streets in the darkness. Even though she generally took along her torch, it having been recently fitted with both new Number Eight batteries and a fresh globe, she rarely used it. Perhaps it was the carrots her mother, with typical wartime economy, had put into nearly every soup and casserole she served, or the fresh bilberries Maggie loved (berries which were keen for the eyesight and thought to give R.A.F. pilots the upper hand over their German adversaries).

Maggie had thought during her trip back into the city with Ruth that a very good place for a fugitive and his "gun moll"—as the Americans so colourfully put it (or at least those Americans who worked on the Warner Brothers gangster pictures)—to go "underground" was actually to *go* underground—that is, to lose themselves among the throngs of Londoners who queued up each night to shelter themselves from bombing raids by descending like Lewis Carroll's Alice into the city's deepest rabbit holes. Maggie could easily fancy her mother and the man who would have become her father, should things have transpired differently, spending long evenings in the Balham tube—and perhaps a good part of their days Underground, as well.

Maggie had nearly convinced herself to take a look when there came a knock at the door. She hesitated. She peeled up one corner of the blackout paper that covered the front window. Through the exposed glass she got a sideways view of the front step…and the man standing upon it. It was Jerry Castle, the person in all the kingdom she least desired to see again.

"I've come to apologise," said Jerry to the door.

"I'm over here at the window," Maggie shouted through the glass, her lips all but pressed against the spot where she'd turned up the gummy paper. "Apologise to me over here at the window and then pop off."

Jerry wheeled round to address the windowpane. "I'm sorry I behaved so abominably. I am an abominable person and deserve to be removed from your life forever. I am without any hope of redemption. Accept this apology and I'll be on my way."

"Apology accepted. Now go."

"I'm going to enlist."

"You're making a list? What list?"

"No. To *enlist*. In the army."

"Oh. Well. Take care of yourself. Cheers."

"I will. Cheers."

Jerry started down the flag walk just as the air raid siren began to blare. He halted and looked up into the sky. Overhead, the silver-grey barrage balloons drooped in limp silhouette, the conical searchlights that would soon animate them not yet switched to full power.

Maggie looked at him for a moment through the spot where she'd pulled the paper away and where the light from inside seemed, she thought, to be escaping with such brilliance as to target her house for a made-to-order bomb drop from an approaching Heinkel or Messerschmitt.

Then she went to the door. Reluctantly, she opened it. "Come inside. We'll go round back and you can wait out the raid in my Anderson."

Jerry nodded and followed Maggie through the empty house and out to the backyard. "Where's your mother?"

Maggie spoke to Jerry over her shoulder. "It's a sad but interesting story. You know part of it already. We'll have plenty of time for me to tell you the rest once we put ourselves beneath the corrugated."

This particular air raid lasted over an hour. With the bombs falling frightfully close and the two feeling that copping it right then and there was a palpable possibility, Jerry took Maggie in his arms and held her closely and protectively. Maggie didn't resist. She had, like Jerry, become a helpless victim to the peril of their circumstances. She was frightened. She was also exhilarated.

Soon Jerry was kissing Maggie and undressing her with ravenous paws. Maggie forgave him for every hateful, stupid, boorish thing he'd said, and even forgave his participation in "the game," for which he blamed Tom Katz, who "had a way of forcing people to do things that were against their generally good natures." And whereas Pat and Molly had been like two adolescents, exploring one another with tender and curious innocence; and whereas Will and Carrie had delighted at the Hammersmith Palais in all the possibilities inherent in "that which could very well be"; and whereas Ruth and Cain had melded minds and joined their two hearts to the extent that their settled penchants permitted them; and whereas Jane had submitted to a seduction that was less seduction and more a brutal conquest of body, mind, and spirit; Maggie and Jerry found in their present situation the opportunity for union of a different species, enhanced by an aphrodisiac of immense potency. They reeled over the possibility that the climax of their spirited animalistic coupling might be death itself in the form of either an advertent or inadvertent gift from Adolf Hitler and Hermann Goering.

It did not end thusly but it *did* end with feelings of receding rapture that Maggie would have been hard-pressed to describe in words.

No. Maggie hadn't danced a dervish with the devil, but there was still the distinct smell of cordite and sulphur in the air.

And it made her wonder…

Chapter Twenty

Bellevenue, Mississippi, February 1997

"Where are my panties?"

"Is that them hanging on that rake?"

"That isn't a rake. It's a yard broom."

Jerry was sitting on an upturned wheelbarrow. He was enjoying the scene of a totally naked Maggie Barton searching the tool shed for all the clothes she had flung off before having impromptu, devil-may-care sex with him. "I'm kind of out of my, um, element," said Jerry teasingly. "I've never had sex in a tool shed before."

"Well, neither have I. In fact, I've never had sex *anywhere* before. That is, if you don't count the times my sick bastard incestor father put his hands inside my underwear." Maggie stepped into her panties. "How can you just sit there naked and freezing your ass off?"

"I'm not cold. I think you really got my blood to flowing."

"Yes. I can see one spot where it's *still* flowing."

Jerry looked down. "Oh yeah." Maggie handed Jerry his under-shirt. "Thanks. Is that why your mom kicked your dad out?"

"That and the fact that he clipped his toenails in front of the television and ate whole boxes of Cheetos while sitting on the toilet.

Would you *please* get dressed so we can go inside and get warmed up? Are these your underpants?"

"Nope. Not mine."

"*What?*"

"I'm kidding. You seem to have a healthy attitude for somebody whose father did that to her."

"Oh, you think so?" Maggie pulled her blouse over her head. "I was a virgin until this very afternoon. That's right, Mr. Castle. I lost my virginity in that thunderstorm. And the other half of my dirty little secret is that I'd been thinking about going the rest of my life without sex until you had to go and look so sexy in the rain."

"You looked pretty sexy yourself. You looked like you were in a wet T-shirt contest." Jerry jumped up and started to get dressed.

"I *knew* you weren't really an asshole," teased Maggie.

Jerry smiled. "Oh I'm an asshole, all right. But every now and then I like to take a little vacation."

"I'm glad you took your little vacation with me. I'm not ashamed of what we did. I've been very tense lately and very depressed. I really needed this." Maggie, fully dressed now, busied herself by folding up the tarpaulin she'd thrown down on the shed floor. "I know I'm acting like my father didn't mess me up big time. He actually did. I was really afraid of boys all through junior high and high school. And that just carried over into adulthood. The whole idea of sex scared me to death. I went through a long period of time worrying that if I let a guy do it with me, he might accidentally pee inside of me."

"I'm not sure that's possible."

"*I* didn't know that. I didn't know anything, except that sometimes fathers come into their little girls' rooms and do things you're not supposed to tell anybody about." Maggie chuckled to herself. "Of course, I wasn't one of those little girls who did what they're supposed to do. I went straight to my mother and told her everything. Maybe this is why I put up with all her weirdness. She *believed me*—just when I really needed her to. She sent him packing that very night. From what I understand, most mothers in situations like that would become like the 'Queen of Denial.'"

"I don't know why we put on these wet clothes. We should have just run into the house naked and then thrown everything in the dryer."

Maggie shook her head. "Not a good idea to go streaking across the backyard in the middle of the day. I have nosy neighbors, and you never know when somebody might be looking over the fence. Didn't you put *your* nosy nose over that fence looking for *me* about an hour ago?"

Jerry nodded. "Let's go inside and get naked again and put all these clothes in the dryer."

"I like it when you aren't acting like a dick. Can you keep on not acting like a dick for a little while longer?"

"Okay."

Maggie and Jerry went inside through the back door off the patio. The second they opened the door, they heard voices. Turning the corner from the mud/laundry room into the kitchen, they saw Clara Barton and Lucille Mobry sitting at the kitchen table. The room was filled with the smell of freshly brewed coffee.

"There you are!" Clara cried.

"Don't hug me. I'm all wet."

"It looks like the two of you got caught in that thunderstorm," said Lucille. "I nearly did, but luckily your mother had come home and she gave me shelter. Isn't this nice, Maggie? Your mother's come home."

"Are you okay, Mama?"

"I'm fine, honey."

"Oh, this is Jerry. He works at the casino. Well, he *worked* at the casino; they fired him today."

"Yes," said Clara, going over to the coffeemaker. "Lucille was telling me all about it."

"Who told *you?*" asked Jerry of Lucille.

"Ruth." Lucille gave Jerry a strange look.

"You're really dripping, honey," said Clara, looking her daughter up and down. "Go upstairs and put on some warm, dry clothes. Jerry, follow Maggie up and grab some of my husband's old clothes to wear while we dry yours. I'm sorry you lost your job, but I'm sure you'll find another one you'll like even better."

Maggie started from the room and then stopped. "Mama, did you find Michael?"

"I found him. I can't tell anybody where he is and that includes you, but I found him. He's thinking about giving himself up, but he wants me to call the assistant district attorney's office first and find out what kind of charges he's looking at."

"Well, the charge would be murder, wouldn't it, Mama?"

"But the question is if he could plea out for manslaughter."

"It wasn't an accident, Mama."

"But he wasn't in his right mind, honey, and I know in my heart that he didn't set out to pitch that poor boy out the window."

"We don't set out to do a lot of things we end up doing," said Jerry philosophically. Then he and Maggie left the kitchen.

After they were out of earshot, Clara said to Lucille, "Don't say it. I don't want to hear it."

"Say what?"

"That those boys are bad eggs. I know they're bad eggs." Clara put a steaming cup in front of Lucille. "I should make more coffee. You look pale, honey. Are you cold?"

Lucille shook her head. "Ruth said the girls weren't having anything else to do with them, but then Maggie walks in with this one."

"Maggie has a forgiving nature," said Clara. "You'd *have* to, to have lived with *me* all these years. Lucille, I don't like that look on your face. Tell me what's going on. We've all been dealt enough shit over the last several days. Please just tell me something else hasn't just happened."

"Maybe nothing's happened."

"For God's sake, Lucille, just say it."

Lucille nodded. She spoke slowly, choosing her words carefully. "Your son—the one you gave away—his name is Jerry. I mean, that's the name his adoptive family gave him."

Clara's eyes widened. "Are you saying there's a chance the boy upstairs is mine?"

"Ruth said his name is Castle. That isn't Caster. It's very similar, but it isn't the same."

"You're right. And this is Bellevenue, and where did Herb say the family moved to?"

"Little Rock. It could just be a coincidence."

Clara sat down slowly. "I did see something in his eyes that reminded me of John." Clara shook it off. "This is silly. We'll just ask him. *Maggie, you and Jerry come downstairs. We need to ask you something.*"

Clara got up. She went to the coffeemaker again. Neither woman spoke to the other. A sepulchral silence fell over the room. It was broken by the sound of Maggie and Jerry clumping down the wooden stairs in the other part of the house. Maggie entered the kitchen carrying a plastic laundry basket filled with their wet clothes. She was dressed casually in a pink sweatshirt and jeans. Jerry was wearing clothes that had belonged to Maggie's father, which Clara had never bothered to throw out: an old Memphis State Tigers T-shirt and frayed khakis. He had slick-combed his wet hair back the way John Barton used to when he and Clara had first started dating in college. Clara suppressed a gasp. Lucille, who remembered John from the old days, looked as if she'd just seen a ghost.

"Your last name, Jerry," said Clara steadily. "Has it always been Castle?"

Jerry shook his head. "It used to be Caster. But I hated it. I changed it."

Clara grabbed the edge of the table. "I have to ask the two of you something," Clara went on, now anything but emotionally steady. "You have to be very honest with me. Are you having sex?"

Maggie shrieked. "*Mama!*"

"I have to know."

"You *don't* have to know. And you *certainly* don't have to know right in front of Jerry and Ms. Mobr—"

"She *does* have to know," interrupted Lucille. "It's very important. Tell us if the two of you are sleeping together."

As Maggie hedged, Jerry stepped in. "Yes, we had sex. One time. An hour ago. Out in the tool shed."

Clara and Lucille exchanged bug-eyed looks of almost comic-book horror. Picking up on this, Jerry made his case: "I'm sure you've heard about the game by now, but the game's over. You have my word. Mags and I—we did it because we wanted to. *I* wanted to. *She* wanted to. She's white and over twenty-one as they say, and she can do whatever she wants to with her own body, so maybe we can all just drop it, okay?"

Maggie gave her mother a cold stare. "What is *wrong* with you—I mean, what is wrong with you *today*?"

"Maggie— Oh God. Maggie, Maggie— Oh my dear God."

Lucille grabbed Clara's hand for strength. Then she looked up into the quizzical faces of Maggie and Jerry. To Maggie she said, "Honey-girl. Forgive the language, sweetie, but you just screwed your brother."

Jerry left without speaking a word.

Lucille volunteered to drive a trembling Maggie to the doctor to get her an ECP. As she and Lucille were walking out the door, Maggie said to her mother, "Please be here when I come back."

"I will, baby. I will."

By now the rain had let up and the skies had partially cleared. There was more bad weather headed this way the forecasters said, but not until tomorrow. Jerry got in the car and drove toward Lucky Aces to clean out his locker and pick up his last check. He took a wrong turn and had to double back.

He nearly ran over a dog.

Ruth had made up her mind. Earlier that afternoon, she'd discussed the whole matter with Maggie on the patio. Under a thick canopy of gathering rainclouds, the two drank Frescas and ate Bugles and bean dip, and Ruth had decided this was a good time—given all that had happened—for her to make a major change in her life. She told Maggie about the very last conversation she'd had with Cain. It was over coffee at Harvey Joe's on the square. Cain had announced to Ruth that he'd decided to make a big change with his own life: he was going to Los Angeles to see if he could get a job working in movies or television or something. All his life he'd loved old movies and wanted to be a movie director.

"But you have to pay your dues," he'd told Ruth. "You have to start at the bottom and work your way up. I'm young. I've got time."

"What about Pat?" asked Ruth.

Cain had laughed, his eyes registering warm thoughts about the man he loved. "I have this fantasy that I become a big Hollywood director and then I bring Pat out to the coast and 'discover' him and he becomes the next Chris O'Donnell."

"That shouldn't be your *only* motivator."

"Of course not. It's just one of 'em. So instead of being a casino cocktail waitress, you should do what everybody else in Hollywood does who's waiting for their big break—you should wait tables on Rodeo Drive. You can slip your screenplays into the briefcases of Hollywood executives when they aren't looking."

"How do you know I'd ever want to write movies?"

"You like to write—to write stories, *right*? Writing film scripts is a way to write stories and get paid obscene amounts of money for them."

"So what are you saying?"

"What do you think I'm saying? I want you to come out to Hollywood with me."

Ruth paused to let a little Fresca fizz escape through her nose. Maggie offered her a napkin. "Anyway, I told him I would. Right then and there. That's why it blew my mind when I found out what he did right after Pat died. I didn't know he was that obsessed over him. I know we're all a little crazy—everybody in their own twisted way—but he was smart and he had so much promise, and Mags, you should have heard how he'd go on about things he was passionate about—politics and gay rights and things you'd never think might live inside that brilliant brain of his. And then he does something like this—something so, so, so *stupid*. Deadly stupid. What the fuck is wrong with people? Why are human beings so fucked up?"

"Don't ask me, Ruth. My family should be on the cover of *Fucked Up* magazine."

"So everybody says Hollywood is this messed-up town and all the *really* crazy people gravitate there, but you know what? I don't think Hollywood's any more messed up than Bellevenue, Mississippi, or Armpit, Minnesota, or any other place. So I'm going out there to write screenplays about messed-up people and see if I can't make a living at it."

"What are we gonna do without you?"

"You don't think we'll be in touch? For Chrissakes, Mags! Herb and Lucille'll be tugging me back home for visits on every holiday that has something to do with either Jesus or the Pilgrims, plus ya'll will all be looking for excuses to come out to L.A. and sleep on my floor, just watch."

"When are you leaving?"

"As soon as I can. Viv won't like it. She's asked me to move in with her twice already."

"Will you miss *her*?"

"Of course I will. I really like Viv, you know that. But I don't like it *here*. Everybody wandering around, waiting for something to happen and then when something *does* happen, it's horror-movie shit. It's like what those people in London went through during the Blitz."

"I don't know what that is."

"Well, I'll tell you: you sit around and drink your tea with nervous hands and talk about puddings and then some German flies over your house and drops a bomb on you. That's kind of what we got now. Mind-numbing boredom followed by sudden apocalypse and then whoever's still standing when all the dust settles gets to go right back to being bored again."

"I think you really *are* going to make it as a writer, Ruth."

"Thank you, doll. Do you want to go over to the casino with me? It might be nice to have someone else in the room when I have to drop the arrivederci bomb on Viv."

Maggie shook her head. "Do you mind if I don't? It's so peaceful and quiet out here on the patio. I like watching the way the clouds darken up before a storm. Sometimes I really *like* storms, Ruth. I like getting blown around by forces that have absolutely nothing to do with human beings. It reminds me that as much as we think we're in charge of our destinies, we aren't. We're just leaves in the wind."

Ruth got up. She walked over to Maggie and kissed her on the cheek. "You're just now figuring that out?"

Vivian Colthurst took it better than Ruth thought she would. Partly because Ruth left the window open for Vivian to move out to Hollywood herself if she liked, "maybe after I get myself established. Otherwise, it would be a step down for you, Viv. I know you like

your supervisor's job at the casino and I don't know how many casinos there are in Southern California, let alone whether you could
find another job like the one you have now."

"I suppose you're right," sighed Vivian. "You know what? As
a little going-away present, I'm gonna time-clock you in for the
next two weeks. That way you'll have a little extra money for
your move."

"That's very sweet, Viv, but won't that get you into trouble with
the casino?"

Vivian laughed and shook her head. "With all the money they're
making here? I feel like I work at Fort Knox."

Will, unlike Jerry, had hung around the casino while payroll prepared his final paycheck, blowing money he didn't have at the
blackjack table. The fleet boss, Mr. Matthews, had gotten word
from Ms. Touliatis in Human Resources that several of the gaming
floor cocktail waitresses were getting ready to file sexual harassment
complaints against the three drivers, and besides, this University
of Mississippi frat-boy posse was bad news any way you looked at
them. One had just died—actually *died!*—from injuries he'd gotten
from some kind of fight he'd been in, and then his friend, probably
high on Angel Dust or something, had jumped to his death out a
goddamned window. In Mr. Matthews' day, the worst you could
say about Ole Miss fraternity brothers was that they were lazy. Case
in point: they didn't lift a finger to keep James Meredith from attending classes at the school, preferring, instead, to keep to their frat
houses and guzzle beer while the upright white citizens of Oxford
(like Matthews) had to do all the rioting on Ole Miss's behalf.

Ruth was at the casino too. She was in the changing room for
female staff. She was alone. It was late afternoon on a weekday—a
slow time. Even the geriatrics had already boarded their senior center buses and were headed back to Memphis.

Ruth was pulling out what few things she'd been keeping in her locker. She was putting them in a grocery bag. She wasn't aware she was being watched. Will stood in the doorway. He coughed. She turned. "You're not allowed in here," she said evenly.

"I'm not *in* there. I'm standing out in the hallway."

"Please go away or I'll get a security guard."

"How are you gonna do that? I'm blocking the door."

Ruth put a couple of other things into the bag and slammed the locker door shut. She stood next to the bench, staring at Will. Will stepped into the room, shutting the door behind him.

"We're not going to do this," she said, still without a trace of emotion.

"Do what?"

"You know what. Take one more step and I'm screaming my lungs out. I have big lungs."

"Of course you do. You're a fat pig."

"What are you? Ten fucking years old?"

"I have a knife."

"Show me the knife and I start screaming."

"I can do a lot of cutting before somebody gets here."

Ruth expelled a large volume of air through her nose. "That's the biggest problem I have with men. They're so fucking, fucking predictable. Whenever anything bugs them, whenever they don't get their way, they just summon their inner caveman and go ug-ga-chugga atavistic on everybody's asses. It gets old real fast, Billy."

"So then you *do* think I have something to be upset about."

"I'm sure you do. It all fell apart, didn't it? That goddamned game of yours. Two of your friends are dead. I can't even get my brain around that. The five of you—you all came from good families. You had your tickets written and you screwed it all up because men do that, don't they? Men never grow up. Mentally and emotionally, they don't seem to get very far beyond the fifth grade."

Will grinned. "Oh, that's *me*, right?"

"To a tee, Hur-ca-lees. You come in here with your tighty-whities all in a wad because I got you fired from this stupid casino that you didn't much enjoy working for anyway, but you're still gonna find some way to take your revenge. What are you thinking about doing, Billy Boy? Are you gonna try to rape me like your friend Tommy raped Jane? Are you gonna cut me all up with that secret knife of yours? Will this make you feel better? What do you want to do?"

"Hurting you sounds like a good plan."

Ruth walked up to Will. She placed herself directly in front of him. "I'll tell you what you can do—to get this out of your system. You can slap me. Show me who's boss. Slap my chubby lady cheek and then feel good about yourself."

"I just might. I just might slap the fat pig that went wee-wee-wee all over my friends and me."

Ruth sighed. "They were never your friends, Will. You—none of you—you don't know the definition of the word 'friends.' A lot of men are this way; do you deny it? Self-centered bastards who can't see beyond their own selfish needs."

"Men sacrifice themselves for other men all the time. Cops. Firemen. Soldiers during times of war."

"*Some* men. The *good* men. But the two good men in *your* little band of brothers are both dead. All that's left are the dregs."

"And *you're* a conniving, malicious bitch."

"So slap the bitch. But here's the thing: I get to slap you back. Because Tommy *did* rape my friend Jane, and you were probably just fine with it. It's the same thing you wanted to do to *all* of us, wasn't it? To compensate for your little pencil dicks."

Will smiled his crooked smile. "Well, you pretty much summed it up there, didn't you?"

"Give me your best shot. It won't be any more painful than the slaps those two tract house witches used to give me when I was five. But get yourself ready. Because I intend to give back as good as I get."

They stared at one another for a moment and then Ruth took a deep breath, scrunched in her shoulders and shut her eyes.

Ruth wasn't bluffing.

Will took this as his opening. He slapped her. It wasn't a hard slap, but it made a loud pop. And it smarted. Ruth rubbed her reddened check. Then she pulled back and delivered a much more robust open-handed smack to Will's face.

He waited a moment.

Then he reciprocated.

It went on like this: back and forth—mechanical, without emotion—like two little hinged figurines in lederhosen on a Bavarian clock. Will wasn't going to stop until he felt Ruth had been properly punished. Ruth wouldn't stop unless the two of them ended even.

As this was going on Jerry opened the door to the changing room. He thought he had walked into the *men's* changing room. Jerry Castle was in a daze.

Will, whose turn it was, paused, his hand poised in the air, and looked at Jerry. Jerry walked over to the bench on the other side of the room and sat down, his gaze unfocused, his look blank, indecipherable.

Will and Ruth resumed, Jerry watching with empty eyes, not really registering.

Thirty minutes earlier, Lyle had succeeded in getting some important information out of a friend who worked the craps tables at Lucky Aces. It turned out that a number of the casino's employees lived in the same newly built condominium complex about three miles from the casino.

"I need the number for the unit where several of the van drivers live. I want to drop off some cookies my sister made."

"How come Jane never makes cookies for *me?*" Lyle's friend teased.

"I don't know, Greg. She don't make them for *me* neither."

"I don't have the unit number, but I can tell you where they live. They use the pool a lot, and I see them going in and out of one of the apartments next to it. Their door's downstairs and all the way to the left when you're standing with your back to the pool gate."

"Thanks, Greg. I'll tell Jane to bake *you* some cookies sometime."

"Chocolate chip."

"You got it."

Lyle hung up and went straight for his pickup. He drove over to the condominium complex. From the cab of his truck he could see the unit that interested him, but there were children playing in front.

Lyle waited. He finished his Big Mac. After a few minutes the kids were called home.

There was a young woman in a deck chair sunning herself next to the pool. Lyle waited until she went inside, until the pool and the area around it was empty.

Until there were no witnesses.

Then he got out of the cab. He went up to the door to which he'd been directed. He gave it a strong kick. It was a cheap door. It was a cheap, poorly built condo thrown up in a few weeks to house transient casino workers, and the door was no problem.

Lyle found Tom Katz sitting on the toilet taking a shit in one of the bathrooms.

Tom barely had a chance to look up from his *Sports Illustrated* when Lyle pulled the trigger, aiming for his head. Lyle's sister's rapist fell sideways against the wall, the broken streak of blood left on the drywall forming something like a red exclamation point above his head.

Lyle flushed the toilet with his gloved hand and walked out.

Chapter Twenty-One

Tulleford, England, September 1859

Maggie Barton had stopped talking. She lay in the bed which Miss Mobry had prepared for her. She lay quiet and still as Miss Mobry and her mother took turns placing wet compresses upon her head and speaking to her in soft, dulcet tones. "There's a good girl," said Lucile Mobry. "You sleep, my dear." Then, turning to Maggie's mother, who stood next to her, rubbing her hands one against the other with maternal unease, Miss Mobry said with whispered concern: "Not a wink? All through the night?"

Mrs. Barton nodded. Then she confided, "Each time I entered her room, I found her lying on her back and staring at the ceiling with open-eyed insensibility. A most frightening picture. And each time I spoke, I could extract not a single word from her in response."

"Her eyes are closed now. Mayhap the cordial I administered will put her into a restful sleep from which she'll awaken feeling more herself. Will you stop here, Clara, or go off to reunite with your Mr. Osborne?"

"I wish I could bring him *hither*. He would know just what to do to help Maggie."

"Clara, I doubt very much that Mr. Osborne's offices would be of benefit to our present purposes. I should think you'd prefer he stay away and not risk exposure to the police."

Clara cast a fearful glance out the window. "They will catch him—most assuredly they will. I begged him to go to London, to Glasgow—anywhere he might lose himself in the throng and create a new name and a new life for himself. But he said he couldn't bear it were he never to see me again."

"And is there anyone else he should miss?"

Clara resumed with a hint of irritation, "Well, of course it should be naturally assumed that he wouldn't wish to part with his daughter—to lose the chance to make amends for what he's done. Next to ruing the violent act itself, that should be his *greatest* regret."

"My dear Clara, the time has come for me to withdraw endorsement of your blind allegiance to Mr. Osborne. A crime has been committed, and if the man is guilty of that crime—as we know he is—then he should be made to pay the price for it. You have clearly failed to learn the lesson *I* learnt long, long ago."

Clara placed herself wearily into the chair next to the bed. "You are bent upon telling me your lesson. Be quick about it. I'm so very tired."

"That there are few men upon this earth who do not bear the mark of Cain. And here I do not mean that unfortunate Mr. Pardlow who inexplicably killed himself, but Cain of the Bible who slew his brother. And here I do not mean all men are murderers—not in a literal sense—although most men *do* own a tendency to murder in the abstract that which is good, that which is beautiful, that which is noble, that which is innocent and should be held dear. It is man's nature—this dereliction. You have now loved two men, each of whom has borne the mark. I dare say if another comes your way, he will be similarly stained."

"Upon my very soul, Lucile! All men are evil save your blessed brother who has been inoculated by God himself?" Clara shook her head with undisguised rancour. "And I thought the scriptures taught you always to seek *good* in others."

"The *scriptures*, dear Clara, have taught me to beware the iniquity of men...a lesson those five girls did not learn from us as they were growing up. And as a result, take note of all the misfortune that has befallen them." Lucile cast a tender glance at Maggie. "Poor, poor Maggie, falling in love with her very own brother. And Molly, giving her heart to a young man with only one purpose to his pursuit. And what has happened to Jane is all but unspeakable!"

Clara laughed ruefully. "Yet Ruth, who follows in the footsteps of her aunt, who will have truck with no man, succeeds owing to admirable forbearance. Pooh and pho, Lucile! How tidy is your view of that cursed gender and how wise it be to avoid all intercourse with its constituents!"

"Clara, I sought long ago a man who would love me and uplift me. Finding no such creature over the long course of time, I abandoned the search. Ruth has done better for herself by never having *looked*."

In the next moment that very referent came into the little room where Maggie slept and where Maggie's mother and Ruth's aunt believed they had been speaking without audit. Yet Ruth had been standing just outside the chamber door and had heard all.

Her appearance drew startled gasps from the two older women. One side of Ruth's face was chafed to a state of rubicund rawness, beads of bright blood bubbling up in spots where the upper layer of skin had been fully abraded away. "Oh my dear!" cried Lucile, going to her adopted niece. "Pray tell us what has happened!"

Ruth spoke without emotion: "You say I have never sought a man to whom to affix my heart for reason of mistrusting and denigrating the whole species. That has never been true, my aunt. I did once meet a man who could be upheld as exemplar of his sex, but he is now dead and gone, perished by his own hand. And there *are* other men, I am certain, of whom much good can be said. It is merely the absence of propitious circumstance that has kept them from society with my sisters."

"Speak to me, dear girl," said Miss Mobry. "Was it one of *those* three who did this?"

"I must correct you, Auntie. 'Those three' are now become 'those two,' for I have just learnt from Holborne that Tom Catts is dead."

"*Dead?*" Clara Barton had sprung up from her chair upon hearing the word.

"Someone has put a fatal bullet into him. I must go and find Jane to tell her. She should know that the man who has hurt her will never do so again. Would that it did not grieve her so to learn the identity of the one suspected of having done the deed."

Now came a voice that had previously been silent. It derived from the bed. It recited a rhyme, paraphrased for a purpose:

"*Five little kittens, standing in a row.*
See them bow to the little girls so.
They run to the left. They run to the right.
They stand and stretch in the bright sunlight.
Along comes a dog, looking for some fun.
Tom Cat is dead and can no longer run."

Maggie opened her eyes. "I don't fancy the dog was looking for fun, though. I think he was seeking revenge." Maggie rose up. The damp cloth fell away from her brow. Her eyes were sharp and there was the gleam of strong purpose in her gaze. "I wish to come with you, Ruth. I have an idea I wish to put to all of you: I'd like us to take Higgins to my uncle's cottage on the Isle of Anglesey in Wales and hide him there."

Ruth went to the bed and took both of Maggie's hands into her own. "It has yet to be decided just *what* we shall do with Lyle, but I would like to say this withal: that your *willingness* to help her brother will be a great boon and comfort to our sister Jane."

Miss Mobry shook her head. "Maggie Barton, I can scarcely believe it. That you should be willing to put your future liberty, perhaps even your very life, in jeopardy to assist a man who has had no match in all of Lancashire for ignominy of reputation! *Lyle Higgins*, who now enters himself into the chronicles of male moral malignancy through this culminant act of degeneracy: the premeditated, gelid-blooded slaughter of another human being—this is the man you wish to help? I must sit down. My legs are weak."

Lucile Mobry dropped herself to the bed, where she sate in awkward repose, her head moving slowly back and forth like something mechanical that was retarding itself to a state of total motionlessness.

Clara Barton was shaking her head as well. "Maggie, you have made especial effort not to forgive Michael Osborne for defects of character, which you were always eager to catalogue with the most complacent glee. You refused to absolve him of his own act of violence, to pardon him for any of those failings which led him to it, refused to help *me* balm the pain that put him in such a bad way. And now you wake from your trance and are ready and willing to aid and abet and secrete *this other man* who has killed for no reason but the pure lust to kill!"

Maggie rose up in anger. "That is a foul and filthy falsehood! What Higgins did he did from love for his sister!"

Maggie's sudden outburst drew an equally sharp rejoinder from Clara, who could not hide the pain which brittled her words: "*And Michael Osborne did what he did from love for his daughter!*"

The room rang with the echo of Clara Barton's eruption. Maggie, her hands now free of Ruth's clasp, sought her mother's fingers to intertwine.

"Don't you see?" wept Clara. "How can you not see?"

And Maggie responded, her eyes brimming with fresh tears, "Yet I do, Mamma. Now I do."

She bowed her head. When a moment later it uprose, Maggie fastened her filmy gaze upon the broken lineaments of her mother's anguish-darkened countenance. "Mamma, take Michael Osborne to Anglesey—to Uncle Whitman's cottage by the sea. Jane and I will do likewise with Lyle. We cannot go together, for it isn't safe that way, but we will all be there in three days' time. I know not what the future holds for any of us, but at least we shall face it with a commonality of strength and resolve."

"And what of Molly?" asked Clara.

"It remains to be seen," said Ruth, "if Molly Osborne can find it within her heart to forgive her father."

Now Maggie looked at Lucile Mobry, who seemed a fading shadow in the room of staunch women. She said to her, "Every man is drowning, Miss Mobry—slowly, quickly, in one way or another; you are right. But it is our charge as women to throw out the lifeline. Some men will refuse our help. Others will try to pull us down with them. Still others will blame *us* for their foundering. But still we must take up the burden of their recovery and ultimate redemption. It is one of the reasons God has put us upon this spinning coil. This I now believe." And then, as she betook herself from the bed, she said, "Mamma, my only regret in rising from this bed is losing the chance to have you attend *me* for a change. But I do fancy that from now on we will make it our business to take care of one another in equal measure. Come, Ruth. We haven't much time, and we must first see to your face."

The two sisters started from the room. Miss Mobry called after her niece, "You never told me why this terrible thing was done to your lovely cheek."

Ruth stopped and turned. "No, I never did. Nor will I describe what I did to *his* face in return. I will say only this: he looks far worse than *I* do."

Herbert Mobry found the girl where he was told she would be, standing where the High Road communicated with the Factory

Road, which led to the Tulleford Cotton Mill. On any given day this corner was traversed by well nigh every resident of the town for one purpose or another.

It was Jemma Spalding's purpose to stand upon a wooden poultry crate and broadcast in a raised and highly spirited voice that which she was convinced would in a very short time befall the planet: its sudden demise.

Or, to put it in more dramatic terms: *The Veritable End of the World.*

Jemma's voice rang loud and clear to Mobry's ears as he approached. She sang out, "The end is nigh! Make right! Make right with the Lord!"

As Jemma came into view, someone else came into view as well. It was Molly Osborne, who stood next to her cousin, tugging at her sleeve and saying in quietly frantic tones, "You must desist, Jemma. What you are saying is absolute madness. And it is frightening the children."

Herbert Mobry touched Molly's arm. She drew back with a start but then half-smiled to see that reinforcements—of a sort— had arrived. "Mr. Mobry," she said, relaxing a bit in his presence, "I cannot do this alone. Look at her. She will not suspend. She will be arrested for disturbing the peace and inciting fear amongst the townspeople."

Mobry swept his hand to take in the growing number who were gathering, as men and women frequently gather to lend eyes and ears to entertaining street-corner purveyors of spurious elixirs. "But who amongst our halfway intelligent fellow citizens should ever purchase such nonsense as this?"

Mr. Mobry's question was answered by Jemma herself: "It isn't nonsense, Mr. Mobry. Every word the gipsy said to me will come true. I know that now. For Madame Louisa has come to me in a dream."

"And what did she say in this dream?"

Replied Jemma, her words delivered with adamant certitude, "That she now knows the very thing the cards have been predicting for over a fortnight. They tell of the end of the world—perhaps within a matter of days, perhaps within a matter of hours. This is what Madame Louisa says."

Though Molly's eyes were narrowed upon her cousin, her own words were directed to the former minister, their character cold and biting. "By all evidence, Madame Louisa no longer speaks to Jemma in person because she no longer resides in the town of Tulleford. Perhaps that venerable gipsy has hitched herself to a shooting star so as to remove herself from this doomed planet entirely. Pardon me for interrupting, Jemma. Please go on."

"I will do it, even though your tone, Molly, is cheeky and irreverent. In the dream, Mr. Mobry, Madame Louisa comes to me and says she has read the cards one last time and they have revealed that the instrument of our planet's finish will be a great explosion—the explosion of our very sun."

"I see." Mobry shook his head gravely, not from subscription to the young woman's unsettling prognostication, but from the sad verity of her crazed and wild-eyed state. Mobry had other questions he was assembling in his head to ask, and to ask quickly, before a policeman should arrive to take Jemma away—among them, one that struck at the very heart of his religious faith: How is one to believe a woman who says she knows when the world will end, when it was none other than Jesus Christ himself who said in the holy scriptures, *"But of that day and hour knoweth no man, no, not the angels of heaven, but my Father only"*?

But Mobry could not get out his question before Mrs. Colthurst, pushing herself through the congregating crowd in the company of a man roughly her own age, drew Jemma's eye and her immediate attention. "I have…returned," Mrs. Colthurst expelled, and then took a moment to catch her breath.

"I'd wondered what had happened to you," said Molly through a sigh of relief.

"I couldn't find our friend Mr. Prowse for the longest time. He'd stepped away from the telegraph office to take a morning stroll with his new bride. But here he is. And there *she* is! Hallo! Hallo!" Mrs. Colthurst waved her handkerchief. "We thought we'd lost you, my dear," she called.

The "new bride," Mirabella Prowse, waved her hand in acknowledgment of the hail as she squeezed and wormed her way to join her childhood friend Molly and the others standing in a ring round Miss Spalding upon her crate, as children will do when reciting the "Ring-a-ring o' roses" rhyme of old.

Mrs. Colthurst resumed: "Mr. Prowse, do tell Miss Spalding *exactly* what you told me. Jemma, dear, you must listen to Mr. Prowse. He operates the telegraph but is also a very learned man—an astronomer. He knows quite a bit about the sun."

Reginald Prowse stepped forward and put himself directly in front of Jemma Spalding, who studied him curiously as if he had more eyes than two, or perhaps horns sprouting from his head. "My dear girl, you should know that a star—and our sun *is* a star—doesn't simply get the notion one day to blow itself up without warning."

"Oh, there is to be a warning," countered Jemma with a brisk bobbing of the head. "There will be beautiful lights in the sky. They will brighten the world to give us all time to say good-bye to one another without our having to ignite a single candle."

"Those lights you describe are called auroras. They are quite lovely to look at, but in my long acquired knowledge of helionomy, they have never presaged any sort of destructive solar activity—let alone that auroras would ever prefigure the fiery death of the sun itself. It makes no scientific sense." (Mr. Prowse wished to characterise such thinking as "sheer lunacy," but in spite of the cleverness of the subtle celestial comparison, he did not wish to imply that Jemma Spalding was a lunatic.)

"And yet it is what I have been told," replied Jemma, unpersuaded. "The beautiful lights: red and green and violet. And then the great explosion that will come in a blink of an eye and put to quick flame every planet in its orbit. A blaze of igneous glory."

"*Glory?*"asked Mirabella.

"Glory in that those who are in God's good grace will be transported in that moment into His supernal arms."

Mirabella nodded (to be polite). Prowse sighed and shrugged his shoulders, then conferred a look of utter helplessness to Mobry and to Molly and to Mrs. Colthurst, and even to his new wife, for whose especial benefit he appended a wink and a little smile which said, "We shall resume our lover's ramble shortly, my love, once my duty here is done."

Mrs. Colthurst placed a hand upon Jemma's. "Let us go, you and Molly and I, and have a soothing cup of violet tea at my dress shop. Our nerves are all so frayed, my bonny child, and yours must be worn to a frazzle with this heavy burden you've taken up."

"I shall be rewarded in Heaven for every soul I save," Jemma nobly replied, "*but* I will take tea for now. I'm very thirsty, and my throat is parched."

Mrs. Colthurst handed Jemma down from the wooden crate whilst mouthing "Thank you" to Mr. and Mrs. Prowse. Then she whispered, "All will be well" to Mr. Mobry, and the crowd parted to let the three women pass, with Molly shaking her head and saying, "Oh Jemma, Jemma, Jemma" in a weary underbreath whilst wondering if there was even an ounce of truth to what her cousin had said. Because, after all, Molly herself had wondered at times how the world should end. Would it come with angels singing in beautiful Heavenly chorus and clouds opening to reveal gates of opal and pearl? Or would it terminate in some great orgy of destruction and then be succeeded in its aftermath by nothing but darkness and infinite quietude?

Molly shivered in consideration of the latter scene. And then she found herself steeped in sadness, for any prospect that did not put her together for eternity with her beloved Pat or her troubled father, for whom there was so much that still wanted to be said and mended, or her four circle-sisters, who were like extensions of her very own self, was an outcome too tragic for her even to contemplate.

It came to pass that Molly did *not* have tea and biscuits with Mrs. Colthurst and her temporarily docile cousin Jemma, for when they arrived at the shop Carrie was waiting there to take Molly to Higgins' Emporium. Molly had not heard what had happened to Tom Catts and who it was who'd done it to him, and the intelligence sickened and crumpled her.

Carrie was frightened by what Holborne and Castle might do in retaliation, not only to Lyle but to all of We Five. What Carrie did not know—what none of the circle-sisters knew—was that Jerry Castle was preparing to betake himself to Manchester, to put himself back into the fold of his adoptive father, the cheesemonger, and his adoptive mother. But first, Jerry Castle wished to bid good-bye to the woman who bore him and who he knew he should never see again. When the day before he had fled from her house and run and run and thrown himself into a farmer's stew pond in shame, he had thought only of the ardency of the feelings he had owned for the girl who turned out to be his sister. Now he came to regret the fact that he had not engaged her mother—*his* mother—the woman who had foisted him upon the world and nursed him at her breast…and then cruelly tossed him to the winds of fate.

It was an interview he now most urgently wished to have before he left Tulleford. And it would take place whether or no that woman wished it.

Chapter Twenty-Two

San Francisco, April 1906

Clara Barton set her valise upon the bed and walked over to the mahogany wardrobe. As she was about to open its doors she noticed out the window, a flock of seagulls circling lazily in the bright afternoon sky. Clara never tired of her crisp "springtime" view of the city from this window, unobscured by rain and fog. She had lived here upon the near-summit of Washington Street hill for all her years in San Francisco. John Barton had chosen this third-story flat for its sweeping prospect—one of the best spots in San Francisco for taking in this rolling, terraced city in full panoply, as well as the scenic landscape that lay beyond. Pacific Heights was Johnny's gift to his young bride. It was given to her at a time in which she felt he loved her and wanted only the best things for her.

Though the view continued to enchant and inspire her, the same could not be said for the man responsible for it.

And now there was another man who had offered Clara his heart—a beautiful gift that had unfortunately become desecrated, even in this early season, by tragic circumstance.

Clara went to the window. She sat down on the cushioned built-in seat her daughter so frequently occupied. From here one could see San Francisco Bay and the shore of Contra Costa. Laid out before her: the great city of Oakland and its neighbor, Berkeley, and across the bay, the sleepy fishing villages of Tiburon and Sausalito. Towering in the distance were the majestic crests of Mount Diablo and Mount Tamalpais. In the foreground: the green tidewaters of the narrow Golden Gate inlet.

Clara looked down at the jumble of roofs that descended, in stair-step fashion, the precipitous slope below. Then came a great confusion of chimneys and cupolas and still more roofs, both gently and steeply pitched. These houses possessed all the architectural ornamentation—the windows in triplicate in a Serlian motif, the arches and dentils and oriels and gables, the classical columns and terracotta panels and gingerbread tiles and fish-scale shingles—of the Queen Anne style—an idiom marked by a predominance of wood and brick and slate in colorful and fussily constructed idiosyncrasy that gave Clara to think on occasion of the Queen herself coming and waving her magical architectural wand and transforming the city into a storybook for the eye. Clara imprinted the scene before her onto the pages of her memory, even as she knew it could not hold. A perched gull, the feathery top of a lone Canary Island date palm, a solitary sailing ship in the Bay, Goat Island in the distance—these things individually she would remember; yet the scene in aggregate would blur over time—would blur and fade even if the canvas were not about to be ripped from the wall altogether by means of geoseismic catastrophe.

The rustic cabin belonging to Clara's former brother-in-law Whit was miles and miles away on the Klamath River. It was an old gold miner's shack Whit had fixed up for the wife who left him. Clara hoped that it would be here that Michael could hide himself until those who were looking for him gave up their search, and here that Jane's brother Lyle would also find refuge. But leaving this city which Clara and Maggie both loved would be painful.

Clara returned to the wardrobe to select the few clothes she would be taking with her. But she'd hardly had time to remove a gingham house frock from its hanger when she was startled by the sound of someone pulling the bell chain downstairs—pulling the chain that signaled the arrival of a visitor to the flat. She went down to see who it was.

Jerry Castle looked pale, almost gaunt. He looked to Clara as if he hadn't slept for several nights, though, in truth, he'd only lain awake *one* night. She detected, as well, the smell of liquor on him—a smell with which she was well acquainted. Standing at the front door, she said, "She isn't here. If you are looking for—" She very nearly said, "your sister," but checked herself. "She isn't—"

"It isn't Maggie I want to see. It's you. Can I come in?"

"Well, I don't— I'm really qu—quite busy," Clara stammered, suddenly frightened by her son's presence, which now felt importunate and threatening.

"So you won't see me?"

"Of course I'll see you," said Clara, and then putting deed to word, she stepped back from the door to allow Jerry to enter. "Come into the parlor. We're allowed to entertain visitors in here if they don't smut the carpet."

Clara led Jerry into the front parlor, which was used by all the residents of the large house. "I have nothing to give you to drink," she apologized as she sat down on the sofa.

Jerry did not sit.

Clara indicated with an open palm an armchair upholstered in gaudy patterned chintz. "Please."

In an act of inconsequential insolence Jerry claimed a leather-seated high-back instead.

"I'm going away, you see," she elaborated. "That's why I can't be a very good hostess at the moment. I'm preparing to take a trip."

"I can very well guess why you're leaving. I don't care about that. There's only one thing that interests me. I want to know why you did it."

"*Did it?*"

"You know what I'm talking about."

Clara, whose eyes had been half-avoiding Jerry's intense gaze, now looked at him dead on. "Maggie hasn't told you?"

Jerry shook his head. "I haven't seen Maggie since I left here yesterday. And I have no need ever to see her again. I'm taking a trip too. I'm going back to Sacramento—the place where I thought I was born, but now I know differently. I know a lot of things I didn't know before—things people shouldn't have waited so long to tell me. Why did you do it? Was it a matter of money? Did you think you couldn't afford to raise me?"

"That wasn't the reason. I wish Maggie had talked to you. She might have said it in a way you'd understand."

"Maggie did tell me about our father's ill treatment of her. Was this it? Did you send me away because you were worried he might hurt me too?"

"I *wish* that were the reason. That would certainly exonerate me, wouldn't it? No, in truth I—well, I just didn't want another John Barton in this house. From the moment you came into this world, I could see him in you. Your face was his, your little hands—the way they bunched themselves into tight, angry little fists. So I got rid of you. I didn't know at the time that it would have been easier to divest myself of him instead. Because eventually he *did* go, and he didn't put up a fuss about it. But by then it was too late. You were gone and there wasn't any way for me to get you back."

Jerry thought about this. He picked up the wooden stereoscope resting on the table next to his chair. He put it up to his face and looked at the composite image presented by the card in the slot. The view was of some place in the Orient. There was a pagoda in the foreground. Behind it were trees that would have looked unreal had Jerry not seen a good many such strangely trimmed trees in the Japanese Tea Gardens at Golden Gate Park. He tried to push from his mind the day he spent at the park with Maggie and her four shopgirl friends, the way he'd forced himself on her, kissing her, touching her rudely upon the hips with his hot hands. The thought came with shame and with anger. It did not have to be this way. If he had known she was his sister he surely would have suspended his pursuit and gone after one of the others instead.

"But I turned into him anyway, didn't I?" he said bitterly. "For all the good your sending me away did." Jerry paused. He studied the Oriental rug on the floor. He didn't raise his eyes as he said, "I had thought about killing myself. I had thought about killing the both of us."

At first Clara couldn't find words to respond. She rose from the sofa. Then she said raggedly, "I think you should go. As I—as I have said: I have packing to do."

Jerry got up as well. But not before flinging the stereoscope to the wooden floor. It made a loud clatter, the handle breaking away on impact, the picture card flying off. Clara started. She took a step back.

"It doesn't look real!" Jerry raged. "They say it's supposed to look real and lifelike when the pictures come together. All well and good, but they're still in damnable black and white. We don't live in a black and white world."

"No, we do not," said Clara, her voice aching with pain. "I—I've seen cards where the pictures are color-tinted."

"Like putting rouge on a corpse." Jerry was breathing heavily. He took a moment to catch his breath. "I can't hold you accountable for what was done to me. You are a stupid, frightened woman. You would have made a stupid and frightened mother, who would have been of no use to me."

Clara nodded quickly in a frenzied travesty of agreement.

"It was better that I was raised by the cheddar-heads."

"I don't—I don't know what that means."

"It doesn't matter. I'm going. I'm sorry for what I did to your daughter. I'm sorry for casting this brief shadow over *your* life. I needed to see you—not for you to apologize—just to face for one last time the woman who would do this. Now I've faced you. But I am not changed. My heart hasn't softened. I thought it might, but it hasn't. I don't wish you well. I wish that the rest of your life were one long trial. And that you'll regret to your dying day the stupid thing you did."

Clara spoke softly: "I have always regretted it."

Jerry left without saying another word.

Clara sank back onto the sofa and wept. She remembered Lucile Mobry's words from the morning—what she said about men, and how, frankly, undeserving they were of redemption, and then she remembered opposing words from her daughter, who felt that a man could be changed through the tendance of a loving, caring woman. Now Clara came to see the truth as it was unveiled to her by the example of Jerry's belligerent visit—the truth that lay somewhere between the two extremes.

She walked over to the stereoscope and picked it up. She wondered if she could repair the handle before her landlady came home from her errands and discovered it broken. She picked up the stereographic card containing the two images of the same Japanese pagoda and scrutinized it. She saw no difference between the two pictures printed side-by-side on the rectangle of thumb-smudged grey-green cardboard. Yet together the images were supposed to create a single picture of fuller dimensionality. Clara shook her head and returned the card to the box of stereographs.

Lucile Mobry and Clara's daughter Maggie had spoken of men and women as if there were worlds of difference between them, but Clara wondered. She saw in each the same elemental needs and then that one great, overarching need: to snatch at happiness whenever one had opportunity, and to use it as a salve for all the aches and throbs that come from human existence. Men and women engaged life, they engaged one another, in very different ways, but in those things that made them most human they were like the pictures on the stereograph: very much alike and very much in need of one another to make the whole picture.

Whatever that picture might be.

Clara climbed the stairs to her third-floor flat, the one with the window and the fine fogless view and the plush seat where one could sit and gaze out and do one's best to push aside dark memories and feelings of painful regret. But Clara did not sit. Instead, she returned to her packing.

She did not hear the wicker of the gelding below, shuffling and unnerved in the street by a portentous vibration below ground undetected by any of the two-legged creatures passing nearby.

Two policemen came looking for Lyle. Will Holborne had told them who he believed had killed his friend in their shared flat on Telegraph Hill. He directed the cops to the Emporium. What they found when they got there were four young women finishing up the last morsels of the supper they'd prepared together. (Ruth had removed herself to the larder, so as not to draw unnecessary speculation as to the reason for her injured face.) Jane was taken singly into the parlor and questioned by one of the two officers.

"I don't know where he's gone," she said in a businesslike manner. "He flew out of here a couple of hours ago."

"So you don't have a clue as to where he might be headed."

"That's what I said. What is it you think he's done?"

"Killed a man."

Jane opened her eyes widely in an expression of shock and dismay that served. "My brother wouldn't kill anyone. It would take too much effort."

"How about you make a little effort to take our questions seriously, Miss Higgins? A man is dead and there's one who said it was your brother who did it. He said your brother had it in for the victim."

Jane was sitting on the sofa. *That* sofa. It could not be avoided. She didn't like the way she felt just being in the room. Everything reminded her of what had happened there only a few days before.

"Did the person who said this—" said Jane, while effecting a look of serious inquiry, "—did he also say *why* my brother wanted to see this man dead?"

"Not in the few minutes I had opportunity to question him. But we know there's a reason there. He said he was nearly positive it was your brother who was the one that did it. We like that phrase 'nearly positive,' Miss Higgins. It tends to make our job easier. Anyway, somebody will get it out of him. Sometimes it can be a simple thing: one man doesn't like another man's politics. Or his religion. Or the way he's looking at him. And they exchange words. And they're both lit, and things turn violent." The policeman sniffed. "Your brother drinks. I can smell it all around the place. We're going to make our search now. You go back in the kitchen with your friends. You have some very pretty friends."

"Thank you. I'm the team mascot."

"You're a funny one. Are you girls having a party?" The officer craned his head to see past the door and into the kitchen down the short connecting hallway.

"Not really. We just like to get together now and then, away from work. We're salesclerks at Pemberton, Day."

"My wife was there only yesterday. She bought a tam o' shanter for my daughter—for her birthday. Maybe you sold it to her."

"I don't think so. I'm in the ribbons department."

The policeman led Jane back into the kitchen. Then he and his partner looked around the showroom and through all the back rooms of Jane and Lyle's living quarters. After searching the house, they went out to the yard in the back. There was a storage shed, where some of the stock was kept. It was locked. Jane gave them the key. Twenty minutes later, the police officers were gone.

We Five agreed to wait in the kitchen until they felt confident the men weren't coming back. They took this opportunity to come to one mind about the fate of Jane's brother Lyle, who was presently hiding in a crawlspace above his bedroom.

"I'm not comfortable harboring a fugitive from justice," said Ruth. "But you know already that this is where I stand. And *I* know that I'm outvoted. The three of you think that Lyle shouldn't have to pay for what he did. And Molly, having yet to make up her mind, abstains."

Maggie, who was sitting next to Molly at the table, the two having lovingly patched up their differences so that they now held hands in sisterly affection beneath the table, said, "Molly's torn in two different directions when it comes to her father. It's too much to make her decide the fate of Lyle Higgins as well."

Molly shook her head. "No, Mag, I *have* made up my mind about Papa. He is my father and I love him, and I don't trust a judge or jury to be lenient with him. As for Lyle, I'll go along with whatever the rest of you want."

Ruth, who had been pacing back and forth, now stopped and addressed the three young women sitting at the table and the tall one washing dishes at the sink: "I was raised to understand the difference between right and wrong. But I was also raised by a minister and his sister to recognize how murky is the swamp that lies in between. Mobry himself has given shelter to men—Negro men, who are alleged to have committed crimes—but in these cases it was to shield them from the lawlessness of mob justice. It's a complicated matter deciding what's totally right, what's *half* right, and what's only a *little* right. And if I'm to be perfectly honest, I'd say that keeping Lyle from arrest is only a little right—the kind of right that comes from selfish love. But it's the same kind of selfish love that would make me do the very same thing for any of you."

"Please take the last slice of mocha cake, Ruth," responded Jane with tearful affection.

"Are you insisting?"

"We're *all* insisting," said Carrie.

It was Jane and Carrie who went into Lyle's bedroom to tell him the coast was clear. Jane tapped the ceiling above his bed. A panel slid back and Lyle dropped down. Jane told him what the police officer had said. Meanwhile, Carrie's eyes were drawn to Lyle's sketchpad on the table.

She opened it and turned its leaves, each bearing a pastel drawing of a scenic landscape.

"Did you do all these?" she asked.

Lyle interrupted his conversation with his sister to answer, "Yes. Yes I did."

"They're really quite wonderful," said Carrie, who could not keep her eyes from them. "I'd like to have one to keep."

"Where will you keep it, Carrie?" said Jane, brusquely. "You don't have anywhere to live."

"You keep it *for* me then, Lyle. *This* one." She turned to a sketch of a seaside village. "That's Tiburon, isn't it?"

"Yes it is."

"Put my name on it. It's mine."

"All right."

"Are you both quite finished?" asked Jane. "We can't stay here. It isn't safe. The police will pay a return visit as soon as Holborne is made to tell them everything he knows. They'll want to ask me a thousand questions. I can't answer a single one. I'll fall to pieces."

Carrie nodded. "And I don't like it that Holborne's still out there—that he may want to come after us. Look at what he did to Ruth's face." Carrie had put her statement in the present tense because Ruth at that moment was coming into the bedroom, along with Maggie and Molly.

Ruth, having already taken charge of matters, was *in medias res* with the other two: "The next ferry to Oakland isn't until early tomorrow morning. Molly, you and Jane and Lyle will need a place that isn't far from the Ferry Building where you can spend the night. If you hide yourselves well enough, you stand a good chance of getting Lyle on the boat without being seen and followed."

"You might as well come with us, Ruth," said Maggie. "You're already packed and you already have your ticket for New York."

"That leaves Carrie," said Jane. "What are you going to do with yourself, Carrie?"

"I've been giving it a lot of thought. There's a music school I've been looking into. It's in New York."

Ruth corrugated her brows with interest. "Are you saying you'd like to come with *me*, Carrie?"

"There's nothing keeping me here in San Francisco. Especially with all of you leaving. Yes, I'd like to come with you, Ruth. I have money in the bank. I didn't put it in my mattress like some do. I put it in a savings account. I'll just withdraw it all tomorrow morning and then you and I can be on our way. If, that is, you'll have me."

"Why shouldn't I have you, Carrie? You seldom get under my skin the way our three sisters do."

Ruth's attempt at dry levity went unacknowledged.

Carrie looked at Lyle. "I think, then, I *will* take that picture from you, Lyle. Because I don't know when I'm ever to see you again."

Lyle tore the sketch from the book. There was a shyness, an awkwardness about him that seemed out of character. But then again, there was very little Lyle Higgins had said or done over the course of the last two or three days that seemed *in* character. He handed the sketch to Carrie.

She looked at it with the loving eyes that her present discomfiture would not permit her to raise up. "I always wanted to live in this little village. I'll look at it and think of you, Lyle."

Lyle swallowed nervously. He glanced up at the ceiling as if he might wish to climb right back up into the crawlspace to escape his present unwonted unease.

Ruth looked back and forth between the two of them, half smiling with curiosity. "How did I happen to miss the first act of this little play?"

"You didn't miss anything at all," chuckled Jane. "It feels to *me* as if the curtain has just begun to rise."

What was also rising at that moment was the color in both Lyle and Carrie's cheeks.

"So just where *will* we be staying tonight?" asked Maggie, returning the discussion to more practical matters. "Holborne knows where each of us lives. Miss Colthurst gave all our personal information to the Katz Agency."

"I'd like to make a suggestion," said Ruth. "You may not like it, but then again, it's not a place Holborne or any officer of the San Francisco Police Department would be likely to go. Cain took me there. It's in Chinatown. We can sleep there. They have little rooms."

Carrie frowned and then ventured nervously, "This place, Ruth: it isn't an *opium den*, is it?"

"As a matter of fact it *is* an opium den. Among other things. But you needn't worry. The opium eaters will be far too torpid to give us much trouble. And as for any lurking white slavers, we'll have Lyle to protect us."

In spite of the reactive gapes and shudders which followed Ruth's proposal, not a single one of its recipients spoke up in opposition to it. It was, after all, the most reasonable choice from a menu of severely limited options. And the tearoom on Dupont Street was very convenient to their purposes; it was only eight short blocks from the Ferry Building on the Embarcadero.

They would spend the night tucked away in the heart, or, if one wishes a less benign description, the *viscera*, of Chinatown, and then Molly and Maggie and Lyle and Jane would rise early and catch the first morning ferry to cross the bay.

And if Ruth were lucky, the tearoom's kitchen would remain open late into the night. Because upon her previous visit to this place with Cain, she'd discovered that she had quite a taste for authentic Chinese cuisine.

All of We Six had been to Chinatown before, but excepting Ruth's luncheon there with Cain, there hadn't been a visit since the Plague. Now, as they climbed Dupont with halting steps and wide-eyed gazes, each appearing equally exotic to the neighborhood's denizens due to their unfamiliar Caucasian countenances and their strange Occidental garb, they felt as if they'd just disembarked into a place out of time and ken. The street was chockablock with crowded structures whose original architectural purpose had been shanghaied by the necessity of reduction and compartmentalization into smaller and smaller spaces. The side streets were dark narrow alleys with opened doors that afforded smoke-clouded glimpses into rooms congested with men crouched over fantan tables. There were staircases that went up and those that went down, and every block was overhung with a plethora of balconies and logia, which to the squinted eye might remind one of a street in Venice.

The fully dilated eye was confronted by colors of every shade and hue: in the bright iridescence of the clothing; the green and yellow and sky-blue and vermilion of the richly painted walls; the gold which outlined the cornices and eaves and window trimmings; and the variegation of intense color to be found in the signs bearing bold but inscrutable Chinese logograms. There were red and gold lanterns hanging from every ceiling and assemblages of fat cobalt-blue pots of red saffron and pink tulips. Some of the buildings were dilapidated and crumbling beneath their decorative ornamentation, like old women with youthful souls.

Molly nudged Maggie to note a little pigtailed man in an orange Mandarin jacket. She wanted to say that this was the same jacket she'd seen their friend Mirabella Prowse wear a couple of weeks earlier. But Molly wouldn't even attempt to voice the observation, for she knew she wouldn't have been heard. The air was too full of the clamor and clatter of too many people in too small a place, all hail-ing and railing and singsonging and wheeling and trundling their carted wares, seemingly oblivious to the inconvenience of their crowded circumstances.

Maggie, who had a sensitive nose, pinched both nostrils. There were pungent wafts in the air of fresh-caught Pacific crayfish and squid and flounders and sole, the rank odor of fast-ripening produce, the strong aromas of sandalwood and smoldering punk and exotic dishes being prepared in upper rooms and vented out into the street.

"Here we are," announced Ruth. "Up these stairs."

"Has it a name?" shouted Jane over the din.

"Places like this don't have a name."

"Oh God," said Maggie and Molly at the very same time. Yet Carrie, for once, didn't seem worried at all. Lyle was holding her hand.

Chapter Twenty-Three

Zenith, Winnemac, July 1923

Sister Abigail Dowell looked her five newly appeared choir members up and down disapprovingly. She reserved her frostiest glare for the male interloper who stood among them. "Sister Lydia isn't going to like this."

"Isn't going to like *what?*" asked that very referent, stepping out of her private office accompanied by her choir director, Sister Vivian.

"Well, *everything,*" replied Sister Vivian's assistant. "They've missed the last two choir rehearsals and we've got full dress at six o'clock."

Sister Lydia rolled her eyes. "I know we've got full dress at six, Abigail. I'm the one who scheduled it."

"And who is *this* person?" said Abigail, pointing at Lyle indignantly. "He can't be here."

"He's my brother," said Jane.

Sister Lydia turned to Vivian. "Fix this, Vivian." And then to We Five: "So nice to have you all back, even though by the looks of all that luggage, one or more of my sweet young songbirds may be getting ready to fly the coop."

"I'll find out what's going on," said Vivian. "Abigail, please go and prepare the rehearsal room. We've got to familiarize these girls with the two new hymns before the dress rehearsal. Run along now, and let me handle this."

A brief moment later, both Sister Lydia DeLash Comfort and Sister Vivian's officious assistant had departed the outer office, leaving Vivian alone with We Five Plus One.

"Just tell me," said Vivian, "that if one or more of you *is* leaving, you'll wait and do it *after* tomorrow morning's celebration."

"We're *all* leaving, Vivian," said Ruth. "But not until after the service."

"So you aren't the only one thinking about enrolling in the University of Winnemac. Your sisters have decided to join you."

"It's far more complicated than that, Vivian," said Jane. "We're all leaving—you're right—but for different reasons."

"Tell me that this has nothing to do with the rumors."

"What rumors?" asked Maggie.

"That Sister Lydia's Square Deal Ministries is in financial trouble. Because let me just say this at the outset: the organization may be floundering, but it certainly isn't *foundering.* Sister Lydia—I love her bushels—but she doesn't have much of a head for business, and sometimes she doesn't plan for things very well. We aren't nearly ready for the celebration tomorrow. The varnish on some of the pews isn't even dry. We're still waiting for five pipes for the organ. They've apparently gotten lost on their way from Cincinnati. And there seem to be problems with the new wiring; lights keep flickering on and off. On the other hand, the Sister's done all this advance publicity and everybody who is anybody in the state of Winnemac is going to be here tomorrow, and she's convinced it will be an utter disaster if we *don't* go through with it. And just when you think she's got enough to worry about already, *this* is when you've decided to turn in your choir robes!"

It was decided that Vivian could be trusted. We Five knew how fond their choir director was of Sister Lydia's Quintet of Songful Seraphim, and especially how fond she was of one of the singers in particular: Ruth. And so it was explained to Vivian that, yes, Ruth would be enrolling in the University of Winnemac in the fall, and that Carrie planned to do the same. She was going to study music. Jane and Maggie and Molly and Jane's brother Lyle would be going somewhere entirely different: to the northern woods of Minnesota.

"Why Minnesota?" asked Vivian.

Ruth placed a hand on her friend Vivian's shoulder. "Sit down, sweetheart. Lyle, go shut that door. Vivian, we're going to tell you what's *really* going on."

Vivian eased warily into the nearest chair. "It's about those awful college boys, isn't it? And the two sad ones who died."

"*Three* are dead now," put in Maggie.

Vivian choked.

Jane looked over at her brother. Her eyes solicited corroboration for the incomplete truth she was about to dispose: "The young man was murdered. And the police think it was my brother who did it. We have to get him out of Zenith as soon as possible."

"*You* have to get him out? And Maggie and Molly as well?"

"There are other parts to it," said Jane. "I'm sure that Ruth will explain it all to you in time. All we can do right now is apologize to you and Sister Lydia for leaving like this, and hope you won't hold this decision against us. Oh, and one other thing. We have a small side favor to ask of you."

"Yes?"

"That we be allowed to spend the night here."

"Right here? In Sister Lydia's tabernacle?"

Jane and Ruth nodded. Ruth picked things up from here: "This is a church. And a church should be a place of sanctuary. We need that refuge tonight. All six of us. I know there are resting cots in the storeroom downstairs—the ones you'll be using for healing services. We can sleep on *them*—down in the storeroom. No one needs to make any fuss over us."

Vivian thought about this. "It's very irregular. But then again, what is regular in a world that seems these days to be spinning right off its axis? And I fear, my dear girls, that we are a long way from having peace and sanity restored."

Vivian got up from her chair and walked over to where Lyle was leaning against a wall: silent, pondering.

"I have to know," she said. "*Did* you kill the boy? Did you do it?"

Lyle traded a look with Jane. Jane nodded that he should answer, and he should answer truthfully.

He tipped his head.

"*Why?*"

Jane sat down. Her eyes began to well up. Molly went to her and wrapped her arms around her neck in a gesture that was both loving and protecting.

"I think I know," said Vivian Colthurst, looking painfully at Jane. "And I also know that the church has offered sanctuary to the accused for centuries—both the falsely accused *and* the rightfully accused who seek divine forgiveness. And why should Sister Lydia's Tabernacle of the Sanctified Spirit be any different?"

Vivian spent most of the next two hours working with her five favorite choir members to teach them the songs that in their several-day absence the other members had already learned. In the meantime Lyle was down in the storeroom making ready the room he and We Five would share that night. It was decided that rather than have Lyle wait until the end of the morning service to leave—and thereby run the risk of being spotted by the police—he'd depart alone just before daybreak. He would drive his 1919 model Oldsmobile "Economy" delivery truck up to St. Agatha. He'd wait there at the depot for the arrival of the Middle West Limited from Zenith. Then he and Maggie and Molly and his sister Jane would continue their journey to Maggie's uncle's cabin by back roads.

Vivian had pointed out to Lyle that if he wished, he need only come close to the heating vent in the basement storeroom to hear his sister and the other choir members singing during the full rehearsal in the auditorium upstairs. "Sister Lydia is quite the showwoman, so you'll miss all the eye-pomp that generally characterizes her theatrical services, but at least you'll be able to *hear* things, if you're so inclined: her sermon—riveting as always—*and* the music. Such divinely gorgeous music."

At five minutes to six, a robed Molly and Maggie and Jane and Ruth climbed the stairs to the north anteroom off the auditorium. Carrie did not. Carrie took a detour; she went to the storeroom to see Lyle. For a moment Carrie and Lyle looked at one another without speaking. Then Lyle said, "Maybe I'll tell you goodbye now, because you'll probably be sleeping when I leave in the morning."

Carrie nodded. She took Lyle's hand and held it up to her cheek. "You've been very nice to me. Jane said you never used to be nice to *anyone*, so I consider this as a big improvement in your character."

"I'm still not a very *good* person, Carrie. I killed a man."

"According to Jane you've killed *several* men. During the war. In the Battle of the Argonne Forest. She showed me your Distinguished Service Cross."

"How could she? I threw it out."

"Well, it didn't *stay* thrown out. She said she found it in the trash and kept it. Why *did* you throw it out, Lyle?"

Lyle took a moment to answer. He did so without looking at Carrie. "I stopped believing what they told me about the war. And then I stopped believing I could ever have been a hero. You can't be a true hero in a war that should never have been fought. And when I stopped believing *that*, why, I stopped believing in anything."

Lyle took Carrie by the shoulders and turned her so they'd have to look at one another now. He kept his hands on those shoulders as he spoke. "Listen to me, Carrie. I know what I did was wrong— killing Catts was wrong in ten different ways. I wanted to hurt him for what he did to Jane. No, I didn't just want to hurt him. I wanted to kill him. You're right. I've killed men before. The army taught us how to do this—how to flip the switch, and then suddenly it's okay to kill, because you're in a war and it comes down to either you or the Boche. And even though the war's been over for five years, it doesn't look like I've lost the knack for flipping that switch when I can find a reason to justify it. That makes me the opposite of a nice person, Carrie, a *good* person. That makes me a *dangerous* person. You're looking at me and seeing somebody who isn't there. I don't think he's *ever* going to be there."

"You don't know that, Lyle."

"If I ever find the Cross, I'm going to toss it out again. Jane was wrong to hold on to it. Look, it would have been something else if I'd walked in on the two of them—if I'd caught him in the act of hurting her and I struck out at him. But I didn't. I went looking for him. The same way I hunted down German stragglers in the Argonne and picked them off like field rabbits."

Through the heating vent came the sound of the tabernacle organ (compromised somewhat by its five missing pipes) playing the anthem "Onward, Christian Soldiers." The anthem would serve as prelude to the procession of Sister Lydia and her large company of choir members, musicians, and various spiritual adjutants into the auditorium.

"You should go," said Lyle, taking his hands from Carrie's shoulders.

"What about *us*, Lyle?"

"I don't know about us. I only know that I can't keep running forever. At least if they decide not to hang me, you can always come visit me in prison."

Carrie glanced at the open door, but she didn't make a move for it. Lyle nudged her gently. "Hurry up. They're waiting for you."

Carrie nodded. She leaned in and stood on her tiptoes to kiss Lyle on the cheek. "My love for you, Lyle—it's very irregular, I know." She laughed. "But in the words of Miss Colthurst, 'What is *regular* in a world that's spinning off its axis?'"

Sister Lydia had chosen "Roses" as the theme for the first service to be held in her newly constructed (or rather, very *nearly* constructed) temple. Roses had always played a big part in her ministry. There were many photographs in the rotogravure pages of the country's Sunday editions of the smiling evangelist, dressed in her simple white muslin "nurse's uniform," a dark serge cape draped over her shoulders, stepping from trains while holding large bouquets of long-stemmed roses, which had just been placed in the crook of her arm by local welcoming committees.

The auditorium was filled with roses. They were spread around the stage as if it had been besieged by a hundred wedding-ceremony flower girls dropping petals and stems wherever their little fingers sought to release them.

The dress rehearsal went well. There were only a couple of minor problems, both having to do with lights that did not come on when they were supposed to, as if there were still shorts in the electric circuits that needed to be addressed.

While the orchestra played a piece especially written for the celebration, the ushers took their places at the top and bottom of the three steeply raked aisles and along the walls of the mezzanine and balcony. Each of the twenty-five women wore crimson sashes appropriate for the rose theme of the day. Once they'd found their spots, a dozen male volunteers wearing their best Sunday suits filed in and took seats upon a riser along the upstage wall. These men represented the pastors of Zenith's various religious denominations, who had promised to attend to show their support for the launch of their colleague's permanent ministry.

The choir entered next, all twenty women mantled in deep burgundy velveteen robes. Once inside the choir box, each went to kneel before her chair. It was through this expression of reverent genuflection that the choir members acknowledged the arrival of Sister Lydia, who came gusting down the center aisle, her cape flapping behind her. As she mounted the stage and crossed to her podium upon a path of broken roses, the orchestra played "Sweet Hour of Prayer."

Sister Lydia knelt next to the podium and waited for the orchestra to finish. When she finally stood up, the choir stood up along with her, and under Vivian Colthurst's direction, they sang a brand-new song in the hymnological canon (written just the year before), but one well suited for Sister Lydia's purpose:

> *Jesus, Rose of Sharon, bloom within my heart;*
> *Beauties of Thy truth and holiness impart,*
> *That where'er I go my life may shed abroad*
> *Fragrance of the knowledge of the love of God.*

When the song was finished, Sister Lydia addressed the four thousand empty seats in front of her, pretending that each was occupied by someone eager to hear her words of happy salutation. "A warm welcome to each and every one of you here today. May God's grace live within your heart and His love anoint your abiding spirit."

Will Holborne had been to see Minerva Quintane twice before. The first trip was made early in his college career when he motored out from Zenith with Jerry and Tom and Pat, each of the four woefully under-versed in the ways of love—even the kind of love that is obtained for a sawbuck (or a shiny Indian Head eagle if one wishes to impress). It was a longstanding rite of passage for the Winnemac Aggie to pay at least one visit to Minerva and her "girls" at some point during his four years at the A&M. Aggies mounted the stairs of Miss Minerva's storied gingerbread Victorian on the outskirts of town as *boys*, and, it was said, descended those same stairs fifteen to twenty minutes later as *men*.

The second time Will went to see Minerva he was alone. She didn't remember him from the time before ("Far too many of you panting-mouthed puppies for poor Miss Minerva to keep track of") but got to know him over ersatz Brandy Daisies in her front piano parlor, which was where she preferred to conduct all her interviews—those little booze-lubricated tête-à-têtes that helped the madam pick just the right girl for every taste. Will, as Minerva quickly discovered, liked big-boned, flaxen-haired Swedish farm girls, of which Minerva had at least two in residence. (Strong, big-boned farm girls, Minerva confided, also came in handy around the place on Monday chore days.)

Today, Will Holborne was making his third visit. This time Minerva *did* remember him. She recalled that he liked girls with an ethnic heritage similar to his own. But today Will didn't want Katrin or Helfrida. He had a very different type in mind.

"Do you have any girls staying here that maybe don't seem to have much use for men?"

"Don't have much use for men?" Minerva clucked like an old hen. "That's like asking do I keep any dairy cows out in the barn that don't give milk. What a silly question!"

Will's serious expression remained fixed. It told Minerva that *he* didn't think the question silly at all.

Minerva stopped smiling. She chewed her lower lip for a moment. "Do *you* happen to know a girl who's that way? Did she break your heart, slugger?"

Will didn't answer right away. He took a drink first. "She didn't break my heart," he finally disclosed. "But she was bad news."

Minerva nodded, slowly comprehending. "Sounds to me like it was one particular man she didn't have much use for."

Will shook his head. "No, Miss Quintane. It was men in general. There are girls like that. You must know a few. I knew a *man* who was like that, but the other way around."

"And if I find you a girl like that, what are you going to do, Will?"

"I'll make her do what nature intended. Whether she likes it or not."

Minerva laughed. "But of course she wouldn't like it—wouldn't like it at all, would she? Will, honey, I don't think you have any business punishing any girl—mine or any other—for what some other girl did to you. There is no amount of money that can get me to arrange something like that."

Then Minerva grinned enigmatically.

"But maybe there *is* a way I can be of service. But only if you promise to be a good boy and play by the rules. Rose. She has a special gift. She can pretend to be anybody you like."

"Is she pretty?"

"She's quite pretty. She *is* a little Rubenesque."

"I don't know what that word means."

"She's *ample*, darling. She's well-rounded, in the physical sense."

"That's good. I like that. That works."

Minerva set her glass down and rose from her chair. "You intrigue me, Mr. Holborne. You're quite a closed book. But then, what man isn't?"

Sister Lydia now spread her arms out to the sides and lifted her eyes to the stained-glass skylights in the dome above her. "I thank You, my loving God, for Your divine presence in the lives of all Your children who've gathered here today. So very grateful are we for the wondrous blessings You've bestowed upon us."

Sister Lydia lowered her arms and re-engaged her imagined audience with a look of fevered passion. She stepped to the side of the rose-covered pulpit and sniffed. "Do you smell it, brothers and sisters? Do you smell that sweet attar of roses in the air? Is there any flower more fragrant? Any flower more delicate in its construction? What is the rose but the embodiment of beauty upon this earth?"

Sister Lydia held out a rose as if she were admiring herself in a hand mirror. "But a thing so beautiful, so ambrosially fragrant can only be appreciated in contrast to those things which *cannot* be thought beautiful or fragrant or caressing of the human spirit. My children, the rose has thorns for a very good reason. As we embrace the Rose of Sharon that is our loving, merciful Jesus Christ, we must realize that faith is a thing to be earned through triumph over adversity, through the endurance of all the pain of life's trials and tribulations. It is a gift, yea, it is a gift, brothers and sisters, of most divine purpose, but we must make the journey that will place us in the garden to receive it. God helps us in our struggles by setting our sights upon the garden, upon the rose that dwells within. There are thorns along *that* path, children, nettles and briars, and spines and needles of the thirsty desert, but we persevere for the love and grace that waits for us at journey's end.

"Our blood is red for a reason, brothers and sisters. It is red to match the blood of Christ in his sufferings upon the Golgotha cross, and it is red to match the exquisite color of that Rose of Sharon which is the floral incarnation of our dear and loving Lord."

Now the choir members rose to their feet and sang out:

Just as I am—without one plea,
But that Thy blood was shed for me,
And that Thou bid'st me come to Thee,
O Lamb of God, I come.
I come.

———

Rose looked nothing like Ruth, but Will drew the similarity in his mind's eye.

And Rose was good. She was very good.

"What are you doing here?" she asked unsmilingly. "Men aren't allowed in this room."

"I couldn't care less," said Will, closing the door behind him.

The two stood for a moment, staring at one another in silence. Then Will began his advance. Each step forward elicited a corresponding step of retreat from Rose, until she was halted by the wall behind her. With no place else for her to go, Will stood before her, his muscular arms hanging at his sides like slaughterhouse slabs of beef, the veins of his thick and corded neck prominent and pulsing. He was breathing deeply, perspiring heavily at the temples. He was regarding Rose with menacing contempt—the jungle predator taking the measure of his cornered prey.

Rose responded. She demanded that he leave at once, hissing the words at him with requisite venom. She was playing the game—just as Minerva had instructed her—but it was all she could do to tamp down the genuine fear she was feeling at this moment—a fear which, left unchecked, could only undermine her performance.

Yet there *was* no performance so far as Will was concerned. What Will saw standing in defiance before him was a woman who could very well have been Ruth—a woman who could have gotten along quite well without Will, without *any* man for that matter.

And how does man subdue, subjugate, subordinate woman if woman is going to muck up the works with all this ridiculous ramping and resisting?

Will would see to it that at least this one woman knew her role, knew her place and did not depart from it.

No matter what it took.

The rehearsal ended after more stirring words from Sister Lydia, performances from several singers—a trio of young men in A.E.F. uniforms who sang "Soldiers of Christ, Arise," a quartet of older women from the choir who sang softly and tenderly the old hymn "Softly and Tenderly," two eight-year-old twin girls in ribbons and pigtails who earnestly belted out "The Church in the Wildwood," with one of the two mostly singing the lyrics and the other mostly doing the "come, come, come"s. Finally, a stout Negro woman from the largest of the city's A.M.E. churches walked out on the stage to astonished gasps from the ushers (who hadn't been apprised of her participation), half of whom were touched by her willingness to contribute her beautiful voice to the day's celebration and half of whom either didn't know or had forgotten the fact that Sister Lydia was fond of Negroes and hoped to make her tabernacle services as racially integrated as her tent revivals had been.

The woman sang "His Eye is on the Sparrow," and three of We Five wept: Molly, who was reminded each time Sister Lydia spoke the words "our Heavenly Father" that the fate of her own *earthly* father still remained in question; Carrie, who deeply missed her late mother, herself a woman of strong religious faith; and Ruth, who recalled that this very song was sung by a member of her aunt and uncle's own racially integrated church at a memorial service for the woman's nephew who was lynched by members of the Indiana Klan.

It wasn't the clean uppercut which brought Will down, or even the not-so-clean-but-powerfully-delivered left hook. It was the liver punch. It left Will on his knees, cradling his gut in agony, as if all of his insides had been violently rearranged. He was left there on the floor by Big Jim, the Negro ex-boxer whom Minerva employed for the purpose of rescuing her girls from the violent drunks, from the all-around women-haters, from the odd ducks like Will Holborne who were either unwilling or unable to take revenge upon the true objects of their wrathful discontent but must seek a paid surrogate to abuse in their stead.

And Rose Sowell was much abused. In the time it took Big Jim to hear her cry for help and then race up the stairs to her room (with Minerva following close behind), Will had taken the opportunity to clabber up the girl's painted face with his pummeling fist and to change the hue of various parts of her pink chubby flesh to red and black and a species of blue-green not often seen imprinted upon human epidermis.

Under his threat of tossing Will down the stairs, Big Jim kept Will on ice until the cops arrived—specifically the two cops with whom Minerva had a special relationship. (They were both on the take.)

"I'm afraid that things got just a little out of hand," said Rose in answer to one of the officers' questions. Ordinarily this particular officer liked to conduct his interview with one of his hands roving absently about the female victim's smooth, conveniently exposed thighs, but for this interview, in deference to the severity of Rose's injuries, he kept his paws to himself.

"I worried that things might go in this direction," said Minerva, tossing a regretful look at Will, who was now sitting handcuffed and wild-eyed upon Rose's quilted vanity chair in the corner of the room.

"Why didn't you tell me?" Rose painfully groaned.

"Oh, I really should have. Here, darling. Take another aspirin."

Chapter Twenty-Four

London, England, October 1940

"Is the professor sick?" asked Molly, sawing a piece of her stewed steak.

"Not sick, really," replied Bella. "Just a little knocked up." Bella, playing to the hilt the role of hostess to her six impromptu dinner guests, passed a serving plate of currant rolls to Maggie, who was seated next to her. "I barbitoned him, you see. The poor thing hasn't slept for the last two nights, so I thought I'd give him a few good winks before the sirens go off again."

Ruth spooned up more new potatoes for her plate. "You take very good care of your new husband. You're taking good care of us, as well. Bella, you've become quite the mother hen in your premature old age."

Bella laughed. "I get lots of help. Mrs. Hood from next door cooked most of this feast. I wanted to give all of you one thumping good meal before you head off to points unknown. Of course they're known to *you*, but I'd rather you not tell *me* in case the police drop by and start asking questions. I can certainly lie if I have to, but it's so much nicer if I *don't* have to."

Jane cocked her head, listening. "He's snoring."

"I'm so glad," replied Bella. "My poor sweet Reggie. He's think-ing about taking a leave of absence from the college. Since the phys-ics lab copped it last month, he's had to teach out of the gardener's potting shed. Not that he's got that many students these days—so many have dropped out to enlist—but he says it's still hard to do anything on the two or three hours of sleep he gets at night *and* with groundskeepers and gardeners popping in and out during his lectures and rattling pots."

Carrie reached across the table and touched the hand of her friend and former next-door neighbour. "Considering what the professor's been going through, you're both very kind to let us stay here tonight."

"You're most welcome. But I seriously doubt you'll get to spend the *whole* night here. Since there isn't room for all of us in the shelter out back, I'm afraid that once that siren starts screaming, I'll have to send the whole lot of you off to the tube station." Bel-la smiled. "*Although*...there have been some interesting rumours flying about lately—that the Nazis are deliberately avoiding this neighbourhood on Hitler's special instructions. They say he adores Du Cane Court and wants to use that whole block to house his SS officers after the inva—"

The words of Bella's explanation trailed off because Carrie had turned away from her in the middle of them. Bella bit her lip.

"I'm so sorry, love. I wasn't thinking."

Carrie spoke without looking at Bella. "Or maybe you just thought the incendiary that ended my mother's life was a Nazi *mis-take*."

"That isn't what I— all I'm saying is that some of our neighbours here in Elmfield Road do believe this, and so they don't bother to take shelter. That's all I'm saying."

Carrie nodded. She turned back to her friend and said, soften-ing, "I know you meant no harm." She tried to smile. "Maybe it isn't Art Deco Hitler likes. Maybe it's all those music hall singers and dancers who live there. Sometimes I walk along the High Road and I can hear them carrying on inside. I know what it's like to lose oneself in music—to forget there's even a war going on. To forget *everything* that eats you up from the inside."

Maggie touched Carrie tenderly on the shoulder. "Like the night we went to the Palais and you were carried a million miles away."

Carrie laughed mordantly. "By a man who probably should have been sitting in a prison cell."

Bella considered Carrie for a moment before speaking. "Carrie, you haven't sworn off men altogether, have you?"

Jane laughed. "Oh, I don't think you have to worry about *that*." At that moment Lyle returned from his trip to the lav, and all the women sitting at the dining room table, save Carrie, burst into laughter. Lyle looked at them speculatively and then checked his flies.

"No, brother, we aren't laughing at *you*," said Jane, and then quickly correcting herself: "Well, of course we are. But not in a bad way."

Lyle, still looking befuddled, sat down next to Carrie just as Professor Prowse padded sleepily into the room from his early evening nap. "I *thought* I smelt Mrs. Hood's vegetable soup. Is there any left?"

"Pull up a chair, Reggie," said Bella, going to her drowsy-eyed husband to smooth back his bed-mussed hair. "I'll fetch you a bowl. You know all the girls. You don't know Lyle. He's Jane's brother. Lyle's a fugitive from justice. These chums of mine from childhood are his abettors."

The professor and Lyle shook hands. "You'll be pleased to know, Mr. Higgins, that I—" The professor interrupted himself to cough away some accumulated phlegm from his throat. "—am a moral relativist. Whatever you did, you had your reason for doing it, and it isn't my place to judge." The professor yawned. "Are those Mrs. Hood's currant rolls? What did we do to deserve that woman's cornucopian generosity?" Assuming there'd be no answer to his potentially rhetorical question, Prowse bit off the end of one of the rolls and continued, "At times of communal crisis, members of society are forced by circumstances to do one or more of the following things, and you'll usually see all of them employed in varying measure. One: 'Extend, amend, or bend.' The rules, that is. The rules of societal and civil engagement. Exempli gratia: Michelle Hood *extending* her wonted liberality to bounteous excess. Elsewhere, female factory workers and Land Girls being permitted to wear trousers. Cooks replacing butter with marg."

"But certainly not by choice!" pronounced Ruth. Everyone laughed.

The professor quickly reclaimed the floor: "A chap puts on a uniform and suddenly he's given license to kill. Or rather, to follow the 'amend and bend' model, the soldier has been provided a 'justification' for murder. By definition, it's still murder, but we fix a wartime rider to the rule to extenuate the consequences.

"Two. 'Break the rules entirely.' Both sides in this war have done their share of *that*. They've broken confirmed promises not to bomb civilian targets. The rules against killing noncombatants are ignored, purposefully flouted.

"Three. 'Anarchy reigns.' All rules simply disappear. It is every man to his own defence, every man by his own conscience—should such a thing as conscience withstand the crucible of communal crisis.

"One of my colleagues—Dr. Haverson, in the astronomy department—he's conducting research on the relationship between coronal mass ejections—those bursts of solar wind and electromagnetic radiation that sometimes get tossed by the sun far into space—which means, on occasion, right at *us*—and thermospheric auroras—the Borealis and Australis—examining the degree to which the auroras are intensified by these solar events. I mention this because he and I had a very interesting discussion the other day about something quite extraordinary that took place in a small mill town outside of Manchester in 1859. It was coincident to the first recorded observation of a solar flare, and the solar storm that went along with it. The storm was the biggest there has ever been—at least since astronomers acquired the ability to recognise them. The result of this event was one of the most chilling examples of mass hysteria ever recorded."

"Mass hysteria?" asked Ruth.

"The whole town, to put it in the vernacular, losing its bloody mind."

"I don't understand. Just because the sky lit up with beautiful colours?"

"It was a little more than simply beautiful colours. Are you going to eat that biscuit? Thank you. The whole sky lit up like noontide in a cloudless desert, even though it happened in the middle of the night. For the people of Tulleford it augured the end of the world. Armageddon. Whatever apocalyptic designation you wish to put to it. I mention this because it's the best example I can think of for the kind of disorder and chaos that hasn't really any underlining purpose. It's the human animal in a state of utter madness. Chickens running about without their heads. This is what happened in Tulleford in the early hours of September 2, 1859. I fear this is just the sort of madness into which we will descend should this terrible war go on for too long. We'll lose every covenant of civilized society. We'll even lose our instinct for self-preservation. We'll be like those who jump to their deaths from burning buildings—mindlessly trading one form of death for another."

Carrie got up and left the table, putting herself in a chair across the room. Molly watched her, along with all the others, and then turned to Professor Prowse and said, "Whatever your reason for bringing all this up, Professor Prowse, I don't see it. It isn't any wonder you don't sleep well at night, if these are the sorts of loathsome thoughts you live with every day."

Bella rushed to her husband's defence. "Molly! What a horrible thing to say!"

Molly's jaw tightened. "I meant every word of it. We're all trying our best to cope with some very trying circumstances, and yet your husband seems to feel the need to tell us about something that happened years and years ago that does us no good whatsoever. I don't want to hear about it and I don't think my sisters do either. We're tired of being frightened. And we're tired of being depressed. And I don't have to sit here and listen to someone who seems to *want* to make me—*us*—even more afraid and even more depressed than we already are." Molly got up from the table.

Professor Prowse rose as well. He looked thoroughly chidden. "I'm sorry I brought up the Tulleford incident. I truly am. Sometimes I forget I'm not standing behind my lectern addressing my students."

Molly wasn't yet ready to suspend her reproof: "I don't fancy your students would much appreciate this sort of talk either."

"You're right, dear girl. There's a proper time and a proper place for dispassionate scholarship, for detached analysis. This is neither a fitting time nor setting. I must say, though—and you must certainly see the inherent irony—that this does return us to my original thesis: that we live in a most extraordinary era in which the human animal is apt to behave in wildly unpredictable ways—ways that aren't governed by any of the rules of conduct we've laid down."

"But we don't toss away everything we are as human beings," put in Maggie from across the room. She had gone to be with Carrie. "The species simply couldn't survive if we did."

"No, Miss Barton. It could not." Prowse sighed heavily. "My lecture for the evening is over. Let's talk about something else. Or perhaps I should finish eating my tea in silence and then return to blissful, oblivious slumber. I used to dream. I don't anymore. My mind becomes an empty blackboard. And I wouldn't have it any other way."

The words had hardly left Prowse's mouth before the local air raid siren began to sound. It was still light outside. This evening's visitation of terror from the skies was coming a bit earlier than usual.

Bella Prowse arched an eyebrow and half smiled. "Ah, now the moment of truth. Do we sit about this table and ignore the howl of—how was it you put it last night, Reggie?"

"The Teutonic banshee."

"Or do my husband and I fly to our Andy and to the tedious company of the Jossers and the Collinses who share it with us, and you flee with all the rest of the neighbourhood up the High Road to the Balham Underground?"

"I'm too fagged to move," said Jane.

"Then I'll carry you," said Lyle. "We shouldn't stay here."

Jane sat up in her chair. "But what about—oh, you didn't hear. You were out of the room attending the necessary. There's a theory among many of the residents of this street that Hitler won't strike here because of a rum attachment to the Du Cane."

"That's daft," said Lyle. "Hitler may like that building. But that don't mean Goering does."

Carrie smiled and shrugged. "Lyle does have a point."

We Five lifted themselves begrudgingly from their chairs. "Take whatever you like from the larder," said Bella. "I also have playing cards, and Ludo, and Snakes and Ladders, and there are books in the study. They're mostly Reggie's so at best they'll put you to sleep for a while. But do put a jerk in it. The station is five blocks away and you haven't time to dally."

Ruth shook her head in amazement. "Look at you. You *have* become the mother hen."

"Just cheese it, Ruth. And you needn't tuck those biscuits away so furtively. Take as many as you want and don't feel the least bit guilty about it."

"You're a love," said Ruth, blowing a kiss across the table.

We Six hurried up Balham High Road to the tube station. All round, others were doing the same—parents holding the hands of un-evacuated children; old men and women, who could not help being reminded that they had done much the same thing during the First World War, that some things seemed destined never to change. Some of those in the road wore haversacks and carried blankets and Thermos flasks, prepared for a long night. One woman scuttled along dressed in only a pink night robe and matching pink swan's-down slippers. But others didn't seem in any hurry at all. They had been through this drill often enough before; someplace else would get the first pasting—that was usually the way, wasn't it? Or they would wait for Balham to sufficiently hunker down before paying their own reluctant visit to the community shelter.

Keep Calm and Carry On.
We Are Open for Business.
Hitler will not defeat us.
I will duck my head when I'm good and ready, you bloody flying monkeys.

During air raids, the Balham Underground ticket window was closed. No one was expected to buy a ticket when the farthest they'd be traveling was down to the end of the station platform. Take your pick: southbound or northbound? As the six crossed the crowded booking hall to step upon the rattling down-escalator, they randomly chose the south platform. Others were choosing the same—people who, before the night was over, would find their lives coming to a swift, tragic end.

Chapter Twenty-Five

Bellevenue, Mississippi, February 1997

"Is it a Duster or a Twister?" asked Carrie, ducking her head inside the vehicle through the open passenger door.

"It's both a Duster *and* a Twister," said Lyle, "and I hope the battery isn't dead, because I don't know where I put the jumpers. I don't drive this car very much. Jane don't either."

"This was your daddy's car, wasn't it?" asked Carrie.

"That's right," said Jane, "and I don't know if any of you remember this, but Daddy had a bad habit of driving Winston around in the backseat. And he *wasn't* in the habit of cleaning up after him."

"What are you saying?" asked Carrie. "That your father, as a rule, would just leave doggy doo-doo in his car?"

"As a rule, it was usually more like diarrhea dribbles."

Ruth groaned. "Oh God, Jane, really! Do you *mind*?"

"Well, I don't smell any bulldog doo-doo back here now," said Carrie, matter-of-factly. "Maybe somebody got in here and cleaned it all up."

"I call shot-got!" announced Molly.

"*Shot-got*? What are you talking about, Molly?" asked Jane.

"I think Molly means shot*gun*," said Ruth. "I also think the Valium just kicked in. Molly, how many Valiums did you take?"

"Two," said Molly. "They were old and I didn't think just one was gonna do the trick."

Ruth nodded. "And are you doing better now, peanut?"

"I'm doing just fine. And I hope ya'll don't think I do this very often. It's just that the dream I had—it was so real. It was so horribly real with the wind and everything. Do you want me to tell you about it?"

"You already did, honey," said Ruth. "Try not to think about it."

"I'll ride up front too," said Carrie. "Next to Lyle. That means Jane and Ruth and Mags—ya'll will have to sit in the back."

Maggie didn't hear this. She was busy arranging all the luggage in the trunk.

"Is it all gonna fit?" asked Jane, coming around to monitor her efforts.

"I think so. Even though it looks like Ruth and Carrie have totally violated the one-bag-per-person rule."

"I *heard* that!" shouted Ruth from the other end of the car. "The rule wasn't fair. Carrie and I have a lot farther to go than the rest of you."

Carrie and Ruth actually *did* have farther to go—*much* farther. They had planned to spend a few days at Maggie's Uncle Whit's vacation house in Bienville National Forest—Carrie's idea; it would give her a few extra days with Lyle—and then Jane had agreed to drive them to the airport in Jackson. By late that night they'd be in Los Angeles and ready to start this much anticipated new chapter in their lives—Ruth pounding the Hollywood pavement and Carrie attending a music school in Glendale.

But first they all had to make it to the vacation house, and the weather wasn't being at all cooperative. Molly walked over to the open garage door and looked out. The rain was coming down in thick sheets, the back mist spritzing her face. Every now and then

the sky would light up, and the steady thrum of the heavy down-
pour would be augmented by the crackle of encroaching lightning.
Molly turned and said calmly and a little slurringly to her friends, "I
think we should probably wait until it lets up."

"And how long will that be, Molly?" asked Jane. "The weath-
erman said it could keep up like this all night. And what if the cops
come back and do a stakeout after the storm finally does taper off?
They'll catch us right as we pull out."

Ruth studied the surrounding wet afternoon darkness. "How
do you know they aren't out there already? Sitting in their patrol car
eating donuts and fixing to make all of our lives totally miserable?"

"In *this* rain?" asked Molly.

Carrie walked over to Molly and said, "It's all planned, honey.
Don't mess it up. Don't you want to see your daddy? The sooner we
get to Mags' uncle's house, the better."

Jane turned to her brother. "Lyle, you should probably hoof it
over to Ruth's house now. Take the back way, like we talked about,
so you'll keep off the street."

"I know the plan. But first I gotta see if this shitty old engine is
gonna turn over for us." Lyle slid onto the front-seat bench and put
the key in the ignition. The shitty old engine started immediately.
He grinned. "I never liked Plymouths. But I'm liking Plymouths
just fine right *now*. Where's my umbrella? Hey, Ruth! Herb and Lucille know I'm coming, right?"

"They know, they know. So skedaddle. Everybody else in the
car. Jane, you gonna drive us to my house or do you want *me* to?"

Jane walked around to the driver's side of the Duster while
Lyle threw on his slicker and slipped out the garage's back door. "I
think it better be me, Ruth. Daddy didn't like just *anybody* driving
his car."

Ruth rolled her eyes exasperatedly. "Your father's been dead for
four years, Jane."

"Humor me."

Molly had moved to the door through which Lyle had just left. She was still assessing the growing storm. On a sunny day she would have gotten a good view of Jane and Lyle's junk-strewn backyard behind the antique store. Right now the cataract of water coming off the roof gave her the feeling she was standing in the mouth of a cave, right behind an enormous waterfall. Molly said, to no one in particular: "Just a couple of weeks ago Mags slip-slided us off the road and right into a dip—a *ditch*. We don't seem to have a very good track record when it comes to riding around on stick sleets."

"Well, the good thing, baby doll," shouted Jane from the driver's side of the Duster, "is that Mags ain't drivin'. I'm not letting her anywhere near this steering wheel. Anyway, once we make our secret pick-up of Lyle from Ruth's house, it'll be Lyle behind the wheel all the rest of the way, and he's never had a single wreck."

"*Sober*," clarified Ruth.

"Which he is right now, smartass. So everybody get in the car and let's get this show on the road."

Jane had stopped mail delivery and put a sign on the window of the antique store that read Closed for Inventory. Will Reopen Soon. Aside from that, no one else had any hint they were leaving town, so as not to raise suspicions, with the obvious necessary exceptions of Herb and Lucille Mobry, and, of course, Michael Osborne and Clara Barton, who were supposedly already at the vacation house and awaiting the arrival of We Five.

By the time Jane had finally pulled the yellow-gold coupe out onto the street, the rain was coming down on a Genesiacal scale. Jane drove fifteen miles an hour to the Mobrys' place—a quarter mile away—to pick up Lyle. The subterfuge wasn't necessary. Nobody was watching the house, and the Duster wasn't going to be followed. The cops had come the night before to ask their questions and had put them to Jane in a very routine, almost bored manner.

They openly registered doubt over Will Holborne's claim that he knew for certain it was Lyle who'd killed his friend and roommate Tom Katz. As it turned out, the Bellevenue police lieutenant who was handling the case and the county sheriff who was working with him had theories of their own having nothing to do with Lyle Higgins and everything to do with a string of recent murders in the area, each potentially linked to a Memphis crime syndicate thought to be muscling in on the casinos' sports betting operations. An unrelated revenge killing based on personal animus wasn't a possibility anybody was considering at this point.

We Six didn't know this. The only thing they knew at this moment was that no one seemed to be surveilling their getaway Duster-Twister as it headed out of town in the torrential rain. And even if they *had* been accidentally observed by the cops driving around in the middle of a major early spring thunderstorm, it wouldn't have elicited suspicion—only the possibility of an offhanded comment by one of the wisecracking officers that "somebody in that Duster sure picked a fine time to run out of Marlboros."

Lyle was waiting. He took the wheel and drove the six of them in the direction of Bienville National Forest in the middle of the state.

Herb and Lucille Mobry, standing side by side looking out one of their living room windows, watched their rainswept departure. "Our Ruthie-girl's leaving the nest," Lucille had sniffled.

"It was only a matter of time before she'd want to try her wings, Sister."

"I hope California treats her nice."

"Ruth can take care of herself. She'll do just fine."

"Do you think she'll call us now and then, Brother?"

"Of course she will." Herb paused. "But regardless, we should probably go ahead and rent out that old trailer. Ruth's boss at the casino, Ms. Colthurst, said one of her new cocktail waitresses is looking for a place. A real nice girl. Kind of quiet."

"Quiet? Well, we can't have that, Herb."

"Why?"

"Because Ruth has spoiled me for girls who speak up for themselves. We'll have to pull this new one out of her shell."

"If you say so, Lucille."

"Jane, honey, do you have any more of those little prepackaged cheese and crackers?" asked Carrie. "I've got the munchy-belly."

"Check the snack sack. I think it's up there with you."

"Here it is," said Carrie. "Molly's using it for a footrest. Molly, pick up your feet and let me look in the snack sack."

"What's that smell?" asked Ruth. "All of a sudden the car smells like old bananas."

"It's old bananas," said Carrie. "I was gonna bake us some banana bread when we got to the woods. They always say the riper the banana the better the bread."

"Well, they're stinking up the whole car," concluded Ruth. "Lyle, how can see anything through that windshield?"

"It ain't easy," admitted Lyle. Lyle turned on the radio and skittered around the dial to find a weather report.

"Oh stop it right there—please, please, please," said Molly. "I love that song. It's from *Ghost*—it's what they played when Patrick Swayze was trying to help Demi Moore turn her pot."

"Not *turn* her pot—*throw* her pot," corrected Ruth from the backseat. Ruth turned to Maggie and said, "But let's give her the benefit of the doubt since she's on industrial-strength tranquilizers."

Molly didn't hear this. "And—and—and—all the clay got all over the place because she was hungering for his touch."

"Lonely river flow to the sea, to the sea," sang Carrie pensively.

"Like us," said Ruth. "All this rain is gonna take us right out to sea. Are you sure we shouldn't pull over for a few minutes?"

"Sure," said Lyle. "Let me just find a place."

"Lonely rivers say 'wait for me, yes for me,'" paraphrased Carrie tunefully.

"I cannot believe LeAnn Rimes was only four when she sang this," marveled Molly.

Ruth muttered, "*Fourteen.* Not four."

Molly went on, "Only four years old and singing this very adult song about rivers and love and shit."

"She was *fourteen*," muttered Ruth.

"Indulge her," whispered Maggie. "It's just nice to see her finally calmed down."

"*I* could use a Valium right now," said Jane, looking apprehensively out the window. "I don't like this. I don't like this one bit." Jane, who was sitting directly behind her brother, leaned forward. "Lyle, really now, honey, find a place to pull over."

"I'm trying to. It's just farms and fields—I mean, from what I can see, and I can't see much."

LeAnn Rimes was gone. She had been replaced by a man giving a dire weather report. "The National Weather Bureau has issued a tornado warning for the following counties in northern Mississippi—"

"Well, we can't just pull off to the side of the road," said Ruth. "Not if there are tornadoes all around."

Lyle groaned. "Well, what do ya'll want me to do—pull over or not pull over?"

Several opinions went up at once, while Molly said, "Do you think Patrick Swayze has soft and supple girl hands? Some say this, but I never noticed."

Jane raised her voice above everyone else's: "Everybody shut up and help Lyle find some safe place to pull off. The wind's picking up. This isn't normal wind. It's blowing sideways."

Jane was correct in her observation. The car was being slammed in the side by forty- and fifty-mile-an-hour wind gusts. Lyle was having a difficult time keeping the Duster on the road.

"On second thought, Carrie," said Jane, nervously, "why don't you keep on singing?"

"And help take our minds off the fact that we're all about to die," commented Ruth in an equally nervous voice.

"I've never been in a tornado," admitted Molly, peering calmly through the passenger window. "I've never even *seen* one except in the movies. Like—like *Twister*, with all the cows and tractors and stuff flying around. But maybe there are also tornadoes like the one in *The Wizard of Oz* that picked up Dorothy's house and set it down all nice and easy in that place where all the midgets lived."

The wind was wailing now. The wind had begun to sound angry and human.

Ruth groaned. "I don't think real tornadoes ever do that, Molly. I believe they're much more violent than that."

"Holy shit, this looks bad, Lyle!" cried Jane from the backseat. She was bent all the way forward now, her fingers curled around Lyle's headrest. "Just pull off *anywhere*."

"I think that's a farm up there. Doesn't that look like a barn?"

"Whatever it is, it's got to be a lot better than this death-trap-on-wheels we're sitting in right now."

"I think one of the tornadoes in *Twister* was tossing around tanker trucks like they were Tinkertoys," said Molly.

"That was an F-5," said Ruth. "F-5s are very rare, as I understand it." Then to Maggie: "Molly needs to shut the fuck up, okay?"

"What number tornado is *this* one?" asked Carrie nervously.

"What makes you think we're in the middle of a tornado?" asked Maggie.

"Because my ears just popped and I can hardly hear myself think."

"Do you hear a freight train?" asked Jane. "They say approaching tornadoes make a sound just like a freight train."

Carrie shook her head. "No. It just sounds like wind."

"Then we're probably all right for the moment," offered Maggie.

Lyle squinted through the windshield. "That gate looks locked."

"Well, we weren't gonna stay in the car anyway," said Jane. "Let's just get out and climb that fence and go inside that barn."

"In the rain?" asked Molly.

Ruth snorted. "Molly, you need to get out of the car. Everybody out of the car. Anybody who objects is gonna get knocked unconscious and thrown over that fence like a hay bale."

Molly said in her poutiest voice, "Would you please stop being such a meanie?"

"It's tough love, baby. Back me up, Jane."

"One hundred percent. Everybody move your asses," said Jane. "Carrie, baby-honey, that umbrella isn't gonna do you much good. It'll just carry you away like Mary Poppins."

"I'm scared," said Carrie.

"I'm right here," said Lyle, squeezing her hand.

We Six spilled out of the Duster-Twister and onto the shoulder of the state highway and then trudged, heads down, into the driving wind and the driving rain toward the old barn, which sat at some distance from a small darkened farm shack whose electricity had already gone out.

Molly tried to remember what happened to Helen Hunt and Bill Paxton when they fled into a barn at the end of the tornado movie. She couldn't quite recall, and then in an instant she *did* recall and a great chill went down her spine, even though she had thoroughly tranquilized herself.

Chapter Twenty-Six

Tutti

Ruth and Carrie were going to America. It had been decided that each would create new lives for themselves on the other side of the Atlantic pond. This made perfect sense, given their present situations. Ruth knew not a soul upon the earth to whom she was connected by blood, and with the exception of her absent and itinerate father, Carrie could make the same claim for herself. And who was to say that Ruth and Carrie's long friendship didn't create a bond which surpassed in steadfastness and affinity that of familial attachment? For has it not been stated time and again (in this story most markedly) that the link which joins female friends may be most sisterly in its strength and complexion?

The plan was made. And then the plan was altered in the best way possible when Lyle Higgins confessed upon the heels of its disclosure that he must be with the woman who had captured his heart, whither she might wish to go.

Would Ruth have it?

Yes, Ruth would have it.

And how would the three of them take themselves from the Isle of Anglesey in Wales to New York City? They would stop in the cottage by the sea for a few weeks and then make their way down to Cardiff, because leaving Great Britain from Southampton could pose difficulties for Higgins, especially if at the time of their sailing he was still being sought for the murder of Tom Catts.

It was a practicable plan, although it first required transportation to Liverpool and then transit through northern Wales. It was decided that they should take the horse and waggon Lyle used for his deliveries, with Lyle safely concealed in the back—that is, until they passed into Wales, where his anonymity would afford safe passage even with him situated upon the driver's box with reins in hand. As for Maggie and Molly and Carrie, they would go by hired carriage, which would be secured in Liverpool.

And where would all six spend those final hours before departure? The women would stop in the emporium and Jane's brother would drowse beneath the hay of the small area stable behind the shop.

Yet Lyle Higgins did not drowse that night, nor, in fact, did any of the others.

At first, thoughts of their impending journey kept each of the travellers from drifting into untroubled slumber. Then later, in the small hours of the night, there came something of a much more compelling nature to rob them of their needed rest—something of such grave importance and consequence that all thoughts of the morning journey were superseded.

It began with cries and shouts in the lane of sudden advent and without explanation. Jane looked out the front window of the family shop and saw that the street was glowing, as if from the light of a great many torches or lanterns, and there was a hazy cast to the luminosity, which made the picture seem not real at all.

Jane stepped out the front door and looked up at the sky. To her great surprise what she saw above the rooftops and treetops was a magnificent display of northern lights—brilliant unfurled curtains and squiggles and swirls of red and green and yellow and purple, the auroras glowing and shimmering with dazzling brilliance. It was the sky itself that lighted the street, and the light that shone down seemed to be growing brighter and brighter as if daylight were coming in accelerated prematurity. There were townspeople wandering about, many of them still dressed in their nightshirts and sleeping gowns, some in bare feet. They had emerged from their homes, just as had Jane, and were staring skyward in rapt wonderment, some clearly delighted and enchanted by the beauty to be found in this unexpected empyreal presentation. Yet others wore looks upon their faces that betrayed a quizzical pondering over what should be the reason behind it all.

Jane was soon joined by her sisters, whose faces were gleaming and radiant in the multihued illumination. "It's so *beautiful!*" Carrie whispered in a reverent, awestruck tone, as if the phenomenon had been handed down by God Himself for the pleasure of His terrestrial children.

But Molly wasn't smiling. She countered with a violent shake of the head and said in a low, fearful voice, "It is exactly what she *said* would happen."

"Who? What?" asked Ruth.

"My cousin Jemma. This is how Jemma said it would begin."

"How *what* would begin?" pursued Ruth.

"I cannot even put words to it."

The shouts and screams that had punctured the night had not suspended, but instead were now increasing in volume and intensity. These were not cries of awe and wonder. There was a more fearful, even sinister, tenor to them.

For there were those in the town of Tulleford who took the celestial array as an evil omen and expressed their horror at the tops of their lungs.

Ruth shifted uncomfortably from one leg to the other. "I'm going to ask Mr. Prowse what *he* thinks this is," she announced. She looked down at the nightgown she was wearing. "First, I'm going to get myself dressed. I suggest you all do the same."

"Mr. Prowse will tell you the same as me," said Molly, up-gazing apprehensively. "Because he was there the day Jemma made her prediction for all the town to hear."

Maggie took Molly by the arm. She addressed her sisters on Molly's behalf. "She's still asleep, you see. Molly has yet to waken from whatever nightmare still possesses her."

Molly turned to look directly at Maggie, the dread evinced upon her face holding fast. "Maggie, you must come with me to see Jemma. I wager she'll have much more to say about this."

"I'll take you to your aunt and uncle's house, Molly," returned Maggie, "but only to disabuse you of this ridiculous notion that what fills the sky has aught whatsoever to do with Jemma's foolish notions."

We Five went inside as others who lived in the lane continued to move about without seeming to know just what to do. Was one to stand and enjoy the incredible beauty of a sky filled with glimmering auroral colour, as if the display were some grand pageant to be attended and applauded? Or was there some *other* purpose to what was happening in the sky—some purpose requiring serious immediate action or *reaction* of some sort?

No one knew anything. Except that on the other side of town there were people screaming, people shouting, and they would not desist.

The night, as it was becoming quite evident, was fast unraveling.

Ruth and Jane dressed quickly and then were off and away to the Prowses' house, which was affixed to the back of Reginald Prowse's telegraphy office. Carrie slipped into a loose frock and rushed out to the stable to inform Lyle—should he not yet know—what was happening in the sky. Molly and Maggie were the last to finish dressing, for Molly's hands were trembling and she could not button herself and lace her stays without assistance. Finally, in a great hurry and flutter of spirits, the two set off for the Spaldings' cottage at the other end of town, Maggie attempting to calm a greatly agitated Molly all the while and to assuage her fear by continuing to aver that the unusual display of auroras was nothing but a harmless astronomical anomaly, for consider how often the Scandinavians witnessed such exhibitions from their Hyperborean precincts and thought nothing of it.

Molly nodded.

"I know this to be true," she said groggily. "I know that San Francisco rattles and shakes as its wont, but it still woke me."

"And now you've woken *me*," moaned Maggie in nearly inarticulate protest. "So do us both the favor of going back to sleep." Maggie rolled over upon the sleeping mat she shared with Molly on the floor of the little Chinese room.

But Maggie had scarcely gotten the words out of her mouth when the foreshock which was its preamble gave way to the great quake itself. The room shook with terrific violence, the crockery and glassware on the room's sideboard falling and shattering upon the floor, the walls shifting and juddering up and down and from side to side as if rattled by a giant hand.

In the next room Ruth and Jane tried to pick themselves up from the floor and could not. Nor could they even see one another through the thick cloud of atomized plaster dust, as strips and chunks and pellets of white plaster began to drop from the shuddering ceiling.

The same was occurring in the next room over, as Carrie, who had been sleeping alone, screamed out in terror, and Lyle, who was in the room on the other side, heard her even above the din and rose to his feet, only to be knocked back down again, and then was forced to crawl like a baby toward the door.

Now the walls and ceilings began to open up, to tear themselves into discrete planks and studs and beams, which snapped and cracked and fell this way and that, and one large beam came crashing down upon Lyle, pinning him flat to the floor, the boards beneath him continuing to undulate like the waves of an angry sea.

And all was a riot of noise from the tremendous quaking, and things throughout the tea house were crackling and fracturing into myriad pieces. And there was a thunderous rumble underneath it all that told the ear what the body could already feel and the eye could already see.

Molly tugged at the closed door that had wedged itself into its frame and she could not open it. Conversely, Ruth and Jane's door flung itself open on its own and, in fact, unhinged itself entirely from its frame, ripping through the drapery hanging in front of it. Through the cloud of dust the two could see the large copper gasolier in the dining room swinging wildly back and forth like a mad pendulum, while beneath it a wooden Buddha rolled its roly-poly self across the rippling, heaving, snapping floorboards like a performing Chinese tumbler.

In her own little cell, Carrie covered her mouth and nose with her hand.

But even in that intermediary moment between sleep and wakefulness, she recognized and registered the acrid tang of smoke.

She was the first to smell it. And she was the one to wake and alert her sisters and Jane's brother Lyle to the frightening reality of it, situated as they were upon surplus army cots in the basement storeroom of Sister Lydia's new tabernacle.

Quickly did they all wake and just as quickly did they spring to their feet. It was Lyle who stated the obvious: "The building's on fire. We have to get out."

There was a little window in one corner of the room, but it was too high and seemed far too small for even Molly, the most petite of the six, to squeeze through it.

Jane was at the door now and pulling it open, only to be knocked backward upon her heels by a blast of smoke from the outside corridor. All began coughing and choking, each struggling for breath as the room became quickly filled with a thick fog of particulates and soot and ash. Each knew that survival meant leaving this room, for closing the door would only postpone the unthinkable. And so into the smoke they went, hands and handkerchiefs and pillowcases covering gasping mouths, each with one hand left free to grab the hand of another. Heads tucked and eyes half-closed, the six shouldered their way into the darkness—commending themselves into the waiting arms of either death or salvation, their fate dependent on how extensive had spread the electrical fire which only a few minutes earlier had been but a tiny spark, though now was something large and menacing and ravenous for the very oxygen We Six required to execute their escape.

In the midst of the darkness each of the six could hear the frightened cries and frantic, desperate shouts of those fellow shelter dwellers who had also been cast into a state of utter blindness by the blast. It was a 1,400-kilo semi-armour piercing bomb that had deeply penetrated the ground beneath Balham High Road just north of the Balham Northern line station. It exploded upon impact with the cross passageway between the two platforms and immediately unleashed a terrific volume of water from severed mains and shattered sewer pipes—the water gushing directly into the stygian subterranean tube station.

We Six could hear the sound of the cascading water as it quickly began to flood the Balham tube. It was Molly who first noted the wetness about her ankles as the gathering stream coursed past.

"Maggie! Maggie, where are you?" she called. Maggie, who was standing no more than two or three feet away, swung her arms about until she made contact with Molly in the blackness and latched a hand upon her arm.

Nearby, but seemingly miles away down the platform, its cowl of darkness being pricked by little pinpoints of light from the engagement of matches and little candles and cigarette lighters, were Ruth and Jane, who had also found one another and each of whom now clung to her sister in cold, silent terror. Carrie and Lyle hadn't similar good fortune. Separated by the panicked thrashings and flailings of those who were rising from their sleeping spots, now sacrificed to that growing river of water and mud and sludge that was once the southbound platform of Balham Station, Carrie and Lyle could only call to one another, though it was difficult to be heard over the frightened screams and the roar of the surging torrent.

The sound rose and now became nearly deafening in its volume. The wind that was its source was fast whipping itself into a maddening circle about the barn. Yet Lyle continued to call out for Carrie to come to him, as he, in turn, tried to make his way to *her*. As the sideboards of the barn flew off and away, the entire structure became a skeleton-like vestige of what had only a moment earlier been wholly intact—a deceptively safe refuge for the five young women and one young man who had sought shelter there.

Ruth and Jane locked arms around each other's hips as they hooked their other arms around a wooden post set into the corner of a horse stall, each debating whether they should flee the doomed structure altogether and take their chances in the open.

Molly and Maggie were considering the same, having watched the horses and the one frightened cow do that very thing without thought in their bestial brains for what might be the consequences. In the end, the two struggled through the churning wind and flying debris toward a large tractor which sat heavy and solid and unmoving in the middle of what was left of the dismantling barn.

As Molly took her few steps in this direction, putting herself upon the doorstep of her cousin's house, she felt something hard and heavy strike her head and down she went. As she sank into unconsciousness, Molly looked briefly into the eyes of the madman now staring down at her with crazed, lascivious eyes. In that next moment Maggie sprang upon the man and began pounding his chest with angry fists for what he'd done, only to be flung to the ground by his companion. As the brace of men moved to make lecherous assault upon their two victims, their advance was halted by Jemma's father, who had at that moment swung open his front door and aimed a gun at them with the threat that he would use it if they did not vacate his property on the instant.

Other men of the town were running wildly and riotously about, smashing windows and tumbling things with hysterical fury. There were women tearing at their hair and their clothes, for it was now believed by many of those abroad that the multi-hued skies had opened special portals through which the righteous had already been uplifted into the loving embrace of the Almighty, and those who were left behind could only presume rejection, denunciation, and damnation from on high. And so they would act upon their unbridled rage over this unfortunate turn of fortune through ravagings and mindless violence and all other acts of brutish depravity, doomed as they now were.

There were still others who saw nothing apocalyptic or eschatological in the goings-on, but were nonetheless motivated to commit theft and sundry acts of mischief as means to survival in a lunatic world now suddenly made captive to mankind's most base instincts.

Reginald Prowse stood at the window next to Jane and Ruth, who had been hurried into the house. Mirabella Prowse brought a salve for his hands. They had been burnt only moments earlier by sparks that had flown from the telegraph instrument and by the small fire the sparks had ignited upon his desk and which he had fumblingly smothered out with a blanket. "It's a geomagnetic storm from the sun, is all it is," he said. "That's what has caused this. Nothing else. But I cannot explain why a scientific phenomenon, easily explained, should have thrown this town into such a state of madness. *Here* is a phenomenon that absolutely beggars comprehension."

"They think it's the end of the wo—" Jane wasn't given leave by circumstance to finish her sentence before a brick came crashing through the window and struck her in the shoulder.

She fell backward as another brick and then another shook themselves from the wall. Ruth had only a moment to pull her sister away from the wall before the whole thing came crashing down before them. Outside the little opium room, out in the dining room of the teahouse, the gas-jetted chandelier finally snapped loose from the ceiling, leaving a large and jagged hole in the wooden floor beneath it—or what was *left* of the floor, for Ruth felt certain it was about to give away entirely beneath their feet.

In Molly and Maggie's room, the two had finally succeeded in wrenching open the obstinate door that had been imprisoning them. Meanwhile, Carrie, having placed herself in her room's doorway (as one is told to do during earthquakes) continued to call out for Lyle, who was still trapped beneath his heavy wooden burden, though he was conscious and making good progress in wriggling himself out from under it.

Lyle answered Carrie.

His voice could be heard above the sound of the crackling, licking flames which now lighted his passage down the tabernacle's burning basement corridor. Carrie's hand, which had earlier slipped away from his, must now be found and drawn back to him. "Where are you, Carrie?" he hacked and sputtered. "Goddamnit! Where the hell *are* you?"

She heard him and tried to answer, but the smoke was too thick for her to open her mouth.

Jane *did* speak. She called back to the others that she'd gotten to the stairs that led up and out of the basement conflagration. "Push through!" she called. "Push through the smoke to the stairs. It isn't far!" Ruth reached out for whoever may need her assistance. Molly saw the hand of her sister and grabbed for it, but suddenly, as if all the blood had fled from her head, she fell into a faint upon the floor.

Maggie could feel Molly now slumped next to her, lying in the raging water, its level having risen well above her ankles and fast moving up her calves. It was becoming harder and harder to stand, and yet with all her might, she pulled Molly to her feet, slapping at her to fully revive her. "Molly! Molly!"

"I'm here. I'm here, Maggie," said Molly.

Ruth and Jane were walking. They were walking, sloshing through the water, headed in the direction of the flow. Others had been moving in the *opposite* direction toward the stairs, but these two—indeed, Molly and Maggie as well, thought it best to move *with* the water, believing that once it rose high enough, it might carry them down to the next station.

Carrie was alone. Lyle could not find her. Lyle called her name in the darkness. She heard him—or she *thought* she heard him. "Sing to me, Carrie!" he called out. "Sing to me so I can find you!"

And Carrie began to sing. She sang out the song that came first into her head, the hymn that was her mother's favorite and was sung several days earlier at her funeral, "Dear Lord and Father of Mankind":

Breathe through the heats of our desire
Thy coolness and Thy balm;
Let sense be dumb, let flesh retire;
Speak through the earthquake, wind, and fire,
O still, small voice of calm.

She sang out in her strongest, loudest (and least calming) voice, and there were some in the Balham Station who thought the girl mad. But it didn't matter, for Lyle was following the sound of the belting, boisterous voice. And he was getting closer and closer.

And now he was there, finding her hand...

Putting her hand in his.

Together they crawled through the storm of flying straw and splintered pieces of spinning airborne wood and other bits and slices and chunks of piercing, clawing, stabbing debris, their eyes shut tight, their heads bowed, in the direction of the tractor that wobbled but did not move—the tractor where Ruth and Jane were waiting for them, and toward which Maggie was dragging an unconscious Molly, who had been struck by a flying bucket, and they were all coming together in that one place where they felt they had the best chance of mutual survival.

Each of the six, now converging upon it—converging upon the emporium, where they had run through the madness and the chaos of this human-driven calamity of marauding mayhem, away from the Spalding House, which had been set afire, and the Prowse house, where men had entered set upon ripping it apart—running, tripping, falling, rising, running again from this phenomenon of aberrant behaviour that turned men into wild beasts who burned and smashed and pillaged and fought one another with fists over loaves of bread from the baker's raided shelves, actions that could not be understood as one can never understand those things which periodically imperil human survival upon a fragile planet—wars and inexplicable institutional cruelties and all the natural assaults upon human body and spirit: the quaking, shuddering ground; the raging, consuming fire; the cataracts of water that flood and drown; and betrayal by the very air we must breathe to live, which will at times gather itself into the greatest concentrated force of nature known upon the planet.

The tornado moved on, taking most of the barn with it, leaving behind a tractor and the six frightened young Mississippians who lay beneath it, either clutching at its belly like Romulus and Remus with their surrogate she-wolf mother, or body-clinging to its oversized rear tires.

Bouncing, stumbling, bobbing by turns like bathtub playtoys, We Six were swept down the Underground tunnel to the next tube station where there was light and safety and life.

The fire had been confined, at least at its outset, to the tabernacle's basement, and reaching the top of the stairs that led to the ground floor the six emerged from the worst of the spitting flames and the choking smoke, and staggered outside the building just as the fire trucks were pulling up and there still remained hope the structure, so dear to Sister Lydia's heart, might be saved.

The ground, after nearly a minute of violent convulsions, settled itself into still and stationary complaisance, the rumbling silenced, replaced now by the sounds of human misery upon a very large scale, expressed by those who had been battered by falling things, had lost loved ones to collapsed chimneys and toppled oriental sculptures and architectural appurtenances that now rubbled the cobbles of Dupont Street. The teahouse was still aright, though it seemed none too safe to remain inside, and so the six hastily removed themselves from it and stepped out into the gloaming that preceded the dawn to find a city that no longer resembled itself and which would soon be further ravaged by a fire of epic proportions.

In Tulleford, the citizenry calmed itself and came ruefully to their senses and were abashed and repentant over everything that had transpired in the preceding hour of madding pandemonium—an hour that certainly gave God Himself pause to wonder why He created man without any thought to the potential flaws in the human machine.

Epilogue

If only the Exto Carapace Air Lock had been breached, We Six would have had seven and one half minutes to evacuate the chamber and move into one of the unbreached adjacents. But instead, the storm had delivered to Chamber 17 a double punch—*two* different meteoric strikes, both of which had penetrated both the Exto and Inner Carapace Air Locks which, upon emergency engagement of the manual Aeropositer, left only a scant one minute and sixteen seconds of chamber equipressurization before the cell functionality was permanently compromised and any remaining occupants permanently de-extanted.

In other words, We Six were very lucky to have gotten themselves out of the chamber in which they were hiding, with their lives intact.

But there was consequence to be borne, and it was the fact that Lyle was now exposed to the human interveillance of the Office of Incident Investigation. Because in the course of learning, consequent to the meteor storm which had struck the Tesla Terranium, that a chamber which had been registered as *un*occupantal did *indeed* have human occupants hiding therein (who were awaiting stowage on a Parenthian merchant ship as an extralegal means to departure), the O.I.I. discovered that one of those occupants was none other than a prime suspect in the murder of a Crewer's Mate by the name of Tom Cates, who had been intentionally de-extanted six diurnals earlier in the sanitroom of his living quarters.

As Lyle was being escorted to the transport ship that would take him to a cell in the Tesla Penal Holding Center, where he was to await trial, there was a tearful exchange between Carrie and her new lover to which all were witness (including two android processitors whose emoticapacitors had been freshly re-actualized following complaints from human analogues that the processitors had been too bureaucratically impassive in their dealings).

In other words, the robots cried just as much as Carrie and her sisters did.

And in a most amazounding turn of events, something very nearly identical took place three quadrants removed in the First Quadrant in which Maggie's mother and Molly's father had been hiding and awaiting similar breakflight: their chamber was identically breached and it was likewise discovered that the chamber's unauthorized occupants included a man who was also suspect in a recent murder. This one involved the gruesome shrusting of one Pat Harrison, also a Crewer's Mate, down the G Station Rubbish Chute from which no human had ever emerged unscissored and unserrated and not in a de-extanted state of unrecognizable man-shreddage.

A freak accident, to be sure, since to fall all the way down the chute to the tooth wheel, Crewer Harrison would have had to plummet down the chute at precisely the moment all three of the upper mesh gates had been retracted, which by tragic coincidence all three had.

In other words, Crewer Harrison died because three different top-level residents of the G Station dormitower chose to shrust their garbage at the very same time.

Molly would not learn of her father's capture for two diurnals. A most difficult time lay ahead for her, due not only to the reality of his incarceration and likely conviction, but also to the guilt of her earlier feelings that he deserved whatever punition was dealt to him.

Carrie sat for a moment after Lyle's wrist-clipped departure and wiped away the last remnant of lachtrickle from her cheeks. She took a deep breath and raised her eyes to look at her four sisters, who smiled the smiles of the well-intended, and gathered about her, Jane sitting the closest in sisterly communion, for Lyle was her brother, and she'd always loved him, but never more so than now, for he had come of late to be the upwardman she'd always hoped he would one day be, only now to find himself whisped off to live the rest of his human analogue life behind transparabars.

"Well, I really see no need at this junxten for us to go to my Uncle Whit's planetoid, do you?" asked Maggie with a brave smile. Though the statement was made in black jest, her companions nonetheless nodded agreement. "So what happens to us now?"

"Colthurst will take us back," said Ruth. "It's too soon for her to have replaced us."

"There may be charges filed against us," said Jane, standing at the observaportal and watching Ramses as it began its final eclipse of Cleopta for that diurnal, the two satellites orbiting one another like dancing dervishons. Jane turned around. "But I think we can convince the judge advocate that it would be a waste to lock us all away when we can be more useful in civic service. Lieutenant Colthurst knows the judge advocate, and can probably put in a good word for us. She'll also remind him that We Five are perhaps the best cooks in the Fourth Quadrant."

Carrie was sitting in the corner of the room staring at the Manipubox spindled to her chair, but keeping her hands from insertion into its plasmatter. Maggie walked over and sat down next to her. She put her arm around her friend. "You're thinking of your mother, aren't you?" she asked.

Carrie nodded. "And you're thinking of your mother too, aren't you, Maz?"

"They'll lock her up just like Molly's father. For how long is anybody's guess."

Carrie swiveled the Manipubox Screen out of the way. Though her face registered a great, nagging sadness, there was a glimmer of a smile upon her lips. "I think it's funny how I ended up as a Quadrant cook, considering how claphanded Mama always was in our own galley."

"And to end up as one of the best to boast!" added Ruth, whose hands were dipped into her own Manipubox, though her manipulation of the holographic images that floated there was more mindless fidget than purposeful arrangement.

A silence followed, broken only by the periodic beep of the vitometer in the corridor outside the Interview room. A few moments later, an older woman entered and said, "You're all free to go now. We'll have each of you in over the next two diurnals for further inquiry. Within half a mensal we should have some idea what the judge advocate intends to do with you."

We Five nodded thank-yous for their release and started down the corridor to the transportation artery. "I don't want to go home," said Molly.

"Nor do I," said Jane.

It was agreed that no one wished to return to their respective living quarters (though the Mobrys would have been happy to see Ruth restored to their loving embracement).

"So what do we do?" asked Maggie.

"I'll say what I'd *like* to do," said Carrie. "It's been months since we've taken a walk in the Outland. Let's suit up and go."

"I don't know," said Molly. "It will bring back so many memories of my excursions with Dad when I was a girl."

Ruth placed a hand on Molly's shoulder. "We're going to make you a brand-new memory, Molly. Today. Right now." Ruth smiled. "And as it so happens, Sisters, I've been holding five trektrak passes since the last time we tried to do this and everything fell agang."

Carrie kissed Ruth on the cheek. "You are such a dearling. I was going to suggest just slipping out without passes and paying the penalty afterward, but now we can do it legal!"

We Five took the arterial to K Station where the Fourth Quadrant's main standport was located. They suited up, choosing rigs in their favorite colors, and Molly requesting a Pulmoassist because the excitement of leaving the Quadrant might accelerate her inhalations and make her expend her standard nitrox allowance faster.

Since it had been quite some time since they'd been in the Outland, it took a while to get used to walking in the heavy suits, but soon they were ambulating comfortably and moving along the paved Prowlpath past holographic markers and informational signage pertaining to the geology and terrain of the Tesla Terranium, which looked very much like the moon except for the occasional bright green takite deposit and the sparkling lemon yellow of the giant xanthite quarry nearby. The Prowlpath had yet to be cleared of most of the debris from the last two meteor showers and there were places where We Five had to sidestep scatterings of inconvenient meteoritic rubble, but there was no difficulty in reaching the observation deck at the terminus of the path.

We Five climbed the stairs and brought themselves up to the highest landing, which commanded the very best view of the sky, set off in sharp perspective by the forewash of the Kepler Peaks.

Not a word was said—though the interpersonal transmitters were still engaged—each sister standing in awe of the deep black, twink-stippled sky. For where were there words to describe such an extraordinary view?

And Molly took Maggie's pudge-gloved hand and Maggie took Jane's and Jane took Ruth's and Ruth took Carrie's, and the five friends who had been friends nearly all their lives, the five sisters-of-the-heart, stood side by side by side by side by side in mesmeric silence and felt tiny and inconsequential in this tuck-corner of a vast, cold universe.

But they did not feel alone.

Not even for a parasecond.

Acknowledgments

The author wishes to thank the following individuals who read the manuscript in early drafts and offered suggestions that were thoughtful and most helpful:

Mary Elizabeth Dunn, Patrick Gabridge, George Ovitt, Jim Davis, Mary Ellen Holman, Tonya Hays, Michael Keith, Carolyn Valtos, Janet Stephenson, Susan Guinter, Laurie Kalet, and Jonathan Odell.

The author also wishes to thank his literary agent Amy Rennert for her many years of support. He is grateful, as well, to be working again with his favorite editor Guy Intoci and his favorite copy editor Michelle Dotter. A special thank-you goes to Patrick Walsh for his fifteen-year advocacy and friendship—happy proof that an Irishman can also be a mensch.